The Tatra Eagle

(Tatrzański Orzeł)

The Tatra Eagle

(Tatrzański Orzeł)

J. Victor Tomaszek

ROUNDFIRE
BOOKS

Winchester, UK
Washington, USA

First published by Roundfire Books, 2012
Roundfire Books is an imprint of John Hunt Publishing Ltd., Laurel House, Station Approach,
Alresford, Hants, SO24 9JH, UK
office1@jhpbooks.net
www.johnhuntpublishing.com
www.roundfire-books.com

For distributor details and how to order please visit the 'Ordering' section on our website.

Text copyright: J. Victor Tomaszek 2011

ISBN: 978 1 78099 522 9

A CIP catalogue record for this book is available from the British Library.

Design: Stuart Davies

Printed in the USA by Edwards Brothers Malloy

We operate a distinctive and ethical publishing philosophy in all
areas of our business, from our global network of authors to
production and worldwide distribution.

Then everything includes itself in power,
Power into will, will into appetite;
And appetite, a universal wolf,
So doubly seconded with will and power,
Must make perforce a universal prey,
And last eat up himself.
William Shakespeare - Trollius and Cressida

Za wolność Waszą i Naszą
(For Your Freedom and Ours)

For the priests

Chapter 1

Young Bolesław Radok sat up with a shudder as a wisp of chilled mountain air swirled between his body and his woolen campsite blanket. The hunter stretched, pleased to awake among the vaulting peaks of his beloved Tatra Mountains, far above the chaos of life below. He sat cross-legged; knees almost touching the fading fire's glowing embers. A hint of color in the otherwise black curtain of the moonless night promised dawn. The rising sun would make short work of the light snow cover.

Mimicking his master, Burek extended his front legs, chest to the ground, yawning. Both man and guard dog celebrated their seventeenth spring. No razor had yet touched Bolesław's cheeks and even when saddened his face shone with the gift of innocent youth. The huge canine, blind in its left eye, its right ear ragged and chewed, a wide hairless line from shoulder to snout from a single swipe of an enraged bear's paw, wore its scars as evidence of years of servitude.

Bolek jabbed a long piece of kindling into the heart of the fire several times before adding a few thin pine branches. While warming his face, he pulled some bread from his bedroll. Equally divided, the companions broke fast, gnawing on their crusts to the crackle and hiss of the snow-dusted twigs. Two butchered deer, shot the afternoon before, hung from a pine branch near the campfire, a result of the unerring skill of the acknowledged master archer of the region. The shepherds would eat well on the morrow.

A cocked head and guttural growl from Burek startled Bolek, his own senses unable to penetrate past the glow of the enlivened flames. With faith in canine perception far beyond human ken, Bolek rose to his knees. The snap of a twig no more than ten yards away transformed the curled ball of white fur into a bristling mass of muscle, intimidating fangs and menacing growl. Before Bolek could attain his balance, a blurry grey-brown shadow leapt through the orange glow, dank-smelling wet fur brushing his cheek. Bolek fell then recovered to his knees, his face mere inches from the merciless glare of an alpine wolf.

Burek's enraged strike at the creature's neck gave Bolek precious seconds to reach for his *ciupaga* mountain ax, his bow useless at this range. Ax raised as wolf and dog whirled round, each vying for dominance, he waited until the beast came within arm's length and swung downward. The blade cut the air and buried itself a hair's breadth from his left boot, his futile curse all but lost among vicious growls.

Snapping jaws each fought for dominance, for an opening. Old Burek, while bred in like size and ferocity to fight wolves, fared poorly against the speed of the expert killing machine. A brutal nip to the haunch sent a yelping Burek to the ground, the wolf at the dog's throat in one motion. Bolek leapt upon the creature's back, arm in a strangle hold around its dank furry neck, twisting, yanking, pulling certain death from Burek's throat. The air rife with steaming breath from the three combatants, Bolek's body jerked left then right as the infuriated predator struggled to free itself. His grip lost, Bolek staggered backward as flesh-rending fangs bit into his left arm, pressing down with numbing force. Blood spouted; Bolek screamed. He groped for one of the eyes with his free hand, digging a finger into a socket. The wolf whimpered and released its viselike grip. A revived Burek sprang at the neck, giving Bolek time to roll through the fire and reach his *ciupaga*. Ax in hand Bolek shoved the ax handle into its face and pushed.

"*Odejdź ode mnie*! Go away!" The feebleness of his own reedy voice shamed him. His left arm quickly lost strength as pain weakened his resolve. The raging wolf wrenched the ax from Bolek's grasp, shaking it in a frenzied rage, giving Bolek enough time to scramble up a nearby pine, taking the rough branches like steps of a ladder.

"*Prosze! Prosze!* Help!" Bolek shouted into the night as the brute below now attacked one of the slaughtered deer, snapping the pine branch the meat hung from with ease. Fumbling for the horn dangling at his chest, Bolek blew out several pleading salvos, alerting any and all to his peril. The alpine valley came alive with hollow echoes, the shouts of men mixed with the agitated barks of Burek's fellow guard dogs. With a dash of confidence, Bolek forced his eyes downward to the sight of stringy red flesh ripped from the carcass.

This could have been Burek's fate. Or mine.

Bolek's eyes locked with his adversary's. Head lowered, body crouched in readiness, the beast glared at Bolek in warning as it swallowed red meat. Bolek shuddered but could not turn from the merciless glare. Tightening his grip on a pine branch with his good hand, he watched in shame as the carnivore hefted the slack deer in its mouth and with one forceful lunge over the underbrush, predator and prey disappeared into the safety of the pitch black forest.

Chapter 2

Confident voices from just beyond the fire's red glow allowed Bolek to leap from his perch. A panting Burek rose with some effort and yipped as he tested his hind legs. His tongue purple and sagging, his once pristine white coat blood-spattered, he looked to his master for comfort.

A stout, black-bearded shepherd strutted through the dying fire, armed with a long knife, his shuffling feet sending coaling sticks to sizzle in the snow as he inspected the scene.

"Only one wolf here and Pan Radok up a tree?" He growled as three more shepherds followed with rusty battleaxes and improvised spears. Speechless, Bolek could only glare at Wojiech, de facto leader of the herding shepherds. Two large mountain dogs greeted Burek, sniffing his wounds, and then converging on the spot where wolf and trophy disappeared into the safety of the woods. They barked in unison as if to challenge the wolf to return.

"Our dogs to the north give chase. The wolf pack flees," Wojiech said. Another shepherd picked up Bolek's ciupaga, deep teeth marks visible, the wooden handle well-shredded.

"It is the blade or the pointed end you should use against a wolf, young master, not the stick." Wojiech said.

This is not the proper tone to address a son of warriors. But in what way have I exhibited any distinction?

From the expressions of the other shepherds, Wojiech could see he had gone too far.

"I am not in the best of spirits at this moment, Wojiech."

"I have never seen the likes of what this wolf did," the slim and boney shepherd called Mathias said, eyes wide in disbelief.

"This winter was particularly long and bleak and perhaps they grow bold with appetite."

"Yours is a bad wound and needs tending, Pan Radok," another shepherd cautioned. "Go home, sir. You have given us meat a plenty. Daylight comes. The wolves won't attack you. They feast this morn."

"They eat my meat," Wojiech muttered.

"Our master bowman felled the deer, Wojiech," Mathias reminded.

"Tend to your mother's farm, Pan Radok. We will tend to the sheep, as always."

Burek yelped again and Wojiech dragged his foot through the embers, sending a cloud of dust at the wounded dog.

"Take one of our dogs with you, sir. This one is useless. We will put him down."

"I will put him down, if needed, Wojiech," Bolek fired back. "Right after I put you down."

All eyes save Bolek's went to the ground.

After allowing Mathias to bind his arm, forcing himself to reveal no sign of discomfort, Bolek ensured Burek's wounds were not life-threatening. Gathering his camping gear, bow, quiver and ciupaga he strode down the mountain path toward home far below; a blood-stained and limping Burek at his heels.

Chapter 3

Birds emerging from the warmth of snow-covered evergreens announced a gentle dawn with celebratory refrains well before the sun began to paint the mountain peaks with color. Song mixed with promise of warmth raised the young traveler's spirit on his trek home. Despite having to stop and redress his puffy arm with strips cut from his bed roll and winter-weight woolen pants, Bolek hefted the ailing Burek over his right shoulder on the steeper parts of the descent, as the faithful dog whimpered and staggered with each step on uneven ground. A grateful sloppy lick to Bolek's face now and then, though little consolation, was tolerated. But it went unsaid that neither of the two beaten and bloody comrades would abandon the other unto the very end. They had grown up together, and each would always be a part of the other's life.

"Do you know what today is, Burek?" Bolek asked as he picked his way over rocks and fallen branches along the narrow, winding path toward home. "It is the sixth of May. Father left on this day one year ago. Only two weeks at home before returning to service." Bolek glanced down at Burek as if to ensure the canine's attention. "Two weeks. Not enough time to go hunting with his son. Not enough time to prepare his son to wield a szabla, an elegant curved sword. He is back skirmishing with Turks and Tatars.

"The next morning you and I set out for Babia Gora. We trekked up Witches' Mountain. I climbed the still snow-covered *Diablak*, The Devil's Peak, at night, with only the Moon as a guide while you barked up a storm below. No Witches Sabbath occurred that night for me to interrupt. Even *Matka Niepogód*, the Mother of Bad Weather, could not blow me off her exposed peak which scrapes the sky itself. As we recuperated for our descent, lightning set a hundred spruce trees aflame. We feasted on elk and deer, felled from my own bow. We triumphed. But I felt no different than I do now. It is as if I am a prisoner in a dream that spins in place like a child's top. But the desires are veiled in my longing dreams.

"Bah!" Bolek cursed as his spittle disappeared into the darkness of the ravine below. "Always the Turks. What are they to me? Father leaves us as victims to these brigands who steal our food, take our livestock, and sell us to the Cossacks or Turks as slaves. Where is Father, Burek?"

Alert for any sound, Bolek reacted with heart pounding, to cracking twigs ahead. A deer crashing through the underbrush. A strange feeling came to him - uncertainty. The wolf encounter had changed him.

I am alone here also.

As a child, Father and Grandfather had often taken him to these high alpine areas to hunt for game. Once he thought himself master of all in the mountains. Fearless. Now, his bow hand trembled as his imagination sensed peril from imminent attack from all sides. His swollen left arm throbbed.

My father is off in the service of others. I pray for his victory and his continued health. Still, I pray harder he returns to prepare me. I am lethal with bow and fair with horse but lacking in sword. I must ride to war and finally home to win Rozalia. Lord God, make it so.

He looked down from *Gubalowka Hill*, at the small village of Zakopisko, some call Zakopane. The picturesque village sat snugly amid numerous glades with their aspens, beech, alders, oak and pine standing firm, the familiar white specs of innumerable sheep grazing in open grassy meadows. The giant sleeping knight, *Giewont Mountain* stood as a silent sentinel above.

An errant step on a loose stone took his already wavering balance away as strained muscles gave way. He stumbled. Burek ambled to him, a cold nose to Bolek's neck, heavy breathing mixed with panting. The sound of trickling water promised relief to the parched throats of the weary travelers.

Their journey took them to *Morskie Oko,* a sparkling mountain lake near Mount Rysy, called 'The Eye of the Sea,' because of her bounty of trout. Famine trout they were called, for fish in alpine lakes were unusual, and this highly prized catch could be relied on during periods of famine.

They stumbled as one, both lapping water still mixed with melting snow from a clear pebble-laden stream as it snaked its way from the vaulting peaks on its unstoppable route to supply the mighty rivers below. Quenched for now, Bolek rolled over for a well-deserved rest. Burek remained in the water flow, allowing the power of the current to cool and massage his tender wounds.

Throbbing pain woke Bolek, and he examined his wolf-bitten arm. He probed it with his finger and groaned. Blood oozed through his makeshift bandages. He caught sudden movement on a mountainside in the distance, something dark and silent; an eagle's shadow on a canyon wall. Pinpointing the plunging hunter in the pale blue sky and her target, a hapless white tail hare scampering along an exposed streambed far below, he marveled at the eagle. Her swift descent made Bolek's jaw drop; her massive feathered wings were elegance in motion as they adjusted to the mercurial canyon wind currents. He admired the ease with which she prepared her long vice-like talons, at the ready to dig into the unsuspecting prey's flesh. As predator and prey embraced, Bolek's eyes never wavered. The initial strain of the hare's weight forced the mighty wings to flap with considerable effort, yet she lofted her stunned quarry from the earth.

At a height deemed appropriate, she spread her talons, releasing the motionless hare, allowing gravity to deliver the bone-crushing deathblow. A sun-drenched rocky ledge fifty feet below, dripped with red as the prey bounced twice then lay still. The majestic raptor changed direction, veering downward in an ever-tightening circle, scanning the terrain for possible danger before scooping her meal from the mountain ledge. He watched in awe as she grew ever smaller on her way home to the solitude and safety of some cloud-hidden aerie and her needy young. *How high must I live to be safe? Ah, to be a Tatra eagle.*

Gauging the hour by the sun's height and the dagger-like shadows creeping up the mountainsides, it was time to move. A hint of moisture in the air and a subtle change in wind direction told Bolek a storm neared. Man and dog continued their trek toward home below. As the trail flattened out, the companions traversed rolling hills; the pace quickened. True to Bolek's mountain senses the sky darkened, then rumbled, flashed, illuminating pristine green and yellow dew-soaked meadows ringed by strands of Silesian willows as they were pelted by fickle winds of the late afternoon.

Up there I would be safe in a secluded cave. Down here I am exposed.

He grappled with two thoughts – the safety of home set against his certainty of the shame that shepherds tongues would soon wag. Halting a cold fury building within, memories of family overwhelmed him – from the aroma of steaming loaves of aromatic bread cooling on the hearth's iron grate, to the odor of freshly plowed earth after a heavy spring rain. He smiled, recalling how Father had once told him even the exotic perfume from the Orient could not rival the fragrance of a simple loaf of crisp and hot Polish bread.

Bolek recalled his mother's face, her wide smile and pale eyes, eyes that were capable of imparting tenderness or anger or a hundred unspoken thoughts in a heartbeat. Father always said the Bolek had her eyes. Next, a vision of the warm embrace from his young sister, Kasia, who scrambled to him whenever he returned from a hunting trip. An image of Rozalia burst upon him in vivid flashes. Here, in all her beauty, he heard the music of her laughter, almost touching her bright blonde hair, recalling the scent of her rose oil. These remembrances drove one foot in front of the other. The pain of the smarting arm faded.

His pace quickened, his heart praying he would not see black smoke nor smell an acrid odor; omens of certain death in these times.

Please God . . .

Chapter 4

Bolek eased his stiff body over the four-rail wooden fence of the Radok compound as Burek slid between two rails. Both spirits rose with anticipation. Well into dusk, the heavens rumbled, the lightning offering staggered glimpses of the countryside. The inviting beacon of the candle-lit windows pierced the approaching darkness with ease. The familiar Radok ancestral weathered timber manor house grew nearer with every burst of light, its thick walls made of felled oak trees, each stuffed with moss, all resting on the mighty white stone foundation standing impervious to any threat. A traditional Góral highlander steep-angled reddish tile lathed roof topped the smooth stones surrounding the perimeter at the appropriate angle to keep mud and water away. Burek announced his presence with a series of yaps at ten paces, the door flew wide and Bolek, bathed in the warm and welcoming light of home, burst into the cottage as Mother Józefa uttered a curse, slapping him on the back of his head.

"Again you do this to me. Again!" She scolded. "Don't you remember the threat lightning brings?" She shadowed him as he threw his shredded ciupaga and rain-soaked bow and quiver into a corner before walking to the crackling hearth where Burek, already curled up in his favorite spot, sniffed the air for food. "You were supposed to be home well before sunset. My mind saw you slain in the road, captured as a slave, lying broken at the bottom of a ravine."

She knelt with a heart-rending sigh as the light from the hearth illuminated the wolf's work on her son's arm.

"A wolf," Bolek whispered. "Burek is hurt. It took a doe from me."

"This needs tending,"

"I am sorry, Mother,' he pleaded kneeling before her, drying his cropped blond hair in her apron as she struggled to cut away the makeshift bandages. "I am home. I am well. Nothing to fear."

"It seems the worst happens when there is nothing to fear."

She shook her head in mock anger, her piercing blue eyes drilling into her son's as he tugged at one of her thick light brown braids hanging in front of her long one-piece *letnik* cotton gown.

"You know how I expect your father's return with every knock on the door and with each appearance of a silhouette in the distance?"

"I do also, Mother," giving the response she expected.

"This is a jagged wound and you will carry a scar, Bolek. Your first. And a wolf's bite. Pray that you do not grow fangs and bay at the moon yourself."

"Are there such things as werewolves, Mother?"

"Men gone astray, their hearts locked away from God. This is what your father always said of ghosts and demons."

"Yet nothing said by him in over a year."

"I know, son. We have no way of knowing. But God gives us faith and hope. Wherever he is, he will make for this very spot when his tasks are accomplished."

"What about the tasks that need doing here, Mother?"

"God's will, son."

"I look for him daily."

"So imagine how it is for me when you are late," wagging a stern finger for emphasis. "Will God ask me to pine for a son as well as a husband?"

"This will not happen again," he said, attempting to wrap her waist in his uninjured arm. "How much did my sister grow in the last two weeks? Where is Kasia?"

"Asleep. She asked I wake her at your return, but it will go badly for you if you do."

"Is some supper left?" Bolek ventured, well aware of the delicious odor still lingering in the rafters. He could almost taste the cheese, garlic and ewe's whey mixed together.

"When is there not?"

She shuffled toward the soot-blackened fireplace, checking on a dented and well-charred iron pot set close to the orange glow. The massive stone hearth anchored the center of the room and had fulfilled its obligations for many generations. Bellowing smoke curled its way upward, past the second-story loft and out through a covered outlet in the roof. This method protected the cottage from the dreaded *Halny Wind*; a mountain tempest capable of turning sparks back down the chimney and causing fires. The deadly storm was known to flatten entire spruce forests.

The Góral highlanders of the Polish Tatra Mountains were famous far and wide for master woodworking skills, their homes always decorated with handcrafted carvings of each kind of wood available in the mountain region. Equally known for a hearty independence, their freedom they cherished the most; *Szlebodu* in their dialectic tongue.

"Wash up," Mother Józefa commanded, setting a bowl and a large spoon on the ornate, straight-legged maple table. She pushed him out of the way a bit with her hip before reaching into the hearth's ashes, extracting a blackened potato, juggling it bare handed before plopping it onto a metal plate.

A large hunk of *placki*, fresh and tasty bread topped with cheese and herbs, the traditional sign of the cross etched into its crust, joined the smoking potato; followed by a steaming bowl of *zur*, a fermented rye soup, presented at table with an onion and some garlic from the previous year's harvest floating on top. The preserved vegetables added salt to the soup and restored the wrinkled greens to their former shapes. Groats, made from millet, barley and oats stored from last year's crops followed as did aromatic cured cabbage.

Bolek sat and dipped his soft bread deep into the bowl. Interrupted by a light slap to his head as a reminder, he mumbled his thanks to God and made the sign of the cross. *Kleb*, fresh bread, baked by tradition only once per week – fresh today in celebration of Bolek's anticipated return from the high pastures. His arm even felt better.

"I'll tend to Burek now," Mother Józefa said.

"Mother, Grandfather must consent to teach me how to wield a sword. With a sword I would have killed the wolf with one slash and then a finishing thrust."

"Last month a great war horse was an absolute must."

"Brigands roam free killing neighbors. Thanks be to God I own a bow and a full quiver. But for close fighting I need a sword."

"Hungry wolves bring down bears, my son. There is little shame in facing such," while kneeling by Burek, inspecting his wounds.

"It was just one wolf. I cowered up a tree. The shepherds laughed. Me and Burek, both bloodied."

"Burek is like your Grandfather, son; their days of war are past."

Burek barked at his name and mother and son chuckled for it sounded as if Burek fully agreed.

The cottage door burst wide, a cold gust from the raging storm invading the area, the hearth growing bright with the huge blast of air. Smoke and ash swirled about as a shaggy white-haired wisp of a man vied with a frigid gust for control of the door. Finally securing the solid oak barrier with a curse, he tossed his coat on the floor, ran to the fire, his craggy face stopping mere inches from the flames, each hand rubbing the opposite arm to stop his shivering.

"Everything is tied down for the night," he announced. "The storm still grows. We are in for it." Surveying the room his eyes fixed on Bolek. "Adalbertus!"

"No, it's your grandson," Mother Józefa said.

Bolek frowned, for Grandfather often thought him to be his father. The old man rapped his knuckles to his head as if in a futile attempt to somehow awaken long lost wits.

"I'm sorry, Grandson. The storm has a thousand sabers tonight and I am thin of bone. The men will secure everything. I fled for the safety of the house, tail between my shivering legs."

We are of the same blood.

"A wolf took a butchered doe from me this morning."

The bent-over patriarch eased onto a stool at the head of the table, while lowering his head to the bowl to spoon his soup, never taking his eyes from his grandson.

"Your ciupaga has been sorely used. The handle is in shreds. You were close to the wolf." But no blood on the ax head. Did you wash it off already?"

Frail as a bird, often in a fantasy world, but still he takes in the whole room, even my weapons.

"The wolf snatched it from me."

"I whittled that weapon from the finest mountain ash. Picked out the tree limb myself. Your father fashioned the ax's head and barbed tip himself. At least you could have drawn blood."

"The beast was as large as Burek and attacked me without a sound. I had no opportunity to—"

"Wolves are not dogs. They only bark in warning to their pack. Burek, you old bag of hair. Did you wet yourself too?"

The curled-up dog yapped at his name, eyes never leaving the food on the table. Bolek flushed. Mother lowered her head.

"A wolf calls your bluff just as a school room bully does," Grandfather said, slathering butter on his fresh bread. "It is spirit that defeats an enemy. Jan Sobieski knows this better than most."

Bolek bit his lip. "His Majesty is a king. I am a farmer and sometimes shepherd. Last week I was a beekeeper when Sasha took a bride. His helpers taught me his tasks grinning all the while at my fumbling."

"This should not be," Grandfather growled as if hearing of this for the first time. Casting a glance at Mother, he continued. "My grandson is of warrior blood," the patriarch replied, now with some steel and heft in his voice. "We have land. We have a history of service and honor. We are fearless."

"And I am ready, Grandfather," Bolek announced in his deepest voice, standing almost at full attention as a power to challenge the storm outside grew within his chest.

In this mood, I am ready for the wolf.

"You are noted for your fine horseshoes, Grandson. This is a start."

"Horseshoes?" Bolek echoed. "Peasants' work. Any fool can make horseshoes. I need a sword. The cost is great, we have no wealth, but you can make one for me. Our family had such skill."

"Remember your place, son," Mother added.

"You do not know what you ask, boy! Take my sword. It is here somewhere. Perhaps in the barn."

"Grandfather, it is rusty."

"That isn't rust; it's the blood of a hundred invaders."

Bolek sighed. Grandfather's sword was a dull shadow of what it once must have been. It would no longer maintain an edge.

Its only purpose now is for cutting the bindings on hay bales.

"Our family's sacrifices demand respect," Grandfather went on undeterred. "All can be taken from you, save honor. When it comes time to fight, Radoks are there."

"I've heard all of this a hundred—-"

"We steward the land while those rich Cracow merchants and nobles sell out the country," the blustery old man shouted, face flushed, fist to the sky. "They acquire wealth on the backs of we who serve Poland. And taxes? Always taxes and more taxes."

"Father," Mother interrupted with a half smile and her eyes locked with her son's. "I'll boil some water and you can soak your feet. Please sit in the rocker and I will come to you."

As Grandfather shuffled in his slippers to the rocker, and nearer the fire, his hands grasping the carved lion heads, he moaned. "Old bones, be damned."

Mother stood on her tip toes, mouth to her son's ear.

"It was not unusual for this man to kill five men in one day.

On campaign he slept in blood soaked clothing. He did not eat for days at times. We honor him for what he once gave. If your blood is noble, act as such. It will be more difficult to do this than maim or kill another soul. God is teaching you now for whatever role you will play."

Bolek nodded understanding.

God's mercy. Thank you, Father, for Mother's wisdom.

"I fought at Chocim with my son in '72, or was it '82," the old man continued, shaking his spoon at Bolek, his ashen blue-veined feet now soaking in a steamy pot.

"Eighty thousand Muslims came at us. King Michael rallied us to victory by will alone. We fought off the Tatars then too. This legacy must be sustained with honor. You should be a wolf hunter now, Grandson, I should have a wolf's fur to warm me. Perhaps a bear."

"Perhaps, Father, you can take him up there yourself and show him how to face a wolf," Mother said.

The old man flashed an angry frown at his daughter-in-law, but it quickly softened. Nodding his head in agreement he reached out, chuckling as he snatched the last chunk of sausage from Bolek's plate.

"Would that I could take my grandson to the highlands. Hell, I cannot even walk to the barn without having to piss twice. *Staroszcz nie radoszcz!* Old age be damned!"

"Don't curse, Father," Mother warned while glancing to the ancient soot-covered blue icon of the Virgin Mary hanging above the door.

"My father, now he was a sword maker!" Grandfather said with pride. "I cannot seem to make out his face anymore. But his voice often comes at night, on the wind."

"When the next wind comes, tell him his great-grandson wishes to learn his trade."

"Bolek!" Mother Józefa scolded, raising her hand but drawing back as quickly.

"When the next wind comes. Ha!" Grandfather laughed from his belly. "This is my father's humor, young Bolek. You also have his quickness and steel mountain legs. But he could never hold his liquor. A ladies man. I bet I have ten bastard siblings."

"Father!" Mother reprimanded, hand to her mouth to hide a slight smile, fooling nobody.

"What does it matter, daughter-in-law? They'd all be dead now anyway. They all are," he said, the last few words mumbled, his eyes looking well beyond this world. "A sword. A sword for my grandson. Son," he continued, "I can barely lift a hammer now. And even if I could hit the glowing steel it would be a weak blow."

"It is Adalbert's task to pass on the skill to his son." Mother sighed.

"Yes, daughter, yes," he replied, with hand to forehead. "If he does not perish in battle or waste away from drink, a Góral lives a long time. I should have passed on with a Turkish spear in my guts and three of the dogs cut down at my feet. My left leg is numb!" he shouted, banging a palm on the table, his flailing feet upturning the pot of water. "Instead of an honorable end, God desires me to die in pieces."

Bolek gazed into the fire, seeing himself on a great hussar stallion, charging into battle with Rozalia watching from a nearby hill, cheering him on.

"God has honored you with an easy end, Father," Mother replied. "So few in our families ever attained such a great age."

"I always teased your grandmother and told her I wanted to be killed by a jealous husband on my one hundredth name's day and be guilty." The old man laughed. "*Sto lat! Sto lat! Sto lat niechaj zyje nam,*" he sang head held high, his arm in the air. "Live a hundred years! Live a hundred years! May you live a hundred years for us."

Bolek spied a face peeking out from behind a drape which led to the sleeping room. Bolek's sister came darting out to her brother, barefoot, in her woolen nightgown.

"Kasia!" Bolek embraced his sister with his good arm. "Mother will whack me now for certain. She told me not to wake you."

"Grandfather's singing woke me." She brushed strawberry-red hair away from her eyes as she climbed up to his lap.

"Careful of his arm," Mother cautioned.

"You are hurt?" Kasia asked, touching the bandage as if it would bite. I dreamt you brought me a gift from the mountains."

"What sort of gift?"

"I'm not sure," she said on a sigh. "I couldn't see it!"

"But it's hard work up there, Kasia. When would I have time to find you a gift?" He replied, feeling more than a bit guilty for teasing his baby sister.

"I don't know. I dreamed it," She crossed her arms with a grunt.

Bolek edged her to one side of his lap as he reached down into his knapsack.

"A bear! A bear!" She cried, jumping up and skipping across the room. "Bolek made me a bear!"

"But it is a smiling bear," her grandfather muttered. "A bear should always be carved in a ferocious position, his front paws up like this, his claws out, teeth bared."

"Well it's fine carving anyway, son," Mother proclaimed. "Your father would be proud. And as a gift for your sister, too. Many hours, much love in the making. God's grace," she added, crossing herself with a show of reverence.

Bolek marveled at Mother's absolute faith in what she learned at Mass. The Virgin Mary was real to her, for he heard her pray each night as if the Queen of Heaven were sitting next to her. Sunday Mass for Bolek meant a chance to see the girl he loved. His praying seemed more habit than from the heart.

A booming knock on the heavy oak door brought Bolek to his feet. In respect for his grandfather, Bolek looked to him for a silent nod to allow Bolek to answer. Grandfather waved part in agreement and part in frustration.

The compound's yeomen and two of his helpers stood with hats in hand at the threshold.

"What news," Bolek asked.

"Word comes that the merchant who mends boots disappeared on the trail to the village," the yeoman spouted. "Man, horse, wagon, gone. Just some blood and a cooking pot left."

"Bah!" Grandfather said. "Some fool rode here in this storm to tell us this?"

"Sir," the yeoman replied with a slight bow. "In these times we must spread news like the wind and in any weather."

"That merchant charged too much and did poor work," came Grandfather's response. "The Devil take him."

Looking to young master Bolek for guidance, Bolek thanked the yeoman and his companions for their diligence and promised to investigate the disappearance in the morning.

Four-legged wolves up in the mountains and two-legged ones down here. I must have a sword. No wolf or brigand would face a noble sword.

Grandfather shuffled off to his bed with his usual generous cup of warm vodka and Kasia soon fell asleep by the fire with her arms wrapped around her wooden bear.

"Mother? Can we send someone to look for Father?"

"When his work is done, he will return," she replied, not looking up from her needlework.

"I need him. I must have a sword, Mother. It is time. Death with honor is better than cowardice and helplessness, is it not? It is unfair."

"Unfair. Yes, I have no husband to rely on. Brigands attack and kill closer to our farm each week. My feeble-witted father-in-law cannot protect us. My son wishes a weapon of war but I could not go on if I lost another loved one. My daughter has no father or a little sister or brother, which I particularly desire. Unfair."

While this reply, given in an even voice, may have masked emotion, Mother did a poor job of holding back the tears welling up in her eyes.

"I will keep your grandfather from his vodka tonight and tomorrow morning," she said, dabbing tears with some wool. "He will take you to the forge. He will do his best to teach you to forge an exquisite Polish szabla. I know nothing of it other than it brought money into our home and the mill. Our men were proud of their craft. My son should be also."

Bolek started to smile but the look on her face froze him solid.

"The men from both sides of your family were well-trained in combat. They wielded sturdy and sharp sabers. They all died, save your grandfather."

"And save Father."

"Save Father."

Chapter 5

Bolek rose with the sun. Stepping outside, the subtle change in morning temperature coupled with a distinct odor of turned fertile soil whispered to him spring had won the battle with winter. A commotion in the area of the forge sent his heart pounding. Grandfather's familiar loud and colorful cursing took Bolek off of alert.

He found Grandfather covered in soot and sneezing. The forge was nothing more than a large rickety shed with a crumbling stone fire pit, an abandoned symbol of better times; now a place where the serfs drank and gamboled. But it was once a magnificent forge where great-grandfather, grandfather and father fashioned Polish szablas, the razor-sharpened blades, badges of nobility and honor which protected Poland.

"Ha! Bolek," Grandfather said while swinging his hands to and fro to sweep spider webs from the walls, anvil and tool table. "My breakfast measure of vodka has disappeared, and your mother ordered me here. Ordered me!"

"I want to forge a magnificent sword, Grandfather."

Grandfather, sat on a three-legged stool, its front leg shorter than the others, forcing him to lean this way or that for balance.

"I hereby give you my szabla, Grandson. Come. Embrace me for such generosity." Arms stretched, he offered the dull reddish blade with a wobbly hilt to his grandson.

"What am I to do with this? Dig onions and potatoes?"

The old man winced. "The bow, the ciupaga and the spear are the weapons for a wolf. Very few men would face the beast with a szabla. Wolves fight in a pack. Those jaws break arms and legs on contact. A bite to the thigh and you watch your life flow out of you within minutes."

"The foothills are full of thieves and murderers. If I cannot face one wolf, how can I face a pack of men?"

"Sit down, son."

Bolek sat on a rotted dust-laden bale of hay as Burek limped in, curling up at his feet.

"I was a pancerny," the old man said with a nod, his lower lip pushed upward. "Armored light cavalry."

Here is a new story, perhaps brought on by the visit to the forge.

"I galloped into battles firing death from my bow, impalement with a sharpened spear, a short stabbing sword for close work."

"Father is armored cavalry too, Grandfather?"

"We are *towarzysz pancerni*. We wear chain shirts and helmets, and carry woven silk round shields, our horses lighter and more maneuverable. Where the winged hussars are eagles, we are the bees and hornets that kill with numbers and speed; our venom, short lance, bow and dagger. I fought on foot occasionally with pike and saber and sometimes with the dragoons."

"Dragoons because your muskets spat fire like the dragon's breath."

Bolek imagined himself on a mighty charger, a veritable St. George, bold in form and deed. Family, friends, the entire village turned out to behold a battle to the death from the safety of the ridge, cheering Bolek on as he slays brigands and infidels.

"Did I give my mail armor to Adalbert? Did my brother take it?" Grandfather asked, eyes bulging.

His grandson shrugged.

"Did we not laugh when, as a boy, you donned your father's *misiurka* helmet and disappeared under its veil of chain, your legs bowed from the very weight? When you were but a tot and your father was home for a time we taught you to shoot a bow. The next year you worked with short lance and wooden saber. Soon you performed the moves, without thinking. Finally. And bareback on my steed."

"But I barely remember, Grandfather. I only see his szabla. I want to make one exactly as Father's."

"Haw! You do not know, Bolek. You do not know what you

ask of me." He covered his eyes with trembling hands for some time before speaking again. "We are fortunate to live near the ancient trade route, Grandson. Many strange men from East and West, their wagons brimming with precious metals and stones, silks, rare spices and deep understanding of other lands and customs come and go. Merchants pass through these mountains over well-worn paths which snake between the peaks. The Amber Road; land bridge connecting the wealthy Western cities and the exotic Eastern provinces."

Fearing another drifting tale, Bolek restated his intention. "I want to make a special sword."

"One night, returning from a hunting trip and loaded with several braces of goose and duck, my father's ever vigilant ears picked up a whimper on the wind. Reining in cautiously he discovered an aged Persian man, beaten bloody and surely left for dead by a caravan. Father took pity, brought him to our farm, nursed him back to health. We knew nothing of his babbling tongue, but he spoke a broken Polish. Timur was his name. Thankful for his life he repaid our hospitality with a secret and forbidden skill."

"To make swords," Bolek said.

"Timur told of a mystic called Assad Ullah, a legend in the mysterious Orient. This incomparable master fashioned blades like none other. Harder than hard, sharper than sharp, they would neither dull nor break, yet remained flexible. The ore for these unnatural weapons came from a mine like none other. The combination of iron and whatever else lay there with the lode forged iron that would not weaken, let alone break. Its location and the process were kept secret on penalty of death."

"Do we have some of this magical ore?" Bolek asked. "I must have such a sword. I will do anything to obtain one. *Anything.*"

"Careful not to blaspheme. Greater ability lies within you in the form of resolve, a love of justice, of family. Even if we did have the ore, we could not create such a sword."

Bolek put open palm to forehead and grunted.

"Timur was never able return home on pain of death. He was quite content to live out his remaining years with us. It took my father ten years to learn Timur's skill. Ten years, every day. I forget yesterday and today, but I begin to see images from long ago."

Images came to Bolek also. The red glow from the forge, the sensation of intense heat on his face, the acrid odor, the well-muscled arm of his father, his jutting bare chest covered in sweat and soot.

"I hear the voice of Timur goading Father, pointing here and there, growling *Yes, Yes* and *No, No* in his thick accent. I hear the clanging of the hammer on steel. The first and loudest clank and the ever lessening ones."

Bolek and his grandfather, eyes looking inward, shared memories, but from lifetimes apart.

"I remember the szablas as Father thrust them into the water; the sizzle and steam," Bolek said.

"Good. Yes. Timur taught Father. Father taught me. I taught Adalbertus."

"But the chain was severed there. Why?"

Grandfather ran his yellowish bony hands through his white hair and pummeled his head, as if trying to wake up his aged brain.

"All superior szablas, save ours, were made in the resource-rich cities. In Cracow, teams of men produce the finest blades. One team is skilled in smelting ore, another pounds and fashions the rough-cut blades, one grinds the edge, one engraves, and one creates the hilt, the last, the scabbard; each craft requiring years of instruction to perfect the individual. All accomplished under the vigilant eyes and supervision of one master.

Bolek purged himself of air and slouched. He cursed his childish imagination, for in his exuberance, he fully expected his own blade by sunset.

"So much toil, years of aching arms, stooped backs spent covered in soot. Skin baked to leather by roaring heat. But with Timur's knowledge and patient guidance, Father and I began to produce exceptional blades here, in this forge. Word spread quickly. Wealthy lords rode for days and sometimes weeks to purchase our ware. This was a tribute to Timur."

Grandfather, now talking more to himself than to Bolek, ranted on.

"Between the three of us, we produced two or three blades a season and paid a princely sum in return."

"But you stopped."

"Timur died. War put your father and me in the saddle day and night."

"And nothing came of it," Bolek said, flicking a scurrying beetle away from him with the toe of his boot.

"Nothing? A Pole with his sword is a Pole with his soul. Only noble warriors carry szablas. Only great knights wield for justice. Each blade is blessed by a priest."

"I never . . ."

"How do you reckon I paid for your father's armor and mine? For our horses? Our retinues? Do you believe our water wheel and mill simply sprang from the ground? Why do you think you were the only farm boy educated with the Pitry boys, week in and week out by Father Czarnota?"

Images poured into Bolek's head. The long, boring lessons in reading, writing, Polish history, Latin and mathematics came to him. Poetry. The taunting of Rozalia's brothers who never let him forget his place – they with their wealth and fashionable clothes but lack of a coat of arms, or royal blood.

"We donated to the Church. We tithed. A significant fortune. The tall wooden spire you see every Sunday? The golden icon of Mary? Radok gold. All pulled from the pockets of the wealthy lords for our steel."

Bolek made a fist, chin jutting farther than usual. "Yet another path closed by an avalanche."

"Still spring always comes again and melts the snow. You whine over spilt milk."

"I will have a sword, a great blade. No matter what!"

This pleased Grandfather who laughed from his belly so hard he slipped off the stool. "Damn it!" he said, "my foot's gone numb."

Bolek watched him struggle to rise, hop to the chimney, reach deep into the fire pit, and retrieve a clay demijohn bottle. Ash blackened his right arm from finger to elbow.

"Women do not like to get dirty; your mother would never look here for my emergency supply. What was I just saying?"

"I will have a sword. It is my heritage."

"You are a Góral. Radok, body and spirit. Pluck. Our family is known for our pluck."

Grandfather took several short swigs, his thin and wrinkled hands squeezing his treasure.

"It is not natural for a man to go without his vodka for long."

"What was the greatest szabla you made?"

"It is called a Damascus blade," he said, wiping the spilled liquid from his chin, licking the precious droplets from his hand. "You can know it by the waviness within the steel. These waves rise and fall as the hills around us. Many think this to be a flaw but somehow it is the key to incredible strength; know it by its blue cast, for there is no bright shine, but neither does it tarnish."

"And it is impossible to obtain one," Bolek said, blowing dust from the workbench. "If I could just see one—"

"You have. You polished it many times."

"Have you had too much drink, Grandfather?"

"In gratitude for saving his life and for giving him a home, Timur stole back to his country and pilfered some heavy metal billets from the secret mine. He brought them here and we hammered and drew them out long, then fashioned the curved edge to perfection. Timur proclaimed the final product a

Damascus blade."

"Where is it?" Bolek demanded.

"It's been passed down to your father. He wears it with pride."

No father. No training. No sword. Only death lies ahead for me.

"How are you two men getting along?" Mother asked, appearing at the doorway with a basket of eggs.

"Better, daughter, better," Grandfather said, raising his jug in salute.

"If vodka were gold, I could build a great castle on a hill," Mother said, glaring at her father-in-law.

"I forget much, Józefa. Vodka makes me forget that I forget much."

"Your father never got the chance to grow old, and you complain about your lot?"

Grandfather rose his jug to hide her glare. "You wound me to my core, woman."

Bolek smiled. "All is fine, Mother. Grandfather and I speak of ghosts. He remembers much."

Mother Józefa shook her head as she left.

"A dragon, that one," the old man whispered, lips curled in a proud snit of resentment. "Pray you have her fire and claws. *Stolat!* Live a hundred years," he toasted, visiting his precious demijohn yet again. "Why I remember when I could drink—"

"Bolek," Mother Józefa said as she returned. "If you are done listening to stories, can you hook up the wagon? We need to purchase a few piglets and get supplies in Skawica."

"Yes, Mother."

Perhaps Rozalia would be there.

Chapter 6

The man most feared in the entire mountain region ambled into the small mountain village of Skawica as if he were on parade in full regalia, on display for all to see, and indeed he was; six and a half feet animated brutality. An ash-gray complexion, mouth frozen in a sneer, a jutting forehead trimmed with bushy black brows making his eyes appear to glow as from out of a dark cave. Those unfortunate enough to have crossed paths with him compared his character to a cave bear's, instantly enraged if threatened. His body dwarfed that of his stout muscled horse, making it appear as a pony.

Villagers froze mid-chore once they spotted him. Blacksmith hammering and carpenter sawing stopped, merchant and customer haggling over prices ceased, the innocent laughter of children hushed by fearful mothers as Gustaw rode into the center of Skawica. Even the bucking chickens, the snorting swine and the baaing sheep stilled as if even livestock sensed approaching danger. Soon galloping hoof beats, maniacal screaming and wild laughter signaled Gustaw's gang's entry into the modest village. 'Lord, protect us!' was the common cry. Bodies dashed for cover. Wooden doors slammed and latched. The roar of heavy wagons followed – the brigands no longer the stuff of imagination. The nightmare rode into reality. Into the village.

Gustaw dismounted, positioning himself atop the lip of the village well, stretching and yawning as if he were completely at ease, above the law, and God himself. The main street, now deserted, save an arrow-riddled dog trembling near death, and a slumped over beggar holding the shaft of an arrow protruding from his belly, wheezing. Neither had moved fast enough for Gustaw's men.

As a two-horse driven wagon slid up to the communal sty, its driver yanked on the reins, three of Gustaw's gang started butchering swine, swinging the piglets round and round by their legs, flinging the carcasses over the waist-high wooden fencing and into the wagon. Blood splattered faces and clothes, the brigands reveling in their fun, white-toothed sneering smiles a stark contrast to blood coated flesh and clothing.

"You!" Gustaw demanded of the village blacksmith who snapped to attention, eyes to his feet. "What are all these flowers here for?"

"A wedding party is planned for tomorrow after the ceremony, sir."

"Jędrzej," Gustaw barked. "Let's have some sport. Follow this blacksmith to the hut of the bride-to-be and bring her here."

Piercing screams drew laughs and cheers as Jędrzej, dragging a maiden, both fists full of her blond hair, swung the girl to her knees in the mud before Gustaw, her parents following with hands clasped to their hearts.

"Master Pan Gustaw," the father pleaded. "Tomorrow is my daughter's wedding before God. The bans are posted. See how she is dressed in our traditional Góral bridal clothes?"

"The sewing is not yet completed," the mother added, kneeling in the mud next to her daughter.

"Why was I not invited to the ceremony?" Gustaw growled. "Do I not protect you from the Ottomans while your men are at war whoring and collecting booty?"

"Yaaaah!" A lone rider, on a roan pony, a cocked spear at shoulder height, rode straight at Gustaw. One arrow, then another took him in the chest. His body collapsed, fell from the saddle, the body hitting the muddy street with a single plop. Even as the horse ran off, the attacker clearly dead, arrows continued to pummel the body from several angles.

The girl, wailing and struggling to rise, could not free herself from Jędrzej's firm grip.

"Brothers!" Gustaw shouted, rising to his impressive height. "I assume the groom has left this world before the sacrament."

Course laughter mixed with heavy sobbing as the maiden, allowed by a nod from Gustaw, crawled to the corpse of her betrothed.

"Jędrzej," Gustaw whispered, "where is that toothless Cossack we picked up a few weeks ago? I have need of him."

A hollow-faced, bruised and unkempt shadow of a man stumbled up to stand before Gustaw.

"Bride to be," Gustaw said. "I am replacing your groom. And we will hold the ceremony now."

Looks of disbelief replaced the crying. Faces turned away. Jędrzej pulled the girl to her feet and shoved the grimy Cossack to her side. He was on to the game quickly and attempted to kiss the girl, his pinkish tongue seeking her lips, his grubby hands fondling her breasts.

"Find the village priest!" Gustaw commanded.

"No need to shout," Father Czarnota said in an even voice, advancing to Gustaw with no sign of fear. "God sees everything. Nothing is missed. You sin deeply."

"Marry these two, Priest, and live to preach another Sunday. Else I will hang you the minutes from that limb."

Chapter 7

"Whoa!" Bolek commanded as a riderless horse appeared on the horizon.

"What is it, Bolek?" Mother Józefa asked as their cart came to an abrupt halt.

"Look there, Mother. A spooked horse is never a good sign."

Jumping from the cart Bolek was able to slow the horse with raised palms and grab the reigns.

"Blood on the saddle, Mother. We must return home."

"No, son. Someone needs help."

Bolek hesitated, biting his lip. "Mother, please hand me my bow and quiver. Drive back home. Put everyone on alert."

Before he knew what was happening, he found himself mounted on the pony in a full gallop, headed toward the village. Realizing he had just given his first command to his mother, and she had obeyed, he wondered if he had remembered to say 'Please'?

Tying up the well-lathered horse by the stream that set the border of the village, with enough reins to allow the animal to revive itself, Bolek crept toward the sound of laughter under cover of a clump of trees and light underbrush. Crouching low, he pushed some scrub aside, and his stomach churned. Raiders. Twenty or more. Wagons. A hysterical village girl, struggling with a brigand. An arrow-pierced body a few feet away. A man and woman on their knees, hands raised to God. Father Czarnota, a brigand holding him in a headlock, a toothless brigand, his arm around the girl's waist, head raised, crowing like a cock at dawn.

With fire in his belly, a hunter's eye and a steady hand Bolek launched an arrow deep into the brigand's chest. The body shuddered, the maiden fell to her knees. A second shaft took the brigand holding Father Czarnota full in the back. Priest shielded the maiden as both collapsed in the mud. Bolek retched. These were no deer killed for food. Rising, he set another shaft and aimed. Bolek, looking down the shaft peered at the enraged face of Evil. Though seventy yards away, Bolek froze, for these were the same eyes he had peered down at from the pine tree a few days before. Wolf eyes. Cold. Merciless.

Panicking, he ran for the pony, raising a full gallop in mere seconds.

I have killed two men. I am damned forever. And the wolf has my scent.

Chapter 8

Loud barking mixed with shouts of alarm greeted Bolek at Radon Manor.

"It's Pan Bolek! He's safe," someone shouted.

Mother Józefa was as his side before his dismount, hugging his leg, a glistening face looking up at him.

"I thought you might be—"

"Raiders. Murdered Walenty. Olenka was attacked. Mother, I, I . . . I've killed two men."

"Get my grandson some vodka," Grandfather shouted. "We must complete this baptism by fire."

"You killed brigands, Bolek?" Mother Józefa asked.

"Yes, Mother."

"The villagers?"

"I don't know. I ran."

"You got two, Bolek!" Grandfather shouted, shuffling his feet in a dance of joy.

"Mother, I, I saw Gustaw."

All chatter halted.

"I was too far away to be recognized, but I think he knows me. Does this make sense?"

"Evil has many eyes, my son. We must be prepared."

"Józefa," Grandfather asked. "Where is my musket? I can take three down before they reach that fence."

"We must all be more vigilant from now on," Mother Józefa replied, "but there is no reason to believe they would come here now. They have the village, so they have the fat. We have time. But we must pray for our unfortunate brothers and sisters."

Queried over and over on what happened, all within the manor house wept, prayed, beat their chests, or shouted curses.

"On the eve of Olenka's wedding."

"To slay her husband-to-be before her eyes."

"To mock the sacrament of marriage."

"To attack a priest. The evil one is on the prowl."

"In the name of Saint Michael, defend us in battle."

"Thanks to God that the fearless Pan Bolek was there to exact vengeance," one farm hand shouted.

"Pan Bolek Radok is the hero of the day," another said. "Brigands will keep a wide berth from Radok Manor."

"Don't talk foolishness, Kasper," Mother Józefa scolded. "How could they know it was my son's work?"

"I shot from long distance and was shielded by the cover of scrub brush."

"Spoken like a true hunter," Kasper said. "And you hit the mark. Twice."

But froze then ran before firing the third arrow.

"Master Bolek was the only one to act," a voice from the rear shouted.

"I believe it was Walenty who died bravely," Bolek said.

"We must use Walenty's example when those dirty brigands are here at our throats," Grandfather said.

"Bolek," Mother Józefa whispered, "Take your grandfather's vodka away. Then we need our rest to repel what comes our way."

Bolek slept in fits and starts that night, though he knew sentries were in place and on high alert. He lay in his bed grasping a rusted war-hammer from the forge. His stomach turned as he eavesdropped on his grandfather's evening prayer.

It has been ten long years, Father. Tatars, czambul raiders appeared from the East, from the belly of the endless steppes. The Ottoman, Hussain Pasha, crossed the mighty Dniester River, with 80,000. Entire Polish villages crushed into heaps of white ash with fire and sword, the stench still in my nose.

Farmers butchered in their own fields, green and golden crops turned black, barns emptied of livestock. Just die, it told us. Just die. Watching the young and the weak starve still wounds my soul. Churches sacked and desecrated; priests beheaded. Young Polish maidens debauched, passed around for Tatar amusement. It steeled me, Lord. Surely Satan rides at the head of this bloody horror again. Brigands. Raiders. Murderers. Give me my strength, Father. Return my youthful strength for one more battle, I beg of you. I beg of you to remove these horrible memories from my mind. Leave me only the thoughts of loved ones from long ago and those I have now. Amen.

Chapter 9

Several farm hands stood together with sickle, scythe, and pitchfork, eyes focused on the area of approaching hoof beats; a single horse, a hurried pace.

Is he being chased by brigands? Is this a call to arms?

As a silhouette materialized and grew in size, Bolek recognized a neighbor from the village, for he rode the only spotted pony in the region. Grips on weapons relaxed.

"The raiders have burned our village," he shouted, without dismounting his well-lathered pony. "They killed—"

"We know, Alexi," Mother Józefa said.

"How . . . Bolek, was it you?"

"It was my grandson," Grandfather said.

"I knew only you could place shafts that quickly and accurately. Bless you, Bolek," Alexi said, making the sign of the cross. "After dropping two of those dogs, they scurried away immediately for whatever devil's lair they hide in. They feared more archers in the woods."

"Alexi?" Bolek asked. "The giant, the one with the black glowing eyes?"

"Gustaw. His wrath erupted when you interrupted his blasphemy. He threatened a few for your name to no avail and seeks your head. We are ashamed of our cowardice and proud of your revenge. Your name will not be spoken by any."

"And we must keep it this way," Mother Józefa cautioned. "Do you understand, Alexii?"

"Bolek's action changed something in many of us. Perhaps it is possible to defend ourselves. None of us were certain of our savior's name, but the name Bolek will pass none of our lips, Pani Radok."

"Olenka?" Bolek asked.

"As expected. We bury poor Walenka today. The flowers go to a funeral in the stead of a wedding. Can you pass this message westward, Bolek?"

"Yes. I will leave this instant."

"Hold," Mother said. "Alexi, you have a sense of our situation, do you not?"

"Yes, Pani Radok."

"We have twelve men here, all forewarned. Your horse needs rest. Let us break this morning's fast together. We must know all."

Bolek stared at Mother.

Five men greet the rider with pounding hearts and fear in their throats. Mother calmly offers a meal.

Fresh bread and eggs were set out in no time. Kasia ran back and forth from hearth to table, helping to serve. After a morning prayer, the dusty rider spoke first.

"Word came to our parish late last night. An Ottoman army does indeed invade Europe again. Tatars ride with them."

Bolek watched his mother, grandfather and Alexi cross themselves.

"The brigands have this news so grow bolder still. They taunt full aware there is no one left to defend us."

"We will defend ourselves," Bolek uttered.

"God will be with us too, my son."

Then ask him to bring me a sword, Mother.

"Newly made widows and their waifs stream into the village," Alexi continued. "Many farms are burning, their supplies from the last harvest, taken. How do we survive spring and summer without food?"

"We will hunt meat," Bolek replied.

"We need to hunt demons," Grandfather contradicted.

"Sir, the Tatar raids move nearer every day," Alexi said. "They challenge our strength, our wills. We muster little resistance. They grow bolder. They are as many as the leaves on the trees."

"Yesterday I rode south," the farm's yeoman said, "and came upon a large pool of blood in the middle of the road. In the weeds lay a headless body."

"Who can do this to our own people?" Mother asked.

"Bah!" Alexi snorted. "They are lower than dogs. They owe allegiance to neither God nor Poland. Gustaw is not our people. He is the devil's own."

Bolek's stomach swirled at the name 'Gustaw' for it was as if evoking a fire-breathing dragon to the table.

The wolf has left his mountain lair and now prowls the flatlands.

"This fiend was a plague on the region even before conscription took the men to war," Alexi reminded all. "He is a Goliath, bold, heartless, said to be merciless with the saber and ax, invincible in battle. Perhaps our Bolek is our David."

"Józefa," Grandfather shouted, "My armor. My sword."

"Pan Radok, they have muskets," Alexi continued. "Szablas from God-knows-where, battleaxes, spears."

"They scavenge after battles like dogs and wolves, under the cover of night," Grandfather said. "I remember."

"Even if we had these weapons we have no skill with them," the yeoman said.

"Let's ride to the village!" one hand shouted, who turned to take his own advice, but was stopped by the yeoman's firm grip on his arm.

"The village is a deathtrap," Alexi said. "The merchants who still have cottages cower behind their barricaded doors. The brigands will burn them out on a whim. That is their strategy."

"We are not soldiers, Alexi," the yeoman said. "We know crops, not war."

Bolek could understand the yeoman's thoughts. While unerring as an archer, fighting face to face, man to man, Bolek was uncertain, untested. His vision of himself on a massive war horse with his Rozalia behind him faded. But he did remember the imposing walls of her father's compound.

"The Pitry manor is protected with strong wooden walls, and his estate house of stone, Bolek said. "Perhaps they would offer us safety."

"When I rode there with the news, Pan Pitry's son laughed and told me to go hide in the mountains. He has trained men. There are at least twenty who can shoot and fight. Wealth solves many problems for him, but there is none for us."

"Perhaps I should ride there as I spread the message and —"

"We need you here, son," Grandfather said. "We will introduce these brigands to Radok steel – steel from the forge and the heart."

"I must go," Alexi said. "God's mercy."

Bowing his head as he mounted, he made the sign of the cross before disappearing into the once protective foothills, on his way to other neighboring farms to spread the news.

Bolek shielded his eyes from the rising sun and looked to the hills. "Alexi heads eastward. I will take the news to the west. Perhaps then we can escape into the mountain pastures, if need be."

"Ha! I will meet them here and give them a cold blade in greeting," Grandfather said. "I must find my sword, my uniform. Where the hell is my horse?"

"Your son has your horse, Father," Mother Józefa reminded him.

"Bah!" He replied, walking away toward the barn. "I have fought and killed mighty warriors. This rabble will not defeat me."

"I will not leave my home, Bolek," Mother Józefa said. "For this is where your father will come looking for us." She wrapped one arm around her son's waist and pulled him toward the cottage. "All my memories and friends and family are here. We cannot abandon those who depend on us. And your father will be home soon. We must rely on God's will."

I am as a ewe caught in the mud, shuddering, expressionless, and I wait trembling as the wolf's jaws draw ever closer.

For the rest of the day all but the most critical chores were put on hold. It was agreed that if unfamiliar riders appeared on the horizon an alarm should be raised. All would assemble at the makeshift barricade in front of the manor house – hay bales, the wagon overturned and bits of this and piles of that for defense. Bolek led the efforts to protect Radok Manor, yet showed no shame in pitching in with common laborers. One and all prepared for an attack from the raiders; each prayed his brother would fight like a lion; all hearts pounded, bodies sweated, hands trembled.

Later, as he headed west to notify neighbors, Bolek passed many refugees, some headed to the Radok farm for mutual protection. Others simply limped and trudged onward. Brigands grew bold. Ottomans and Tartars drew ever nearer.

Chapter 10

Bolek awoke later than usual, bone weary from the previous day and night ride through the countryside to warn his neighbors of increased brigand activity. Grandfather stood before him at attention, at the head of the table, dressed in a faded blue floral zupon coat, his rust-pocked curved szabla at his side hanging from a thin leather belt under a bright crimson Turkish sash, his knee-length yellow leather boots stained and cracked.

"I am prepared," he told his grandson.

"You look remarkable," Bolek said.

Mother explained that aged men wandered off a bit in their heads and tended to repeat their proudest memories while forgetting the repetition. His grandfather never tired of talk of war, and while the same tale over and over was maddening, sometimes a never-before-heard memory came to Grandfather, and Bolek listened, mesmerized. Indeed, he was proud of the long line of family warriors, somehow gaining personal stature and hope for a future from the deeds of ancestors.

From so many years in the saddle, their eyes and labors off their own needs and desires, the Radoks had fallen into the realm of almost noble and once-well-off poverty. Still, each generation passed on a lingering hope of personal honor, service and memories of recognition for unwavering service to the crown. A fist full of medals lay in a bag stored somewhere.

"I have this wool zupon," Grandfather said as he ran his fingertips down his faded and dusty coat. "No expense spared. Notice my boots. None but a noble could afford leather such as this. I once rode a splendid Arab horse too but have misplaced him. No matter! He will wander back soon."

"But they all saw you, right? Dressed so?"

"I made sure they saw me at Zamosc. The Swedes lusted for our fertile land and thought Poles to be less than human. It was a deluge. *Potop*! As many men as could cover ten large fields of wheat died at their hands in a single afternoon. Our blood watered our own rye fields."

"So many? So fast? It is not possible."

"Dear God, son, nearly one half of our people were put to the sword by the Swedes. And to our shame many Polish nobles went over to their side. Dogs! I stood at Zamosc, in this coat, an eagle on my shield. The peasants and the burghers rose to fight. We loved Poland because Poland loved God. And our resolve was to keep them both intact, together."

"Your szabla is still sharp," Bolek said from rote, tracing the dull curved blade once honed to a razor's edge on both sides for the last eight inches.

"It is this szabla and the Virgin who keeps us free," the old soldier said, his trembling chin jutting upward. "I buzzed and stung like a hornet at the throats of the arrogant Swedes at Jasna Gora. The damn Protestants came to dishonor the Virgin nearly thirty years ago. I fought on foot, backing up our troops as they spiked some of the Swedes' massive cannons.

"Here!" he said, commandeering the table and moving bowls, plates and spoons around to represent the famous battle. "Our brave cavalry cleared a small opening at this point, and it fell to us to hold the line here, giving our men little precious time."

The table, food and condiments came alive for Bolek as his grandfather moved objects like chess pieces.

"The Swedes had to gallop past me, this brightly dressed target," he growled, pounding his chest and pointing to an onion he had designated as himself, "to get to their cannons, this goose egg, and when they charged I cut one down."

Bolek laughed from his belly as his grandfather's fist came down on the egg, spattering the table map and its imaginary armies with yellow goo.

"My sons, Jan and Stefan, your father's brothers – your uncles – they watched me do it."

Bolek stared into his grandfather's faded blue eyes, wishing he could experience the inner vision, to see the faces of the uncles he did not remember.

"A father could not have been prouder." The old man paused, catching his breath and gathering his memories.

"A knight on a giant charger as he comes at you standing your ground is a terrible thing to witness. He raised his saber to slash me, but, at the last possible instant I dodged to his left, under his horse. Driving forward, I skewered him in his armpit with my spear, on his unguarded side. He tumbled like a sack of wet wheat, and I finished him off before he could stand. I crossed myself and said a prayer for him, but I do not know if it had any merit. Protestant Swedes under Charles Gustavus came to sack our holiest Christian shrine. They made war on us, slaughtered children, and all because Sweden was broke and needed wealth. It is said he told the self-righteous English dog, Cromwell, that when he was finished with Poland there would not be a papist left. What kind of men were these?"

"I wish I could have seen all of these things, Grandfather, to be at your side, to add my arm." Bolek's imagination was afire. "Was that your proudest moment, sir?"

"Perhaps. Yet, in '58 I fought next to the famed Castellan of Kiev, Stefan Czarniecki. Our eyes met, fellow Poles battling side by side, protecting the right flank. He nodded. Struggling with difficulty to keep my balance, knee-deep in blood and gore, I nodded back."

For Bolek, the incident with the wolf again seemed pitiful. Grandfather, one among a thousand outnumbered brothers, had stood against invaders who wanted to take his life, his land, his way of life.

"For that moment, the master hetman commander and I were equals on the field of glory. We ripped them off of their saddles in droves. Polish noble and peasant became one, the peasants attacking with scythes, axes, and pitchforks. We citizens risked all, unselfishly, to regain both our homeland and our withered souls."

"How withered souls?"

"We were dead in spirit then, and Poland as a country ailed, drifted. We were not one made of many but many with only self-interest in our hearts. Before we repelled the Swedes at Jasna Gora, we didn't care if they came into Poland. We expected others to repel them. We let our chosen representatives in Cracow deal with them diplomatically. Ha! Politics. Compromise. A meeting of self-serving beggars. Traitors like the Lithuania's Radziwill. A curse on political dogs, Bolek, a curse!"

Vivid recollections of age merged with the naïve dreams of youth.

"Then, when there was little resistance or effort from the self-serving bureaucrats, we said *'Why bother? Is not one ruler, one politico, the same as another?'* We thought nothing would change for our rural lives. We thought ourselves entitled.

"But once this invader moved to destroy the shrine of the Black Madonna, we somehow awoke as one and began to act as one. Something deeper was at work here. It was as if God had breathed a new spirit into our nation. You are too young to understand that the things you can see and touch are not as meaningful or lasting as those you cannot."

"So you all awoke to glory and repelled the invaders. How proud you all must have been."

"I buried two . . . sons, my boys, on that day, Grandson. We had been through so much for so long, taking care of one another, protecting one another's flanks. Both boys fell within minutes of the other." He collapsed into a chair, breaking into tears and a sob. "I couldn't get to them in time. I . . ."

"Burek!" Bolek yelled through the window. "Stop that barking."

"The nightmares come, son. I see my boys, bleeding, slashed, faces skewed in pain. I try to rise, to reach and comfort them, but my legs will not move."

Yet again Bolek shouted at Burek to stop his incessant barking. Grandfather took a moment to recuperate from his mental anguish. Perhaps the dog was upset at Grandfather's emotional outbursts.

"After the Swedes had abandoned the field, I took my slain sons bodies to the woods and buried them deeply, so deeply the wolves would never get at them."

"Let's take the cart and find them now," Bolek said. "I don't care how far away it is. We could bury them here. At home."

"You're a good lad, Bolek," putting his cold hand over his grandson's. "I did return to that awful place several times. I searched. I searched again. But I could never find the spot. It all appeared so differently when there were no bodies, no blood, and no smoke around. Death had left that place by then, and well fed."

"Both the best time and the worst times for you. How can this be?"

"It was not nearly the worst time. Leaving my boys buried in a strange place hurt, but it was in Polish soil. Reclaimed Polish soil. Coming home was worse. Your grandmother spied me walking up the path. I winced as she cocked her head and looked beyond me. When she understood no one was trailing me, stumbling home . . . my heart twisted in my chest as she fell to her knees, her arms pulled over her head, her shrieks echoing through the mountains. She moaned all night. I think I did also. I always wanted brave boys, Bolek, but I wanted alive brave boys, even though I feared such a thing cannot always be."

Bolek again ran his finger along the sorry and pitted blade as his grandfather took a moment to control his trembling lips.

If I fight, I die. If I do not fight I work the soil until I grow old like Grandfather or am killed by Turks, Tatars or brigands.

Bolek, growing tired of the deep pain his grandfather's words brought, peered through the window facing the path to the farm, wishing his father's image would appear in the distance.

Everyone would be so happy. Everything would be all right. They could face the wolves and brigands and Turks together, fashion sharp and strong szablas . . .

"I have enjoyed helping to raise you, Bolek, despite my cranky dotage. But I'll be dammed that for every tooth you grew, I seemed to lose one. I keep the mill up and still prevent the

peasants from lolling around and stealing us blind. I think a grandfather should grow old to see at least one grandson survive." He patted the back of Bolek's head.

"When your father returns, his wagons plump with booty. We'll finish your training in smiting and wielding the sword. We'll harvest the greatest crop ever and go to Cracow to get you horses, armor, a retinue and wagons. Real horses, Polish steeds. You'll be a soldier of resource and wealth then and will go join the hussars and maybe ride with King Sobieski, the wizard king, king by his own hand. They say the Ottomans and Tatars flee in fear the moment his name is whispered."

"A hussar!" Bolek exclaimed, for this was too much to dream. "The Winged Horsemen? Not the infantry? I could become a hussar?" Visions of himself riding into Rozalia's rich manor with shining armor and atop a magnificent steed filled his head.

"Why not?" Grandfather asked. "We country nobles can dream too. Who could prevent us? Next week, we'll go hunting, Bolek. We'll search for wolves. We'll make a blind, shoot a deer, butcher her, and string her up. When a wolf comes a hunting, you'll use your bow. We'll put a respectable wolf skin on our wall. And once you kill a wolf, all their kin will see it in your eyes, smell your confidence, and fear you."

"Were you always brave, Grandfather?" Bolek asked, wondering if training for war made one certain and, therefore, brave.

"Ha!" What a question. In my first fight I trembled much, sweat poured in streams, and then I turned cold, had no spit; I wet myself."

Burek's intensive barking caused Grandfather to shout army curse words at him and beat on the table with his szabla before the barking subsided. "A dog does not bark simply to bark. Perhaps he has caught an unfamiliar scent in the air."

Bolek ran to the door and then outside to have a careful look around. Nothing. No Turks. No Cossacks. No Tatars. No Father.

As he re-entered the house, Kasia appeared from the bedroom, her hair tied in braids, her woolen pullover *letnik dress*, looking like new.

"Has Papa killed many Turks, Grandfather?" she asked.

"Kasia, you are a perfect Góral doll," the old man said, picking her up and twirling her around and around, despite his four score years. "And your brave papa has killed so many Turks, my little princess that his right forearm measured twice as thick as his left."

"*Is*, Grandfather, *is*," Kasia corrected. "Father *is*."

"Is," the old man repeated as he returned his granddaughter to earth. "Last night I dreamed I saw him, on the steppes, slashing invaders, brigands and murderers. He keeps our farm safe. We have not suffered the same fate as others in this region. No one takes our pigs or plump geese. No one!"

"Stop bragging, Father, please," Mother Józefa begged, as she entered the room. "Praise God and praise Mary for sparing us. And we entreat her to end the suffering of those who have been less fortunate. So many."

"And so many more soon to come," Grandfather added.

"It is time to leave for Mass," Mother announced. "Enough of this frightful talk."

"Mass?" Grandfather repeated. "*Psaw Cref Choletta* – God's blood! We go nowhere this day. God will understand."

"It is a sin—"

"I will not die on the road cut down by a horde of scurvy dogs. We will defend our ancestral home."

"Yes, Father," Mother Józefa said with a slight bow. "Kasia, you may change from your Sunday clothes."

"I may be a fading shadow, but I have smelled fresh blood in the air a thousand times. And I smell it now."

Chapter 11

Bolek's role as sentinel brought him to the top of the strategic hill again. It felt uncomfortable being at home on a Sunday morning. This was God's day. He could not remember the last time he had missed Mass.

A chilling breeze caught him by surprise and brought a shiver. Cold air from the high mountains would sometimes invade the lowlands and lower the temperature by many degrees. But this time it seemed a unmistakable omen to the young sentry. The grayish-blue mountains still ringed him, but he now regretted his vain boasts that no army could penetrate his mountains. The mountains now seemed like a box he found himself and his loved ones locked within. Knowing the highlands as well as he did, he remembered the gaps where horsemen and wagons might pass. There were a thousand places he knew to hide where no man could find him. But some of these glens were assuredly known by the brigands also. Ominous clouds swirled around the peaks.

"Therefore, brethren, stand fast, and hold the traditions which ye have been taught, whether by word, or our epistle."

He remembered Sunday Mass, not for the communion with God, or the wisdom of Father Czarnota, but for the promise of a glimpse of Rozalia. Ignoring the priest's words, as usual, he always strained to look over the barriers of kneeling neighbors within the old wooden incense-tinged house of worship. But a fortuitous gap in the crowd always appeared and revealed Rozalia's profile. For Bolek, it was as if the warming sun had popped over a mountain and banished the surrounding cold and uncertainty. What was once a dark and damp church, designed for prayer, reflection, and penance now transformed into a golden temple, ablaze in beauty and the promise of love.

Rozalia always knelt and prayed in the front row, amid her family, her corn silk hair set in delicate braids, dangling to the middle of her back from beneath her white *peremitki* head scarf, worn in reverence to God. Always bored by Father Czarnota's indecipherable chanting, Bolek often recalled a particular cherished memory of an evening spent at a wedding celebration last year. Those golden braids swung in captive measure as Rozalia turned left, swayed right, spun round as elegantly as a butterfly in the air, fused with the melody and harmony, the scene embraced in music and laughter.

An elbow from Mother reminded him the ancient rite now called for the faithful to stand; his vision of Rozalia blocked like a dark curtain draped over the golden sun. But always a few bodies shifted weight or swiveled a hair this way or that and Rozalia's profile reappeared briefly. For him, her image eclipsed the very gold adorning the altar.

As the congregation rose, as one, to file out of the church, Rozalia came into view. The sight of her never failed to freeze his feet in place and dizzy his mind; the moment of genuine recognition, the mischievous twinkle in her eye, the delicate nose and rounded cheeks. He forced an enigmatic smile, presented so as not to betray any indication of what was stirring within him.

Unlike the larger-boned Radok women, Rozalia was petite, yet every inch a woman, in manner, in words and lately, in curve. Bolek found himself having to tear his eyes from her whenever she was near. Freckled as a fawn, he wanted to count them all. Though he thought the Virgin Mother and his own mother stood for what women were supposed to be, something else seemed at work as his body reacted differently when Rozalia neared.

Is this sin I feel? Am I evil in nature because of what I sense and am driven toward?

As Rozalia's prune faced father passed, a black drape was again thrown over the sun, the icy canyon wind swirled around Bolek. Pan Pitry never failed to size Bolek up from boot to crown, oozing displeasure, forcing Bolek to adjust his highland garb, for it somehow did not fit properly under the scrutiny of Pan Pitry. The merchant family adopted the refined shop-made fashions of

Cracow, which lay fifty miles to the northeast, with their dyed silks imported by caravan from China and Persia, styled with well-tailored lines and a tight fit. Pan Pitry and his wife announced their wealth dressed in elegant flowing *delias,* costly fur-trimmed capes. Rozalia wore the Krakovian style of white linen, her skirt dotted with red and green flowers, her pure white blouse adorned with puffed lace at her neck, a bright red vest with polished brass decorations sewn into the fabric. Her braids were tied with blue linen flowers, the ends brushed out into puffed balls bigger than a man's fist. Her red boots were the same color as her conch necklace.

Bolek reminded himself to feel no shame for his light and fitted homemade Góral clothing, for it was clean, well-made, the wool, mixed with flax, and spun from the fiber of his own sheep, and the style had been worn proudly, unchanged in design by generations of the Góral Tatra folk. Yes, he was proud of his dress from the tips of his black moccasin-like *kierpce* shoes, up to his white pants with the green embroidered seams, held up with a wide leather belt with sturdy brass buckles, to his fitted white linen shirt, decorated with bright red and green designs at the chest and shoulder. He held a traditional large, round black felt hat in his hand, the band trimmed in red and white, a goose feather jutting out the side.

Outside the church, when an opportunity presented itself, Bolek offered greetings to Rozalia's mother. The formidable lady always frowned or pretended she did not see him. Both of Rozalia's brothers saw Bolek for certain, for each cast threatening glances and silent growls his way. Once on the wagon ride back home, Bolek asked his mother why Rozalia's family disliked him when he had done nothing to vex him.

"Ha!" Grandfather said. "Your sin is that you have been born both in a family with a tradition of noble military service but lacking in gold or silver. Pitry gold can be taken away. Your ancestors' deeds cannot."

"Father," Mother Józefa said, attempting to prevent his further comment.

"The Pitrys are merchants. They sell kielbasa sausage, Eastern spices, and probably women's under garments."

Mother gasped.

"They have money," Grandfather continued, "but have never lifted a sword in Poland's behalf. They despise you, Bolek, because we are their betters no matter how nicely they dress or how many racehorses and buildings they own."

"Bolek," Mother Józefa said, putting her hand on his as he guided the cart with the reins, "some of what your grandfather says is true."

"Bolek," Grandfather asked through a grin, "I must be going more deaf. Did your mother just admit I told the truth for once?"

A glare silenced Grandfather. "Wealthy nobles will rarely marry those with less gold. It seems there is never enough for those who have it and too much seems to somehow blind the heart. It is the nature of this world. But the value of our lives has little to do with gold."

Bolek frowned, unable to understand his mother's words, for his sole purpose was to obtain Rozalia's father's permission to marry his daughter. Whatever it would take, he would do it.

"You will dance at my wedding, Mother."

"I pray I do and you choose your bride with love, commitment and respect."

"Then it shall be Rozalia."

"Bolek, we have a large farm, with unusually favorable soil. Our extended family, our serfs, they are treated fairly, kept in our confidence as family; we manage our farm with dignity for all. We embrace God and our country before everything. We have given that which is most precious to Poland. We are rich in the things one cannot see, the things which will last through eternity. Rozalia comes from a life different from ours. Can you honestly imagine her living happily among us?"

Grandfather snorted. The horse snorted. Bolek lightened the pressure on the reins. The rest of the journey home was spent in silence, Bolek's jaw set in concentration.

The Pitry family snubs always dealt a serious blow to Bolek's intentions. As youngsters, Bolek and Rozalia's brothers had been schooled together twice a week at the church. But the Pitry boys eventually were sent to Cracow for what they deemed a formal education. When they returned for the summer last year, an acquaintance called Mateusz came with them. Not only did he stay at the Pitry manor, but Bolek sensed this new boy was a threat; he had an obvious admiration for Rozalia. The thought that Mateusz slept under the same roof as Rozalia often set Bolek's blood to a boil. An uncontrollable urgency for action, of any sort, came to him. Bolek became a veritable knight in his dreams. The Pitry boys and Mateusz became Turks and brigands. Swords were crossed; heads cleaved from shoulders, blood ran in rivers.

Rozalia's family was powerful and influential, with strong political and business contacts in Cracow. While there was little hope for an insignificant Bolek of winning such a highly placed maiden for a wife, still, he decided to boldly proclaim his intentions.

The spring prior, he'd decided on a traditional maypole ritual as the way to express his intentions. He selected a long, straight forest spruce – one bigger, he hoped, than any rival could wield. He cut it down with an ax and saw in the dead of night, meticulously trimming the limbs and removing the bark. With no access to the great city of Cracow to obtain the appropriate paints for the demanded decoration, Bolek, employing the master wood-carving skills his father and grandfather taught him, lovingly engraved hearts, lambs, and other symbols of love onto the body of the pole.

One late afternoon he carted his maypole to the Pitry estate with the imagined stealth of a Tatar thief. With obvious amusement, the farm workers all stopped their labors to enjoy this unfolding scene. Following a thoughtful plan, he dug, pounded and bound the pole and turned to the Pitry estate hat in hand Rozalia immediately threw wide her bedroom window and leaned out, eyes dancing with merriment, hand to mouth in what Bolek saw as appropriate maidenly shame. In a time-honored tradition, Bolek had declared his intentions for all to see.

But the next step in the ancient tradition was never acted on, for Bolek was neither invited into the Pitry home for dinner; nor recognized for his declaration of intention. As dusk came, he stood silent next to his unacknowledged maypole, facing an ever-darkening stone silent manor house he knew to be filled with people. When no candles flamed in the vast estate house as night blanketed all, Bolek departed. Before entering the black forest, he turned in his saddle and noted the estate windows now ablaze with candlelight. He hurt with a deep pain of rejection and unworthiness.

On the route home, he vowed to become more than he was, to be deemed a worthy suitor by Rozalia's family. This meant wealth. This meant respect. This meant war and plunder. His will would overcome all obstacles.

Chapter 12

Another day and night of anxious anticipation came and went. Then six riders, known to be Pan Pitry's men rode into Radok Manor, each wearing a haughty face. Bolek was handed a letter.

I have an immediate need of your skills. This contingent will guarantee your safety. You will be paid in kind.

Pan Adam Pitry.

His head swam as he read it several times. Pan Pitry would not call him for common labor, for he had many laborers. This must be a request for something to do with the sword, for the Radok reputation for this craft was still alive. While he was no authority, Bolek reasoned he could handle himself well in sharpening any weapon. Or perhaps word of his deeds in the village had leaked out. No one could know he ran. The shame of his trial with the wolf? No. Pan Pitry was making amends; handing Bolek a much-desired olive branch. Folding the letter and sliding it into his pocket Bolek resisted the urge to fly to Rozalia's manor house.

After announcing his new prospects to the family, Grandfather grumbled one could always tell a rich man by how he advertised his waste. Ornate houses, overly plush robes, a stable of horses not meant for labor or for war but for amusement. A bejeweled szabla which never tasted blood. Grandfather's message was clear: stay away from the Pitrys. But Bolek could no sooner do this than stop breathing.

He thanked God Rozalia wasn't there to witness his ignoble entrance upon the farm's draft horse into the Pitry Manor. Her older brother, the rotund and nervous Maciej, received him with a brisk gesture and pointed to the mill house with a thumb. Bolek marveled at the numerous and well-tended buildings and equipment Pitry riches could muster – a wealth allowing the family to pursue leisure activities while others tended the countless acres of wheat, rye, oats, barley and millet. Even the fences were well-maintained and painted. Painted! The outbuildings used for storage for food and equipment reflected the sheer size of the farming operation. Every time Bolek came to this exotic farm he discovered something changed, unlike his own farm where nothing had changed for years.

He noticed a new stable to accommodate the numerous horses needed to plow the vast acreage, the wood not yet fully weathered from age. Another structure, stretching for twenty paces, served as shelter for the many workers needed to tend to the fields, judging by the bunked beds visible in rows through the double doorway. A granary, smokehouse, cheese room and general storage building formed a wide arc, surrounding Bolek in what seemed to him a small town.

Grandfather had warned that fortunes could be made by selling and trading supplies during wars and that the rustle of a skirt was not a valid reason to get involved with the Pitry family. Bolek was blind to this advice – just so many words. But rumors of ever-growing merchant contracts, political contributions and valuable contacts in Cracow abounded with the Pitry name attached.

Bolek counted ten well-armed laborers just within his own sight, a number capable of discouraging all but the largest raiding party. Pitry Manor was a fortress, made safe by wealth. The security that money could obtain was not lost on him. Someday . . .

As he walked toward the Pitry manor, a whistle turned his head. Maciej stood at the forge and beckoned as if calling a dog. Bolek could not help but notice the sheathed saber hanging at Maciej's side. The inlaid jewels and gold scrollwork told Bolek this was a ceremonial blade, used for format attire, and not one suitable for fighting.

Maciej pointed into the dark smiting barn. Bolek stooped and entered. A thin, soot-covered serf stood next to the blazing hearth and bowed to Bolek. The Pitry smith, a diminutive man, wore bright red welts which stood out from the grimy flesh on his face and arms. He stared at Bolek in childlike anticipation.

"I hope for your sake, Radok," Maciej hissed with every bit of condescendence he could muster, "Father will be pleased with your shoes."

"Shoes?" a confused Bolek asked.

"You were summoned to craft a set of shoes for Father's new racing horse," Maciej muttered as if it hurt his pride to hold a conversation with Bolek. "This fool has made an expensive stallion lame with his inferior product."

Bolek forced himself not to divulge any hint of reaction to the insult Maciej expected to see on his face. Visiting Rozalia's manor to consult on the crafting of a soldier's saber for Pan Pitry had, in fact, been a summons for a farrier to forge some iron horseshoes. The letter had been unclear. He had fallen into the trap like a lamb to the slaughter.

"Where is the horse?" Bolek asked.

"What does it matter?" Maciej asked. "It is a large horse. Therefore, large shoes."

"Then tell your father you have decided on large shoes and I can depart now."

"Father wants your opinion," Maciej replied, while chewing on his lip.

"Each horse is unique," Bolek explained. "Each animal's hooves are of a different size, each grows differently, and some horses may need a shoe shaped specifically for each hoof."

Maciej, on the defensive, attacked his own smith. "You fool Gawel! You did not know this?"

Bolek bit his tongue while desiring to reproach Maciej for not knowing this either. But confronting Rozalia's brother on any account would lead to no good. "Go get the stallion," Maciej shouted at the smith.

Bolek looked around the Pitry forge. The huge hearth, the hammers, anvils, pincers, nippers, rasps were all lined up within easy reach. Chunks and bars of iron lay stacked in the corner. The one thing missing here was the knowledge to construct a proper saber.

Knowledge I do not possess either. So I will make horseshoes. The hapless serf returned with the tall dark bay stallion. Bolek could only marvel at the stallion's beauty and strength. Here was a horse appearing as if it could rival the south wind in speed and never tire.

What would such a prize be worth?

Bolek asked the serf to tie the stallion to the post and began his investigation as Maciej departed with a belch.

"Master," the serf whispered, "I've only experience with plow horses. Can you teach me to shoe such a beast?"

"Yes, stay close. It is knowledge usually, with some skill. Watch."

Bolek patiently explained each step of the process to the attentive serf and answered all his questions. He showed first how the animal's hooves had been improperly trimmed, with too much slant, and how to correct it. He explained the marks from the previous shoe nails had been pounded too near the center of the hoof, giving the horse immense pain. It was no surprise this spectacular steed was not winning the races he was bought to run.

"The shape of the hoof is key, the weight and thickness of the shoe important," he explained to Gawel. "Hot shoeing, where the iron, still soft from the fire, can be bent to a necessary form is ever better in many cases."

By mid-afternoon Bolek and his intent pupil had fashioned four iron shoes tailored for the racehorse's unique hooves. Gawel expressed confidence he could duplicate Bolek's method and thanked the 'Master'.

"An undeserved title, Gawel,"

Gawel's eyes went wide looking beyond him and Bolek turned to stand before Pan Pitry. Pitry motioned with a finger and Gawel understood to lift the horse's hind leg to reveal the new horseshoe. Pitry studied the stallion's hooves from various angles.

"On the surface, this appears to be masterly work, Radok," Pan Pitry announced. "You employ hot forging as they do in Cracow."

"Yes, Pan Pitry."

"You learned the technique from your father?"

"Grandfather, sir," Bolek responded, feeling no discomfort in the presence of Pan Pitry, content to let his work speak for itself.

"Has Gawel paid close enough attention to duplicate this work?"

"Yes, Pan Pitry."

"Let us hope so."

Bolek took pleasure from Master Pitry's smug smile as the landlord ran his hand over the precious stallion's rump as his sons joined him.

"Now, perhaps this overpriced lump of horse flesh will run as promised when I purchased him."

"I am sure of it, sir," a daring Gawel promised. "Master Radok—"

"Let us hope young Radok is a better farrier than a shepherd or keeper of bees," Pitry said.

Though Bolek's ears burned, he showed no emotions as the comment elicited a round of laughter from Pan Pitry's sons.

While he had been proud of his ability and skill today he now relived his cowardice in the mountains. Shepherd tongues had wagged, and now proof that the whole countryside knew was before him. A report will certainly be brought to Rozalia by the lord's two sons. Here he stood, shirtless, covered in soot and sweat, while these two dandies chuckled in their lavish silks and rattled bejeweled sabers.

"Master Radok, payment waits at the manor house," the lord said.

"May I wash first, sir?" Bolek asked.

"No need for formalities. Service done and compensation required."

Approaching the sprawling wooden manor, with its cross-gabled roof, peaks for each separate bedroom window, and the tallest for the lord's grand hall, each support wrapped in elegant wood designs the Góral people were known for carving, Bolek took in a deep breath. With war and violence springing from every corner, this county merchant bought treasures to fill his home, rubbed shoulders with Cracow politicians and raced and wagered on expensive horses. Was war only a concern of soldiers and farmers? The poor its only victims? Did Muslims and brigands leave wealthy merchants and politicians alone?

Chapter 13

Entering the residence of a member of the Polish elite and master of the entire Góral region was something new. On passing thorough the elegantly engraved double-doors, pulled wide by a house servant, a world unimagined appeared to the young Pole. The fear of starvation and brigand attack did not exist here.

Gold-colored tapestries hung from most walls. The oaken floors gleamed, covered here and there with Eastern carpets of which Bolek had only heard. Candles, each held dear in the Radok manor, were in abundance, and with flame during the day.

What must it cost to light this splendid hall?

This manor was a carefully planned cornucopia of color and richness. Paintings hung here, and ornate hand-carved bookshelves stood there, scrolls spilling out on long tables, books lined up in rows. Curios and adornments filled spaces between each wonder. An army of Góral woodworkers must have labored for months creating the numerous carvings and decorative touches – a scene from the Passion, an entire alcove reserved for the image of the Queen of Heaven.

As he moved deeper into Lord Pitry's great hall, Bolek spied a copy of the *Merkuriusz Polski Ordynaryjny*, the famous Cracow newspaper, lying prominent on a lone table. By the date, it was but a week old. Such things were rare in the country. News this early must be ridden in on a regular basis.

The ceiling vaulted two stories. A large wooden wheel, a candle mounted at the end of each spoke, hung suspended by a black chain from the top beam. Bolek could tell by the color these were beeswax and not made of common sheep tallow.

Swords, shields and other mementos of war crowded the walls. An ornate musical instrument Bolek could not name anchored one corner. A matching stool stood before it and matching bowlegged chairs sat on either side.

A cry from behind made Bolek turn with a start.

"Boleczek!" Rozalia cried, using an affectionate form of his name as she ran to him, stopping abruptly as she got a close look at him. "Mud on your shoes! On Mother's carpet. I would allow you to kiss my hand, but yours is filthy. Am I not worthy of a presentable Boleczek?" Her sparkling blue eyes wide in question.

"I wanted to wash, but your father ordered me here for payment."

He laughed as she brushed soot from his cheek before placing a peck of a kiss on it.

"You are too easy to tease," she said, rubbing her lips and chin to ensure no soil stained her. "But you must wash. Father and Mother are coming soon. You must be presentable. Out! Wash!"

Boots in hand and heart in throat, there was no choice but to withdraw outside to the well. His attempts to clean a day's work of labor and grime from his clothing were unsuccessful, yet after a credible effort, he sauntered back to the manor door expecting to be greeted. The massive door was closed and did not respond to his knocks. Soon he circled the house to possibly get someone's attention from a window.

"Why did you let this unkempt beggar into my home?" Rozalia's mother voice floated out of an open window.

"I see their eyes meet regularly in church," Pan Pitry replied. "She has feelings for him. Just now I made him appear as he truly is, and here in her own surroundings. You should be thanking me. She will come to realize on this day he does not belong in our world."

"You are such a schemer, Roman," she chuckled. "Pray we are done with this peasant suitor from now on. Do you remember the maypole? Gad."

"Do I not have our daughter's best interest at heart?" the lord asked.

Bolek bolted to his thick horse, tearing a feed bag from its head, bridled and saddled it roughly, fleeing from his shame. On reaching the safety of the forest, he attempted to calm himself as cold fury shook him to his core. He wished he could push his heavy horse into a gallop, but the old gelding could end up lame from such a pace.

Reacting to the sound of approaching hoof beats from behind, he guided the horse off the trail and into the safety of the trees and thick brush.

Chapter 14

"Rozalia!" he cried out.

The young girl turned her Spanish mare with ease and rode to Bolek's side as he emerged from the thicket.

"Why did you leave?" she asked. "If I embarrassed you, I am sorry. I only wished you clean so Mother would not scold us both."

He was touched she had followed him, but the overheard ridicule and cruel trap set by Pan Pitry still stung.

"Your father summoned me to make iron shoes for his horse. I finished the work and left."

"Not true," she said, urging her horse parallel to his and cocking her head with a coy smile. "You came to see me."

"True, Rozalia. I will not deny it. I came to see you."

"And you are still mad about the maypole and my family's rudeness."

He nodded.

"But you are happy I rode fast and hard to catch up to you," she said through an impish smile.

Another nod.

"Then everything I say is true?"

"There are no lies in you," he whispered.

"Why are you always so sad, Boleczek? Why do I have to work so hard to make your radiant smile bloom?"

"Sad? I am sad because I am but a skillful worker to your father, sad because I am a timid shepherd to my family, sad because your parents make it clear I am less than a desirable match. I am a noble without nobility."

He did not expect the short giggle in response.

"*I am only a small boy,*" she sang in a lilting voice. '*Who knows no Latin, who knows little, will tell you little.* Join me, Boleczek. We are Górale and noted for our singing."

Reluctant at first, he joined her in the old Easter song, sensing

65

she was trying to lighten his spirit with music, the language of the soul.

'I will tell you news, that today we will eat eggs and salt pork, and colored eggs and cheesecake, and blessed pork, and bitter horseradish which will curl your nose.'

They both pinched their noses and said the last few words through laughter.

"Remember my sixteenth birthday," she asked, "when you gave me the doll you carved? The one you were ashamed of?"

"Yes," he admitted.

"I knew you were embarrassed because, as I opened presents from others, you grew redder with each gift and more solemn. You thought your present the least, but it was the most. I still treasure it. So intricate, so lovingly made."

"It will last forever," he boasted.

"Unlike the expensive hat from Cracow which is now horribly out of style and lies smashed under other discarded things in my wardrobe."

"Remember when we danced, and the adults made fun of us thinking we were trying to mimic them?"

"I do," she replied. "But we are now older by several years."

"But we are still as we were?"

"Not if you run away from our hospitality and refuse payment for your work."

Bolek shrugged; again, no words. He wanted to proclaim his love for her then and there, to take her away, to go and make his fortune with her. But she turned a certain way, and he saw something of his sister Kasia in her. She was a woman but yet an innocent girl. And he knew he had to stay on the farm and be the man of the house – to protect his family. It was acceptable to dream, but he would never abandon those who needed him.

"I see your brain working, Boleczek. What are you thinking?"

"Of my place in the world."

"Father told mother you are a master iron-worker."

"It only matters what you think of me, Rozalia."

"What I think? I think as you do. We are childhood friends."

I love you, Rozalia. Yet you call me friend.

"There," she said. "Again it seems as if your thoughts are high up in the mountains rather than here with me."

"What is to become of us, Rozalia?"

"Once these senseless wars are over things will return as they were. Father says wars fill his gold chests, so they are good."

"Good? They keep my father away fighting and the brigands at our throats."

"But they will end. Father says they always do. I'll wed some prince and my brothers are to continue in father's business ventures. One day the Pitrys may be ennobled by the king. Others have. It can happen."

"And me?"

"Bolek Radok? The great archer, son and grandson of warriors? You will go to war and keep Poland's borders safe. We each have our destiny, no?"

"Destiny?" Bolek growled. "Me on the borders bleeding for the wealthy and you in the bed of a prince!"

He understood he spoke too crudely, too truthfully as Rozalia's face flushed, contorted in shock.

"Bolek! What has gotten into you today?"

"Something wears at me, Rozalia. I apologize. Something closes in on me, as if I belong nowhere. It is not your fault. I supposed I want to be that prince," he admitted.

A strange look came to her now, and he knew she recognized his intentions for the first time. She flushed and turned her eyes away. Things would never be the same between them ever again.

"You are of two minds, Bolek," she said after a painful pause.

Bolek could feel a wall separating them now.

"Rozalia, at times you are a girl, all giggles and rustling skirts and you look at the world as a new puppy does. The next minute you are a woman of the world, wise, confident, guarded. Which are you?"

"I am your friend and you accept me as I am. Who knows what will happen to you and me. We must see the world for ourselves. Mustn't we?"

"Yes, Mistress," he teased, bowing from the waist as best as he could in the saddle. "We must."

"You have forgotten your just payment," she went on, laying her heels into her mount until she was knee to knee with Bolek. He took in her exotic perfume. "Speak with your mother and have her teach you how to wash and dress. Then, perhaps my father will agree to allow us to see each other in more social settings."

Hopelessness followed by a ray of hope. What am I to think? The way she moves her eyes and her lips and how the wind plays with her hair. Let me gaze at her forever.

He resisted an urge to embrace her.

"You have heard about my shame in the mountains?"

"My brothers delighted in the telling of it."

There! There it is. She knows. So help me I will never run again. Never. Better to die.

"And I told them when they are both fat-belly lazy bankers with melancholic and fatter wives you will be someone of note."

"They are really fat in Cracow?"

"The women mostly look like overstuffed sausages in their expensive dresses," she said while leaning forward as if to ensure none might overhear. "And few if any of the merchants have your honesty or strength."

"So you are not ashamed of a poor noble boy who runs from a wolf?"

"If I were ever in bodily danger I would want you and none other to be at my side. If such ever happens, I will whisper your name. And you will appear."

Again he resisted the urge to hug her.

"After I save you could we dance again, together, as we did

those three years ago?"

"You are my only partner," she said offering a leather bag of coins. "Now take this. I grabbed it from the table where my father left it for you when you ignored his shouts to return. He will *not* be pleased with me."

Bolek accepted the payment and stuffed the heavy bag into his shirt.

Rising in her stirrups, Rozalia kissed him on the cheek. He blushed and smiled as he watched her ride away.

"Be careful," he shouted, then cursed himself for sounding like a mother.

"Don't worry about me," she cried, "I am in God's hands as are you."

Bolek's spirits were as light as air now and he wondered how a woman could have such an immediate impact on such a morose one as he. Someone of note, she had called him. At least of note in the future. But by the szabla, the plow, or as a merchant or a master sword maker in Cracow? How to become of note? What path?

He trotted home with the waning reddish sun peeking through the tops of the swaying trees. Forgetting his place and the times, his sole concern for a great future, he filled the darkening woods with music from his flute, an old Górale folk song and then gave it words with a strong voice, as the Polish highlanders often did when spirits were high. The song told the story of a young Góral who sadly left the mountains of his childhood.

Chapter 15

Mother Józefa was forced to pursue Grandfather several times around the table before he stopped bellowing crude barracks songs. Bolek and Kasia chuckled and applauded the mock anger and cat and mouse game.

"You will surely go to Hell, Father."

"It cannot be worse than what I've already been through."

The patriarch eventually collapsed on a stool, his jug of vodka cradled in both arms.

"It is a wonder how you men believe you can fight when you are drunk," a breathless Józefa said.

"If you knew war, daughter-in-law, you'd wonder how it is a man can fight sober."

No riders brought distressing news for two days now; not one brigand sighted. Word came that there had been some talk of Cracow sending soldiers to the area. While farm chores took precedent over sentry duty, Grandfather was aching for a confrontation. And the vodka flowed.

"We must ride to the village," Mother Józefa announced. We still need supplies, and perhaps a young pup for Burek to train. He barks all the time and his wounds do not heal properly."

"Booowlek," Grandfather said, slurring his grandson's name, "be sure to find a replacement for me too. My sole job these days is to turn vodka into urine."

This admission caused the old man to laugh, singing something unintelligible in a screeching, off-tune falsetto.

"Kasia and I will get the wagon ready, Son."

Bolek half filled a bucket with water and dug a heated warming stone from the hearth, juggling it from hand to hand then tossing it into the bucket. The sizzling steam relaxed him as he knelt and dunked his head until it pressed against the stone. He blew bubbles as he massaged his scalp, oblivious to the world around him, holding his breath for as long as possible.

Muted vibrations; creaking floorboards. A solid thud snapped his dripping head from the bucket. He rose just in time to catch his pale grandfather.

"By God, I got one," Grandfather rasped, spitting blood onto Bolek's face before the old man's full weight slumped into him. Clearing his eyes with his forearm, he saw blood spurting from a long gash across his grandfather's stomach. Grandfather moaned, shuttered, and went still.

Shouting men, Burke's bark, laughter, high-pitched shrieks. Just like the village. Raiders! Grandfather murdered!

Running toward the door, he stumbled over a body writhing on the floor. A strange and grimy face, gurgling blood, both hands pressed to his neck in an effort to suppress the red gushing. Grandfather's szabla lay next to him. Bolek realized the two men had grappled and exchanged saber slashes at the doorway. Bolek grabbed the szabla and ran to the screams.

Smoke clouded his eyes, dust choked him. Horses galloped this way and that. He made out two brigands on horseback blazing past him toward the barn, hacking and laughing as they slashed at defenseless serfs.

"Not the child! Please, God," from somewhere beyond the dust cloud took Bolek's full attention. Squeezing the hilt of the szabla he charged into the haze with a scream of rage.

Five short paces brought him to a writhing brigand on the ground, straddling his bloody-faced mother who, despite her predicament looked to her left where another brigand dragged Kasia by her hair. Reaching his mother and her attacker in two strides, he plunged his szabla into the brute's back. As he drove the blade aided by his whole bodyweight, the saber snapped at the hilt. Bolek dragged the still body off his mother, and helped her rise to reach Kasia.

A blow from behind and Bolek staggered, seeing stars, fighting for consciousness. A knee in the stomach, he lost his breath and crashed to the ground. A boot to his chest pinned him. Recovering his eyesight he stared up into a madman's leathery face, a pitiless grin, a battleaxe rising over his shoulder, both hands on the hilt.

Lord, please do not let Kasia's scream be the last thing I hear.

Chapter 16

As the ax reached its zenith, now ready for the death blow, Bolek caught the blur of horse and rider pass extremely close to him. This somehow changed his executioner's expression to one of surprise an instant before his head tumbled down his chest, hitting Bolek's shoulder before bouncing along the ground. The beheaded body fell backwards.

Turning his head while rising, he stood mere feet from a wild-eyed, hatchet-faced uniformed soldier, spinning round and round on an equally wild-eyed horse. Wielding a blood-dripping saber, Bolek's savior beckoned brigands to come to him. One, then another of the monsters was dispatched with deft precision. This one took a spear thrust to the face at point blank range, his body thrown backward like a toy; another was knocked flat by the horse's haunch then skewered with the same spear. The wild horseman then launched the spear at the brigand grappling with Kasia. Hit in the upper back, the man fell, attempting to dislodge the spear.

As more brigands attacked the rider, Bolek awoke from the spectacle, grabbed the battleaxe that was meant to cleave his head and ran to help the soldier. Meeting the eyes of an onrushing murderer with a szabla Bolek shouted and charged. He was again startled as one then a second arrow whizzed past his ear, burying themselves in the man's chest – dead before he crumbled to the ground. He turned to face two more uniformed men, airborne, their horses hurdling the corral fence, both releasing shafts at the top of their jumps. Brigands all around him now fell dead with a brutal efficiency Bolek could never have imagined.

Mother Józefa's cry brought reality back. Kasia, on her knees and shaking wildly, staring at the dead villain lying before her trembled, but Bolek could see she was not seriously injured.

"The cavalry!" Mother Józefa rasped as she reached and

embraced her daughter. "Thanks be to Jesus!" She shouted, running with a limp to the safety of the house with Kasia in her arms, attempting to cover both of them as best she could.

Glancing around for any imminent threat, Bolek's heart sank and tears welled as he spotted Burek lying still near the sty, an arrow embedded in his ribs.

Even my dog.

None of the plundering dogs was left standing. Bolek counted four uniformed soldiers each atop a war horse, on full alert, as if they welcomed attacks.

Only four are able to deliver this mayhem against a small army?

By their armor, he could tell these were members of the renowned Polish armored cavalry – *pancerni*.

What miracle brings these warriors here and now?

All four now gazed off into the distance. The tall one, angular, with a chiseled face, a drooping black mustache flapping in the wind, nodded to his companions. This is the one who saved Bolek.

"*Psaw Cref Choletta* – God's blood!" Bolek heard him exclaim. "Other than a girl dancing or a Baltic ship with her sails full with the wind, there is nothing more beautiful than a galloping horse."

Looking for what this cavalry *pulkownik* (captain) studied in the distance, Bolek spotted the sole surviving brigand galloping off across the fields.

"Czesław, it is unduly windy," the captain said, never taking his eyes from the horizon.

"Even the wind is no match for No Arc," the red-haired, lantern-jawed giant replied.

"Note how it moves," the leader continued, "a mare, I think. Some Kalmuck in her methinks, but taller, longer."

While Bolek's heart still pounded, his mouth dry and breath short, these men were engaged in calm discussion mere minutes after a life-or-death struggle where they dispatched three times their number without a scratch.

"Head up," the cavalryman continued, "gliding over the prairie like a stately white arrow slicing through the air. Look at the muscled haunches." He pointed his blood stained szabla at the distant image. "She does not deserve to carry that coward. I want her, Czesław. Can you make such a shot?"

Bolek gazed in rapt curiosity as the redheaded giant unsheathed an arrow, notching it to the string of a thick blue bow.

No man could make that shot. A waste of an arrow.

Suddenly he effortlessly pushed hard on his stirrups and sprang into the air, his feet landing balanced on his saddle, his mount never flinching. It seemed he took forever to gauge his shot as the fleeing raider gained distance with each second. The rye in the fields and the higher branches of the trees seemed mere captives of the gusting wind, somehow daring the bowman, echoing the bald one's challenge.

"Can you make the shot?"

"Yes," the bowman answered, pulling back on the bowstring, straining the recurved structure to its limit.

"Kill that horse and I will take your mount," he cautioned, twirling one side of his mustache between thumb and index finger, yet never taking his squinting eyes from the distant horse and rider.

"Thank you, Priest," the bowman nodded. "Your confidence does me honor."

A solid twang. The arrow disappeared. The fleeing brigand lurched forward, flailed this way and that, and then fell from his mount, the shaft lodged squarely between his shoulders. The swift white mare slowed, came to a halt, looked back briefly, and drifted off to graze.

The leader, the one they called Priest, standing upright in his stirrups, put two fingers to his lips and whistled three short bursts. He repeated this action twice again before the horse turned and made her way to the call. Bolek's eyes darted from one to the other as the four warriors dismounted, discussing what to do with the slain bodies as the white horse ambled back to the farm and trotted up to Priest, who took the reins dangling from her bridle.

Priest or witch?

Eavesdropping, Bolek learned the horse was indeed a mare, Kalmuck, most likely with Turkish blood. She was strong, able to live on a wisp of food. The Kalmuck still had feral blood but a willing temperament. The Turkish Arab in her made her malleable. She could be trained to engage in battle, and a thief had no right to own her. She would bring a king's ransom in Cracow.

A Pole without a horse is a man without a soul.

Bolek had heard it at table a thousand times.

Priest slapped Czesław, the archer, on the shoulder then walked over to Bolek.

"Are you hurt, son?"

"No, sir. But my grandfather is dead and my mother—"

"The women will look after each other. They are well used to it. But go attend to them. We will remove all this garbage for you."

As Bolek entered the house the servants had already wrapped his grandfather's body in a sheet, while others washed the blood from the floor, their buckets and rags full of pinkish water. An attendant was sewing Mother Józefa's soiled smock together where it had been ripped, her face bruised, her left eye puffed shut, holding Kasia, hugging her while ignoring the child's plea of 'I am fine. Let me go.'"

Bolek glanced at the bucket he had washed in and pondered what had changed since he had pulled his dripping head from it. He took one last long look at the sheeted figure on the floor. He had known his grandfather his whole life, and Grandfather had been an old man for that entire time. But not too old to defend his family, for Grandfather had killed a brigand.

Grandfather dead. My mother and sister attacked. Myself seconds away from death. Burek gone. Pancerni here. What is happening?

Chapter 17

You are the man of the house now, Bolek." Mother Józefa said with little energy. "Until your father returns. Go out and help our Good Samaritans. Thank them. Say I will have food for them within . . . soon."

"Mother, these men are like Father and Grandfather?"

"Of course they are, Bolek. These are Polish knights. Much higher in rank, but yes, comrades in arms. We are honored to serve them at our home as they serve Poland."

He returned to help his saviors as they dragged bodies to the nearest hay wagon, hefting the dead weight into the wagon bed like sacks of grain. Boots, belts, hats, bows, arrows and swords were piled into a heap near the main corral. The one called Priest barked instructions to his men and the serfs. The soldiers' faces betrayed no emotion as Bolek pitched in with the trembling and unquestioning serfs to strip the corpses.

These are warriors and are familiar with death. They've performed this cleaning up after a battle many times.

Lugging a saddle to the weapons pile, his eyes fell on the giant blue bow leaning against a hitching post. It had killed at such a considerable distance and was larger and thicker than any he had seen.

"It has been Christened No Arc," one soldier said, barely looking up, busy stripping boots from one of the dead brigands. "Czesław is its owner and is capable of hitting any leaf you can see on any tree. An arrow dispatched from its jaws will pierce armor and beyond to the bone."

"Why is it called No Arc, sir?" Bolek asked.

"Because it is so powerful you do not have to aim a shaft above the target to adjust for the pull of the earth. Take true aim at your intended mark and let the shaft fly. No Arc. That is if you can bend the bow to its limit."

"Where did he get it?"

"He did not get it, he made it. And it does not treat Ottoman, Tatar or brigand with any special deference."

"How do I make one?" Bolek demanded.

"Thinking of revenge so soon, lad? The one called Czesław answered, a bear-sized hand on the Bolek's shoulder. "Sharpened barbs in cowards' bellies? Why much of the blood here is not dry yet."

"How is one made?"

"Ash is the best wood, but maple will do. Deer sinew for the backing, horn of cattle for the belly, fish glue and boiled tendons to bind everything. And then two years of trial and more trials to get it all right. I patterned it from a captured Tatar bow, noted the combination of materials, design, and learned each nuance of creation from my any failures."

"No other bow maker would believe such a thing could be fashioned," the kneeling knight added. "Czesław was as a man possessed while he built it."

Mother Józefa appeared, shuffled to the edge of the porch, heaving a bucket of bloody water off the side.

"Nine dead, Tadek," Priest announced. "They packed lightly. I doubt their camp is far. Their comrades will soon be wondering as to their fate."

"Do we follow their mounts to their camp?" Tadek asked.

"Or wait here for a reprisal?" The dish-faced one called Piotr added. "Only well-treated animals return to loving care. These all bear the scars of the whip. They will drift out onto the prairies and graze."

Firearms, sabers, bow and arrow, horses. They know these things as I do my daily chores. They are indeed like Father and Grandfather.

"Strap one of the bodies on the roan gelding, Tadek. He has seen better days. Send them both on their way. With a rider on his back, he may run to the camp and deliver a stinging message."

Again Bolek's eyes darted from one speaker to the next. He

knew much of the Polish light cavalry, was familiar with descriptions of many of the weapons they wielded and the expertise they employed. While his imagination pictured new and shining weapons, it took him back to see these men wearing mud-splattered armor and wielding dented and scarred weapons. The chain covering their bodies was rusty and dull. He'd grown used to the polished breastplate and helmet of his father and remembered the hours he'd spent buffing it, working oil into the leather, honing szablas to razor fineness.

Priest, as the others called him, commanded respect with his terse firmness, deference shown to each command without question. Sharp features, a bald head, a solid black and gray mustache. He wore a long red woolen *zupon*, a travelling garment. Though stained and dust covered, it was of a richness Bolek had only seen on the Pitry men. It flowed from a tight-fitting Oriental collar to the waist, where it flared, rich gold brocade lining all edges. Six rows of sparkling *pelticami* braids fastened with golden buttons ornamented his chest. A red Turkish sash, gold buttons and matching calf-length goatskin boots, marked him as a nobleman. His red fur-lined cap, a wool *kolpak*, sprouted a three-hawk-feather plume, kept in place with a large gold brooch pinned to its left side.

Nothing is as I imagined it. I would not look resplendent in the least wearing dull armor like this. The sun would not reflect my war helmet. Rozalia would view me as an ordinary horse soldier.

A Hungarian-type sheathed curved szabla dangled from Priest's leather belt, next to a menacing looking war hammer with a sharp pick at the end, capable of piercing the toughest opponent helmet and skull with ease.

The one called Czesław, the bowman, was a red-headed giant with a baby face. It seemed his natural countenance was a smile, which revealed a gap in his teeth on the upper right. Gentle giant, yet deadly bowman. He dressed in a rougher and plainer style, in a tan unadorned *kontusz*, a simple green sash, an oversized yellow kolpak cap trimmed in what looked to Bolek like wolf fur.

The quiet one, Piotr, the shortest and roundest of the group, reminded Bolek of a pious monk with his bald pate, fine features all wrapped within a moon-shaped face. A modest brown robe hung under his chain, torn and faded blue pants, brownish boots visible under the long riding coat. Like the others, his horse carried a long *koncerz* thrusting sword, and a shorter one, for close combat, called a *pallasz*. Bolek remembered how each employed these with deadly skill and speed. An ornate sheath holding his szabla hung from his belt.

Up until now I have only heard stories of many of these weapons and their uses. Still, these look as if they were dug from the earth rather than fashioned in a great forge. But the szablas sabers are sharpened. Their swords are their souls. The last, Tadek, shocked Bolek as he removed his helmet. A Cossack; the first Bolek had ever seen. He retreated one step as Tadek sneered as their eyes met. Cossacks were spoken of locally through family lore at evening fires. Although not a people of blood, but of profession, these semi-nomadic people were legendary as skilled sailors and ferocious warrior-horsemen, controlling many of the Eastern Rus rivers and tributaries, forcing all who passed to pay tribute. They offered their services to the highest bidder and sometimes fought against one another for booty. Comforting allies in battle and vicious foes said Father.

Tadek's features were of the Orient, with a wide, flat nose and a pale wheat complexion, his face scarred like a cutting board, with tiny whitish nicks and gouges running at every angle. The most prominent scar, finger-thick and irregular, ran from the right temple to his chin, and rose and fell when he tensed his jaw, which was often. Wide shoulders; a thick neck tapering down to a narrow waist, his chest pushing against the buttons of his *zupon*. A single lock of black hair, the thickness of a man's wrist, sprang from the top of his otherwise shaved head, dangling to mid-back. A wisp of a mustache. A scowl seemed frozen on his face. He also wore the grayish ringlet mailed armor and carried a bright red, round *kalkan* Tatar shield on his back, a Mongol bow, a Tatar quiver.

These men were pancerny, armed to the teeth light cavalry. While the legendary Polish Husaria wore heavy iron armor and rode giant horses, the pancerny wore intermeshed iron ring mail and carried a variety of weapons. Their small and swift horses offered speed, agility and endurance. Their armor allowed protection during extremely close contact with an enemy.

"Your grandfather was a soldier, I take it," Priest asked.

"Yes, sir. And he took a brigand with him. Slashed his throat with his szabla. A brave man and a good way to die."

"And what part did you play?" Tadek asked Bolek, his black eyes unblinking.

"I . . . I . . ."

"He skewered that one there hard enough to separate saber from hilt and quickly made the headless one pose for me," Priest answered for him. "Quick work for my *szabla*. A clean slice."

"Grandfather's szabla was old and rusted. This is why it broke."

"That does not make for as interesting a tale, young lad," Priest said. "But I admire your honesty."

Warming to Priest, Bolek could almost believe he had contributed something to the melee. But he trembled as he fought, holding back vomit and dizziness. He'd stared, body frozen, into the eyes of the man who'd been about to take his life. Images of the battleaxe blade accelerating downward kept playing in his mind.

"Lash the headless one to a horse and send him out onto the prairies, Tadek," Priest said. "This is an even better message, no? If it were harvest time, we could have fixed a pumpkin to it."

"One serf is moaning like a stuck pig, skewered with a small lance," Czesław reported. "He is tended to by the women and should improve. One has a slight slash wound to his back but squeals like a piglet. None of the peasants helped much."

"This is why they are servants." Tadek replied, never taking his eyes from Bolek, who struggled to maintain his gaze.

"Mother says food will be ready soon," Bolek announced in his most adult voice. "You are all welcome at table. We thank God for your help."

"Did you hear that, Piotr? Czesław? Tadek? We dine as guests tonight."

"We would have eaten here anyway, Priest," Tadek fired back.

"But we have been invited." Priest glared. "What is your name, son?"

"Bolesław."

"Clan?"

"Bończa."

"Your father's name?" Priest asked.

"Adalbertus Radok."

Four expressions soured instantly.

Has my shame with the wolf even spread to the pancerni?

"Tadek," Priest whispered, "the *szabla*."

"This is not the proper moment," Piotr cautioned.

"Would it ever be?" Priest replied.

An uncomprehending Bolek was alert for any hint of understanding. The Cossack, Tadek, strode to his horse, withdrew a long cloth-wrapped package from behind his saddle. Cutting the twine and unrolling the cloth Tadek handed an unsheathed szabla to Priest, who handed it to Bolek. The blade was bluish in hue, with waves running throughout the entire curved blade. The familiar grip, once too thick to hold when he was young, fit his hand now.

"Your father was killed in a skirmish with the Muslims these two years passed. Out of necessity, in unwelcomed territory, we buried him where he fell. This szabla is a masterfully crafted blade. Exceptional balance. Tadek, here, has always fancied it. But we honor a fallen soldier's final wish and present it to our brave comrade in arms heir."

"God took him before he could tell us where he came from," Piotr whispered.

"In war we often know little of the previous lives of our comrades and prefer it that way," Tadek added.

"We've been searching for its rightful owner," Priest said. "I'm sorry this is returned to you under these circumstances. But this is your father's legacy."

I have what I thought I wanted more than my soul. I wished for a szabla with every fiber of my being. I begged God for it. And so I hold my father's Damascus blade. My grandfather and father are gone. But I grasp what I said I wanted above all.

"Now I will use this to kill all of them," he told the soldiers. "All of them."

Chapter 18

"You hold that szabla in a death grip, boy," Tadek scoffed. "You could not land a single blow against Tatar or Turk like that."

"Then show me," Bolek growled, turning the point of the szabla inches from Tadek's face.

"These Górale," Tadek chuckled, moving forward until the blade's shaking point touched his cheek. "One must admire their spirit. When cornered they are as wolverines and even the bear backs away."

"Teach me. Teach me now!"

Priest grasped Bolek's saber arm and steadied the shaking point.

"We do not have time for fencing lessons, young master. Have you had no training?"

"Grandfather was old and Father always away. I am an expert archer. And now I am even unsure of that after seeing this one's display with bow and shaft."

"Góralu," Piotr said, "I call him Góralu. The one from the mountains. He is wasted here, Priest. Too much fire in his belly to farm."

Bolek's heart raced. At that moment, he wanted to destroy everything evil in his world with a single blow.

"Yes," Czesław added, his long chubby finger rising in the air. "But it is numbers that defeat an enemy, not spirit."

"You have this backwards yet again," Piotr said.

"Do you have brothers, uncles?" Priest asked.

"No brothers. My uncles all died in the wars."

"We must help him somehow, Priest," Piotr said.

"Piotr," Priest replied, "this boy is now the head of this household and master of the farm. He has just inherited his responsibility."

"So when you leave, I and mine die," Bolek challenged.

"*You* are not our responsibility," Tadek growled. "We have

already saved your life, ungrateful whelp."

"Teach me the blade, and I may someday save your life in return."

This made Priest laugh from his belly. He preened his thick shank of a mustache, a lock between each thumb and forefinger.

"We are of the Royal Guardsmen, son," he continued with head held high. "We live or die at the King's whim and expense – the crimson and the white." He pointed to the pennant draping the rump of his horse.

"I will support the king, as my father and grandfathers always have," Bolek responded. "But I must learn. I ride. I shoot. I will learn the sword. It is my legacy. I will be ennobled."

"Son," Piotr whispered. "Courage is a foolish thing when it is not rooted in wisdom."

"Then show me wisdom."

"We would, if we had any," Piotr replied. "Wisdom is like hen's teeth. And unlike the Western Europeans, nobility is not inherited in Poland. Though many present a façade, or purchase a title, nobility is not passed down to heirs."

"Then I must become ennobled."

"You are not a trained soldier. Where will the money come from for your horses, armor, and supplies, your retinue?"

Bolek shrugged, searching for jewels and gold to spring from the very soil.

"Where is my father's armor?" Bolek asked. "His helmet, his shield?"

"The szabla comes to you by a solemn promise," Priest said. "A fallen warrior is stripped of all precious armor before burial. It now serves others in need."

All was silent, save for the crickets.

"Adalbertus was a great comrade," Czesław said, pushing red hair from his eyes. "He could sing folk songs until the sun rose."

"*Biedna to, biedna ta nasza kraina, gdzie chleb się kończy, a woda zaczyna.* (Poor, poor is our country, where the bread ends and the water begins),"

Czesław sang in a light tenor voice.

"And hold his vodkie," Piotr chuckled.

"I know all those songs," Bolek stated. "And I can play all of them on this, as well," He fired back while pulling his flute from his shirt pocket.

"We must bring this boy to face the Muslims with us, Priest," Tadek said. "He will attack them with his hollow stick. I freeze in my tracks."

I hate this Cossack dog.

"We do not train boys to make war," Priest said. "Swords, arrows, axes are merely tools. The man is the weapon."

"Pani Radok requests you gentlemen to wash for dinner," a family servant said, saving Bolek from yet another embarrassing response.

As the guests followed the servant to the house, Bolek oversaw the stabling of the first war horses seen in the mountain region in recent memory.

Entering his home, now in control of his emotions, he smiled as Kasia, refusing to retire to her bed, helped out as best she was able, with preparations for the meal, despite her upper lip swollen to three times its normal size. Tonight they would dine with guests in a traditional Polish rural way; the mountain way. The Górale way. Bolek had learned in childhood that mountain life, though difficult at most times, was celebrated to the hilt for any ray of light found in the overwhelming darkness of the times.

Mother nodded to her son. She seemed entirely composed despite some bluish black bruises, holding her head high, as if nothing had happened. But when she saw the szabla dangling from her son's right hand, the light went out of her eyes. She shuffled toward it, took it slowly from her son, lifting it with both hands, peering into the blade as if it could reveal her husband's image staring back at her, perhaps even to hear his laughter for the last time.

"They knew him?" she whispered.

"Yes. Riding companions. A whole year. So long ago."

"Suddenly we know what we always knew," she said, returning the szabla to her son, leading him to the head of the table, the place reserved for Grandfather since Bolek could remember. The servants stood silent, eyes avoiding contact, heads bowed, as if they wished to be invisible for this small but significant ceremony. Two generations of Radok warriors had passed. The next in line takes his place.

"Your grandfather died proudly, Bolek. Like your, like your . . . father. It is rare than an old man can die defending his family. Good stock. And on the same day your father's szabla comes home. A good sign for an only son. A good sign for the last Radok." Crossing herself with her right hand, she caressed her son's cheek with her left.

"We will wait outside, Mistress," one of the servants said.

"No need, Leokadia. You are all family."

Her jaw tightened, and Bolek knew she was holding back strong emotions. While they would be let out, later and in private, this was neither the place nor the time to grieve.

"Now this is your seat, Pan Bolesław Radok," she said while pulling the wooden stool out from under the table. "Put your father's szabla through your sash. I will find Grandfather's scabbard to protect it properly."

Great loss today. Father's szabla come home. So much change in so little time.

"Be a strong host for tonight's dinner. You must taste your first vodka and offer several toasts."

"I've tasted vodka before, Mother, and I hold my own." He regretted his boast as his mother lightly slapped his cheek.

"Where are my manners? I should not swat the head of the Radok house."

Bolek promised himself to guard his tongue on this night.

"But I can still pray to Mary for my wayward son who has obviously disobeyed me by drinking."

The servants came to life with smiles and knowing nods. Mother kissed her son on his forehead and he hugged her, careful not to betray any sign of the emotion welling in him.

Bolek marveled at the strength within his mother. Today she had been attacked, saw her father-in-law murdered, he daughter threatened, learned of her husband's death and yet could still ensure a family tradition was followed by helping her son begin his new responsibilities with the proper ceremony.

There are others in the world besides me. Others suffer. Others endure. And the brigands will taste this steel I now wear.

Chapter 19

As the Polish knights appeared at the doorway, all eyes went wide, several bowed clumsily, one knelt, and others shuffled backwards. The dust of the road washed away, the chain armor gone, and worn travel clothes were replaced by bright colors and embroidered *kontusz* robes retrieved from saddle bags. The veteran warriors bowed formally as one to Mother Józefa and Bolek before a nod from Bolek allowed them to enter. Their colorful clothing and presence had never been seen in the Radok home in memory.

"It is good to see a crucifix over the entryway," Czesław said.

"If it were missing," the Cossack, Tadek, added, "an umpry could catch you at the door and beat your head with a bucket and use that very bucket to drain your blood to hold his evil meal."

All in the cottage fell silent as if a dark shadow just blotted out the sun.

"This is a Christian home," Priest announced. "May God bless us all."

Tadek returned the perplexed stares with a menacing grimace.

"We know Cossacks are as Christian as any here," Piotr told Tadek. "If there are any umpry man-bat blood suckers in this region we will dispatch them with relish."

"It is time for Grace," Bolek announced.

The warriors and the Radoks sat at table, the servants, farm workers and families sat on dusted off benches and stools brought into the cottage from the barn and work areas. And so it was for the first time in his life, Bolek led all at table in Grace, thanking God for the meal before them and entreating Mary to take care of Grandfather on his journey to heaven and for Father who had been there for some time.

"We are sorry, Pani Radok, we were late in arriving," Priest said as bread was passed. "It was not known to us that raiders were in this area or that they would be so bold. While local nobles have beseeched the king to clear the countryside of this predatory lawlessness, it was not our mission. It seems fate brought us here. I speak for my comrades at arms also when I say we suffer for our tardiness."

"My son, daughter, and all these good people on our farm owe our lives to you," Mother Józefa replied, with a dignity that made her son proud. "We are thankful you came when you did, risking life and limb for strangers. God's blessing, fine gentlemen. Warriors of Christ."

"Mother," Bolek said, "is there any vodka at hand?"

"Of course, young master of the house."

Mother nodded to one of her helpers and a large clay flagon appeared, tiny -colored cups distributed and filled with mouth-watering anticipation by all.

"To my brave grandfather and father," Bolek toasted.

"To Radoks," Priest added.

"To Radok!"

"*No to strzemiennego!*" (Cheers) from Piotr.

"*Zdrowie wasze w gardla nasze!*" (To your health; down our throats)," from Czesław.

"*Na druga nozke!*" (On our second leg) from Tadek.

Once the bottle was turned on its head, a dead soldier given its just due, dinner commenced. A beet and cabbage soup served with steaming bread made up the bulk of the modest feast. The unexpected addition of a few links of smoked kielbasa sausage spiced with salt and garlic along with dried mushrooms brought to the table with ample fanfare caused all to further toast, and toast again.

While the fare was simple, the Radoks would eat like birds for the next month, at the least, and each guest understood this and was grateful for the gift of a meal.

After appetites were sated and hearts lightened, some Góral heavily salted smoked sheep cheese, *oscypek* went from cellar to table; Piotr pulled a bowl pipe from his coat and showed it to

Bolek, who nodded approval for smoking. The other soldiers each extracted his own pipe as Piotr passed around a well-stuffed bag of tobacco. The men packed and lit their pipes, a pleasant aroma soon permeating the room.

"English tabac from their colonies," Piotr instructed. "Not a luxury. Good for the body. It prevents infection."

Bolek, a bit tipsy from his first serious experience with vodka, took out his flute and began playing a familiar mountain song, but hesitated as he remembered the darker events of the day.

"This is not a time for music. I am sorry, Mother."

"No. Play, Bolek. Play to honor your father's memory. Play to honor you grandfather's heroic passing. Play for our saviors here and for all who surround us here this day. Let us all join in song."

Bolek now played with inspiration.

At first a few weak and uncertain voices began singing the words to Bolek's tune. As another vodka bottle was passed, more and louder voices joined in the fast-paced mountain air. The giant Czesław danced with feet as light as those of a cat. The slight Piotr spun round and round with a serving woman and together they stumbled as one to the floor, rising to continue to applause and laughter. Tadek danced a Cossack dance to a fiery tune, his body in a sitting position with no stool beneath him, his legs a blur as each pushed from the floor in proper time to keep his body from collapsing to the earth.

Greater laughter and cheers ensued as Czesław fell to his knees, vowing to protect Kasia always. Her first marriage proposal was declined, to her mother's satisfaction. At this, Mistress Radok's eyes welled with tears, whispering to her son, "Your father has sent these men to us."

The dance brought on a powerful thirst and a call for more vodka. Bolek joined the King's guards at the table as a roar of sound raged around them.

"You are a wood carver, a smith and a musician, young Góralu," a sweating, out-of-breath Piotr said. "I am impressed."

"Bolek carved his own flute and made me this bear," Kasia told the warriors.

Priest inspected it closely before returning it to Kasia. Rising from table, he excused himself, returning quickly with an aged violin, a thumb-sized hole running straight through the body near the tailpiece.

"I would rather an arrow had pierced my heart than this, my treasure," he told Bolek. "This came all the way from Austria. Is it possible to make it sing again, highland wood carver and musician?"

Bolek accepted the fractured instrument, inspecting it from all angles. "Yes, but it will cost."

"Bolek!" his mother scolded. "These are our revered guests and saviors."

"How much, wood carver, musician and now merchant?"

Bolek hesitated, biting his lip before blurting out: "The horse."

"Which horse?" Priest almost shouted, leaning forward, his nose nearly touching Bolek's.

"The white mare."

"Ha!" Tadek grunted. "For what? To pull a plow? Or a wagon filled with straw? A waste."

"We owe a debt to Góralu's father," Piotr reminded.

"A brave man and a patriot," Czesław added.

"A debt, yes. A war horse, no," Tadek said, his arms crossed, his white scar pulsing.

"She can be sold for a heavy purse," Priest told Bolek. "What would you do with such a horse?"

"I would defend this region on her back, armed with my father's szabla and provide proper warning of danger to the villages and farms. No brigand could catch me on such as she."

"She was trained for a warrior," Priest noted.

"Your violin is a precious instrument," Bolek replied, holding Priest's stare with the courage from vodka. "Is your playing worthy of the bargain?"

"Bolek!" Mother Józefa shouted, the back of hand covering her gaping mouth.

Czesław erupted in laughter, pounding his fist on the table, so hard the wooden spoons became airborne.

"Góralu, you can stand up to Priest," he said. "I admire it. He matches you scowl for scowl, Priest, oath for oath, test for test. If you want your fiddle fixed, you must pay the boy in horseflesh. A prized desire for a prized desire."

"And for the mare you will repair my violin?" Priest asked, his eyes darting from Bolek to damaged violin and back.

"It will sing as sweet as a morning songbird."

"Done!" Priest shouted, extending his hand to Bolek, who took it to the sound of cheers and applause.

Soon the fanfare weakened, then died as tired bodies and happy souls departed. The soldiers and Bolek sat on a bench near the hearth amid the scent of burning pine logs, as wisps of pipe smoke curled and twisted to the roof. Bolek played a sad song on his flute as each man gazed into the fire with personal thoughts. The wounded farm hand they thought would die appeared to be recovering, his wounds bandaged, his contribution to the defense of the farm ever growing in his account of his involvement. Burek was buried in the family cemetery, a stone to mark his place in memory. Most evidence of the morning raid has been cleared away. Thoughts turned to the future.

Piotr cleared his throat for attention. "I will teach Góralu to sit a horse."

"How is this, Piotr?" Priest exclaimed. "You never volunteer for anything."

"Because I am beguiled by the delicate and exotic sound of the flute. It calms me so. Will you teach me to play, young Góralu?"

"I will certainly teach you to play," Bolek replied, "even though you can offer me little in the way of training to ride."

This brought a mountain of laugher from Piotr, Czesław and

Priest. Tadek shook his head, expressionless.

"Stand, gentlemen! Up!" Priest rose, his stool tumbling over. "Out to our new war booty, the white mare. I want to see if she is worthy of our young expert rider. Show us now, Piotr."

With a few small fires lit to hold back the impending dark, Bolek found himself standing outside, at the exact spot where Priest had saved him from certain death. Among his family and servants in the chilly spring twilight, he was watching a Polish cavalryman about to mount a dead man's horse. With his hands clutching the mare's mane, Piotr raised his right leg to the level of his head. Then sweeping the leg in a backward arc, the momentum vaulted his body onto the bare back of the white mare.

Again, Bolek cursed his boasting. This Piotr mounted the horse as nimbly as a squirrel moving from branch to branch, landing as softly as a butterfly to a flower.

What more do these men know? What are they capable of?

At first the animal fought against the bit, grunting, twisting her head this way and that, lifting and pulling at the iron mouthpiece, struggling for dominance against a new master. Kasia put her hand in her brother's.

"The bandits mistreated her," Piotr noted. "She's trained to respond to pain and has forgotten how to work as one with her rider."

Bolek's eyes widened as Piotr and the white mare began to move together, almost gliding, as one. It seemed that changes in Piotr's weight distribution and gentle leg pressure were easily read or remembered by the mare. The monk-like soldier was soon spinning her in tight circles, first clockwise and then counter, his balance never faltering. She whinnied as if proud of herself. Now he paraded the white beauty sideways, her legs shuffling and crossing under her like a dancer. Piotr pointed her toward the corral, squeezed her barrel with his calves, and she lunged forward, clearing a three rail fence with ease. Man and horse circled the corral at a gallop before a returning jump, ending mere inches from Bolek, her hot breath on his face somehow invigorating him.

"Strong, willing, and sure-footed," Piotr proclaimed, while sliding his lithe body from the saddle to stand before them. "A trained war horse, certainly captured by the brigand dogs. They do not know how to prepare a war horse. She is in need of more precise instruction."

"Not like your Hector, then?" Priest asked.

"Not like my Hector, your Mieszko or Czesław's Ajax nor Tadek's Parabellum."

"Strange names for horses," Bolek remarked.

"I'm sure our names are strange to them also." Czesław remarked. "Piotr's Hector is as mobile as a bat and as sly as a fox."

"Piotr," Priest said, "show Góralu here – who already knows how to ride – the difference between trotting off to church on an ancient nag and engaging three infuriated Turks at once."

Beaming with delight Piotr whistled for Hector.

"I'll untie him and bring him here," Bolek offered.

Czesław put a large hand to Bolek's arm. "No need. Even the Gordian knot is no challenge for Piotr's well-named mount."

Kasia put her hand to her mouth as Piotr's dark bay stallion ambled out of the barn, trotting to his master. A confused servant followed with Hector' saddle, and after a few adjustments, Piotr took his seat atop the cunning animal. He twirled the stallion in a circle, and then horse and rider bowed low to all, Bolek clapping like a boy.

"How does one teach a horse to bow?"

"A carrot offered between the front legs brings the head down, and then it's easy to pull the right front hoof backward," Czesław replied.

Piotr and Hector began a methodical dance, the horse's forelegs moving up and down in an intricate pattern invisibly dictated by Piotr. The pair performed as one.

"A Turk at your back," Priest shouted to Piotr, and Hector kicked out high and long, driving both rear hooves into the imaginary adversary.

"A Turk at your breast!" Tadek cautioned, and Hector reared and drove his hooves forward, finishing with lateral cow-kicking maneuvers to the left and right sides, pummeling imaginary adversaries as he landed.

"Two Tatars on each side," Priest warned. Piotr dropped the reins and wielded imaginary szablas in both hands as Hector spun round and round, his agile muscled body sweeping danger away in its wake. Horse and rider were as one, swerving away from szabla thrusts, kicking imaginary enemies. The rider parried numerous saber blows with ease, the horse knocking invisible enemies to the ground to be trampled.

For the first time, Bolek could see how a war horse performed and why their bravery in battle was legendary, their value and their cost attainable by only a few. Piotr and Hector were as the Centaur of old. Invincible, with man and nature fused together.

"My horse will need lessons, too," Bolek admitted to all.

"And its new owner?" Priest questioned, raising an eyebrow.

"Priest, I stand both corrected and humbled by Piotr's great art."

"Piotr," Priest commanded. "Enough. Leave a few Turks for the rest of us. Give Góralu some lessons with his new mare. That's teaching two at once."

The white mare!

Every fiber in Bolek's body bristled with joy. She had run with the wind, her mane flapping, her tail pointing upward with pride. She was controlled fire. No such horse existed in the village or on the farms. Not even at the Pitry manor, Rozalia's home. This horse could outrun hers, he thought, picturing the blond beauty following him, doing her best to keep up on her expensive Cracow-bred mare, her hair streaming in the wind, begging Bolek to slow his pace.

"Her name," Priest said, drawing his gleaming szabla and pointing it toward the white horse, "is Quo Vadis. Góralu atop Quo Vadis."

"*Where are you going*," Bolek said, stumbling with his Latin.

"Yes," Priest replied. And fitting for you young Master Radok."

"In the name of your father and his father's services to our beloved Poland, we give Góralu this feisty mare."

"This is a horse of the endless steppes, Góralu," Piotr said, hand on Bolek's shoulder. "Her Kalmuck blood gives her incredible stamina. But you must earn her trust. Do not command, but suggest."

Bolek couldn't speak. His father's sword. A war horse. To be taught to ride by men such as his father. It took an effort to hold back tears.

Mother came into view, her cheeks glistening with tears, her face set in resolve as she knelt before Priest, wiping her cheeks with her apron.

"My mother gave my father and my uncles for Poland. I gave my husband and my brother. The dark clouds gather again, protectors of Holy Poland. Yet another storm comes. I ask you humbly, to train my son to war. I give my son for Poland. God's will."

Priest stiffened.

"Is there no path to overcome adversity in Poland other than teaching our sons to butcher?" He growled, walking away without further word or gesture.

Chapter 20

The soldiers rose before the sun, and were out to reconnoiter the area.

"The gift of the horse and teaching the boy her true worth is more than enough," Tadek said, looking off at the farm's fertile fields, the rolling hills and the purple peaks in the distance.

"Perhaps the madness will not reach these mountains."

"You hope against hope, Czesław." Priest said, poking the tip of his szabla into the soil and turning over a few black clods. "This soil is rich and fertile; created for crops, unlike the Eastern steppes. Those are for grazing only."

"Your point is the East will always want our farmlands," Piotr said.

"The Western population grows. They will push at Poland's borders for more land." Tadek said.

"You have all read the latest dispatch. The Ottomans have declared war on Austria. Last month we pledged our offensive and defensive support to Austria. Whether the Ottomans drive to Vienna or to Cracow, it is only a matter of time before we must face them."

"And if we fail to repel them," Piotr added, "the crucifix displayed over the door of that farmhouse will be replaced with a half moon within a year."

"The boy will slow us down." Tadek frowned. "We seek gaps in the mountains, places to ambush a Turkish or Tatar force."

"Góralu knows these mountains; we do not," Piotr said.

"We could garrison ourselves here," Czesław said. "The loft doesn't leak or smell of pigs or chickens, and the food is excellent."

Priest glared at the giant redhead. "You wish to do this, Czesław? Does Poland need another murdering dog like Gustaw?"

"I like Góralu," Piotr said. "The boy is two parts naïve

innocence, one part fire and—"

"It is that last part," Priest growled. "Is it a mix of hatred, anger and a desire for cruelty?"

"I sense the anger in him," Piotr replied, "yet I think it springs from being wronged. He seeks justice. That is a God given right"

"The idealism of youth is a two-edged sword without guidance."

"Were you not young once?"

"I have forgotten." Priest asked.

"Then revisit it through the boy. His entire male line has stood against the Swedes, Tatars, Cossacks and the Muslim Ottomans," Piotr said, biting down on a crust of bread pulled from his coat pocket. "He lives in an impulsive dream world now because he does not understand the harsh realities of his world. There is no grey for him yet, only the black of night and the brightness of day."

"As we are inspecting the passes and searching for Gustaw, the boy could serve as a guide and training for him is then possible," Czesław said.

"Góralu reminds you of home, red beard?" Piotr asked Czesław who smiled and shrugged.

"He has no sword training, brags of prowess with bow and rides a plow horse," Tadek argued. "He has not been broken, molded and then tempered like a sword."

"You sound like a Turk, Tadek. He has free will and may choose his own way."

"And will die an untrained ignorant fool, unable to fight back with anything but raging spirit," Piotr shot back. "If we ignore him, we betray the sacrifice of his ancestors."

Priest raised his head to the sky and growled.

"What is the chance of finding Adalbert's son, saving the family from a brigand attack and returning his szabla all within a few moments? Perhaps we were brought here," Czesław said. "Perhaps we have a task before us."

"What task?" Priest shouted. "What will God have of me now? Can he not see my failures?"

"Wise Czesław has a point," Piotr noted. "Do we leave the boy to be butchered by Gustaw or do we train him?"

"Rather ask do we take the boy's innocence and make him a war-scarred soul-dead murderer."

"I am back from soul-dead," Tadek said. "The thought occurs to me that we might search the mountains to uncover both its secret passes into Poland, as well as Gustaw's lair, and do a favor for a fallen companion."

"Also, this is a perfect location from which to scout the area and protect the locals," Piotr said. "And to train the boy."

Piotr withdrew another crust from his coat pocket and tossed it to Czesław who had been eyeing Piotr's breakfast the entire time.

"Well said, Master Piotr!" Czesław replied as he munched on his prize. "There's food a plenty here, gents, we are welcomed as saviors, and the locals will feel safe. I propose we make this our temporary encampment."

"I agree to this," Priest said, "but I will not turn children into monsters. God help me!"

"The boy is a son of Polish patriots," Piotr said. "A delicate dilemma for us, comrades. Our Góral child either dies in ignorance by Gustaw's hand or Turkish sabers or is trained in battle by ours."

"The odds favor death by Turk," Tadek said. "The youth may also show cowardice on the field and run. A coward in a small world who finds himself a coward in a much larger world will quickly crack."

"My penance," Priest whispered, his gaze a thousand miles away. "Piotr, what are we to do?"

"I will help him and the mare bond. Tadek could easily teach him a few sword maneuvers, Czesław the bow. Then we will see what talent and what spirit spills out of him."

"What will Priest teach the boy?" Tadek asked.

"The only thing any good priest worth his salt is able to," Piotr replied, to a hearty laughter from all.

"You will teach him to take life, Tadek. I will hopefully teach him how immense a sin this is."

"What is the plan?" Tadek asked.

"We scout out and map possible invasion routes from the south and east, those that are suitable for barricades and ambush. The boy serves as our mountain guide. We keep an eye out for the brigands and will deal with them when we come upon them. We graciously accept the Radok hospitality while we teach the last of their sons to die by the sword. Do we agree on this?"

After unanimous nods and a deep breath Priest said, "Summon him."

"No need," Piotr said, pointing toward the barn. "He comes now, and at a lively clip atop Quo Vadis."

Chapter 21

"A favorable omen. A good beginning." Czesław said as the knights watched Bolek gallop to them. All four crossed themselves.

"I was up as early as you were," Bolek shouted, jumping from Quo Vadis before she had come to a stop. "But I had chores. I want . . . I want to apologize for my mother. You have saved us all, given me a magnificent horse, and I—"

"Walk with me, son," Priest commanded, pointing out into the rolling hill above fields with his unsheathed szabla, his comrades in tow. "Polish farms are generally small ancestral strips. How do you come by so much land plus a forge and a water wheel mill?

"My grandfather's father built the mill and forge and bought much of the surrounding fields. Some money came from szabla making, some from booty from war. But now I am the only one left, neither soldier nor saber maker."

Priest, slowing the pace, stoked his pipe. "This is an idyllic place, Góralu. Fertile lands, rolling hills, vaulting peaks in the distance, reaching to heaven itself. Abundant game. Firewood. Mountain streams. Precious salt and iron. A self-sufficient life."

"Until a band of devils come over yonder ridge and cut us down like stalks of wheat."

"So you seek to wield a saber for protection?"

"It is my father's blade and now rightfully mine."

"Some men use a blade to demand a false respect; some for revenge; some for show. Some enjoy killing. Fewer still employ it in defense of righteousness."

"I want to drive the blade into those who deserve it," Bolek announced.

Priest squinted.

"You would enjoy killing?"

"For those who seek to kill my mother or sister, what other

choice is there?"

"Do you pray?"

"At first only to please my mother," Bolek confessed. "And lately to ask God for things I feel I deserve. But Grandfather asked God daily for help, and look where he is now. I think God will neither give me a good crop nor protect me from evil men. It is up to me."

Priest looked back at his trailing comrades who turned their heads away.

"I have been given the most difficult part of the master plan, gentlemen, and you curl your tails between your legs."

"What plan?" Bolek asked. "Once trained I will clear this region of evil."

"By becoming evil yourself."

Bolek was confused.

"Don't you go to Mass, boy? Where is your head and heart on Sunday mornings?"

Bolek thought of Rozalia and had no words.

"Live by the sword, die by the sword. Love one another as I have loved you. Do these wisdoms simply drift in and out of your head?"

"It is honorable for a Pole to die by the sword. Father said this repeatedly."

"That was accurate in his case, for he understood the task before him. Few others do."

Priest ran both hands over his bald head as he and Bolek ascended a small knoll, the three comrades in arms trailing at a respectable distance.

"You do not truly understand your situation, son, do you? Have you studied your Polish history?"

"Of course, I know—"

"Don't rattle off what your local priest has told you of long dead heroes, meaningless ceremony or local superstitions."

Is this man a savior or yet another devil?

"The beauty of Poland is also her curse," Priest said.

"We are the bastions of Western civilization!" shouted Czesław, who was silenced by an icy glare from Priest.

"We hold our Christianity in our hearts and not just in ceremony or pious words," Piotr put in.

Priest shook his head in frustration.

"All of Europe and Asia is aflame with political intrigue and each of you shouts boasts into the wind. Is this what you wish to equip the boy with?"

He and Bolek now continued up the hill in silence, the comrades falling back, just out of earshot.

"We stand between Paris to the west and Moscovy to the east," Priest said, pointing with his szabla.

A geography lesson?

"We have saved the West from the Eastern invasions for many centuries. These events and sacrifices have seasoned Polish culture. We are a warrior nation, our hands awash in blood. The West has grown wealthy and sophisticated and at our expense. Most of the nations to the west conveniently ignore our contributions to their peace and prosperity. They sometimes even march eastward to help themselves to our land. We are encircled by the Orthodox Rus, the Protestant Swedes and the Muslim Turks. It is Polish blood and Polish spirit always on the front line, and once again we are threatened with death or enslavement."

"I'll never be a slave," Bolek replied with his chin held high, "I am entitled by Polish constitution."

Priest guffawed. "Entitled simply for being born here, are you? Sleeping snugly in your bed, protected by a two-hundred-year-old admirable intention written on a thin scrap of paper. Your constitution is melting; its power sucked from it, stolen from you day by day, word by word, in amendments, in monstrous interpretations. When it no longer lives in our hearts, it is dead."

I don't understand what these words have to do with my szabla or my bow.

"Góralu, does a seed magically sprout from the soil, a gift from nature? Nay, for we must plant it carefully, cultivate it; work the soil, struggle with weeds, and then harvest."

A fleeing jay squawked high above with two smaller birds diving incessantly at it. Bolek watched the scene, happy to take a moment's respite from Priest's words.

He sounds like Father Czarnota. How can this come from a warrior?

"Polish eyes on Paris; Polish hearts on Rome; Polish sabers on Russia," Bolek found himself saying, remembering a frequent toast Father and Grandfather offered.

"Yes."

"Perhaps no one will attack, Bolek ventured. "Perhaps we can put all the brigands to the sword and be left alone, forgotten by the Turks."

In response Priest again pointed with his szabla. "There lies the Baltic. The Swedes invaded us in an overwhelming deluge to capture our rich fishing and trading ports. Always keep a watchful eye turned northward.

"There," he continued, sweeping his outstretched arm from due north to a bit eastward, "sit our brothers, the Lithuanians. They require our protection from the brutal Eastern Rus. And with our attention on the East we often lose awareness of the Muscovite Rus to the east. Eastern Orthodox. When they travel west toward us, they come in countless numbers. Always keep an eye there."

Bolek began to feel surrounded by enemies, yet he knew Priest had not finished.

"And there the mighty Rus stronghold Kiev," the rising wind pushing at the skirt of his coat and the locks of his mustache. "Over four hundred years ago they came at us. The Golden Horde, some call them. Mongols. Scourge of God. From beyond the Ukraine. They came like locusts, driving their ponies westward looking for grazing land and plunder, finding a bevy of their desires here in Poland, killing everything before them. The only gift from the merciless nomads was to show us how to fight with fast horses and deadly compact bows."

"And there," Priest went on, now pointing his szabla to the southeast, "lays Moldavia. Beyond that, Constantinople. Many there thought they too would be forgotten, left alone. Now the holy city is called Istanbul. A Turkish stronghold where Mass is no longer said."

"After we slaughter the brigands I will ride with you and we will liberate this Christian city."

"We have more than enough dreamers of glory in our armies, young son. It is a terrible thing to look into their eyes once they discover the true nature of war. Afterwards, most are never the same."

"I am not afraid of the Turks."

"I am. They embrace the Saracen religion and grow stronger daily. The Ottoman Muslims they call themselves now. They grasp the Black Sea in a cold and inhuman fist. Be watchful to the south and east."

Bolek looked up toward the soaring peaks of the Tatra Mountain range.

There, there is safety.

"And to the south, Priest said, as if reading Bolek's mind, "over your mountains, there lies the splintered and troubled land of the Huns, Hungary, currently in rebellion against the Holy Roman Emperor, Leopold. They bargain now to accept Ottoman domination. No matter what pact they sign, soon they will spill out of their dens, come up the Danube basin and either lay siege to the Habsburg city of Vienna or Cracow itself. Your Carpathian Mountains will not save us, for the passes through the mountains are ancient and well known. Keep an eye there," Priest repeated.

"So many," Bolek whispered, imagining himself surrounded by marauding horsemen of every possible language and dress.

Only my mountains offer safety.

"See, boy!" Priest shouted, "A little knowledge of your true situation, and you want to abandon your countrymen for the highlands, leaving them to fend for themselves. How noble, son. We consider teaching you sword and bow so you can shrink and hide in your mountains. Good men gather at this moment to sacrifice all. These are men of pride. Of honor. And you wish to flee."

As confused as Bolek was, instinct told him a test was being put to him. "I do not know what is being asked of me," he replied. "It is clear we do not have enough swords."

"We will endure. But not with our szablas." Priest rebuked him.

Piotr, Tadek and Czesław rejoined Priest and Bolek at the top of the hill. The majestic mountain vista ringed them. Bolek searched their eyes for some clue to their questioning.

These men offer a way off the path of tedious farm life, a way into Rozalia's heart; a way to face the wolf. What do they want of me?

Priest sheathed his szabla.

"So, young Master Radok, what unites us more than blood and is sharper than any sword? Ponder this riddle," he instructed, turning and stomping off toward the house.

What do they want to hear? God help me break their riddle. God.

"God, Priest, God is the answer!" Bolek shouted out, surprising himself. "God unites us in blood, and his truth is sharper than any sword."

"There! Piotr exclaimed. "The boy understands."

Thanks be to you, God, for I've told them what they want to hear.

Priest froze and turned slowly.

"A fir tree once boasted to a bramble bush, 'You have no reason to exist; while I am everywhere, used for houses and roofs.' The bramble replied: 'You poor creature, call to mind the axes and saws which are about to cut you down, and you will soon wish you had grown up a bramble bush, and not a fir tree.'"

Piotr helped Bolek. "A choice is offered you, Góralu. An invisible mountain boy or a warrior with a target over his heart?"

"I love the mountains, it is true, for there are few men there," Bolek confessed. "I think of glory and wealth also and desire to overcome that which I fear. I am of two minds."

Priest's face softened to Bolek before turning in frown to his companions.

"The sword, horse and bow are straightforward, my friends. So many have those savage skills. But teach him to replace his self-directed youth with wisdom, his innocence with understanding, and his lack of purpose with direction, commitment and compassion. Which of you can teach him our butchering skills and put a heart and a brain behind them?"

None but the howling wind spoke on the grassy prairie for what seemed an eternity.

"Tadek," Priest commanded, hands clasped at the small of his back, eyes to the earth. "Teach Góralu the secrets of the blade. Czesław, the bow. Piotr, the horse. May God help him. And me."

Three Polish knights and a farm boy watched the lanky Royal Guardsman stride toward the farm.

"Priest is like a storm, son," Piotr said. "Those first spears of lightning and the rumble which follows make you afraid. But soon you become accustomed to it."

A bright-colored uniform will be mine, an exotic plume atop my helmet, a fist full of gold in my left hand, my right arm encircling the waist of fair Rozalia. One day I will travel to the great city of Cracow on Quo Vadis, magnificently dressed, the crowds cheering and shouting my name.

Piotr sighed. "*Si vis pacem, para bellum.* If you desire peace, young Spartan, ready yourself for war."

"I will."

"That smile will be the last you will wear for some time, Góralu," Tadek cautioned, tracing his baby finger along the jagged path of his hideous white scar. "Soon will begin a trial of pain. You may soon wish we never crossed paths."

Chapter 22

Word of the bold assault upon the Radok farm seemed to spread on the wind. Neighboring farmers visited to offer condolence, gifts of yarn, milled flour, lambs and chickens. Many also came to marvel at the Polish cavalry, something extraordinary to behold in the rural south. To have mounted soldiers in the region taking up quarters at the Radok farm was an immense relief to all. The terrible Gustaw shrank in stature for the moment.

Bolek commiserated with the visitors feeling every bit the lord of the manor when his advice was solicited. Knowing his saber training would soon begin, he began work on his end of the agreement for his horse, Quo Vadis. At night, he labored in secret on Priest's arrow-damaged violin with the woodworking skills he'd garnered from his father and grandfather, wielding the specialized carving tools he received as gifts on his Name Day, over five long years ago.

He chose spruce for the wood and a combination of tree sap and pitch to patch the offending hole. Taking apart the worn, fragile instrument, he gained respect for its craftsmanship. He could not easily discern the reason for the various angles and curves, initially taking them for more show than function, but he was true to these designs and patterns as he mended the entry and exit holes in the body.

Once he deemed the project completed and well out of earshot, he put bow to string. The nasty scratching and hissing sound he could only evoke from the instrument made him wince. It was an awkward tool to make music with, nothing like the ease of operation and the beautiful tone that emanated from his flute. Still, he had heard the violin often and knew it could sing with elegance and passion. He reasoned that in the hands of Priest he'd get a better idea of how well he had repaired it.

The very next evening, feeling pleased with himself after solving a lingering problem with the mill that morning, followed by a good meal, some vodka, and a few old funny stories and reminiscences from the war veterans, Bolek produced the mended violin, as promised, in return for his horse.

Priest's eyes widened. After cleaning his hands on his coat and pulling on each lock of his mustache for luck, he accepted the delicate instrument with an almost reverent nod to the woodworker, then cradled the violin in his left arm and ran the fingers of his right over the patched hole. The scars were visible, yes, but the patch was smooth as the rest of the body. The hole was plugged.

In a measured pace, he placed his treasure in the crick between his left shoulder and his jaw. He adjusted it until satisfied with the placement, then proceeded to pluck each string, adjusting the pegs accordingly, nodding to Bolek who blew notes on his flute until the tuning was the same as the flute.

Now satisfied with the tuning, Priest stretched an open hand across the table, and a pleased Bolek gave him the bow. All at table leaned forward, the creaking of the stools the only sound. Positioning the bow to string, Priest performed an up bow then a down bow. Then again. Then he scowled.

"Dull! Dead!" He scrambled to his feet. "There is no life here!" Grasping the violin by its neck, he hurled it across the room and into the fireplace, where the dry wood caught fire within a few seconds

Bolek felt as if an arrow had pierced his chest, and he sank deflated into his chair.

After what seemed like an eternity of silence, watching the once beautiful instrument disappear in the flames, Priest sat back down and raised his cup to the fireplace.

"To my old friend," he growled. "Yet another true and faithful companion falls. This is not your fault, Góralu. You worked magic. But we cannot heal the dying nor raise the dead. I applaud your effort. A bargain is a bargain. We will continue to use our combat skills to help choke out your innocence."

"I don't wish to be innocent anymore, Priest," Bolek replied.

"Eve's very words to Satan." Piotr chuckled.

Bolek's training began promptly the next morning as a reddish sun popped over the distant peaks. The dew, still heavy on the prairie grasses, caught each blade, turning the fields into an endless sea of shimmering jewels.

The training regiment was not as he expected, with one skill first, then another – but sword, bow, and horse together. Numerous threats required frequent and varied responses; there was little time for thought; response must be spontaneous.

While Piotr barked commands to turn Quo Vadis in one direction, Tadek demanded Bolek parry an imaginary saber attack. Czesław ordered imaginary arrows to be drawn and fired much faster than Bolek thought necessary. When the bone-weary student pleaded dizziness and confusion, three voices berated him in a bitter harmony. Next, the instructors shouted commands in unison, chastised the young highlander without respite.

The nights were full of dreams as an exhausted Bolek heard the voices of Tadek shouting, "Slash!" Piotr barking "Pivot!" and Czesław shrieking, "Release!" But soon, the wisdom of the strategy came to him. He discovered that while leaning over his saddle to concentrate on a szabla slash, he relaxed, his innate sense of balance finding the proper center on its own. His composure atop Quo Vadis improved with each session. As he spun his mare in a tight circle, or backed her up with a mere shift in weight, he learned he could respond at lightning speed to a threat from any direction. His father's szabla began to move as part of his wrist and arm, almost by instinct. He gave tireless dedication to his combat-trained warriors. Within a week, he could nimbly protect his weakest flank or strike at a vulnerable enemy opening. In war, a man did not have the luxury of relying on a single skill. Not if he wanted to survive.

On Sunday next, at Mass, with news that Rozalia was in

Cracow, Bolek's attention was on anything but the sermon.

They instruct me with vigor. But how can I live up to my promise? I could not repair Priest's violin any more than I could cast a sword. They give, but I am failing them.

The warriors still confused him. These fabulous Polish knights were almost worshiped by the local people, not only for their extraordinary deeds in the service of Poland but also because they were somehow congenial to all. Here at the old wooden church they knelt at Mass, not as hardened warriors but as men among equals, following Father Czarnota's Mass in a childlike call to worship.

Bolek, humbled and on his knees, hands clutched, eyes closed, wondered if this complete devotion to God helped them in their tasks, and so he emulated them, praying to God for guidance and understanding and not for objects.

Dear Lord, how do I hold up my end of this agreement with Priest? My attempt to repair his violin was a failure. How do I repay my debt?

A *Eureka* moment of 'Yes!' echoed through the church like a cannon shot and at a most solemn part of the Mass. Heads turned in surprise to the source of the interruption. Faces frowned in disapproval. Father Czarnota grimaced, pointing a threatening finger at Bolek, who shrunk down to hide his face. But he thanked the Lord, grateful for the lightning-bolt instant solution.

Though beaming an ear to ear grin as he exited the church among his peers, it was clear Mother Józefa was not pleased with his outburst.

No matter. God had answered my prayers. I will find another violin and purchase it.

His mother crossed herself many times that day as she viewed her son's enigmatic smile. The four cavalry men thought it to be signs of fever.

Bolek confided in Wiktor, the farm's factotum, of his dilemma, for Wiktor's father, the old toothless and ever-smiling Cyr, was a fair balalaika player and often strummed along with others, including violinists. Wiktor's father seemed honored the master of the farm had come to him for counsel and advice.

"While the balalaika is an instrument of the plains," the musician pontificated, "a soft spruce and a rock-hard maple marriage is the best for its body. In times of dire need, a balalaika is also a potent weapon for head bashing. The gut of cats works best for strings. But the violin, there's another story, an instrument of another caliber, young master. I know nothing of these things."

Disheartened, Bolek pained over how to lay his hands on a violin. Unexpectedly, it was Wiktor who found the answer, noticing how dejected his master appeared, and aware of the reason.

"There is a Cossack shoemaker who lives on the outskirts of Skawica, Master. In the hills. He has two violins. I have seen them together with these eyes. The Cossack played one. Sweet as the birds in morn. Perhaps he'd part with the other. He can't play two at once. He is a hermit with no friends."

After explaining his plan to Mother, she agreed a white lie was excusable, if confessed by both, to God. So, the following morning Mother told the warriors Bolek actually was coming down with something and needed to travel to town for some medicine. His torturers reluctantly gave him the day to himself while they rode to search for invasion routes though the mountains. Once out of sight of the farm he raced his white steed, racing with the wind toward Skawka. He was directed to the old Cossack shoemaker immediately as everyone in town knew of the 'touched in the head' craftsman.

His shop was little more than a shabby lean-to, a heap of sticks and pieces of wood tied together with a tarp over the top to provide protection from wind and rain. The shoemaker, a leather-faced old man with wrinkles like spider webs, smiled a toothless grin and bowed as Bolek entered. Forced to shout his predicament several times, for the man was more deaf than even his grandfather, Bolek asked to buy one of the precious violins.

"Tell me about the cavalry man," the old man said. "What sort is he?"

The story became easier to communicate by Bolek speaking into the large end of a ram's horn with the smaller end inserted into the old man's ear. In groping for words to describe Priest, as well as having to repeat a few words several times, he realized how dear Priest had become to him in such a short time.

"Problem solved," the old man declared. I got two! And I can't hear either one. Only need one to jar memories. The vibrations are pleasing against my ear, and this is a great comfort to me in what time I have left."

After a few moments of rummaging through a pile of furs, rags and moldy smelling clothes, which evidently served as his bed, the old shoemaker pulled an ornate oaken case from the pile, blew a layer of dust off it and presented it to Bolek. A flick of the delicate golden hasp revealed a striking polished violin resting in red felt.

"This must have great value," an awed Bolek said.

"Just the thing for a warrior priest musician,' the wizened old Cossack yelled. "It's from Mittenwalt. Forged by a master. You can see his name and city glued there on a piece of paper. I can't read, but that's what the noble told me it says. He said it was worth its weight in gold."

"Noble?"

"A raid from our Cossack river boats. When I was young. I was but a camp follower. They killed or wounded most everybody. Took everything. They lit the manor house afire. I was late getting inside, and the plunder was already picked over, the best taken. I saw a stately old gentleman, well dressed, hair trimmed. I took him by the arm to lead him from the fire because it was already on the roof and the ceiling was all smoke, but he wouldn't leave the house. I just got him out of that room before that roof collapsed. He had vodka on his breath. I asked him where he stored it, and he showed me. I drank greedily 'til my gizzard burned. Then I noticed they had chopped off the fingers from his left hand. He drank with his right hand but never took his eyes from the bloody stump. 'They had taken everything,' he moaned, 'except for all these magnificent books. Barbarians, all.' I broke a window to get away from the fire as it grew, but that brought the fire closer. He still would not leave his home. He said it must have been like this when the barbarians sacked Rome. Then he asked me if I played music and me, with my pants almost burning, said, 'Yes! I make sweet music.' So he gave me this very violin. Pulled it from behind a smoking curtain, said the damn Cossacks had missed the greatest treasure. Then he just walked into the flames. I watched his clothes catch on fire and saw him collapse. He never screamed. Damnedest thing I ever saw. I jumped through the window with a demijohn of vodka in one hand and this fiddle in the other.

"I played it once. Like molten gold and velvet. Rats almost got it two years ago. See those chew marks on the case. You better take it."

"What do you want for this?" Bolek asked. "Pigs, chickens, ducks? Tools. Name it."

"I eat like a bird. It would just go to waste. And tools?" he chuckled. "I can't even stoke a fire anymore."

"You can't just give it to me."

"I can, and I do," the old Cossack replied with emotion. "When I was young, like you, different things mattered to me than now. But there is something that would please me."

"Name it."

"I see you at Mass, young sir. I see you look at a nobleman's young daughter. Sixty years ago I sat where you did in the very church, and I was doing the same thing as you, staring at a young beauty from my time. But I only looked. She married. I still see her sometimes. She looks like me now. There is more to a woman than just the burning in your loins, young lord. They are our other and better half. Don't miss your time. Go make music. This is the price."

At the waning of the sun, Bolek secured the precious instrument in its protective case and wrapped it further in his wool blanket then road toward home. As his sure-footed mount navigated the mountain path with ease, he was lost in thought, paying only passing attention to the forest around him. Who could catch such as him on such a steed?

Chapter 23

A startled Bolek rolled out of his bed to a deafening uproar, his first conscious thoughts reliving his grandfather's death. He rose to witness an expressionless Tadek shaking a cow bell, shouting something about getting into the saddle. By the time Bolek's full wits came to him, he was mounted on Quo Vadis amid Priest, Piotr, Czesław and Tadek, moving with them at a swift trot toward the mountains.

"Word comes a wild boar has mauled a young boy," Piotr explained. "The villagers beg us to hunt the beast down."

"We give boars a wide berth," Bolek replied. "They grow huge around here, with massive razor sharp tusks."

"A boar's tooth is a great hunting trophy," Tadek said.

"I have seen a man your size tossed high into the air by a mere flick of a boar's neck."

"Then our first task will be to render that neck useless," Priest said, without turning in the saddle.

"I caution you all. A grown boar weighs and much as three men and can grow as long as Czesław is tall."

"Excellent," Tadek said. "There will be meat enough for all."

After querying the villagers as to the location of the attack, the hunting party approached a marshy area where reeds grew tall and broad, well-nourished by the moist earth. Amid the splashing of cloudy water from the horses' legs and the sucking sound as hooves sank in mud, each man searched for telltale spoor.

"We announce our presence," Bolek said, riding next to Priest.

"Yes. We ask the pig to ready himself as we invade his territory."

"This is dangerous. We should dig a pit and lure the boar to it, not attack him where he is strong and ready."

"What is your greatest fear, Góralu?"

"First yours."

"Not being a dutiful enough servant to my master. Now yours."

"You never say something straight. I must think of every word over and over. You twist my thoughts."

"This makes a tightly woven braid that once understood, is stronger than a few strands. Does this hunt scare you?"

"Not yet."

"Your expression belies your words. Perhaps you are afraid to speak the truth."

Bolek took care to ensure the others were still well out of earshot. "My fear is I am a coward, and I'll run, that I'll hide in that tree and watch the wolf devour my sheep, the brigands kill my mother and sister, the boar slice off your leg, and I do nothing."

"And you blame whom for this cowardice? Quickly!"

"My father!" A teary Bolek fired back.

"Your face is the color of a turnip. Stay close to me on this hunt. It is often the case the hunters are found first."

"Oftentimes I would rather be up there," Bolek said, pointing high up to the peaks which now surrounded the hunters on three sides, "up at the great hidden lake, the sun warming my body, with cool water to drink and game to hunt."

"You wield your father's szabla well in practice, Góralu, but the iron stick does not make courage. It is the desire to do something for others that makes one courageous."

"I think I have the desire. Some desire."

"Góralu, if you heard the screams of your mother and sister right now or those of the poor child attacked by the boar, you would ride straight into the fray. How do I know this and you do not?"

"I would not be here if it were not for you. Boars are to be trapped by stealth, not hunted head on with szablas."

"This will be my first boar hunt," Priest said matter-of-factly.

"I am here because I must be."

"Other than my family and you four, few have ever done anything for me. So why do I need them or should care for them?"

"Our parliament meets daily to discuss just these things – how best for man to live, and how our people should be protected."

"They do a poor job then. Who are they to make decisions for me?"

Quis custodiet ipsos custodes? Piotr said, riding up and splashing muddy water in all directions. "Who will guard the guardians themselves?"

"Who are you to make *no* decisions and allow all this murder, rape and chaos to continue while you blind yourself to it?" Priest asked of Bolek.

"*Panem et circenses*." Piotr recited. "Common people are only interested in bread and circuses, and leave their governing to the wolves."

"I am not responsible—"

"There, Góralu! You have said it all. You are not responsible." Priest stopped his horse in its tracks forcing both Bolek and Piotr to rein in.

"You! You are not responsible. But *I* am. And as I stand before you and as I live and breathe I know your soul can only be saved if you have the desire to act. That is what you are here for. To understand and then to act."

"I think the rest of us will ride ahead," Tadek said, his face dotted with specks of mud. Czesław, Piotr and Tadek nudged their mounts into a healthy trot, disappearing around a bend among the reeds.

"Grandfather always said politicians all do the devil's work and are evil to the core."

A frustrated Priest shook his head. "Góralu, Evil is not some horned and hoofed creature you can conveniently point your finger at and blame for you woes. Evil is the abuse of your free will; your selfishness. And it alienates you from God."

"But in the village—"

"Live the superstitious, the ignorant, and those looking for others to blame for their miseries. Some desire freedom to do what they will. Some desire others to control them, to tell them what to do. But between the freedom of chaos and the control of total submission to another lies acceptance of God's law. Know your evil. Then overcome it with love."

"I attend mass. I confess. I take communion."

"And you do it as part of your culture and from pressure from your community and out of superstitious fear."

Is this soldier now a priest?

"Our sacraments give us visible confirmation of what we cannot see. The Holy Spirit is in our heart, not within our normal senses. How do you know your mother loves you?"

"Well . . . she does. She cares and—"

"Her actions reveal what is in her heart for you. And you the same for her. You cannot see the wind, only the evidence of it. You cannot see love. But it is there and is the light of the world."

"We read daily from the Bible—"

"The Greeks were keen philosophers and showed us how to reason to find God. But their knowledge came by abstraction. The Jews spoke with God and their covenant offers eternal life with faith. And our ever-faithful saints have merged faith and reason together in deed, and in the lives they've led as example."

"Do the politicians in Cracow – do they know this?"

"Many give themselves up to the sins of self-interest. Their reach always exceeds their grasp. Pity these men."

"Still at it?" Piotr asked, awaiting the dawdlers. "Tadek says he's run across a trail. The den is surely near. He also says the boar thanks you two for announcing our presence and sharpens his tusks as we speak."

The hunters stopped before entering a small reed field with

most of the growth taller than a man, the water deeper, vision limited to a few feet, the soggy ground hidden.

"We will tie our horses here and walk now," Priest announced.

"Wouldn't we be safer on horseback?" Bolek asked.

"It would be safer for us, but not for our horses," Piotr said. "This is not their fight. They have an innate fear of the boar. There is no need to have their legs slashed and have us thrown to the ground to boot."

"Although they are dumb beasts, we have a responsibility to them," Priest added. "As we do for those sleeping souls in Cracow, and for you. We hunt from here on foot."

"Horsemanship is easier to learn than politics, is it not, Góralu?" Czesław asked Bolek, his eyes twinkling.

"For now, draw your szablas and ensure your knife pulls easily from its sheath," Priest cautioned as the men began to penetrate the marsh. "Ears and nose will suit us best."

The hunters spread out in a semicircle, each perhaps ten feet apart, their feet sinking into the foul-smelling, clinging mud, sucking at their boots and threatening balance. To steady themselves, each began grasping clumps of reeds with a free hand.

"He is near," Bolek whispered, fanning gnats from his face and neck.

"Really?" Tadek said.

"No frogs croaking. The entire marsh listens and whiffs the air."

"Then the forest must smell your fear," Tadek chuckled.

"Move away from me, Góralu," Priest commanded. "Always remain at least a sword's length away when danger is near. I'll hack an opening through these reeds. You protect my back."

He puts trust in me.

Bolek was on high alert as the hunters slashed the reeds at their base, allowing them to collapse in a heap on the marsh floor, offering better footing in the spongy mush, and better visibility for a killing view. Sweat, mixed with the odor of foul water and rotting brush darkened the mood.

The marsh quickly grew shallow and hard ground soon attained. Immediately a dull rumbling to the left; tall reeds pushed over as trees in an avalanche. Each man, knees bent, readied for impact. A massive black head burst through the thick reeds, a long and thick yellow tusk on each side, sweeping left and right in menacing arcs. Deafening grunts from deep within the dank-smelling body challenged all. Bolek took an involuntary step backward, raising a trembling szabla. Priest sprang forward, howling his own challenge at the enraged grunting beast. It pivoted in the blink of an eye, its enormous tusks aimed at Priest's thighs. At the last possible second, the swordsman sprang deftly aside, the boar's tusks missing his leg by inches, Priest's szabla slicing down hard on the boar's neck, severing the behemoth's spine.

Silence. So fast. So certain.

"I claim these tusks," Priest announced, digging into the jaw of the slaughtered beast with his knife. "And we will all eat heartily this week."

"I hope it will taste better than it smells," Piotr said.

"Poor beast," Czesław muttered.

"How so poor?" Bolek asked. "He wanted to kill us."

"We invaded his territory. He defended his sows."

"He is locked into his nature, unlike you and me, Czesław," Piotr added. "He did his job."

"Yes," Priest replied. "As soon we must all do ours."

Chapter 24

As one, the victorious fivesome made short work of butchering the giant hog and hauling it out of the swamp. Distributing substantial severed haunches among their saddles, they gave Bolek the honor of towing the body and head of the boar behind Quo Vadis on a makeshift two-pole cart, the consensus being that Quo Vadis needed strengthening.

With Priest leading the triumphant hunting party on its way back to the village, they sauntered onto the main dirt road of the quaint hamlet, brandishing bloody tusks and cock sure grins. A lone cry of 'Thanks be to God,' was all that was needed to announce the victorious hunters. Ample cheers echoed the prayer.

The news spread like a lightning fire on a dry prairie. The villagers poured out from thatched-roof homes, from the mill, the nearby pastures and the river bank of the alpine village. Young girls, abandoning their chores, ran with milk pails, the white liquid sloshing this way and that. A saw left in mid cut in a log, a peg half-pounded into a scaffold, a horse left untied. Villagers amassed as one, splashing mud on everything, applauding the triumphant foragers, and the end of the boar.

"It appears nothing like this has occurred in this village before," a puffed-chest Czesław said.

"They usually see only raiders and death approaching. They face starvation much of the time. They merely survive, and spectacle is celebrated for it surely will wane. " Piotr said.

"Let us act like what they expect us to be," Priest said.

As the horsemen pulled up before a small inn, children ringed Bolek and Quo Vadis, prodding the giant boar's head and body with sticks, the braver ones with fingers. Dismounting to cheers, the hunters learned the injured boy would recover without loss of a leg. When the pale and heavily bandaged youth was carried out to the crowd in his father's arms, Priest made a grand display of bestowing one of the boar's tusks on him. At first, too scared to touch it, the ailing, tear-streaked boy soon gave in to gentle prodding by his mother and poked at the bloody fang. Finally, he grasped his new trophy in his little fist, growling like a boar and slicing the air with the great tooth.

Priest graciously distributed a few gold coins to the boy's family, offering the villagers a healthy share of the meat, the entire hide, and the innkeeper was given the boar's formidable head, which would hang proudly on the inn's wall. Keeping the lion's share of the tastiest parts for themselves, the horsemen rode for the Radok farm.

The trip to the farm was sheer delight for Bolek, riding amid men who fought like his father and grandfather, men who had seen the same things, conquered the same fears and now somehow maintained an inner calm, a deep certainly they would each respond nobly to whatever challenge appeared before them whether boar, brigand or Turk.

These are the experiences my father was supposed to give me. Why these men? Why now?

"A great day for us, Góralu," Piotr said as he rode next to the scowling boy. "Yet you seem troubled."

"None of you had fear during the hunt," Bolek said.

"Had he not the courage to make the kill," Tadek remarked, "Priest should not have been there."

"I killed one once with a pike," Czesław bragged.

"The ax on a pole kind or the fish?" Priest teased.

"Pole."

"Much smaller, I am certain," Tadek replied.

"True," Czesław answered. "But my boar was faster. It took more skill."

"It's all about who eats whom after the battle." Tadek declared. "That's the reality of war. Priest will dine on pork tonight, so he is more than the beast was."

"You would not fear raiders ambushing us right now from

this mountainside?" Bolek challenged.

"It would break the monotony of the ride back to our billet."

"The boy is trying to make friends, Tadek." Piotr said. "Is your tongue also a sword?"

"We four know war as you know the land and crops." Tadek told Bolek. "We've pledged our souls to a cause. I am what I must be by my nature. I could not be a farmer."

It was the most Bolek had heard Tadek say at one time.

"I am a soldier of Poland, Góralu. What fate will you embrace?" Tadek asked.

A vision from the world of his mountains came to Bolek. "I would be an eagle," he replied without thinking. "Yes, a Tatra eagle!"

"Why that?" Czesław asked.

"Because nature is free of moral concerns?" Piotr asked before Bolek could speak, causing a guffaw from Priest.

"An eagle soars above the earth," Bolek explained. "She has terrible talons and a fierce beak. She is fearless and lives high, well above the dangers of the prairies and fields below."

"Yet she must come to earth to get food to feed her young," Priest noted.

"Just as we bring juicy roasts to the farm," Czesław added.

It now was essential to Bolek to make them understand.

"Where I am timid and awkward, she is aggressive and precise in her attack. She dives directly at her prey and does not deviate."

"And you do not know if this is in you," Priest said.

Bolek shrugged.

"Perhaps in her own way she believes deeply in something," Priest told him. "Those who believe in nothing have no courage. They live in constant fear. They block their memories of the past because it is full of the stench of cowardice. They abhor the future, for failure tomorrow is also a certainty. They exist in the present only. Rootless. They are like these brigands we search for, the ones who hide in holes as they scurry from us. Today, the boar committed all. And your eagle? She has courage because she lives for her young. Her life is not too grand a price to pay to support them. She nurtures. She gives. This is the source of courage. If there is nothing you would give your life for, you have nothing to live for."

"The legend of the White Eagle, makes this point," Piotr put in. "Do you know the story, son?"

"I only know we Poles love the eagle."

"Yes, we do. For her wings are like faith and reason. *Fides et Ratio*. Wings which allow the human spirit to rise to the contemplation of the truth."

"Here comes yet another tale for surely," Czesław said.

"Priest is a great storyteller," Piotr added.

"A preacher of sermon upon sermon," Tadek said. "And now, as a dam burst, the waters will surely gush with pity for nothing in its path."

Chapter 25

"Before your great great grandfathers' time, there lived a Duke named Lech," Priest began.

"There were no cities then, only hovels and a few scattered and small villages. The Goths pushed into Poland from the West and the Huns from the East. These raiders took our food, our cattle and our lives. Farmers were forced to become warriors simply to protect themselves from death and starvation. It is a fool who believes civilization makes Man, for it is the other way around. And we desired, by our own sweat and perseverance, our own nation, to be free and prosper, so we could live in our own way."

As Priest related how Lech became the leader of the Western Slavs, uniting small tribes one by one, and how they slowly began to repel the repeated attacks by growing in strength, Bolek listened with rapt attention, for this story was somehow his story.

All his senses were tuned to the words as the soldier spoke of how mighty forts sprang up, as Bolek's ancestors proudly taught their children their laws and traditions in schools and at home. Unity brought strength, and the customs became sacred. The Poles solidified their common values with one common language. A society which honors the noble deeds of ancestors, the dignity of all men and women, the unique traditions that help define them, somehow connected those long dead with the current generation and with the hope and faith of those yet to come. An eternal relationship between past and future was forged.

Bolek knew much of this, but somehow Priest's telling parted a dark veil to expose the truth. Culture and faith. Art and industry. But always a sharp szabla in a strong arm. And Lech was foremost in the balance of war and peace. So illustrious a leader was he that even the Muscovites of that time often called the Poles Lachi, after Lech, and the Muslims named Poland Lechistan, or the country of Lech.

Father knew this. Father believed it. Father bled for it.

"Not only was he a valiant warrior, he was also a wise ruler, in the mold of Alexander, who brought Greek culture to barbaric Asia. Both men had a taste for learning. Soon we could do more than merely survive, for we Poles were able to keep our harvests, prosper, and there was time for reflection and learning.

"This Lech, like all Poles, loved hunting, and threw all his vitality into it, as he did in battle as he did in building a united Poland. As he killed bear, boar, fox and wolf, he admired the brave heart, fierce spirit, the unwillingness to quit, true courage, and be it man or beast.

"Lech developed a taste for the Western sport of falconry and had many goshawks and peregrine falcons. One day he was inspired to capture and train an eagle to hunt, and though his falconers had advised it was an impossible task, he tried many times, each attempt leading to failure. But he would not relent in his desire, for he thought the mighty eagle would be swifter and stronger in the flight after its quarry than any other bird that ever lived."

"Go on," Bolek begged for the story to continue.

"On one such quest, Lech rode out ahead of his party, his favorite hawk on his arm, hooded and at the ready. At the summit of a high hill, he spied a magnificent white eagle with a massive curved beak, long, deadly talons, a proud demeanor, and her young around her screeching from their aerie perched high on a rocky crag. He resolved to capture one of the young eaglets and train it."

"This occurred at a place much like this, Góralu," Piotr added, as the group of riders rode out of the woods and into an area of high bluffs.

Bolek looked around, involved to the hilt in this tale of long ago.

The tale continued, and the young shepherd learned how Lech had leapt from his horse, climbed towards the nest, the white eagle eying him intently, her mighty wings shielding her defenseless eaglets. As Lech reached for the nest, the eagle, with a swift movement, pecked him in defiance. It stung, but Lech persisted. Pulling out his dagger, he pointed it at the majestic bird's breast, reaching again for her young. But now the enraged mother-bird was upon him, deftly avoiding the deadly blade, fearlessly pecking at his hand, ripping flesh with no thought of her own pain. Again and again Lech sought his prize, to no avail, for while the eagle bled a bit, Lech's hand and arm were a bloodied mess. Soon Lech's heart was touched by her unyielding noble courage, for she could easily fly away and be free, but chose to stand and fight, and at any cost. Lech became ashamed of his desire to take the freedom from her young and rob their mother of her life. He relented. Climbing down the steep mountain wall, his blood staining the rock walls along his descent, he rested upon a stone outcrop. There, with the vista of the great lands of Poland lay before him for as far as he could see. His country, which he loved with all his heart, held him in its bosom.

The majestic eagle risked death to resist his mere whim, to own and train yet another bird. The wind, whipping through the canyon walls and between the trees whispered *vanity* into his ears. Soon, it came to Lech, with a steel resolve; he would defend Poland unto his death just as the eagle had defended her nest. At that moment, the raptor rose from her aerie, soaring triumphant above him, cawing in pride, in victory, but also of the honor of the struggle. Saluting her, he swore this impressive raptor would become the symbol of his country. From that day forth, Poles would shed their blood in their defense with an eagle's outline as a coat of arms. She would ride before Poland's armies, and never yield. Thus to this day, on the shield and standard of Poland, is blazoned the white eagle on a crimson field.

"And Duke Lech built a castle near that very spot, just as the eagle that inspired him had build her nest," Priest said. "The castle and the city which now surrounds it are named 'Gniezno,' which in language of those days meant, 'nest'. His people became known as Polonie – field dwellers."

"The day may come, young Góralu," Priest said, "when your heart will pound with an immutable beat, your blood will course in sacrificial warmth, and your arms will be of iron, your mind clear and alert."

What he says is so real. It is what I desire. How do I pull it to my breast?

"Suddenly I feel an unquenchable desire for vodkie," Priest declared.

"And pork. To vodkie and pork," Tadek shouted, causing five szablas to slash the air in toast, the blades ending pointed at heaven.

Chapter 26

"Mother Józefa?" The orphan girl, Marianna, who was taken in when she had no place to go, addressed her matron. "What if the outcome of the hunt is less than desired? Would not a feast be a heart-breaking greeting?"

"I will not think of such things today, Marianna. My son is hunting with Polish knights. I pray they return tomorrow in victory. We will celebrate. In these times, we need it. We shall empty our cupboards, storm the winter cellar and cut the meat from the smokehouse rafters on this day."

This celebratory mandate produced a flurry of activity as every soul on the Radok farm agreed a feast was in order. With invasion talk rampant, with raiders at their throats, with boars attacking children, it was time to raise a toast to life and fill one's belly with its bounty. Mother Józefa ordered riders, despite the threat of raiders, to invite locals to the feast.

Spring vegetables were harvested, peeled and trimmed, flour mixed with egg and water, then kneaded for breads and pie crusts, preserved fruits from last year's harvest were soaking in tubs, chunks of cheeses appeared from the cellar and stood for cutting, cows were milked, butter and cream prepared. Sealed demijohns filled with spiced wine were secured to trees with rope and placed in the cooling waters of the mill stream. The entire farm labored through the night and into the day, alive with anticipation of a feast, a time for family, friends, for life.

"They are coming!" A farm hand announced from his perch on the cottage roof. Kasia bolted in the direction of the lookout's outstretched arm, her dress pulled up to her knees to run as fast as she was able. The others stopped their various labors, eyes fixed to Kasia. A mighty cheer arose as five riders appeared, each sitting tall in the saddle, each with success written in their demeanors.

Bolek dismounted and scooped Kasia in his arms, raising her

petite body to heaven. Priest, Piotr, Tadek and Czesław road to the cottage as if this had been just another uneventful trip. But the meat they each carried spoke volumes. Cheers, heartfelt salutes and clumsy bows greeted the warriors. The scene was much like that experienced at the village. A hundred questions were asked at once, a thousand thanks given.

"It was a giant. A beast. Look at that tusk – a szabla in its own right. What was the hunt like? Were there injuries? What of the poor injured boy?"

Each question would be answered in its own time, and the story of the hunt would be told, retold, drawn out and embellished with this spice and those herbs for years to come by those who were there on that day and those who wished they had been or knew someone who had. The boar was a dragon; the Polish knights each a St. George.

While meat simmered in stew pots or roasted on spits, Czesław gave an archery exhibition in a nearby paddock and the young boys tested each other by measuring how far they could bend the mighty No Arc. Bolek laughed at their efforts, much as Czesław had at Bolek's effort when the marksman had given him archery pointers.

Setting up six like targets the size of a man's head, and attaching them to ropes hanging from tree limbs, Czesław asked some of the boys to give each target a swing, then get quickly away from the trees. At a full gallop, while standing in his stirrups, Czesław was able to hit all six targets, the final mark made while jumping a fallen tree limb. Given the distance from the targets, and that they were in motion, and Czesław on horseback, this feat gave the spectators a feeling for the skills of the Polish pancerni armored cavalry who defended them; and also for any brigands who might be watching from a distance.

After the demonstration of Czesław's mastery of the bow, Piotr asked for volunteers to mount his magnificent steed, Hector. At first there were no takers, for the horse stood a full head higher than any of their work horses, snorting and stomping as if he were about to stampede of to the vast steppes and never return. But after Piotr winked at Kasia and she accepted the master horseman's challenge and Hector became a quiet and gentle horse under her seat, a line quickly formed and local mountain farm boys would tell stories for years of how they once rode upon a brave Polish war horse.

"Are all Polish horses from the city so large," a young girl asked.

"Hector is only of medium size," Piotr said. "The hussars ride horses that outweigh him by three hundred pounds or more and are several hands taller at the withers.

"This is a mixed-breed horse," Piotr continued, patting Hector on its thick neck. "He is a Tatar steppe pony bred with a larger and stronger European mount. Speed and strength, he has, yet much-needed endurance also." The children gasped at the mention of the word 'Tatar', for their mothers often threatened to tell Tatars if the child misbehaved.

"My saddle is from Hungary. It is of Asian design, deeper in seat for better back support," Piotr continued, enjoying the innocent expressions of the children as he spoke of the Magyar warriors who had once raided heavily in southern Poland. Now gone, only the essence of their culture remained. "I ride with my knees up higher than European riders, so I can absorb the impact of a collision with another horse or an infantryman without losing balance. Remember this, children: It is the Polish cavalryman on this horse who allows us to breathe freely. Our speed, our weapons, our determination and our love of God's commands allow us to be masters of our land."

For those whose passion was the szabla, Tadek did not disappoint. With Bolek as a sparring partner, the deadly power of the saber was made apparent as the blinding speed and cunning maneuvers of the swordsman pushed Bolek to the limit.

"Think of your szabla handle as a gentle bird," the stone-faced Tadek instructed the children as he attacked Bolek. "Hold her too tightly and you will choke her. But too loose, she will fly away. Good! Good! Better, Góralu. Anticipate!" Tadek growled. "My body will tell you what action I will next make. Anticipate!"

Later, with the aroma of spiced meat and fresh baked bread in the air, all eyes turned to Bolek, who was instructed by Piotr and Czesław to ride at several bales of hay, stacked to the size of a man, while atop Quo Vadis. True to her command, the mare rode at the bag until Piotr shouted, "Turn!" At the last possible second and horse and rider, as one, brushed the hay.

"This is more than just a game," Piotr instructed his audience. "In war there is no time to instruct a horse in the heat of battle. One does not command in war. War commands."

"If only they would take to their catechisms with such attention," Priest noted, as he watched the young eyes fixed on horse and sword, their mouths making the letter O, their eyes fixed and bulging.

"How does our young Góral do?" Priest asked Piotr in a whisper.

"He takes to horse, bow and sword like a fish to water."

"That is not what I asked."

"These things are not as easy to attain as are the tools of war. But he begins to understand what he owes his country, his duty. And for the right reasons."

A hint of a smile and Priest walked away. Piotr continued with his attentive audience of young children until they were snatched away as Bolek atop Quo Vadis hurdled over one then another corral fence, firing one arrow then a second not more than a finger's width apart into one of the cottage's wooden pillars.

As Bolek dismounted and handed Quo Vadis to a servant for tending, Mother Józefa greeted her son with eyes afire.

"I cannot whack you this time for acting foolishly, but I can think the deed," she whispered so as no one else could hear her. "You fire arrows into our very home as you fly by on your horse like a madman!"

"Sorry, Mother," he said, lifting her into his arms. "I lost control of myself for a bit. How is my dinner coming along?"

"There is no vodka on your breath, so I hope this is a temporary madness."

"But there will be vodka on my breath soon," he answered, spinning her in a circle over her protests to be put down.

Soon the Royal Guardsmen, Mother Józefa and Bolek entered their home, to the smell of roasting pork, garlic, and a cacophony of minor aromas. Priest sat well away from the table, his wooden chair cocked back on its rear legs, a wicker-wrapped demijohn of vodka in his left hand, while he made a point with his right. Czesław, Piotr and Tadek sat across from him on the long bench, laughing and elbowing each other in response to Priest's words. The farm yeoman and his wife, son and two daughters were there also, with Kasia joining the young maidens in song, led by the yeoman, who added an off-color verse about a gray horse and a feather blanket and was promptly smacked by his wife.

"You did well today, son," Piotr said to Bolek. "And it is a blessing to be welcome guests at a family feast."

All toasted Mother Józefa, and she accepted the compliment, thanking the soldiers and her son for the gift of precious meat, the main course. This was to be a traditional feast for upon the table sat grain in the form of bread, from the field, vegetables from the garden, dried fruit from the orchard, mushrooms from the woods and fish from the water. God's bounty lay before all on one table.

A feast rarely surpasses anticipation, but this one did. The front door was kept open to create the feeling of an inclusive celebration with the somehow ever growing numbers outside, and servers moved from the indoor table to the courtyard tables, where the farm hands shared in course after course of the earth's bounty. Loud talking and relentless toasts mingled with the warmth, light and color of firelight. Wine and vodka bottles were drained of their fiery liquids at an alarming rate. The boar meat from the spits was unending.

The yeoman had surprised the crowd with a homemade batch of *krypnik*, fire vodka, with honey and water and a few exotic spices added which he refused to identify. But with the bulk of the concoction being vodka, all enjoyed it. *Piwo*, a barley and mead beer was served in gallons. By the time the sweet breads, the plum dumplings, the *szarlotka* apple cake and dried fruit compote cakes were set out, the feast was a dance of delight, the house aglow with grace, solidarity and harmony.

At the head of the table, his face set in rigid lines, Bolek stood straight and stiff, glass raised. He stood silently until a few noticed, then more, then a cloud of silence pervaded the room and those from the courtyard, numbering over a score, elbowing their way for better positions at the doorway and open windows, heads bobbing to see and hear all.

"Join me all in raising my cup to our distinguished friends who are responsible for our safety," he began in a confident and respectful voice, "and as providers of the main course of this wondrous feast. Family and friend, I give you the King's Royal Guardsmen."

A thunderclap of voices roared as the angular Priest, the slight Piotr, the giant Czesław and the bull-like Tadek acknowledged their praises.

"To the Radok manor!" Priest responded in kind, cup raised high.

"To the King!" Tadek countered.

"To the Virgin," Czesław said, besting them all, prompting bowed heads and solemn signs of the Cross.

"To good times," Piotr added, wiping his face with the end of his shirt. "And how we appreciate them so much better because of the sorrows we face daily. Enjoy the enjoyable while we have it. May it always flow in such abundance."

Cheering, all gave thanks to God and most pressed hands and embraced with teary eyes.

"There is one thing missing," Bolek shouted as he leaned forward, his hand in the chest pocket of his newly made *zupon* coat. The room went silent.

"My friend Piotr is an expert horseman and teacher, as all of you know. And he has asked me to teach him the flute. And this I will do. But as much as I love and honor him, I do not want his greasy boar-meat-stained lips upon my own instrument. So, my honorable friend, I present you with this humble tool of music."

With this Bolek pulled out a long pine flute, intricately carved with miniature horses in various poses. The crowd cheered as Piotr stood, his eyes wide in disbelief, his fingers tracing the intricate carvings. All around him leaned forward as he put the flute to his lips and inhaled.

"Hold it like a bird, Piotr," Bolek said with a wink, echoing Tadek's own words to Bolek. "Too tight and you will choke it. Too loose and it will fly away."

The sound, when it came, was hollow, full of air, pitiful. Piotr, along with his expectant audience, winced in pain.

"Ah, the student will now teach the master in at least one discipline," Priest said, consoling the novice flutist, to which Piotr agreed fully, bowing formally to Bolek with his precious gift cradled in both hands.

"Let us hear the master play," Tadek challenged Bolek who drew his flute from another pocket, made a motion to play, but paused in mid breath and asked for violin accompaniment. A serf quickly walked to the middle of the floor holding his violin (for what would a Polish feast be without music), put it to his chin and awaited a signal from Bolek, who responded with the opening notes of a familiar Góral folk song. The violin joined in, and all began to clap in rhythm and sing.

Priest, Bolek noticed, was smiling happily but clearly lost someplace in memory. Immediately, as the song ended, Bolek left the table for a moment, returning with a leather-wrapped package. Placing it on the table with extreme care, he opened it carefully, never taking his eyes from Priest. Out of the straw emerged the toothless old Cossack's violin. Bolek cradled it by the neck and extended it to Priest to reveal a new and delicately carved eagle on its back.

Priest accepted it as he would a newborn child, his fingers running over each nuance from scroll to keyboard to bridge. Bolek produced the accompanying bow, made from horsehair in just the correct lengths and thickness, and he offered it up to Priest as if it were a finely honed szabla. Accepting this also, with wide-eyed pleasure, Priest examined it and nodded his approval. He lifted the violin to his chin; the room, silent. Plucking on a string, then another, he asked Bolek to play an A on his flute. He twisted the string's tuning peg until the notes met in pitch. He gently dragged the bow along the strings. Both eyebrows rose. With initial caution, he plucked, he added vibrato to up bows and down bows, then assertively slashing the bow across the strings to test it to its core.

"Well," he said in mock anger, "Piotr got his flute, you got your horse. It was about time for my violin," he said, throwing out a wink only Bolek was privy to.

Bolek played the first few notes of yet another popular Polish folk song and Priest echoed the challenge with an appropriate response, adding vibrato to his sound, and the fingers of his left hand shaking to and fro to create emotion with music, the language of the soul. And indeed the violin resonated through the manor house as no violin in memory ever had. The din erupting at song's conclusion was only stilled when the notes of a fiery Hungarian gypsy song took everyone's breath away and commanded their feet and hands to respond as Priest looked possessed. The serf's violin joined in the air and Bolek added his flute in trio. Pots beaten with hands and wood spoons on knees kept the beat. The tables and chairs were pushed to the walls, and everyone began to dance, the floor itself shaking from the many feet flying, pivoting and landing. Bodies spun in the dance of life, all souls sated with equal measures of joy and thanksgiving.

The pandemonium broke up only when lightning illuminated dark clouds, and echoes of distant thunder in the west broke up the happy evening.

Chapter 27

Word came to Radok Manor the Pitry Manor's mill had broken down. This was disturbing news since the entire region relied on but a few local mills to grind grain into flour. In such cases, an inoperative mill required expert repairmen and appropriate parts dispatched from Cracow. Bolek had been taught to repair the Radok mill and was capable of forging his own makeshift metal gears and such. As master of Radok Manor, he determined it was his sworn duty to provide milled grain to the Pitry's in their time of need and so, excusing himself from his training and farm duties for half a day, he filled a cart with bags of flour and guided the draft horse toward Rozalia's home, eager to lay eyes on her and for her to see not only his sword but his newly muscled body, a welcome and unexpected addition to his relentless training.

The first thing he noticed as he drove his flour laden wagon through the Pitry manor gatehouse was a tall, imposing black war horse tied to a rail; a hussar's horse, easily a head taller than Bolek's Quo Vadis. Anticipation turned to caution.

Reining in at the entrance to the mill, Pan Pitry's authoritative voice barked commands from within. He hoped his arrival would save the laborers from such demeaning demands. In his own mind, Bolek entered the estate as savior. Radok wheat flour from the Radok mill would feed his love's family for a time.

Food is life. Gold means little without it.

"For you," Bolek said to the Pitry yeoman, as he jumped from the wagon, pointing to the load of flour. He searched for Rozalia, wishing to be thanked by her, wishing to reply in return that it was nothing, no trouble at all. But she was nowhere in sight, although Maciej, her eldest brother, did appear from inside the manor house with a Polish soldier, a hussar, evidently a gentleman and certainly the owner of the war horse.

Tall, fair and slim, a flowing well-trimmed mustache goatee combination, gave him a model hussar appearance, the kind

Bolek had only seen in drawings, the kind father and grandfather attempted to imitate.

Dressed in a tight-fitting riding coat, like Bolek's grandfather used to wear, a szabla hung from his belt, its ornate scabbard resting along bright red pants and down to his knee length leather boots. But the most impressive part of the soldier, to Bolek's mind, was his magnificent felt cap; a beautiful green of a hue unfamiliar to him, not even in the varied leaves or mosses of the mountains matched it. The cap was trimmed in sable, a king's ransom for sure. Numerous hawk feathers attached to the cap lay over the left side as he wore it cocked to the right.

Knowing full well his own pants were soiled, his shirt stained, his boots mud splattered Bolek knew instantly today's imagined role as savior at the Pitry estate was shattered. Catching Bolek staring at his companion, Maciej smiled an inscrutable smile, and then ignored Bolek as he guided the gentleman caller to Bolek's wagon.

"More milled grain has finally arrived," Maciej told the hussar, his back to Bolek. "Service is so inconsistent here in the country. Not like in Cracow, eh?" Guiding the young hussar into the mill house and without turning to acknowledge him, Maciej said, "Get on with it, Radok. Be useful for once. Help the men unload."

Both men shook their heads and disappeared through the door, sharing a chuckle. Bolek, red-faced, jaw locked, hefted a bag onto his shoulder and joined in with the unloading process. The wagon soon emptied, a much-welcomed ladle of well water was offered to him. Perspiration and flour dust covered him.

As a sweet voice called his name from behind, he spilled the last of his refreshment on his shirt. He turned into sky blue eyes, a petite nose, a bright white smile, all framed by flaxen hair. Rozalia. Grabbing an empty flour sack, he attempted to remove both the sweat and the spilled water from his face and chest, leaving him coated in still more ghostly white powder.

"It's been weeks since I've seen you," Rozalia chastised as she attempted to brush flour from his face in a motherly manner with her handkerchief. "Much has been happening. I have news and no friends to share it with. I haven't been to Mass here. I've been away. And I've missed you."

"I'm sorry. Things have happened to me, too."

He saw her eyes widen.

"Your grandfather," she said, raising her hand to mouth. "I am so sorry, Boleczek," she added, using an affectionate form of Bolek's name, which pleased him. And despite his sweat and dusty soiled person, she hugged him. She smelled like wild flowers, and he longed for the embrace to last forever, but afraid to hug back, lest he never let go.

"I am so sorry," she said, stepping back. "I loved him too. An old patriot. They say it is an honor to die as he did. But I don't know how dying can be honorable. But I hear you accounted bravely for yourself as well."

"Not really. It was the cavalry men, my new friends, who should be thanked. Real soldiers like my father. They saved us."

"The whole countryside speaks of nothing else," she assured him. "First they talk of their new feelings of security and then they praise the Radoks for killing a whole raiding party. 'Let that be a lesson to the other raiders,'" she said in a deep voice, with a wagging finger, mimicking a typical farmer's throaty voice and mannerisms.

"I am in training for just such a thing, Rozalia. Come and look at my szabla. Let me show —"

"Later," she said, taking his hand and looking at him from beneath long lashes. "I have recently returned from Cracow, and I have something private to speak to you about."

Now that I am a warrior, my Rozalia seems more womanly with me; more attentive.

"Rozalia, you are summoned to the house," came a stern cry from her brother. "You must show off your trophy, yet again."

"Coming," she replied, locking her arm into Bolek's while pulling him toward the manor house with its long lace curtained windows and spring flowers in boxes beneath the windows.

"I have something wonderful to tell you," she whispered. "In the house. You are my favorite childhood friend, and should be among the first to know." The puzzled Bolek followed, his heart pounding from the effects of her physical contact as she guided him, arm in arm.

The moment they entered the manor hall, the visiting hussar glided to her, cradling her forearm, separating her from Bolek, ignoring him, guiding her into the formal parlor and to her parents' side. Pan and Pani Pitry were dressed in their finest – both in expensive silk *delias*, their bodies appearing bloated from the puffiness of the robes while their heads seeming small. Bolek remembered the haughty attitude the gallant presented outside and how he now wore a cheerful smile, mostly given to Rozalia.

While left unacknowledged in the entranceway feeling somehow he was eavesdropping, his heart filled with pain as understanding came. The trophy Rozalia had spoken of was not a trinket, nor a new horse nor a fashionable hat from Cracow. Her parents and brothers were extremely warm and attentive to the hussar, as they had never been to him. As if the soldier was family also. Her words from a few moments ago echoed in his ears. She had called him her "favorite *brother*."

"Bolesław Radok, come and meet Jerzy," Rozalia demanded, extending her arm with a dramatic turn of her hand. Meet my cousin."

"But distant enough to become much closer," the gallant soldier said looking straight at Bolek as he approached.

Bolek's jaw was tight, aware she had not called him by his familiar nickname, Boleczek, but used his formal name. As introductions were made, the two men's shook hands; not politely but as rival boars courting the same sow, each circling the other, searching for a weakness, an unguarded spot in which to sink its teeth. An instinctive rivalry. Rozalia's parents and brothers stiffly acknowledged Bolek, and he nodded. The verbal confrontation began immediately.

"So you're a local miller," Jerzy asked, taking Bolek's measure head to toe.

"Bolek is a fine wood carver," Rozalia told Jerzy, "a singer, a son of patriots. And he has recently killed a multitude of brigands."

"A multitude? Did you kill ten? A hundred? Or thousands?" Jerzy asked, winking at Rozalia's older brother. "Even a hussar could not accomplish as much."

"I killed but one," Bolek told him, his hands squeezed into fists.

"Only one? Wounded, then. How many did you incapacitate?"

Bolek glared.

"Some of the king's Royal Guardsmen saved you then," Jerzy suggested. "A more correct statement, no?"

"Yes," Bolek admitted, his face burning and his feet ready to fly.

"King Jan has commissioned several parties of cavalry to patrol areas where raids have been taking place," the hussar explained to his hosts. "The peasants are unable to defend themselves, and it is left to us. I suppose one of these patrols arrived at a fortuitous time for your young friend here, my Rozalia."

The words *my Rozalia* uttered by a rival made Bolek lose what little restraint that was left in him.

"They did come, but not before the brigands killed my grandfather. He also killed one. He stood at Chocim. Did you?"

The change of expression told Bolek he had hit his mark.

"No," Jerzy muttered. "And I counsel you to adopt a more civil tone with me, farm boy. Or else you might be forced to draw your shiny new szabla from its sheath for the first time?"

"Bolek!" Rozalia cried. "I want so much to have you two become friends. Jerzy has asked for my hand today. And I've consented. I will soon be a countess."

Turning, bolting for the door, pushing both wide, Bolek's feet pounded the ground on his way to his wagon, his intention to leave the Pitry manor forever. But the hussar was at his heels.

"A moment, sir. I have a right to ask your history with my fiancée. For there is clearly something I have not been told. "

Bolek turned so suddenly the two collided, both stumbled, righted themselves, and Jerzy drew his szabla.

"I do not slaughter lambs, farm boy," Jerzy's blade inches from Bolek's heaving chest. "But I will have an answer to my question. Now!"

"And here it is," Bolek replied, drawing out his father's unsheathed szabla from the bed of the wagon.

Before Jerzy could react Bolek was upon him, furiously employing every move he had been taught. At first the hussar cowered at the surprise onslaught. Bolek heard Rozalia scream as she and her family streamed out of the manor to witness her fiancée cowering, fighting for his life. But Bolek was soon on the defensive as he gasped for breath, his sword arm leaden, his guard weakened and the hussar recovering his wits.

In desperation, Bolek lunged at his opponent, scoring a slight wound and a cry of pain, but, in kind, a paralyzing pain to his right shoulder forced him to wince and drop his szabla. Something hard smacked him on the side of his face; exploding stars in his head faded to blackness.

He awoke in his wagon, lying on straw, looking up through the limbs and branches of towering oak trees at billowing white clouds floating in a clear blue sky. The right side of his face throbbed as he explored the swelling in his cheek and lips with his tongue. Moving his head slightly, he could see his right shoulder had been securely bandaged. As he tried to rise, he yelped in pain.

"Easy, son," one of the serfs who had helped Bolek unload flour cautioned. "We're on our way to your farm."

Exhausted, Bolek drifted between the worlds of dreams and reality. At first, he cursed his defeat and wished to die, but upon hearing the sounds of the forest, to feel the wind brushing his face, he began to long for his mountains, to fly with the eagle, and to leave the shame behind. And his Rozalia, gone! What was there now to live for? But spying his father's szabla lying next to him, a tinge of blood on the point, *Farm boy,* he said to himself. Nobody will ever call me that again as he renewed his vow to become like them, like the Guardsmen. Someday he would meet Rozalia's young hussar, the one with the bright green cap, and things would end differently.

With his one functioning arm, he reached for the crucifix hanging around his neck. Grasping it to his chest, he prayed to the Virgin to allow him to face Green Cap again. The next time he would show no mercy. The next time he would be more than a match for any man who drew breath. There was work to do.

Chapter 28

"He needed a lesson," a bed-ridden and shamed Bolek moaned back at Priest.

"Lesson? Lesson? He gave *you* a lesson. When you returned in the condition you did, we did not trust the wagon driver's account of things. Indeed, we visited the Pitrys and questioned them."

Bolek's pride now hurt more than his shoulder as he recalled his defeat in front of the Pitrys, and how the king's Royal Guardsmen must have confronted them.

"Rozalia?" he asked like a mouse.

"She is angry and hurt. And that petite beauty matches you in fiery temperament."

"It was the hussar's fault."

"He was in the right. Rozalia is his wife-to-be. She accepted his offer and with the blessing of her parents. You had an obligation as a gentleman to honor their bond and answer his question. What were you thinking?"

"Will I ever hold a szabla again?"

"For what? To squabble over maidens with other young bucks?"

"She was my . . ."

"Was. That *is* the correct word. This issue is past."

"Will it be a life of digging turnips for me as a one-armed farmer?" Bolek asked, his shoulder smarting so much he feared he would be a cripple from here on out. "Will I ever hold a szabla again?"

"A sword? So you can slice up one of our hussars? Do you know what those men do? I hope you live to see it once, boy. One hundred men, lined up to attack, each wearing the eagle, the red and white cross. Ready to give their country all. Ah!" Priest cried out. "Why waste words. Your wound is a good wound. It runs in line with the shoulder muscles. And not only will you wield a szabla again, you will begin tomorrow."

"But how? I cannot even make a fist without pain."

"God gave you a second arm, another shoulder, and another hand, with which to grasp a sword. Tadek is equally adept with szabla on both sides. In war, you cannot ask a Turk to fight you on your strongest side. In fact, he will attempt to meet you on your left. A naturally left-handed warrior has an advantage, since, for the most part, his adversaries use their right, and he is used to engaging right-handers. But a right-handed warrior does not often face a left-handed fighter. You will learn to use your left. Beginning on the morrow."

"Perhaps I lost control of myself," a somewhat regretful Bolek admitted.

"He had every right to kill you in his own defense. Instead, he wounded you and then smashed the broad side of his szabla into your head. I want you to take this as a lesson."

"What do the others think of me?"

"Piotr has nicknamed you the Apostle of Ignorance."

"That's not so bad."

"Then he told Tadek he taught you to ride a horse like a lion, but Tadek taught him to wield a sword like a lamb. Czesław told Tadek he taught you to shoot an arrow with an eagle's eye, yet he could capture your szabla armed only with a single blade of wild steppe grass."

Bolek's stomach swirled, overcoming even the pain in his shoulder.

"Tadek's blood boils to think he alone has failed in training our pupil. The Cossack bull is aching to get his hands on you. He would drag you from this feather bed right now, if I let him. Tomorrow."

Bolek mouth dropped.

"Next week we will include you in our patrols. This way we can work on your training day and night."

"Patrol? Can I be trusted after losing my first duel?"

"You lost to a hussar. Though a virgin in war, he has been trained with little regard for cost. He is the mainstay of Poland's greatest line of defense. There's no shame in your loss. And let me tell you of your mistake, a trap we all have fallen into." Priest pulled up a stool to Bolek's bed and spoke softly, as a father might have done.

"In practice, we are all relaxed, at ease, for we are among friends and enjoying sport and education. Our feet are fast and our breath steady. And this is the way we should learn. But it is dangerous to assume a training experience is the same as that of war. Death is in the air then. You will smell it, taste it, hear it, and see it. Your greatest fear will be that you will feel it. So in your first battle your heart will pound, and your feet turn to lead. Your muscles will tighten, and you will chew up breath too quickly and gasp for air. Your feet will stop moving to conserve energy; your arm will grow heavy with blood. All training will be forgotten and then you are no longer a swordsman but a target."

"That is as it was," Bolek admitted.

"We will visit the Pitry manor next week while we are on patrol and you will apologize."

"You are always right, Priest," Bolek said, nodding sadly from his bed.

"It is a curse." Priest smiled. "The next time you fight for your life, do not become angry. Do not attempt to defeat your opponent with brute force. Fight as you train. You admit you were wrong. Therefore, there is hope for you. We will continue your education. As of tomorrow, Tadek will begin to make you a precise warrior or you will break like an egg. Few things matter more to him than his pride. I pity you."

"Thank you, Priest."

"One more thing. The villagers told us of your exploits against the brigands. You killed two. Why did you not tell me of this?"

"I ran."

"Why?"

"I vomited after the two men fell, recovered, put arrow to bow, aimed, and stared into glowing evil eyes."

"Damn." Priest shouted, pounding his fist on his leg. "A giant of a man? Their leader?"

"Yes. Some say it was Gustaw."

"You had him in your sights?"

"It was as if he could see me, see into me. I ran."

"It appears you and I are connected in many ways."

Putting his face nose to nose with Bolek, Priest hissed at him. "You run from a dog yet attack an innocent hussar. If you ever use these fancy tricks we teach you for your own vanity ever again, I will come for you."

"But I—

"Enough!"

Chapter 29

The next day Bolek pitied himself as he faced a grimacing Tadek.

"Fear immobilized you. You must make your position unassailable. You will learn now to give all and yet give nothing."

He took Bolek's left hand and made him take his father's szabla, forcing Bolek to recall the encounter with the 'victor' in mind-numbing detail and repetition.

"Imagine the hussar in front of you. Recall each motion, each step, each transfer of weight, each feint, and each thought or inclination."

Once satisfied, Tadek grunted, and a new level of training began.

"Again!" "Again!" "Again!" Seemed to be the only words the unrelenting fiend of a swordsman spoke as the ailing Bolek, right shoulder swollen and burning, left failing in unfamiliarity and overuse, slumped to the ground.

"Although the loser, your initial attack was excellent," Tadek finally said. "Tight, uncontrolled, but the correct moves. You rushed your moves and were furious but unconfident, showing all you knew in the opening seconds of the engagement, wishing it to end as quickly as possible. Still you engaged. A coward would not have raised his sword."

Not a coward!

"So I—"

"Quiet! Your motive was wrong. It put you at death's door. The victor was well-trained. It is that which saved you. You have three choices. Continue using your emotions instead of your reason and die a fool. Learn to fight with reason, passion and for righteousness. Or become the coward and ignore every slight, every threat and die like a mouse battered by the cat's paw."

I will learn. I thank God I did not have the ability yet to hurt the hussar. But I did hurt Rozalia. I thought only of myself.

"Your footwork failed you and your szabla became a hammer instead of an instrument. Think of this," Tadek said, "taking Bolek's szabla from him, "as a finely wrought violin. Play it with the respect warranted to a fine instrument and it will serve you well."

Tadek threw the szabla at Bolek who fumbled with it left-handed. "So we know you will engage, Góralu. Perhaps a fool, but not a coward. Progress has been made. Let us now work on your head as well as your hand."

Encouraged by the touch of humanity from Tadek, he pushed the daring and stoic swordsman, speaking what he was longing to ask. "How is it you have no fear of death, Tadek? How does one learn that?"

Spitting into the soil and looking away from his student, Tadek whispered. "One night my father drank more vodka than usual. He came home, knocked my mother to the floor, and then turned on me. I fell to my knees and struggled to stay conscious from his kick to my stomach. He raped my sister in front of us. When her screams annoyed him, he warned my sister to shut her mouth. When she persisted, he choked her until she wailed no more. He dragged her body outside, lashed it to our work horse and kicked it hard in the ribs. He sent his sins off onto the steppes. Mother and I recovered. Then deed was never spoken of. I fear life, Góralu, not death. What you see in me is not courage. You see controlled rage. Each man I kill has my father's face. Courage for me springs from the rage of hatred. My death will end my misery."

From that moment on the szabla was no longer cold, dead steel to Bolek, but an extension of his being. He would not become a helpless young version of Tadek. He would die before allowing such travesty. He would sacrifice for love of others. Day and night and night and day was spent in left-handed szabla sparring until his left shoulder grew larger and comfortable as his right. His fingers ached. His wrist numb. But Tadek never once relented. When the szabla fell from an all but paralyzed hand, the master swordsman made the student dance, skip, and jump, telling him to imagine the earth as a bed of hot coals, and he could never rest lest his feet turn to ashes.

Soon Bolek had no time to think about his wound since every other part of him hurt more. In the few moments he had to himself, he would collapse in the mill stream and allow the water to cover and cool him, the current massaging his throbbing body. On one of these occasions, Piotr appeared, smiling warmly and began to massage Bolek's muscles.

"You prepare well, Góralu."

"I begin to hate Tadek."

"As iron sharpens iron, so a friend sharpens a friend."

"I do not have a head for your sayings."

"Tadek told me that based on your explanation of the spat with the hussar he was but a mere inch above your measure in skill. We will now stretch you to a greater height."

"I am prepared."

"But you must learn to understand as well as you prepare for battle. Often, there will be no time to think. Your body will react to what you've taught your muscles with repetition, but that is not enough. At these times, you must let your heart guide you, not your brain. If it is a true heart, built on love and wisdom, it will not let you down. If an old professor such as I learned this truth, so can you. This is the wisdom of Solomon."

Soon, even as Bolek imagined the sun was simply rising and falling to the rhythm of Tadek's relentless torture, Bolek began to improve – the sword was becoming second nature. What was once only tactics soon gave way to strategies. Some evenings Priest would play a fast violin piece while Piotr practiced the flute as Bolek attempted to hold off Tadek's parries and lunging attacks. The swordsman in training worked hard, learned and never complained, keeping his agreement. And the Royal Guardsmen kept theirs.

Eventually it was not so easy for Tadek to touch Bolek with saber point or broad side or to even pass under his guard. And the first time Bolek tipped Tadek's coat with his szabla the teacher's eyes doubled in size.

"Touché," the stoic cried, "as the French dandies say, Góralu. A clean touch." Tadek bowed. Tadek bowed!

Chapter 30

"He is fast, open to instruction and surpasses my expectations," Tadek said as the four guardsmen walked together under a ghostly sun blocked by heavy fog.

"He ran from Gustaw and exploded upon a hussar," Priest said. "Perhaps he is a bomb ready to explode, and we fill him with more and more black powder."

"During the brigand raid of the village, where no villager put a finger on their attackers," Piotr counseled, "Bolek killed two. The first animal murdered the groom-to-be; the second mocked a holy sacrament and threatened a maiden."

"But he ran from Gustaw," Priest replied.

"The boy begins to understand," Tadek said. "I would be confident with him watching my back."

"This from you, Tadek?" Priest asked.

"He but lacks experience."

"Then we put him in the saddle with us. Prepare him."

Bolek's bandages were removed from his right shoulder to reveal a long, straight, red and swollen scar.

"The stitches will hold," Priest proclaimed. "The skin grows together, and there is little festering. Piotr doctors well. Your first battle scar. The women will love you now. The wolf fears you. Tomorrow we ride."

True to Priest's word, well before dawn, he found himself atop Quo Vadis in the middle of a Royal Guardsmen patrol. Though they had been out many times already, this was the first time he rode as one among them. This was not a hunt for game, but for villains. During the past few weeks, Priest was in contact with Cracow concerning the Royal Guardsmen mission – analysis of mountain passes. The king and his generals had chosen their route based on this intelligence. Orders were now for the company to meet up with the advancing army as it approached. Even Priest was not aware of the pass the Polish army would choose to ride through, if Vienna was besieged. But he had his suspicions, which he kept to himself. He would use this time for personal reasons and search for Gustaw.

Priest's plan was to explore some of the lower ground closer to the mountain passes. He was sure the raiders camped somewhere in a ravine off of a canyon or a well-hidden glen at a location where few would travel and protection easy. So the search party moved down into damp and misty darkness.

With the horses heads sagging, rain dripping down their manes, they picked their way through a stony stream, and the moss-covered black canyon walls rising on each side, echoing the clickety-click of hoof beats. With Priest followed by Piotr, Tadek, Bolek and Czesław bringing up the rear, Piotr began to play notes on his flute. As Piotr mimicked the songs of birds with some staccato notes, Bolek's mood picked up measurably. Then the first few notes of a familiar melody rang out from Piotr's carved wooden tube, and a strong tenor voice from the rear of the squadron rang out as Czesław gave voice to the well-known folk song to the accompaniment of Piotr's flute.

Bywaj dziewczę zdrowe, Ojczyzna mnie woła,
Idę za Kraj walczyć wśród rodaków koła.
I choć przyjdzie ścigać jak najdalej wroga,
Nigdy nie zapomnę, jak mi jesteś droga.

As if on command, Priest, Tadek and Piotr launched into the song's chorus, the darkly moody canyon was somehow transformed into a warm and vibrant hall of camaraderie and nostalgic singing. For the second verse, Bolek, his own flute to his lips, ornamented Piotr's song as Czesław's heroic voice boomed and swirled, reaching every crack and crevice.

Po cóż ta łza w oku, po cóż serca bicie?
Tobiem winien miłość, a Ojczyźnie życie.

Pamiętaj, żeś Polka, że to za Kraj walka,
Niepodległość Polski to twoja rywalka

The horses' heads rising, bodies and tails swaying to the rhythm.
"Góralu!" Tadek, always the mind reader, cried out. "This was a favorite of you father. Add your voice."

Polka mnie zrodzila, jej piersi wyssalem
Byc Ojczyznie wiernym, a kochance stalym.
I choc przyjdzie zginac w ojczystej potrzebie,
Nie rozpaczaj, dziewcze, zobaczym sie w niebie.

The melancholic song, its theme of duty to Poland before personal love, filled the gloomy canyon with uncommon fervor and a sad but loyal passion, the voices floating upward, into the sunlight and high pastures, serenading all within earshot. The forest listened with a thousand ears and not all of them friendly.

Chapter 31

Bolek, now playing the scout, knew the mountains as well as any in the region. Together they rode, singing loudly, joking, bold yet mindful and alert for any sign of danger ahead. Soon they were off exploring the highlands, crisscrossing virgin pine and beech forests, plummeting ravines, invading hidden meadows filled with sheep, riding through gushing mountain streams.

"Always keep your bodies even with the trunks of the trees," Bolek instructed as his mounted companions moved cautiously down a steep and wooded hill, the others struggling to keep their balance. "The trees grow upward to the sun, and this is the way we must align ourselves to balance our weight on our horses."

Taking full advantage of being in his element now, he enjoyed the lessons, although his companions responded with sneers and insincere smiles.

"This is the source of Poland's mighty Vistula River," he told his comrades as the patrol crossed the White Little Vistula River at a shallow point. The patrol had been crossing streams, creeks, brooks and rivulets fingering their way down the mountain ranges for some time eventually coming upon this main artery.

"It begins here with the melting snow and drainage of the Beskid Mountain Range," Bolek explained. "From this point we could boat our way into the Baltic Sea and pass Cracow, Warsaw and Gdansk. And at one point farther north, the Vistula comes so close to the Dnieper River it is said one could easily portage over well-worn trails and launch a boat into the Black Sea. From here water either flows into the Baltic or the Black Sea. If East meets West in you famed Eastern city, then north meets south here."

Although he did not know from experience what he was saying, he was proud of his speech for he had memorized it from his father and grandfather's authoritative lessons.

"The great Eastern city you speak of is Constantinople, now in Muslim hands," Piotr said. "Istanbul, they call it. It has gone the way of Alexandria, Damascus, Antioch and even holy Jerusalem. When it fell, over two hundred years ago, the trade routes to the East collapsed."

"Why is the fall of the Constantinople such a big thing?" Bolek asked.

"At its fall," Piotr replied, "the scholars, few of them willing to submit to Islam, flew westward, to Rome. They brought forgotten Greek culture and its philosophies to the West, resulting in a 'rebirth,' a renaissance. In a sense, Man was elevated and God relegated. The Protestant Reformation came quickly. Schism. We've now been fighting for centuries, and many believe the collapse of the Eastern city was the beginning of our suffering. Now Vienna, the new Rome, is threatened by the Islamic Ottomans."

"Neither Vienna nor Cracow will fall as long as I draw breath," Czesław muttered. "Look at all this beauty around us."

"*Plynie, plynie, plynie . . . Plynie Wisla, Po polskiej krainie*," Bolek sang, inspired from the natural beauty of God's earth which enveloped him. "The Vistula is flowing along the Polish countryside."

"This is a magical place," Czesław said, inhaling the fragrance from a grouping of spruce rowan bushes ripe with orange-red berries with slender birch trees sprouting all around. "May it stay untouched forever."

The wind hissed through the beech and fir, and the fresh pine aroma intoxicated the visitors. Woodpeckers, with their distinctive tapping for insects, abounded. At one point, from high above, an eagle called to her mate, floating on the air currents high above the treetops. When two of her feathers floated downward through the trees, Bolek was able to grab both before they fell to be trampled on the forest floor.

"A sign, young Góralu," Piotr said as he wiped the sweat from his forehead with his sleeve. "My cap only sprouts falcon feathers, while yours will display those of the mighty *tatrzanski orzel*. The Tatra Eagle has gifted you. It is your brother, your protector. One feather, one wing. One is Reason, the other, Faith."

Priest nodded in agreement and motioned Bolek to secure the feathers to his Magyar styled hat Priest had sent for from Cracow and surprised Bolek with it when he least expected it. He said Bolek could not ride with Royal Guardsmen wearing his old farm hat.

At least when I apologize to the hussar, it will be with my own hat adorned with these gifts from Lech's eagle.

The companions shared a meal of dried sausage and oscypek cheese, replenishing their leather water bags from a virgin stream. From their hilltop camp, they enjoyed the vista of the rich farmlands ripe with growing food, pristine prairies and wildflower patches dotting the overgrown grasslands. A myriad of butterflies floated atop the buds, the majestic Carpathian mountain range circling the entire scene as damp and misty air obscured the mountain bases. The soaring snow-capped pinnacles, disembodied from their underpinnings by fog, made the peaks look as if they hung like mythical fortresses in mid air.

A single musket shot echoed through the foothills and brought all to their feet with immediate attention. Within seconds, the five mounted riders sped down the hill toward the stand of pines where Bolek pointed.

Chapter 32

"Are you sure?" Priest asked him. "Sound plays tricks in the mountains."

"I am certain, for the mountains brought the sound up to resonate behind us. There is a path to the village where the shot rang out. This way."

Soon the horsemen stood silent atop a gently sloping hill amid a stand of wind-scarred pine trees. Looking down to the path Bolek said would be there, a covered wagon, no more than one bow shot away raced for the trees. It was clearly under attack by two raiders, a wiry gray-bearded wagon master doing his best to defend his property and life with a long musket. The raiders split up and attempted to approach from opposite angles. They were both grimy and lean, well-armed with pistol and bow. A lifeless body was sprawled well behind the wagon, obviously the wagon master's companion. Bolek moved to attack, but Priest grabbed his reins.

"Look there, Góralu, toward the edge of that summit."

Bolek's eyes followed Priest's nod and spotted three mounted men, their attention on the same distant struggle.

"Góralu stays with me," Priest ordered. "You men, introduce yourselves to the spectators there. Let them see your colors, and if they run, dissuade them."

Piotr, Tadek and Czesław were off in a heartbeat, moving swiftly and silently, veering between the widely spaced pines.

"We are going to ride down to engage," Priest murmured. "Keep to my right. Be silent. And for God's sake keep your head."

A puff of smoke and another report was heard. A miss. But the two attackers moved in for the kill as the wagon master fumbled with reins, gun and ramrod to reload.

Standing upright in his saddle, Priest raised his bow and launched an arrow, which lodged itself in the ribs of the brigand closest to the wagon master. He fell out of the saddle, his leg tangled in his stirrup, his horse dragging him out into the prairie. The second brigand, following the path of the arrow to its origin, spotted Priest and Bolek and signaled to his comrades on the hill, who were now in heated retreat followed by the three Guardsmen. The brigand turned his horse and galloped

off with Priest and Bolek in pursuit. Mieszko and Quo Vadis easily closed in on the fleeing raider. Another shaft hissed from Priest's bow, striking the rider full in the back.

"Magnificent shot," Bolek shouted, the wind rushing past his ears as he galloped neck and neck with Priest.

"I was aiming for the horse," Priest replied in exasperation.

With both attackers down, Bolek turned his attention to the other pursuit and watched as his comrades cut the three fleeing sentries down with precise arrow shots. Two died at once and one was wounded, having fallen from his horse with an arrow in his shoulder. He rose with a szabla in his hand as Tadek came at him on Parabellum, who at the last possible moment veered his nimble steed to the other side of the waiting man, changing sword hands, taking the Brigand's head off his shoulders in one swipe.

"That's good form, Góralu," Priest said as they watched Tadek finished his slash, his szabla tip pointing forward and up.

"A great victory." Bolek proclaimed, his heart pounding in his chest even with the danger now past, as the pair reached the wagon.

"A failure." Priest replied, pulling the trembling wagon master to his feet. "Five brigands attacked. Five brigands killed. One left alive would have been easily persuaded to tell us where the others hide."

"Thanks be to God and you, my saviors," the red-faced old man said, bowing. "My lord will be pleased you saved his shipment of vodka from brigands. His generosity is legendary."

"Vodka, you say, friend?" elbowing Bolek. "Well, Góralu, you were right. This is a tremendous victory."

The wagon master frowned.

"Yeoman, we are of the King's Royal Guardsmen. We protect you from brigands, Turks and Tatars. What master do you serve?"

"Master Jadaszewski. A wise and noble lord."

"I know of him. The Battle of Zhovti."

"Sir, I was his retainer there. We mourned Hetman Potocki's death together."

"Only the Hussars stood firm. Cossacks deserted or changed allegiance in battle." Priest's expression was grim as he kicked some dirt. "Pan Jadaszewski is a bachelor, is he not? With many serving girls?"

"The very same."

"When you arrive at your lord's manor, thank him for his gift of half the vodka."

"Half?" The wagon master repeated, his eyes bulging, his word dying in his throat.

"Better to return home with half than with none, and your life forfeit, no?" Priest asked.

The yeoman could only nod in agreement, though frowning.

"We will send two of these brigand horses along to your lord as tribute. They are worth more than all the vodka. Tell him we will thank him personally when the call for assembly comes."

"Assembly?" the old man asked.

"Do you not know Asia and Europe moves toward war? That we are invaded?"

"No my lord," the old man replied, head lowered.

Priest looked to the sky. "You know of the Radok manor, over there, outside of the village?"

"I think, yes."

"Take our share of the vodka there. Keep the brigands boots, weapons and saddles. Leave the flea-bitten gray at the farm."

"Yes, my lord."

"Góralu," Priest ordered, "Help Czesław put the body of the yeoman's companion on the wagon. Then take that sorrel. Lash one of the bodies to it and send it on its way."

Once all the tasks were completed, and the wagon teetering lazily on its way to drop off its precious cargo, the Guardsmen rode up the hill. At once finding a suitable campsite, they settled in a circle, each with a bottle of vodka in hand, recalling the deeds of the day.

"These godless dogs live somewhere close," Priest muttered. "A cave or hidden glen. They often travel and attack in small groups, but there is a larger pack of them. They have a camp. And it is someplace remote enough to allow cooking fires without threat of discovery, someplace where a night fire would not be easily spotted or smelled. Do you know of any such place, Góralu?"

"Only a thousand," Bolek replied with palms to the sky. "There are ravines that have never felt a man's eyes on them. We know giant bears live in these caves because of the pile of bones that lie scattered about the entrance. And then there are ghosts, demons and worse there."

"Ghosts?" Piotr said. "Well, the place they speak of ghosts is a place we must investigate."

"That would be where I would hole up if I were a murdering thief," the inscrutable Tadek mumbled.

"Take us to one of these places where ghosts are rumored to inhabit, Góralu," Priest said as he examined his bow. "But one near to a road or trail, for they need quick access to come and go. Somewhere a wagon could come in and out of to unload booty."

"These raiders become fearless with success, even despite our presence and our warnings," Piotr cautioned.

"Life is cheap when food is scarce," Czesław said.

"What the hell does that mean?" Tadek asked.

"He means food will soon be scarce. War is coming," Piotr said, "and we will all soon be pulled into it. The soldiers moving west will requisition food and conscript every able-bodied man and supplies. Many will grow hungry, there will be few to protect the weak, and the laws of the jungle will prevail."

"Leaving the raiders free to do as they like." Czesław said.

"They are godless dogs," Bolek spat.

"They once were men." Piotr replied.

"How can you say that?" Bolek demanded.

"Well, none of them have attacked a righteous hussar over a women," Tadek teased straight-faced.

The barb hit home, and Bolek clutched the hilt of his szabla.

"Careful, Góralu." Priest warned. "Tadek has not taught you even half of what he knows."

"Czesław," Priest said with a demonic smile. "Ride with speed to the wagon. Acquire a few more demijohns of vodka. Bring them back there, to the hill where we originally saw the wagon. But with caution. The brigands are near."

Chapter 33

"So it is time for the vodkie razor dance," Tadek chuckled.

"We are going to dance?" a puzzled Bolek asked.

"At first. But after a while it becomes more of a struggle to remain upright. And with a razor to your throat," Tadek added as he put a finger to his throat.

"But why do we need vodka?" Bolek continued.

"Because it strengthens the body and extends one's life." Piotr added.

"*Spiritus vini,*" Bolek heard Priest mutter.

"A natural lubricant. Before vodka, I do not know how an army marched or fought."

"Or danced a gallows jig," Tadek added. "If the air around you is thick with the odor of vodka you are near an army."

"It is we Poles who invented vodka," Priest declared, tapping his chest. "The best comes from golden rye. It can singe the hide off a hog. *Na zdrowie!*"

"And the best of that comes from Gdansz," Tadek said, "distilled in boilers as large as cottages."

"Gdansz used to be surrounded by forest," a more animated Piotr continued. "But the firewood required to heat the boilers soon took its toll. Gdansz now sits upon a prairie," his palm stretched outward to indicate he swore it to be the truth. "Now wagons loaded with wood move north to feed the spirit boilers, regularly returning, as this one just did, laden with our *aqua vitae.*"

"A good place here for our dance," Tadek said, surveying the campsite. "I can kill anything and everything that comes at us. We have the high ground."

"But they will see our fire from a hundred bow shots away." Bolek cautioned.

"Let them," Priest said, twisting the left side of his long black mustache round and round between index finger and thumb. "I want this murderous horde to know we are here. I want them to remember their numbers diminish each time we embrace, to realize soon we will meet face to face, and the bill for their evil will come due."

"And it must be soon," Piotr said. "There is little glory in chasing thieves. One day soon it will be time to face the Turks."

If they leave, I am left alone to face Gustaw and his murdering demons.

"Why can we not simply police the farms and live as we do now, like this?"

"In the East, it is said Emperors ask how they may profit their nation," Priest told him. "Lords ask how they may profit their house. And men? They ask how they may profit themselves. You give credence to the saying, Góralu."

"Where is the error in tending our own flocks and what we labor for?" Bolek asked. "I know nothing of these Muslims."

"But they know of you," Tadek replied.

"The world around your little mountain village is controlled by monarchs, warlords, petty tyrants, gangs of raiders," Priest tutored Bolek, "and it makes little difference to the weak if they are called Holy Roman Emperors or brigands."

"They are very far away, and the world is wide."

"Your 'every man for himself,' Góralu," Priest said, "is commendable if each man were just. But chieftains desire to become Emperors. Emperors, in turn, seek more power, more control, ever wary of those who seek to dispose them."

"Thus government is a sea of discontent, always churning, always in turmoil," Priest continued. "And the land is ultimately controlled by the cruel and greedy few, men who put themselves above God. Caesars."

"Politicians are not born, they are excreted," Piotr said as Czesław rode up, his arms full of demijohns of vodka.

"Excellent, Piotr," Priest said. "Your tongue matches your szabla in sharpness."

The men continued to sip their vodka, sitting in a circle on the grass around a charred area, a remnant of a long-dead campfire. After their confrontation with the brigands, the outline of the majestic Carpathian Mountains, both timeless and soothing, off in the southern distance, was a welcome respite.

"Gentlemen," Priest said, raising a demijohn. "Here is to our governments, which distrusts human nature, and to human nature, which distrusts our governments."

"To the only unchangeable thing in this world, I toast," Piotr chimed in. "I raise my bottle to human folly."

All was silent, save the wind whistling through the pines as the men reflected on their toasts to hopelessness.

"If I were home now I'd be eating *Kwaśnica*," Bolek said, "*a sauerkraut and meat soup.*"

"It must be nice to have a home," Czesław said.

"Bah!" Priest said, "To hell with sad feelings. I propose a toast to righteous men, brave men and to the mothers who raised them to be so."

"I smell another fable coming," Piotr said, shaking his head.

"At the very bottom of Wawel Hill, in a dark and damp cave," Priest said, in a deep voice he saved for serious words, "there once lived a mighty and terrible dragon named Smok, who dined on the local cattle and such was his appetite many went hungry and perished from his gluttony. Brave and righteous warriors engaged Smok in battle, but flames spewed from its mouth before a sword or even a spear could pierce its scaled flesh, and each of the greatest knights died horribly, consumed in flames.

"In desperation, the king who ruled in those dark times, sent heralds to announce he would give his daughter's hand to any righteous man who could slay the dragon and save his people from its unholy grip of fear. Many came from near and far, tempted by the offer of a royal marriage and wealth, but all were vanquished.

"But then there came a lowly shoemaker named Krak, and he

used his wits as well as his courage to devise a plan to defeat the vile fire-belching dragon. He found a large ram and poured sulphur down its throat until the beast was fat from it, and Krak placed the offering at the entrance to Smok's foreboding cave. The insatiable dragon, tempted by the meat, devoured it in one mouthful, without a thought. But soon the sulfur began to burn the dragon's throat, and it coughed heavily and spewed flames in vain, its agony heard for miles around. In desperation, Smok slithered to the Vistula River, and drank deeply, gulping gallon after gallon of water, so much water that Smok burst apart. The dragon had been defeated. Krak's cleverness had vanquished the terrible monster and saved the people from starvation and terror.

"The king, true to his word, gave Krak the cobbler his daughter's hand in marriage. And years later, after the king's death, Krak ascended to the throne. To honor the new king, the people named the town for him, the town which had grown to be Poland's eternal city, Cracow."

"So clever wits rather than a deadly sword arm can defeat a foe." Bolek said.

"See, Piotr? See?" Priest said. "He begins to see."

"As I begin to lose my sight," a mellow Czesław said.

"Here is to men who cower from their wives and cannot speak a word at home," Priest toasted again, "but dress up in their finery, perfume themselves, take on airs, regale themselves in meaningless medals and come to the Sejm to speak and politic."

"Goose feathers," Czesław announced. "Always use goose feathers for your arrows, Góralu. They provide the best flight."

Bolek kept up with each toast, his face burning, head spinning.

"*Nihil novi nisis commune consensus.*" Piotr raised in toast.

"How is your Latin?" Priest asked Bolek.

"Nothing new without the . . . agreement . . ." Bolek replied.

"Consensus. Nothing new without the consensus of all. For

nearly two hundred years, this sentiment has been at the heart of Polish freedom. The king cannot make laws without the complete agreement of his people," Priest said.

"Not its *people*," Piotr corrected. "Its *nobles*. Yet God gives us our fundamental rights, not kings, warlords, hetmans or lawyers, or wealthy nobles who have a greater taste for the riches of this earth than those of heaven."

"The nobles are important because they have the most at stake." Piotr objected. "They own the land, the basket that grows our bread."

"It is the land that is power." A glazed eyed Tadek grunted.

"Each man is from God's image, has dignity and, therefore, must be protected by a virtuous constitution," Piotr said. "Else the strong rule the weak, in the never-ending thirst for personal profit. A curse on all demigods!"

"A curse on all bedbugs," Czesław said before drinking.

"To our Polish king. To Jan III Sobieski!" Bolek shouted.

As Tadek hurled his empty clay bottle at a tree with a crashing sound and sending pieces of fired clay everywhere, the others followed suit, except for Bolek who had not drained his bottle yet and was reluctant to part with it as yet. The soldiers coaxed their young ward into downing the last of his bottle, laughing hardily as he clumsily flung it at the tree and missed by the length of a man.

"He's ready," Tadek advised. "Let us begin."

"Draw your szabla," Tadek commanded of Bolek, as Priest, Czesław and Priest all rose with some effort. "With your right hand."

Bolek first tested his scarred right shoulder by extending his right arm, rotating it in large circles. It was a bit stiff but no longer sent daggers of pain up and down the arm. Tadek leapt at him, szabla raised high, forcing Bolek to draw his own weapon for a block. The swords clanged with the unique sound of well-crafted and tempered steel against steel.

Crying out from a pain in his belly, Bolek looked down to see a second szabla's point at his stomach. Tadek had hidden a second sword behind his back.

"What coward's trick is this?" Bolek challenged his instructor.

"One you should have anticipated, drunkard." Tadek replied as he positioned both szablas across his chest.

"Who fights with two?" Bolek challenged for he had never heard of such a thing.

"You do now," Piotr chuckled. "We need the vodka to deaden the pain for this stupidity."

"If we can fight two-fisted, dead drunk on vodkie, and still keep our reflexes and our heads, then we can certainly fight sober," Priest said, drawing his own szabla, tossing it to Bolek who easily caught it in his left hand.

"Go ahead, Góralu" he said, motioning the young man toward Tadek.

Bolek's head was reeling and his feet unsteady as he held and inspected Priest's szabla closely for the first time.

"Ha!" he said, "your blade is flawed. Defects rise everywhere."

"Bah! Not flaws," Tadek growled. "While your flaws are known as Mohammed's Ladder, Priest's szabla was forged from sky stones. Balls of molten iron are thrown down from the heavens to lodge in the earth. This szabla was forged from such a gift from heaven. Sky stones."

"A drunken Bolek with one wavy steel Damascus blade and one pocked szabla made of sky stones," Bolek said aloud. "Make perfect sense," he added as he launched a fierce two-handed attack on Tadek, who was goading him on. The sound of four swords clanging in unison exhilarated Bolek, and he was amazed at how easy it was to wield two at once. The hours of left-handed training had also improved his right-handed skill.

"Ah!" He cried as Tadek scored with a slash to Bolek's forearm.

"Fear not, Góralu," Piotr urged. "As the vodkie works it magic soon it will not hurt."

"But it will hurt me tomorrow," Bolek complained as he collapsed on the ground searching for something with which to wrap his bleeding arm before raising his bottle to his lips.

"Here's to Tadek's right arm," Bolek said, while trying to keep his balance.

"What kind of toast is that?" Czesław demanded.

"Because after this bottle is drained," Bolek slurred, "I will reengage Tadek and his right arm will be here, next to my saddle and no longer connected to Tadek."

All laughed as Bolek lost his footing and collapsed on completing his boast.

Priest took out his violin, Piotr his new flute and together the company made merry atop the flat-topped hill with the expanse of the great plains of Poland unfolding below them as far as a man could see, miles upon miles of grains and prairie grasses, all moving like waves on an ocean, fueled by the invisible wind. Forests, glens, dales, marshes, unfolded before them and in the distance, the mighty Vistula River. Indeed, the beauty of Poland seemed wider than the sky itself.

The world around the comrades seemed to dance in rhythm to the clanging of four swords as Bolek and Tadek whirled around each other in mock combat. After Bolek collapsed, praising a tireless Tadek, then crawling to reach for his bottle, Piotr joined with Czesław to gather sticks and dried grasses. Lighting a fire with flint, they heaped on thicker branches and then a few thick limbs. Once a fire was blazing Czesław gathered some wet grass, and wetting it from his water bag, tossed it onto the flames, producing thick white smoke.

"Here is where we will line up," Tadek said. "The smoke will water our eyes to near blindness."

Priest stood next to Piotr with Czesław and Tadek facing them, leaving no more than a span of ten feet between them, each armed with a single blade. Bolek, groggily watching the scene with much curiosity, was commanded to stand. Taking a szabla in each hand, he approached the Royal Guardsmen with a menacing smirk.

Once a farm boy with only a bow, now I stand facing four Polish knights.

Once I owned no szabla. Now I have two.

Once I knew too much. Now, little or nothing.

What other surprises lie in this world?

Bolek well understood the challenge. He would be defending his flesh against four expert swordsmen, two on each side, while drunk, his cheeks tear-laden, eyes stinging and near blind from the acrid smoke. He forced himself to stay alert and keep his balance.

"You may only defend, Góralu," Priest instructed. "It is your task to keep your soft, white, virgin skin scar free."

"Come on, boy, Czesław shouted, "I think Tadek could teach a bear to wield a sword. But a Góral highlander? Impossible."

Holding both szablas out wide, he began to slash the air as he staggered into the gauntlet.

"Ouch! Ouch! Damn imposshhhibility!" He exclaimed as his body, legs and arms were slashed; his clothes shredded.

"Because you tried to run through us and didn't keep your guard up," Tadek barked. "Patience. Think. Have confidence in your abilities."

The biting pains from everywhere on his body slightly cleared his head. He engaged again, this time parrying blows with some success, using his peripheral vision to prevent and not react to sharpened steel slicing skin; he began to anticipate. This time he was hit but twice and was cheered. In response, he tried to bow only to stumble to his knees, retching.

"What a defense," Tadek complained. "An opponent who attacks with digested supper. But well done, Góralu. Well done."

"I agree," Czesław added, embracing Tadek "You, my

brother, are capable of miracles. A Góral swordsman is born."

"You are a good sport, Góralu," Priest said, helping him to his feet. "You did not respond in anger to pain. I gain faith in you, daily. Careful not to slip in that mess, though."

Bolek accepted the compliment with a respectful nod as he pulled his blood soaked shirt from his chest and back. "I am as a dead chicken with her feathers plucked, Priest."

"Drink no more and warm yourself by the fire and you'll feel better in the morning." Priest said.

"All except for your head," Piotr added.

"I'll take sentry duty tonight," Czesław said. "I cannot sleep. My heart is racing with pride. Jesus made the blind see, and Tadek taught a Góral to fence."

"A miracle," Piotr proclaimed. "Now we will do this dance at every opportunity. We have five now. Better for the dance."

"Here's to the Pope," Tadek toasted, "Who recently made a blind man deaf and cured a ham."

Bolek awoke to the sound of a saber rattling inside an iron cooking pot placed next to his ear.

"Off to hunt for snakes," Czesław said. "Brigands for lunch, maybe."

"I cannot move my arms," Bolek complained.

"You'll forget about them once you move your head."

True to prophecy, as he attempted to stand, Bolek collapsed on his blanket, cradling his head in his hands as white lightning bolts shot through his throbbing brain. His comrades were slow-moving also, waxen-faced, eyes squinting nearly shut when facing the sun. Bolek found he could not tolerate the full sun either, and kept his hand to forehead as shield.

"You'll get used to it, Piotr assured him. "Next time will be better."

"Next time? I will never drink again."

"I've said that more than a few times myself. Czesław replied. "The brigand dogs are sure to have a cache of vodka. So, perhaps tonight we will celebrate their demise."

"What if there are a hundred of them?"

"More glory for us, and certainly more vodka," Tadek answered.

"A hundred would still be outnumbered by us."

"Four men against a hundred?" Bolek asked.

"I count five." Tadek answered, throwing Bolek's boots onto the young man's lap. "Rise. We move within the hour. We are done using our szablas for sport. They need to drink our enemies' blood."

Chapter 34

Bolek led his companions on a tour of the more remote and obscure parts of his mountains, some of which even he only heard stories about and had never seen. These were some places Priest reasoned the brigands would select for a camp since wagons could haul booty unseen in and out of the area.

The stout trees surrounding them stood close together, the upper branches choking out the sun, leaving the lower gnarled branches grayish brown or dead. Shadows of swaying treetops created a flickering, foreboding and unnatural. It was easy to understand how a place like this could evoke fear and make the imagination reel with odd impressions and myths to explain it.

Eventually Priest called an end to the search in this area, reasoning if five horsemen could not move easily here neither could raiders with their spoils.

As the hunting party reached more level ground where the trees thinned, they moved in the direction of the Pitry estate, and Bolek's anticipation grew as he thought of his Rozalia.

What do I say? Apologizing to both her and the hussar – I must find the proper words. She loves me only as a brother, her affection toward me, one of a devoted sister. But why did she not believe me a worthy prospect for a husband? Gold? Fine clothes? In my deepest soul, we are married, with five healthy sons like me and five daughters with her shining eyes and flaxen hair.

"Do you bear ill-will toward Rozalia's hussar," Priest asked as he rode next to Bolek.

"No. She has chosen him over me. I do think ill of her parents. They have shamed me many times."

"I saw the arrogance in the Pitrys when we visited after you were wounded. They care more for their own comfort than anything else and will never find peace on that path. You should pray for them for they are in more pain than you."

The horsemen, weary now from a full day of travel, their

mounts well-lathered, dismounted and walked past the ruins of a castle, the once stately tower crumbling from neglect, the walls stained a sooty black, the scars from siege still evident. The ravages of man and the relentless wind and water of Mother Nature were returning the manmade fortress walls into individual stones, many of which had been carried away by locals to build houses and sheds, to shore up low spots in dirt roads and to build the local shrines. Weeds popped through what was left of the bastions which had once been present to repel cannon balls.

"It seems the whole world is continually at war." Bolek remarked to Priest.

"Far to our west they have time for society, art, science and scholarship. Yes, they have skirmishes, but they are rarely overrun. More of the populace begins to have time for the finer things once they are able put the sword down. But Poland? We live in the devil's playground."

"It would be nice to give Poland the gifts the West enjoys."

"And so we shall with men like you in the saddle, Góralu." Piotr said.

"It all seems so hopeless," Bolek said.

"Once there were people occupying this castle," Priest said nodding toward the ruins. "Living, breathing, human beings. And there was laughter and love, respect, honor and sacrifice, music and dancing, tradition and authority. We have lost one in three of our people to wars in my lifetime alone, a staggering number of souls."

"I think a great lord and his lady lived here once," Bolek said, "with many fat children and happy servants. They danced and sang and flowers burst from every window. They were capable stewards of the land and valued citizens also. They lived to a ripe old age and had many glorious moments."

"You have a poet's soul, Góralu," Priest replied. "I imagine a just lord who sacrificed much to build and defend these walls.

He fought for those who could not defend themselves. And God rewarded him. But sons grew up in privilege, thinking advantage as an entitled right. They turned inward and no longer cared for their neighbors, or for the country that bore them. Where an armful of kindling is impossible to snap and a single stick easily, these men isolated themselves, becoming single sticks. Their sacred beliefs were still echoed in grand but hollow words, their flags merely decorations to hang on walls. Their children were taught avarice before good will. They forgot to study and honor their history, the sacrifices of our ancestors. A great house, like a soul, needs attention and care, or it turns to rubble as this one has."

"Christ's Blood, Priest," Piotr said. "What a cold breath you bring to Bolek's warm imagination. Look at these ruins with hope, Góralu. One day you may purchase this castle. It abuts your Rozalia's manor, I think. And who knows what the future holds? The land here lies fallow. You may one day restore the keep, the barn, and shore up the walls and hire an army of farm workers to bring the property back into bloom. You could fill it with family and friends. The lord of all you survey, one who loves and is loved."

"Your peace could be wider than the sky." Priest added.

"Smoke!" Czesław yelled from ahead, riding hard for his companions, causing all to mount, nostrils up, ears straining for any telltale noise, eyes scanning the landscape in all directions.

"Piotr, ride ahead and investigate further," Priest ordered. "If you run into horsemen, act surprised. Turn and run as if alone and seek to escape. Bring them this way. We will meet them there by the slope, near that boulder. Czesław, up a tree. Fire from there just before we engage. This time leave at least one alive. Tadek, Góralu, up the hill with me. We'll rush them as if we planned to engage, but if they hold ranks we will veer at that spot. We can take at least ten of them with arrows before we will need to fight man to man."

"You are always a prince of foxes, Priest," Tadek said.

All was silent save Hector's galloping hoof beats as Piotr rode toward the billowing smoke column. Soon the sounds of the forest and meadows returned. Frogs croaked, birds chirped, bees buzzed, and a few wind gusts caused the trees to creak and the long prairie grasses to hiss. Bolek found it somehow incredulous that a battle could soon be fought here, blood spilled, men screaming in pain. Death among so much life.

"Remember, Góralu," Priest said gruffly, "you can fight low, on your knees if you must, and cut a leg. You can fight close and prevent a saber thrust, and once you sting, you can follow through. Most men will hesitate for a moment to take stock of an injury, whether received or given. That is your time to act."

Hoof beats. Moving fast. An arrow put to Czesław's bow. Priest and Tadek high in the saddle. Fingers to bowstring. Indeed, there was calm about the knights, as if they sat in church accepting the Gospel while Bolek's heart pounded in his chest.

Piotr appeared, hurdling over a fallen tree trunk, shouting as he reined in Hector. "It's the Pitry manor! Burnt! No evidence of raiders. Judging by the fire damage it has been several hours since the attack."

The manor burnt! And Rozalia! What of her? A different kind of fear now possessed him as he kicked Quo Vadis into motion.

"Slowly, Góralu," Priest cautioned. "We go in as a group."

Ignoring the advice, Bolek urged Quo Vadis into a gallop.

"Czesław!" Priest shouted. "If he does not stop, shoot his mount."

Priest's command forced Bolek to rein in, his heart racing as he followed the knights, moving quickly yet cautiously toward the smoke, his Rozalia's name on his tongue, his eyes searching everywhere for her image, his ears for her melodious voice, his nose for her flowery perfume.

The Pitry Manor, the finest in this region, was now a charred and smoky shambles, flames belching from windows, roofs collapsing with a rumble, the mill, a fiery hearth. The large barn collapsed into dust as the companions rode up. The smell of burning flesh. Blackened and bloodied bodies of men, women and children littered the ground. Some with arms, legs or heads sliced off, arrows protruding from still bodies. Not just dead bodies – tortured bodies. Dismounting, szabla at the ready, Bolek forced himself to look at each wretched face, praying he did not discover his Rozalia.

"It may be they took her for ransom," he shouted to Priest. "We have to find them."

"We will. For now, there may be wounded to tend to."

But further investigation revealed only two survivors and both with little time left. The rest were dead; each tortured before death or hacked to pieces after. It was clear some victims, with deeply slashed bellies, were able to witness the blood of life spill out on the earth. Others, those with unnaturally contorted faces, had spent the last moments of life in dreadful pain.

By examining the tracks, Tadek estimated least forty brigands, and a large two-horse driven wagon. As for the smoldering manor house, it had been looted of any and all fineries. The sty and the chicken coop were empty. Even the dogs were dead.

Like Burek.

"They have too much of a lead on us," Piotr said. "And ample time to cover their tracks."

"Priest," a frowning Tadek shouted, coming up from behind the house. "Come and see what those dirty bastards have done. Do not follow, Góralu."

"We need eyes on the West, son. Stay here, on your guard," Priest commanded as he followed Tadek behind the smoldering manor house.

Bolek continued his search for what he dreaded to find. Perhaps she was captive, but unharmed. Who would kill a young girl? They wouldn't harm her if they expected a ransom. She has rich relatives in Cracow. They might know that. She was worth more alive than dead. Then a dark thought of an image of her in the arms of the greasy, bearded brigand who had been about to kill him when Priest had first arrived at the Radok farm filled his thoughts. His stomach turned.

A pale Priest appeared at his side.

"The family is dead," he muttered. "Behind the house."

"Rozalia?"

"She is there too," grabbing Bolek's sagging shoulders. "You do not want to see this. You *will not* see this."

Bolek was stunned, body and soul, as he fell to his knees, withdrawing from the world and into the safety of his golden memories and romantic fantasies.

I see you, Rozalia. In my mind's eye, I feel your eyes and smile as they warm my heart and send my stomach awhirl.

"The last she saw of me, Priest, I was trying to kill her future husband. How do I make amends for this? I wanted her as part of a selfish dream. Not as the living breathing girl she was."

"She is with God," Priest said, his voice cracking.

The hardened warrior quickly turned from Bolek's gaze but not fast enough to hide the tears glistening on leathered cheeks.

"The last I know of her was a scream. I attacked her true love. If I could only have that moment back."

"We all have those moments buried deep within us," Piotr whispered.

"The brigands also? The Turks feel this?" Bolek growled.

"Perhaps not now, but once."

"We must ride to the village for help," Tadek said. "There are too many for us to bury. We can do nothing here now. Mount up."

Bolek followed, as if in a trance and rode as a shadow among the living, toward the village.

"The time grows ever nearer when we shall embrace, Gustaw," all heard Priest whisper in a steely voice.

"Did she suffer?" Bolek asked Tadek.

There was a long silence before Piotr whispered, "He deserves to know."

"Was she . . ."

"Yes, son." Tadek replied.

"Tell me all," Bolek demanded. "She has been in my heart since I was a boy."

Even Tadek could not look Bolek in the eyes. "The hussar fought well."

"Then I owe him a debt even greater than apology. He died bravely. And in her service."

"All debts will be paid in full to this lot." Czesław swore.

"The girl's parents were hacked up horribly," Tadek continued. "There were too many. The family and serfs had no hope."

"Unlike my farm there were no Royal Guardsmen for the Pitrys."

"The brothers died in the house killed from behind. Perhaps they were fleeing. The hussar fought with sword at the rear of the house. He dropped a heap of bodies at his feet, but others came at him from all sides."

"Good man," Bolek said. "He should have been a brother to me as well as Rozalia's husband; not my enemy."

"The hussar did not die immediately," Tadek continued. "He remained conscious, lashed to a chair. His hands were sliced off at the wrists."

"Did Rozalia see this?"

"Yes."

"Enough of this!" Priest ordered. "

"I want it all. I want it seared into my memory for when I meet them face to face. Tell is all, Tadek. I beg you."

"When they were done with her . . . I found her . . . her severed head in his lap."

Bolek's body convulsed as he grasped his horse's mane to keep from falling.

"Gentlemen," Bolek asked in a soft voice, breaking a long and awkward silence. "Please allow me to go back and bury my Rozalia. I am composed. And I know she would want me to do this one last thing for her and her family. She was my sister, and I have a family duty to perform."

"Ride, son," Priest said. "We will return with help from the village."

"Priest, what if the raiders return with only Góralu there alone?" Czesław asked.

"The cowards got what they came for," Priest said through gritted teeth. "They will never return. But let's pray they do return to meet Master Radok."

"Aye!" Piotr and Czesław said as Bolek coaxed Quo Vadis into a turn to meet his Rozalia for the last time, praying all godless brigands, as well as every heartless demon from hell, would ride down upon him – for the former cowering shepherd no longer feared the wolf.

Chapter 34

Bolek threw himself into his duty as he arrived, digging the graves for the family himself. From the village word was sent to the relatives of the Pitry family as well as those of the servants, notifying all of the great misfortune, while Priest wrote to the fallen hussar's regiment commander in Cracow, and recommending the slain soldier for a medal for bravery and service. Perhaps it would be some consolation for the boy's family to know he died heroically, and for others.

Fear grew again in the mountainous region, for if an estate the size of Pitry Manor, with the number of men, the protective walls, and the weapons it possessed could fall, then none were safe. The village quickly emptied to help bury the Pitry Manor dead. The countryside responded as one to news of the tragedy. Spread over miles, these rural folks, though fiercely independent, could always be counted on to come together in times of disaster or serious need. Father Czarnota held Mass in a Pitry paddock and prayed for each soul by name.

Priest was silent, watching the exhausted Bolek, who, after two long days and nights without rest, finished burying the Pitry family and the hussar, refusing any and all offers to help. Allowing the local volunteers to clean up the rest and concerned about his own family and farm Bolek finally road home with the Royal Guardsmen. But Bolek seemed to hover between this world and his own thoughts.

"Hold to your faith and your reason." Priest cautioned.

"Faith? Reason? I long for revenge. I long to face Gustaw."

"So do I. But to prevent him from causing pain to others. You speak as an executioner filled with a raging emptiness. This is how Gustaw feels now. This is why he gives no mercy. He hates all of mankind. He hates himself."

"Is this what Father and Grandfather had to endure? It is horrible."

"The doorway to your soul is guarded only by you. You determine what you allow into it and what you ban from it. Hatred and revenge should have no place there."

"I want to hack Gustaw with my saber until he disappears into nothing."

"God tests you here, Góralu. This is not swordplay. Feel sorry for yourself. Burn with rage. Kill and become just like what you hate. Or learn to give all."

"I feel only madness and rage. I have nothing to offer."

"Not to your mother, your sister?" Priest shot back. "Making sense of the horrible death of your Rozalia is not your greatest struggle."

"No? Then what is? But do not give me talk of stupid ceremony with empty words of ghosts and repentance."

"I will tell you of your struggle, Góralu, if you will listen."

"Oh, my ears are yours, but your words will not enter my heart."

"Then, like those you despise, you are doomed; soulless. Satan is pleased."

"The only devil is her murderers. How do they live with themselves? How can we call them human? How can you profess to understand my feelings on this?"

"Each of us who ride with you has lost a Rozalia," Piotr replied. "And look at the villagers. They are well-practiced at burials and prayers and making this all look like it never happened. It is an old story. We all carry Rozalia in our hearts."

This advice reached Bolek. His mother surly knew this feeling. So had Grandfather – his sons killed before his eyes.

Have I been a blind and selfish child kept safe in the mountains; shielded from all that is real? Spoiled somehow, living in a dream world of boyish wishes and demands.

"Your greatest struggle is mine also, indeed, all of ours," Priest counseled. "It is to surrender who you are to whom you ought to be."

"Ha. Like I said . . . words."

"Words impart ideas, young soldier, and defective ideas enslave men," Piotr cautioned. "That is Satan's doing. Never belittle the power of ideas."

"From where springs all this cruelty around us, Priest? From where?" Bolek asked, his shoulders sagging, his head hanging low.

"From our free natures. Given by a loving God. But a god of love is also a god of laws. You can go with God or into your own sinful desires."

"How do I go with God?"

"Perfect your nature, son."

"How exactly is that done?"

"Through wisdom. Practice virtue. Avoid sin."

"Rozalia was sinless. She had wisdom and much virtue. She died in shame and terrible pain."

Priest reined in his horse forcing Bolek and his companions to follow suit. The horses grazed; the riders in a semicircle.

"You must learn to know which path you will walk or condemn yourself to hell," Priest said, locking unblinking eyes with Bolek.

"This is my hell," Bolek responded, wishing now to end all thinking, to forget all memories, to have the pain within him dry up and blow away. "I thirst now for vodka."

"If this is hell," Priest replied, barring the way as Bolek tried to ride on, "it is because you are alienated from God. You have recoiled from the murderous deed you've just seen. It is because there is a morality in you. You feel for others. And this feeling is a seed that must be nourished. Each man, every man is deserving of natural dignity. This is an absolute right. We must cultivate this flame through our sacraments and the recognition of our sins. Through communion with God."

"While others ride on, hacking innocents to death?" Bolek countered.

"They violate God's law. They do it because they can, because they believe that might make right. This world, they believe, exists solely for them. No one else matters. It dries up their souls and they hate themselves, and so they hate others more. They have allowed personal desires to diminish their eternal flame. Note the power of flawed ideas."

"And what do we do about all of this when they break God's laws?" Bolek asked.

"Those who have the ability to do justice have the added obligation to do justice."

Bolek felt the urge to argue, to resist Priest, but he did not have the energy, his insides tied up in knots, and his body bone tired. Yet, he held his tongue.

"Now listen to the power of truth," Priest said, the wind in a sudden lull.

"The meaning of life is to strive for the ultimate union of the knowledge and love of God, for truth is an intimacy with God. And to achieve this state we need to learn, to experience, and yes, to suffer. All of this leads to understanding if we obey God's commandments. We need to define all things, all experiences, put them in their proper place, and order them. Then comes wisdom, which is acceptance."

"I do not have your wisdom," Bolek replied.

"Jesus has conquered death, and He will also raise you up when it is your time, and you will be with Him and your Rozalia. And this is why I do not seem as heartbroken as you, Góralu. I strive to be closer to God. If I keep my faith and my hope, then I am immortal. And I will meet all of my loved ones, those no longer with me, those whose bones have turned to dust and those whom I miss sorely. I wish now I was with my family, at a meal, laughing, singing, and holding each of them to my breast. Instead, I am here. God's will."

Twisting his body in the saddle and prodding Mieszko, Priest galloped off, disappearing over a low hill.

Chapter 36

Bolek set Quo Vadis into a gallop on Priest's heels, the others held back.

"Faith?" he asked of Priest. "I still do not understand."

"Czesław," Priest said, slowing Mieszko to a walk, "returned home from helping build a neighbor's barn to find his family massacred. Wife, parents, sisters, cousins, all. He went from a loving family member to orphan. He fights to protect and not for revenge. Piotr was a Cracow scholar, a slave to the cult of scientific reason, a master of debate, employing all the modern tricks of language and the cult of academic arrogance to impress others. Yet something was missing in him. He sensed he was more than an animal with a brain; a clever baboon. Something was calling to him. He listened. He left his prestigious Jagiellonian University, a comfortable life, a secure pension behind and embraced his soul."

"Tadek was always strong, fast, and aggressive with the szabla. He found his talent was in killing, and so he did. He followed a warmongering Tatar Caesar, leading a raid one night on the trail of gold and women. They utterly surprised the wretched camp, but Tadek found himself face to face with some of his own relatives. He pleaded in vain with his fellow raiders to stop the impending slaughter, but the wolves had already tasted blood. Wild with rage, guilt and shame, he changed sides, killing the nameless Caesar, and was in turn attacked by his former comrades and left for dead. But the powerful heart stirred the next morning, the only survivor. Now, as the others and I do, he serves Sobieski. We serve a just king. We serve Poland. And we have faith."

"Each of them is strong of will. Piotr's reason and knowledge, Czesław eagle eye and lack of arrogance, Tadek's expertise and utter fearlessness."

"And you?" Bolek asked of Priest as the other riders caught

up.

Priest dug his heels into Hector and rode away yet again, this time, violently, his horse bellowing with surprise.

"Why is Priest so nicknamed, Piotr?" Bolek asked as the three comrades caught up to him.

"Because he is a defrocked priest."

"What?" a stunned Bolek cried.

"Priest is the one who trained Gustaw."

Bolek looked upward, cursing the heavens.

"How . . ."

"The stench of blood is a sweet aroma for Gustaw. Where we have reason, he has cunning. Priest did not recognize this and Gustaw kept it well-hidden. Gustaw has alienated himself from God and Nature. What we do becomes what we are.

"We must find him now."

"If fortune permits. But an infidel force assembles to invade Europe for an unjust reason. King Jan Sobieski will ride at the front of this liberating army, and we are the King's Guardsmen."

"Leaving Gustaw to murder at will."

"I may plan my strategy but God directs my steps. We are Poland's servants. And soon, God's madmen."

This is too much! Too much for right now.

Bolek dug his heels into Quo Vadis yet again and rode after Priest.

"You were a priest," Bolek growled. "You were excommunicated by the Pope himself."

Bolek winced at Priest's wounded expression.

Lord God, I do not want to hurl my anger at this man but at Gustaw. Please help me.

"What did you think I am, Góralu, Saint Adalbert come to life?

"How does our great and noble king let you serve him so?"

"Our mothers were sisters."

"Why . . . how . . ."

"Góralu, I was captured as a young boy; raised as a slave of the Dnieper Cossacks. I was swept along with the hordes to raid the Black Sea Ottomans even before I could shave my face. I've traveled on the Gobi Desert upon camels, crossed the Urals, and navigated the icy currents of the Volga. Always as a slave with no regard for my will or well-being. I am a product of the Zaporizhska Sich, beyond the Dnieper Rapids, an island fortress where Cossack's alone rule. In 1648, when I was close to your age, I marched into Kiev as part of Hetman of the Cossacks, Bohdan Chmielnicki's retinue, heard him cheered as the ruler of the Rus and liberator from the Polish yoke. I fought at Beresteczko, with and against innumerable soldiers. I watched Polish knights slaughtered by Cossacks and Tatars at Zhovti Vody and Korsun. I rode on raids to free Cossack captives from Ottomans and Tatars. For my weight in gold, I was ransomed home to Poland by the grace of God and His Majesty. I am no longer property. And never shall be again."

Bolek left Priest alone with his thoughts and himself with his. It was quite some time before Piotr, Czesław and Tadek caught up.

"I know Priest well," Piotr said, waving his two comrades forward and waiting until they rode out of earshot. "I am certain he hasn't told you the whole story, Góralu. To grow up a Cossack slave is to grow up as a dog raised by cruel masters. Many such slaves die; nearly all are broken to the yoke. But Priest never submitted, and he was too ornery to die. Starved, whipped, and shunned, nothing broke him. He fell, recovered, rose, fought back. Such is his mettle. Soon he became an amusement for his captors. One heartless devil taught him a few sword tricks certain he would soon be dead from the knowledge."

"How is it he survived and has not become cruel and bitter?"

"Fortune had him lost in a card game to a Turk. The same abuse and test of endurance continued. Once, defending himself with his fists while encircled by some drunken Muslim warriors, one threw Priest a saber in jest and beckoned him on. Priest severed the warrior's hand at the wrist, spat in his face, then slashed the man's throat. The angry mob seized Priest, but word of the debacle spread through the camp from tongue to tongue. Priest was saved from losing his head by seconds, for this story amused a sultan. Priest was trained; saber, bow, spear and horse. A trained pet Christian monkey. Soon few could match his skills. All feared him. This eventually presented a dilemma for the sultan. A Christian capable of besting Islam's greatest fighters? Again Fortune intervened when a well-timed letter arrived from Poland asking for Priest's release from captivity. The sultan saw a way out of this disagreeable situation and a chance to win a tidy profit to boot."

"So Priest came home?"

"In a way. He was taken in by the righteous fathers who follow Saint Thomas Aquinas and was taught his people's religion both spiritually and intellectually. Again he excelled. He took the sacrament of Holy Orders and became a priest."

"And he was defrocked. He failed."

"Did he? The one called Gustaw was a poor young wretch, beaten, abused a thousand ways, abandoned like Priest. Gustaw's only accomplishment was with the bow. Priest felt for the boy and improved Gustaw's gift of archery with expert training. The sword naturally followed. Priest wanted to give Gustaw what he himself never had; someone who cared; a compassionate mentor. This blinded Priest to all the signs Gustaw exuded. While Priest offered only kindness and understanding to the boy, Gustaw turned sour. Instead of learning confidence, patience and forgiveness, Gustaw's new skills fueled his cowardice, employing his newfound power to bully, maim and torture as he had been. Revenge. Priest threatened, refused to teach him more, and eventually disowned him. That night Gustaw slew two monks in a drunken rage and disappeared. Priest was defrocked. Gustaw leaves a trail of death to this day."

"With Priest's training."

Piotr nodded, eyes closed.

"So he is defrocked. There is no redemption for him?"

"His removal was political."

"Politics, again," Bolek spat.

"Priest does not want to be reinstated. He has done much penance. And yet neither you nor he yet realize that you are his redemption."

It was Bolek's turn to close his eyes.

"You are no Gustaw, Góralu. Priest fears for your life. Does he send you back to your home to be butchered by Gustaw and his band of like demons or watch you die fighting the invaders? No. He keeps you at his side. He counsels you as a father would."

"Then we must find Gustaw and make him pay now!"

"Pay? Gustaw pays daily. He is alienated from God. There is only pain and loneliness in his world. The ultimate terror; loneliness. We Royal Guardsmen would give our lives for one another and for you, son. But Gustaw lives alone, within a cell built with his own body and soul, one he has locked from the inside with his own hands."

"Gustaw is five mad boars and a hundred werewolves. He must be stopped."

"The Turks are a hundred thousand Gustaws."

What is the answer, Master Piotr?"

"All I know is that I must embrace the cardinal virtues and make them habit and bring them into harmony with reason and nature. What is your best choice? You must answer your own question."

Each of them knows my pain and feels for me. And I know each has experienced his own measure and more. Yet they ride on, for others. No stench of self-pity, their hearts steeled in spirit and ready for action, prepared to give their lives to prevent the same horrors they have endured. At any cost. These are the eagles upon which Poland builds its life and very soul.

The wind picked up, with dark clouds and distant lightning blanketing the sky. The sound of faint rolling thunder soon became like cannon fire. Four horsemen rode undaunted, into the storm, with a fifth closing in behind.

Chapter 37

"Up, Jędrzej," Gustaw barked. "It is time for us to return to camp."

"I will come later, Captain," the thick-bearded thick-necked bandit replied as he stretched this way and that on the ground in an attempt to find relief. "My back hurts. I cannot rise. One hour. That is all I need."

The 'Captain' as Gustaw was referred to, demanded unchallenged obedience, and could accomplish it by appearance alone. A permanent scowl was frozen upon his pockmarked face, his upper lip split from whatever blade made the mark. He looked out at the world through two cold, black eyes. Rumor had it he had no teeth, for no one had ever heard him laugh or crack a smile.

It had been Gustaw's plan to build a group of raiders large enough to prey on the richer farms and well-protected wagon trains and even the occasional caravan. All were given a chance to join; those who showed any doubts, weakness or mercy soon disappeared.

"Your back fails you more and more, Jędrzej. We each must carry our load."

"I carried the heavy eastern carpet out to the wagon, did I not?"

"Yet there was no sign it pained you when you rode the girl," Gustaw said, followed by the laughter of the men who gathered behind their leader.

It had been their largest score of booty yet, forcing all of his band to participate, but their wagon was overfilled with rich oriental carpets, vases, jewelry, many things the Ottomans and the Cossacks would trade for gold. By Gustaw's absolute law, no living creature was left alive during the raid to tell the story. As their heavy wagon rolled on slowly behind two struggling draft horses, a small detachment was more than a mile behind covering the retreat to their hidden camp.

The booty wagon moved too slowly for Gustaw. They took too many breaks. He sensed the men were on edge, close to unruly, something he did not allow. Still, since this, their first significant raid had gone so well, a celebration was in order. Gustaw did not allow drinking until all were safely returned to camp in the secret mountain ravine. Even he could taste vodka on his tongue. He yearned for it. But the no drinking rule was iron. A reminder of his authority and the price of disobedience was death.

As the ailing Jędrzej rose to his knees, Gustaw stepped behind him, silently drew his dagger and slit the kneeling man's throat, ear to ear, holding the head in an arm lock until the body ceased struggling.

"There! No more pain," Gustaw said, standing up with his knife at the ready and his eyes on his men as the lifeless body crumpled to the ground. "See how Gustaw can heal backs. Adrik, strip him, gather his things and leave the body for the wolves. You may have his horse. The wagon will reach camp soon, and no one has followed us. We ride."

Jumping upon his large steed, he sped away. When he was out of sight, his men ran to the body and began striping the corpse, fighting for the sword, pistol, and boots.

Deserters, ex-mercenaries, failed farmers, unsuccessful merchants, escaped prisoners, outcasts, runaway serfs and life-long thieves, melted together under Gustaw, who surpassed each of them at their own particular skill. It was rumored he had been a Cossack assassin, sent by tribal chiefs to smother rivals, and making it look like a natural death, thereby avoiding revenge. These were men of Tatar blood, Polish, German, Cossack, French, English, Rus, Austrian, English and Prussian. Gustaw's brother, Koyla, who rode with the wagon, was nearly as ruthless as Gustaw, trained in the sword by Gustaw to a fault; the brothers watched each other's back.

It was Koyla who had wounded and overcome the Polish soldier at the Pitry estate. It was Koyla who had proposed that day's entertainment in which they all played a willing part. It was Koyla who had taken the girl's head and tossed it into the lap of the dying hussar. And it was Koyla who led the chorus in laughter at the hussar's screams, moans and whispered prayers. It was Koyla who now sported the hussar's striking green Magyar cap with many prominent feathers, a memento of their most ambitious raid to date.

Nearing camp, Gustaw became more guarded, even though he expected to hear, see and smell nothing of the secret camp his cohorts now approached. If he could ride into camp without being noticed by the sentries, they would be bound and gagged and tossed into the giant cauldron. It would be filled with water, and a fire lit beneath. Bets would be taken to see which man survived the longest. Here, the cost for a mistake was death. The penalties for failure were well understood.

An arrow, then another, lodged itself in a tree a mere foot from Gustaw's head. He looked up to the top of a row of tall pines in front of him, spotted the two bowmen, thirty steps away and nodded, well-pleased with his lookouts. He dismounted, lit his pipe and sat on a log, waiting for his wagon filled with treasures.

Tree trunks and brush piled twice the height of a man shielded the gap in the mountain side to prevent a fire being seen at night. Smoke was guided deeper and higher into the cave by a natural draft, the sloping ceiling as high as ten men were tall, rising higher still as it disappeared into the blackness of the endless cavern. The dense trees and surrounding foliage gave excellent cover and masked sound within the dead-ended ravine. A thin stream snaked its way down the middle of the ravine, offering more than enough water for the raiders. An old abandoned and long-forgotten road, not much more than a tree-shrouded deer path, running along the ridge across from the cave was the only possible position from which enemies could see the cave or approach it. This one exposure was well-guarded day and night by the eyes and shafts of the two deadly and reliable bowmen. The path the riders and wagons took to exit and return was regularly covered with brush, swept and invisible to most. Pine branches dragged by the last two horses in the caravan erased all traces of their tracks.

The heavily laden wagon soon arrived, and the riches were stored away, deep inside the cave, where several men stood guard, to discourage any temptation; even honor among thieves was not honored here. Now celebration was in order.

A wisp of a smile came to his lips as word came a Gypsy girl had been captured in the woods and was tied, nude, gagged and spread eagled between two pine trees. No one would touch such a prize unless Gustaw gave permission.

"Has her will been broken?" Gustaw asked as his eyes moved over her body.

"Yes, Captain. Her back is aflame with the marks of a hot poker. She no longer hurls curses or spits on us. She now begs for your mercy."

"My pleasure."

Taking a fistful of her long hair, he jerked her sagging head up to look into her glazed over eyes.

"How did you come by her?"

"The Gypsies were abandoning their camp. Some of their numbers have disappeared in the deep woods. Scavenged bodies have been found. Headless horsemen ride the fields. There is talk of a werewolf in this region."

"Werewolf? Is she a witch? Gustaw asked, releasing his grip and stepping back, her head falling limply to one side.

"Who knows? Gypsies follow evil and evil follows them."

Gustaw cut the gag from the girl with his blood-stained knife and paddled her face until she regained consciousness.

"If you scream you die. What is this about a werewolf?" he demanded.

"Woods . . ." she gasped, blood and tears trickling down her swollen face, "by marsh. It killed three . . . a child. Throat torn out."

"Are you a witch?" Gustaw asked, "ready to steal my seed to create more beasts of the night?"

"No . . ."

"What is your wish, Gypsy?"

"Anything . . . no more pain," she groaned.

"Good. My men need their entertainment. It would have gone better for you if this werewolf had found you first."

Chapter 38

The rumor of a werewolf in the area reached the cavalry a few hours after the shocking news the Ottomans had besieged Vienna on the fourteenth of July. King Jan III Sobieski was desperately trying to raise an army. Messengers rode in all directions from Cracow. A call to arms echoed throughout the stunned nation.

"The Sultan grows bold," Tadek said, sucking on his pipe, his eyes squinting from the smoke filling the Radok cottage. "His plans for domination are now revealed in action."

"They give us a choice," Piotr said. "Submit or die. To them government and religion are the same, with the caliph as the absolute ruler. *Dar al-Islam* or *Dar al-Harb. Choose the abode of Islam or the abode of war.* Will Europe play the wolf or the lamb?"

And what will my part in this be?

"We must rejoin our regiment," Tadek said. "We ride for the king."

"Yes, but only when the king rides, when he makes his move. He is a fox as well as a bull, and will bargain for time with cunning to assemble an army. We have time, but not much," Priest replied.

"Why do Poles care for Vienna?" Bolek asked. "Let the Austrians defend their own city."

"Vienna is the seat of the Holy Roman Empire," Priest explained. "And as Christians of the Roman order this makes it our city."

"If Vienna falls, Góralu," Piotr added, "the Ottomans will stream north, and the Hungarians will follow. As with Constantinople, God only knows what they would rename Vienna or even Rome. One thing is for certain: We Poles will have Muslims in our backyard within a few months of Vienna's demise."

"So we four must ride," Tadek added. "Better to embrace on

Austrian soil than Polish. Góralu here may want to join us."

"I have business with Gustaw and his kind," Bolek said. "Alone, if it must be."

"You cannot take on several score of men by yourself," Priest cautioned. "Even a rat will fight hard when cornered. You need us with you."

"Careful, Priest. We think now of abandoning our king and country to pursue criminals?" Tadek asked. "This is treason."

"I ask for one more attempt to root out these cowardly dogs, Tadek. I'm thinking a few dead bodies made to look like a werewolf attack would keep folk away from that area of the mountains."

"An excellent idea!" Bolek exclaimed. "Do we ride?"

"Did I hear you say we hunt a werewolf?" Czesław asked.

"Such do not exist, Czesław," Piotr replied.

"Yes, we ride. And now," Priest said.

Being back in the saddle had become habitual to Bolek and the only thing that pleased him. The loss of Rozalia made him feel empty, as if pleasure or joy would never return. Plus he reasoned this Vienna business would take his comrades away from his search for her murderers.

Lord, I beg of you to keep these comrades with me to find Rozalia's killers. I am not up to it on my own. Please help me obtain justice.

He was familiar with the area whence the rumors of a werewolf sprang. It was a secluded spot, attained only by an ancient, narrow mountain-trail, abandoned in winter because of frequent avalanches, and in spring and wet summer days due to rockslides. But when dry, Bolek believed it was wide enough for a wagon. And all raids had been carried out on dryer days.

The terrain was rugged, ringed with high bare cliffs, unsuitable for summer grazing, and though this trail was a short cut, saving many miles by taking a straight line to Bolek's farm and the nearby village, it was rarely used. The only people rumored to travel it were Gypsies, and for the isolation it offered.

This added to the avoidance of the area and helped fuel tales of the supernatural, covens, curses and spells.

The patrol rode at a slow trot through a shallow stream, the horses pleased to be relieved of the tiring suction of swampy ground, their hooves splashing along in the shallow, flat pebble-lined water now. Soon there appeared hoof and wagon prints crisscrossing the stream, evidence of human activity.

"*Cyganie*," Priest declared. "Gypsies originally from Egypt, it is thought. The clan around here would be *Roms*, most likely. Their black-magic potions and devil cards, which tell the future, bring the superstitious, eager to know what will come, to their wagons."

"Devils?" Czesław asked, his eyes scanning the forest around him.

"They do not wish to assimilate into our ways, but they have a place here. When a country is strong and just, there is room in harmony for all."

"Fiery songs and hotter women," Piotr commented.

"The fact a werewolf appears near their camp tells the whole story," Tadek said.

"What will protect us from a man who is an animal?" Czesław asked. "From something that is in alliance with demons."

"The sacraments," Priest answered, causing Czesław to cross himself.

"How in hell do they get their wagons up here?" Tadek asked. "Even my Parabellum struggles with his footing."

"Mules," Bolek answered. "Their mules pull and the men push, for mules are better suited for hauling loads than horses."

"It is as we do with our cannons when we take them over mountains," Priest added. "Back-breaking work."

"How do you know of this road, Góralu," Tadek asked.

"My father took me hunting here often, when I was a boy. It lacks people and, therefore, is teeming with game."

"I glimpse shadows often here. What game thrives?" Tadek asked.

"Bear, mountain lion, wolverine, everything that shies from the company of man."

"Perhaps werewolves, gypsies and raiders team up and stalk us now in the cover of thick forest," Tadek said, actually cracking a smile at Czesław's wide eyed response.

Bolek rode at the rear, ever alert for an attack; each knight's back protected from arrows by their kalkan shields.

"Were you always a great marksman, Czesław," Bolek asked his riding companion who held No Arc at his chest and three arrows in his fingers.

"No, Góralu, an acquired skill, born of pain."

"How so?"

"They told me, after my family was killed that eight horsemen were seen riding away. Only eight to kill everything I loved. All lost for shiny metal and some food."

"No man could stand against eight."

"Not as I was. But with my practice and No Arc I could now slay eight and many more in moments as they tried to ride me down."

"So you ride—"

"I ride because I wish I was with my family now. Home. Safe. With my wife. Perhaps children. How I long to be called Father. All gone in an instant, Góralu. No man should know such pain."

"You saved me, my mother, my sister."

"So I ride on until the last monster is secure in hell."

"But—"

"Camp smoke!" Priest said, forcing all to reach for the reassuring touch of bow, ax or saber.

The patrol continued forward and upward, cautiously entering a raised clearing just off the narrow trail. Shadows soon materialized into men, who waved, then nodded. It was a small group of Gypsy men, stepping out from the underbrush, their swarthy faces and jet black hair in contrast to their distinctively colorful dress; the bright blues, reds and yellows somehow too ornate for the forest. The search party was waved on to follow them.

"A trap, Priest," Tadek whispered.

"Keep your wits and your swords at the ready," Priest said, leading his men through the brush as he followed the Gypsies. "They make a ready spectacle of themselves. Keep an eye out for archers. We charge them as one if it is a trap."

Small covered wagons, set in a circle, with mules stabled in makeshift log pens soon came into view as the horsemen entered a clearing. The smell of fire and cooking meat calmed nerves.

"Greetings, *soldats*," a stocky man, with a strong, pleasant smile and shoulder length black hair streaked with white announced with a respectful bow in a thick accent.

"I am Vardo."

He sported a wooden peg for a right leg and hobbled as he stepped forward, hand open, to greet the hunting party.

"We have food and drink. You are most welcome to share it with us."

"Thank you," Priest replied. "We mean no harm."

"That is well. Rarely do mounted soldiers journey up here. We usually deal only with those on foot who seek to ask what will come to be in their futures. At first you alarmed us."

"There is talk of trouble in these parts," Priest said, dismounting and offering his hand to the Gypsy leader. "Can you not read your own fortunes?"

"How do you know this?" The Gypsy asked, the men behind Vardo looking to one another. "Do you have the second sight, too?

"Rumors of devils and half-man half-animal filter down to the flat lands, Vardo," Priest said.

"We believe there is a curse on us at present," Vardo replied, crossing himself.

"Do you blaspheme?" Tadek demanded.

"Hold, Tadek," Priest said turning to his short tempered friend. "He means no disrespect. Gypsies embrace the god of whatever country they find themselves traveling through."

"You've been among our people before?" Vardo asked of Priest.

"Yes. Fiery drink, tales to chill ones bones, spiced food and vibrant music."

"And we shall have all this today!" the old leader said, turning to one of his men. "Summon Halina and Jadwiga and we shall . . ."

"Hold," Priest said, "We have tasks before us. We need to settle scores with some brigands who rape, murder and rob below and who probably slip into the guise of demons up here."

"We know of the raids," Vardo admitted, silencing his chattering comrades with a raised hand. "We are not guilty of this. We are also victims of this werewolf. We have also seen headless men riding off in the moonlight. You may inspect our wagons and our persons."

"You are not suspect," Priest said. "We are here to put down raiders and werewolves both. We must talk. Now."

Bolek sat on a fallen tree trunk with his comrades, facing their hosts, who, having offered their guests some drink in wooden cups, squatted on the ground before them, perfectly comfortable. It seemed three men, a girl and a child had died mysteriously in the woods over the last two months, at their former camp, an hour's walk to the north, the bodies found with horrible wounds and their throats torn out. Not cut, the old Gypsy stressed, but torn out, by fangs.

"*Vilkodlak*," Vardo said. "A werewolf. If a witch has cut a large piece of human skin and draped it over the threshold of a house in which a marriage is being celebrated, one could be transformed into a werewolf."

"Do you have such a witch here in your camp?" Tadek asked.

"No, sir. We do not defile the dead."

"Where are these sights seen," Priest asked.

When Vardo described the location, Bolek declared he knew the area, a peat bog, always dark and damp.

"Indeed, young sir," the Gypsy leader answered. "There are many ancient trees, small and large, covered by clinging mists which sap a man's warmth as if drinking his blood."

"Nose of Turk and Tatar's lips," Piotr recited as he sniffed before sipping the liquid.

"Piotr, what is this stuff?" Bolek asked as he sniffed at the fluid in his wooden cup. "It smells like goat cheese mixed with chicken crap."

"It's *śliwowica,* a local plum brandy. It will put hair on your chest."

Bolek poured his measure into Piotr's empty cup.

"We go on foot," Priest said as he rose. "Our hosts will tend to our mounts while we are away. This will be no place for horses."

"I question the wisdom of leaving our mounts with them," Tadek complained as the five men walked through knee-high grass toward the place where the bodies had been found. "They might eat them."

"Werewolves before us and Gypsies to our backs. A fine plan, Priest." Czesław added.

"Their only fault is their inability to accept our ways," Priest counseled. "They are a bit too superstitious and clannish, perhaps. But they are still men."

"What if we walk into a camp of brigands?" Piotr asked. "Without our horses, and in a closed-in area, we will be at a disadvantage. Numbers over skill with dictate the outcome."

"If we let them see us first," Tadek said, "we would deserve our fate for our stupidity. Keep eyes, ears and nose ever alert."

"We are simply scouting now," Priest explained. "We can ill afford a neighing horse. If we find a camp, chances are it will be too well-protected for a frontal attack. Keep your eyes open for sentries, especially high up in the trees." Priest pointed high. "Sagging or moving pine branches will give them away."

"And what if we find a werewolf?" Bolek asked. "We are moving into the darkest and gloomiest of this mountain's secret belly as the sun sinks in the sky, and where night belongs to the demons."

"Do you carry your crucifix?" Priest asked, picking his way between stones and fallen branches.

"Of course," Bolek replied.

"If you truly believe in its eternal message no evil can harm you."

The men walked for what seemed forever, such was the hard going, and the unnerving, draining feeling something unnatural was inches from them, hidden in the ever-encompassing brush. A ghostly howl in the near distance froze all five in their tracks as crows abandoned the trees, disturbed by the chilling sound. Czesław fumbled in his robe and clutched his crucifix, holding it before him.

"The wind is at our face. Whatever screams is too far away to catch our scent," Priest whispered. "Still, we go quietly now. Make each step silent and each word a whisper."

"What if there is more than one?" Bolek asked.

Priest looked him in the eye. "You've faced four sabers in the dance while drunk and blind. This will be more like sport."

"Is it a wolf we'll be facing?" Bolek asked, anxious to test his father's szabla and himself but apprehensive of the unknown.

"No," Priest replied. "Wolves do not hunt humans unless they are starving. And food up here is in abundance."

"What will we encounter then?" Bolek asked.

"Your own fears."

Chapter 39

With the sun dipping behind the peaks above, the light dimmed quickly, a chill rising from the ground. A rolling fog soon obscured their feet. The trees faded to gray, clammy fog quickly at their waists. Approaching the area of the murders, twigs snapped under their feet inadvertently, for they were even unable to see their sabers. Balance became difficult and vision worse. The fog now rose to their chests as the temperature plummeted.

Another howl, this one much closer, no more than a bow shot away; a loud, hefty growl.

"Walk by faith not sight." Piotr whispered.

Each looked to his brother for confidence and assurance as Priest signaled them to move apart. Bolek's eyes set on an immense shadowy oak to his left, its ancient curled branches stretching down into the fog-covered ground. The forest was in pale shadow now, the cloud-filled sky offering only occasional moonlight. Bolek's imagination conjured up images of an enormous red-eyed devil inches from lunging at him from behind the tree, ready to run him through the heart with a glowing crimson pitchfork. The demon soon turned into a man-like creature, covered in matted hair, his emaciated arms reaching for Bolek's throat, terrible yellow fangs dripping venom in anticipation of the embrace. Remembering the time in the mountains, when he watched helplessly, frozen in fear, as the merciless wolf captured one of his deer, he shook his head to dispel the image of a clawed and hairy, blood-soaked hand as it grasped for him from deep within the black shadowed pine, suddenly clutching at his neck. He squeezed the hilt of his szabla to ensure it was still in his trembling hand.

A slight breeze forced the trees to rustle. Imagination turned the sound into an unknown language, as if the forest was whispering secrets to itself, alerting ghastly apparitions of

Bolek's whereabouts. The forest now seemed to know of his presence. Something was coming.

Czesław slipped, fell to one knee and cursed. All stood still, expecting an attack from any direction, for the beast certainly had their position now. A thick branch cracked. Something heavy was moving at their right flank.

Who is the hunter? Who the hunted?

"Back to back. In a circle. Watch all directions," Priest whispered. "Keep a sword's length apart."

"My bow is useless here. I can see nothing," Czesław complained.

"Szabla and knife," Priest said.

Another branch cracked, shattering an uneasy silence. A lone gust of wind pushed the fog down to waist high.

The ghoul's breath?

To Bolek, it seemed as if the forest had gone mute, afraid to call attention to its very self, in the presence of whatever strange entity approached.

A guttural growl from a few feet in front raised the hairs on his neck.

What if there are more of these demons in the trees, looking down on me? What if the one moving in the woods is a diversion? What if its teeth are barred, claws ready to take me from behind? Will I offer a response? What if it is a hundred feet tall? A dragon? Lord God, keep my arm strong. Allow me to wield my szabla.

The hunters formed a rotating spiral, each facing outward, stepping both forward and to the side; each guarding the others' backs and sides. They halted on Priest's command, in a small clearing, not more than twenty feet in diameter, waiting, listening. Bolek, chilled through and through, tensed his jaw so as not to shudder. Dampness robbed the heat from his muscles and numbed his toes. His visible breath mixed with the fog, which had become fear itself. What if the beast was below? What if it grabbed his legs and pulled him down, to drown him, to carry him off to hell?

Holy Jesus, how did I happen to come here? Let me be strong, Mary, for what this creature does is wrong. I cannot allow what happens to the innocent happen anymore. Let me be strong. I beg thee."

What came to Bolek in response was one of Priest's lectures.

Let your heart guide your thoughts. Judge the unknown by the known, the uncertain by the certain.

An image of Rozalia filled Bolek's mind, in all her radiant beauty, her musical laughter, and her sparkling eyes. The fury he felt over her brutal murder was displaced by a warm breath of renewal.

A hellish yowl, the stench of rotting flesh, yellow eyes, barred fangs and outstretched claws emerged from the fog. Without thinking Bolek twisted his shoulders, leaned forward on his left leg and swung at the hideous apparition. The jolt of his blade confirmed he hit something real and did not pass harmlessly through a ghostly aura. A thud, the smell of blood; whatever it was, it was of this world and Bolek's blade had cut through it.

"Praise God," Priest said. "Góralu has made two werewolves out of one."

As one, the hunters fanned the fog away with their szablas and hands until all could see what lay at their feet; a mass of putrid smelling rags and matted hair. A sudden gust of wind, the parting of clouds, and the austere light of a gibbous moon forced each hunter to cross himself.

"These are omens," Czesław muttered, "The beast has passed on."

"But not as a werewolf," Priest said, kicking the heap of offal over. "Only as a man possessed."

The moonlight revealed the headless body of a waif of a man. The head lay a foot away, its wild eyes, frozen in sudden death, stared out at nothing. Shoulder length greasy hair, tangled and clumped with mud, a gaping mouth, two protruding fangs, black blood still pulsing from the neck.

"If thy head offend thee, cut it off," Piotr recited.

Priest knelt to examine further. "Look here," he said, digging his dagger into the mouth and extracting a fang.

"Bear fangs have been hollowed out and fitted over filed down eye teeth. This wretched monster insults the bear and the wolf. Look at the fingernails. Long and filed sharp as arrowheads."

"What was this?" Bolek asked.

"A corrupted soul," Piotr replied. "Lost from God. A life lived in hell. And Góralu has sent him to his just reward. Sword of the Spirit."

Priest clasped his hands together and recited in unison with his comrades as they knelt around the horror.

"Diabolus enim et alii dæmones a Deo quidem naturâ creati sunt boni, sed ipsi per se facti sunt mali."

Piotr translated for Bolek. "The Devil and the other demons were created by God good in their nature but they, by themselves, have made themselves evil."

"Can there be more?" Czesław asked, looking all around. "A nest?"

"No. This was a lone madman in a sane world," Priest said. "I have seen this before."

"I pray for all the poor victims of this abomination. May their souls be at rest," Piotr prayed.

"Are we certain there are not more?" Czesław asked.

"Even if there were," Priest said, "after watching the Góral blade in action, they have turned their posteriors to us and are all flocking back to Hell in fear."

The laughter of relief banished the spell of evil.

"Tadek, bring the head," Priest said.

Bolek was not the only one confused by the order and looked to Priest.

"A three-pronged strategy, gentlemen," Priest explained. "First, we must prove to our Gypsy friends we killed their werewolf; they are safe. Second, because they are still slaves to superstition, it is our duty to prove to them the werewolf was nothing devilish. And even if it were that just men will prevail."

"And third?" Bolek asked.

"The appearance of this demon's head in their Gypsy camp will produce elation, then celebration, and, therefore, food and drink."

Tadek drove the point of his szabla into the base of the severed head and raised it well away from his body as the hunting party began to follow their own tracks back to the Gypsy camp, now with steady moonlight, each believed, as some kind of divine reward for their efforts.

"You were the only one certain we did not track a demon from Hell," Bolek said to Priest as they boldly stomped back to camp, having no reason now for stealth.

"It did not matter where this pathetic thing came from," the old soldier told him. "For God would never set something in our path that could not be overcome with courage and faith."

"Perhaps He has more faith in you then, than me."

"Satan is a spirit, and limited in earthly power," Piotr added, crossing himself while looking around just for safety sake. "This poor wretch was enticed by his own desires to become this abomination."

"His heart and mind were open to temptation, the fertile ground of our fallen nature," Priest added. "Have I still not convinced you yet, Góralu?"

"I thought of Rozalia just before he attacked," Bolek admitted. "I became full of rage but then prayed to the Queen of Heaven for peace for Rozalia and guidance for me. I was no longer afraid."

"Push your chest outward and up, Góralu," Priest said, "for tonight Providence has aided you to defeat Satan. Your prayer to Mary was answered and you acted accordingly. Rozalia, resplendent in Heaven, smiles for you."

He knew full well he would never forget this night. Though a life had been extinguished, perhaps a soul had been freed. And its evil will not harm anyone again.

No more mind-numbing fear. Feel. Think. Mary answered my prayer, for I asked for peace for Rozalia and nothing for myself. I was thinking of others when I was freed of my hatred and fears.

"Pray you can stand up to what comes next, Góralu," Piotr cautioned, "for you have defeated one of Satan's demons in single combat and the Beast surely knows of you now."

"Don't expect my saber instructions to deliver you from a pissed off Satan," Tadek growled.

Chapter 40

"Put the bear tooth back in the head, Tadek," Priest told his companion as the reddish glow of a fire appeared ahead. "The Gypsies need to see the human beast in its full regalia."

Tadek, who had carried the severed head like a trophy flag spat in disgust as he complied.

The Gypsies recoiled at the sight of five men appearing from the shadowy moonlit forest, fog at their knees, under a hideous and bloody head fitted to a sword's point. The campfire with its flickering and dancing firelight casting eerie shadows only added to the scene. The Polish soldiers had indeed killed a werewolf and were returning to their camp with its head as a trophy.

After two determined breaths, Vardo, the king of the Gypsies, ventured forth, eventually grasping the severed head by its hair and raising it to the moonlit sky with a roar of joyous victory. Gypsy man, woman and child to the last, inspected the abomination before Vardo, swinging it round and round to whoops and hollers of joy, flung the ghastly head into the center of the roaring fire, thus symbolically banishing the evil spell that had fallen over his people, to the fires of hell.

"Brothers," Vardo said to the five hunters, "in gratitude I humbly ask if we may celebrate your courageous service with a celebratory feast we Gypsies are famous for."

"We must soon leave, Vardo," Priest replied, his comrades staring incredulously at this. "But perhaps one drink."

Vardo made a motion to which the entire camp responded as one, erupting in a flurry of activity. Women appeared from behind the safety of the wagons holding clay bottles, bowls of vegetables, cheese and rye bread. Squawking chickens were scooped up by their legs two at a time, their wings flapping and throats clucking in protest. A lamb was pulled by its collar to an out-of-sight location. Logs at thick as men were dragged into a circle, creating a makeshift arena for the soldiers and their hosts to sit. A table was assembled from a foundation of logs and the slats of wood that made up the walls of a large cart.

Children ran to the woods and returned with their arms full of firewood, the littlest ones returning with kindling, the older with thick branches and men dragging whole limbs until the fire lit and warmed the meadow and its inhabitants. The ever-growing flames were constantly stoked by two attendants with long wooden poles, flames shooting ever higher, sparks crackling and logs sizzling and hissing as the fire gained power.

Bolek stopped counting people at fifty. Each was in motion, actively pitching in as one to create a celebration of thanks centered on him and his friends. It was not lost on him that these exotic Gypsies acted much like family, friend and neighbors at his own celebrations. How different they were than the evil tales he had heard told of them.

One must experience a man before thinking evil of him or his.

These folks were working together, to please everyone; smiling in innocent anticipation. Toddlers giggling as mothers kept shooing them from under foot, yapping dogs at their heels. Men darting from one task to the next.

And pray tell what tales do they tell of us Poles? While we instruct our young that Tatars are fiends and Muslims ghouls. Or that Hungarians are devils, while we still enjoy some of their delicious recipes and claim them as ours, dress in their hats, ride their horses, play their songs while substituting Polish words for their strange tongue. Goulash, paprika. The more I learn the less . . .

One of the Gypsy boys, not much more than knee high, eyes of coal and curly ringlets of ebony hair, approached Bolek, bowed his head while boldly shaking his hand, thanking him in perfect Polish for being so brave to kill the demon who had murdered his cousin. A woman stood twenty paces away, a look of motherly pride on her face; no doubt the boy's mother; a child in training for manners.

Vodka was poured and hoisted, banishing the chill from deep within Bolek's bones. He graciously accepted toast after toast, his cup replenished faithfully by an adolescent girl who stood next to him with a large clay pot of the *aqua vitae*. As he, his comrades and the Gypsy men drank together, empty cups were filled without delay by the girls. Knights and Gypsies began to warm to one another, relax, laugh and toast, then brag and embellish. The threat of a werewolf was over, their losses of family, of precious life, avenged.

The Gypsy hosts were extremely pleased when they learned the heroic slayer of werewolf was a Góral. The very word meant highlander. The Polish mountain people were known for the fierce

independence and isolation from the flatlanders so the Gypsies felt a blood bond with their alpine brethren. Both groups were equally known to resist change and resent laws and restrictions imposed by others – primarily those of the distant and pampered cities below. Who were they to tell us what to do?

"We roam as free as the breeze," Vardo said loudly, his mug raised to Bolek, "We can live as we please. Open road, open sky!"

"Traveling thieves," Tadek said, under his breath.

"You seem a happy people," Priest said, puffing on his clay pipe, "although you are dealt with harshly by most."

"We are friendly and at ease for we have Polish cavalry here, my friend, to protect us this night. And also because we have the werewolf's head roasting in our fire. We have learned to appreciate an enjoyable time when it comes for it is a rare thing. Here, try our honeyed wine."

Vardo passed a large clay demijohn to Priest, who tasted without delay, swishing the liquid around his mouth, proclaiming it excellent. He drank again, deeper this time, passing it along the line to Czesław's thick, greedy paws.

"You should have our young Góral here, a slayer of werewolves, carve your leg," Czesław said, looking at Vardo's outstretched wooden appendage. "He is an expert."

"Perhaps," the good-natured Gypsy said, lifting up his wooden limb for all to see. "Perhaps you can carve it into the form of a beautiful woman?" he said while cupping his hands at his chest to snide laughter.

"Did you lose your leg in a battle?" Tadek asked him.

Vardo's heavily accented tenor voice turned deep and low. "No. An angry Polish lord took it in revenge when his wife died in childbirth after her fortune was told by one of our women. Everything is the fault of Gypsies. We are easy to blame."

"But you are paid to see the future, no?" Tadek asked.

"Yes, but only as a means to hope. We tell widows they will come into money, plain-faced maidens they will marry handsome princes, and barren wives that they will soon conceive. It resurrects hope; a glimmer of romance, of wealth and security, the promise of happiness. All harmless dreams."

"It is said below you once traveled to graze but now graze to travel," a smiling Piotr said, the remark taken as a compliment by Vardo with a deep bow.

"As men of God," Vardo countered, "let us sing tonight in harmony and not just in a forced unison."

When Bolek finally received the passing bottle of the honeyed wine, he gulped the liquid, feeling the full warmth of *spiritus*, of the illusion of spirit coming to his head. All fears from the recent few hours were banished. Recalling an old Gypsy song he knew, a bittersweet tune of lost love, he raised his flute and picked out the tune. A Gypsy violin caught on to the melody. Bolek, knowing nothing of the Gypsy tongue, but able to remember and mimic any language, began to sing the words in Vardo's tongue.

As Vardo heard a familiar song, sung by an outsider in his own language, the Gypsy king's eyes lit in amazement. He rose, cocked like a crow and spun around on his wooded peg, calling for more musical accompaniment before joining Bolek's fluted melody with the words of the second verse. Soon there were five violins, several horns, some drums to keep time and more than a few flutes, including Piotr's, all making music to the tingle and jingle of innumerable tambourines. Two gypsy men, arm in arm, rocking left and right, sang the words in full voice, leading all in a third verse, made up at that moment, telling of a Góral highlander who beheaded a werewolf to revenge Gypsy lost lives.

Priest, Czesław, Piotr and Tadek roared with laughter, swaying their bodies and their cups along with the music. Now all were singing at the top of their lungs, not caring what the words meant for all folk songs spoke of the same simple yet most valuable of things; love, happiness, family.

Priest left for a bit, returning with his prize violin, and vigorously joined the other fiddlers. Even the crickets stopped their song in deference to the master. Not only did Priest's violin have the sweetest sound, the loudest tone and the surest vibrato, but he added something of himself to the music, something deeper than the communication of note, timing and melody could go, something, as they say, where music becomes the language of the soul. Grown men were unashamed in their tears, and, at the end of the song, Priest received their greatest accolade, a moment of silence, while each man remembered better times, safer times, golden memories of youth, love and companionship.

After catching his breath, Priest catapulted the pace a level higher, fiddling the melody of a fiery well-known song. Fueled by applause, the other violins joining the master in harmony, to his melody. Devoid of any reserve, Bolek vied to sing the loudest as sweat poured down his face, his body a slave to the rhythm. For one brief instant, he locked eyes with Priest, who flipped the violin so Bolek could see the eagle he had carved upon its base. Priest nodded and Bolek raised his cup then bowed deeply.

The women began to serve food and the men ate with their hands where they stood or sat. As for Bolek, he was not hungry for food and took a refill of spiced wine from his personal demijohn. As it came to him that more and more women caught his attention, he thought these Gypsy women all looked at him differently than Polish girls did, for down below in the valleys and in the villages, girls would sometimes glance his way, nod in recognition and modestly look away. But here, these dark, black-eyed women gazed deeply, almost as if they were offering some kind of a challenge. Deep within, something began to stir, to awaken and he noticed each woman as she walked, served, smiled, winked and bent over, completely unashamed to move and pose in ways Polish girls did not.

"Gentlemen," Vardo announced to the fluid mass of flesh as the serving women were forced to scurry between tipsy bodies to clear the tables and bring more food and drink. "A surprise for you tonight. My niece, who can shoot and ride with the best of us, my niece who has been to the great city of Istanbul and beyond, will dance for us tonight."

"Alina!" the gypsy men shouted. "Alina!"

"She has been trained to dance in the old way, the way a woman can dance to appeal to much more than men's eyes," the old man told his Polish comrades drunkenly. "But keep in mind she is the greatest archer in our clan. She is a deadly shot. And she is not squeamish."

The main table was disassembled and the wagon walls quickly rebuilt as all sat tightly packed around the roaring fire on the makeshift log-seats; the glowing meadow instantly transformed into a performance stage. A lone violin floated a melancholic and seductive introduction to an exotic Eastern melody. It was followed by a passionate refrain. Soon a second violin joined, then a tambourine. Leather-topped drums began to accentuate the rhythm. A barefoot young woman, not much more than a girl, chin in the air, posture arrow-straight, glided into the center of the celebration and froze; arms slightly extended, each finger at a different angle. She held every eye. To Bolek it was as if a painting stood posed before the fire.

Her hair hung loosely and well down her back, blacker than the midnight forest on a moonless night. Her eyes were darkened with cosmetic kohl; lips red as blood, cheeks reddened also as if in constant blush – a striking contrast to her flawless marble skin. She wore a red silken skirt, cut well above the knee, a thin white muslin blouse baring her midriff. Large circular golden rings dangled from her ears.

Within the pulsing and seducing music, she began to move slowly and fluidly, arms high in the air, hands undulating, seductively reminding the men of something that needed no words. As the pace of the music accelerated, her body curled, swayed and rolled as if each part of her was free of the other. The entire world disappeared for Bolek, for all he saw was Alina. Sensual. Bold. Painted. Adorned. Unrestrained. Vardo's words were true. Her dance awoke and then aroused timeless desires within Bolek and the others.

The wine, the vodka, memories of the maidenly Rozalia, of the exhilaration of his triumph over the werewolf all vied for and infused with this Alina, swirling within every fiber like a whirlwind, with she at the center of it all.

As the music reached a fevered pitch the young beauty gyrated as if she herself was the musical essence itself – music made visible. Bolek's eyes followed her unsecured lightly covered breasts as they swayed to and fro under her thin blouse. Snatching up a tambourine, she struck the rhythm of the music as she twirled. To Bolek each time she spun it seemed her skirt rose higher and higher, teasing him with what lay under it as her breasts threatened to burst apart the seams of her blouse.

Commanding a change of tempo with her tambourine, the glistening Alina imitated a snake as she twisted and turned, jutting her hips in a motion whose heat rivaled that of the frenzied bonfire. Bolek sweated, but not only from the fire, the temperature of his blood rising with each seductive motion. He froze in mid breath as she caught his gaze and smiled. His eyes were captive to hers and she seemed to welcome them, raising her skirt to a point where snow-white thighs were visible, where Bolek felt he would soon explode with the music's finale. She moved closer, turning her back to his unblinking eyes, mere inches away, hips and shoulders swaying, arching her back until he could see her face upside down, her mountain-like cleavage glistening in the firelight.

How like the earth is a woman's body.

The music stopped abruptly and the dance with it, there was no sound but the crackling of the fire and beating of hearts, for all the men held their breaths, each lost in a timeless desire. The girl recovered her balance, smiled with radiant snow-white teeth, bowed and tip toed childlike toward the wagon at the edge of the wood, with every eye upon her. Only then did the men applaud and cheer.

I am possessed.

Bolek's companions, eyelids heavy, slowly returned to slurred revelry. Bolek fought to recover control of himself as another familiar song began and the fete continued, men and women dancing and singing; all save Bolek, whose blood seethed. The drink had made him forget his head. The girl had made him forget his soul.

He watched the men shouting out the words of yet another well-known song, some while dancing around each other, arm in arm, some stumbling, leaning on each other, some losing balance entirely, and singing on their backs from the forest floor. He looked at the women, busy at the other end of the camp, some furiously scrubbing pots at the stream, preparing more food and drink or gathering more wood to feed the insatiable fire. They too were oblivious to Bolek who rose and moved with stealth, using the underbrush between the meadow and where the covered wagons sat. He crept up to the wagon Alina had disappeared into, throwing the heavy animal skin drape to the side. He stepped in, the drape closing behind him. He found her fully naked, kneeling in the wagon, using a towel to dry her glistening body from the exertion of the dance. Her eyes went wide as she attempted to cover herself. Her single scream was lost amid the noise of drunken festivities.

Mere moments later Bolek stumbled out of the wagon to the sound of laughter before him, weeping behind. His lust satisfied, he was certain he had not been missed. He had power now, power to kill werewolves, to be honored in a gypsy camp, to be treated as an equal by renowned warriors, power to take what he wanted. She should be proud, he reasoned. A Góral swordsman and archer, owner of a war horse worth five hundred oxen, and killer of a werewolf had noticed her, favored her. Catching his boot on a rock he stumbled and fell outstretched to the ground. He crawled into the cover of the forest, and did not stir until the morning chilled him.

Chapter 41

The crowing of a rooster taking credit for the dawn found Bolek watching his four comrades rise slowly from their drunken sleep. Vardo's offer of a morning feast was declined. Smoked sausages, salt pork and cheese were stuffed into saddlebags.

"Why so glum, Góralu," Priest asked as they carefully guided their horses single file along the narrow trail. "Is killing werewolves exhausting business or it a pounding head and a sour stomach?"

As the others trailed, dosing in their saddles, Bolek motioned to Priest to ride out of earshot of the others.

"Can you hear confession?"

"I am called Priest now through habit, but I no longer stand in Christ's stead. What is troubling you?"

"The Gypsy girl."

"Ah, yes," Priest chuckled. "That one could warm your bed in winter without the need of blanket or fire. Has she bewitched you with her charms?"

"Do you think Satan could have struck at me last night for killing his wolf man?"

"What have you done?"

"I . . . I took her."

"Against her will?" Priest demanded.

"The way she danced I—."

"Did she struggle against you or submit willingly?

"She struggled."

"You have stained two souls."

"I was drunk."

"*In vino veritas.* Is this your true nature?"

"No, but the way she danced. I have never seen a woman do . . ."

"That was but a dance. Lustful, but harmless. Eastern girls are trained early to accommodate themselves to the needs of men.

She was commanded to dance, enthralled by the attention of men, yes, but naïve to their deeper desires. She is no different than your . . ."

"Don't say that! Rozalia was pure."

"So you have one kind of woman to worship and one kind to use. That is an Eastern trait, not a Polish one. Do you judge your mother and sister as Marys and all other women Eves?"

"What can I do?"

"You will remember this self-indulgent transgression long after the fleeting explosion of ecstasy."

"It is both wonderful and terrible that I have met you men."

"At least you do not revel in your sin, Góralu. If she admits the deed to her father she will be exiled from the tribe by Vardo, or sold to a Muslim for his harem, as a concubine, or worse, sold to the Cossacks. And that, my friend, is a fate to fear."

"All because of one incident?"

"An irreversible incident."

"What am I to do?"

"Go back. Face her. Beg forgiveness. Take her to wife before anyone knows of this."

"She wouldn't have me now."

"She might. Even marriage to a Pole would be better than the wrath of her people or slavery."

"What would my mother think if I brought home a Gypsy wife?"

Priest scowled. "Tell your mother you now know how the brigand at your farm felt when he attempted to take her by force."

"You are cruel, Priest."

"Yet, only in words. You are cruel in deed. Which is worse?"

"My children would be half-Gypsy."

"They would be your children. Besides, who in this country can boast of a pure bloodline? Everyone has invaded us. Our wide cheekbones, Góralu, come from Eastern steppes. Our blond

225

hair, from the north. Those of us of swarthy complexion spring from the south. Who knows what blood lies generations behind each of us? It is true the Gypsies live apart from normal Polish culture and are often blamed for many things. But all men have dignity. Therefore, we must not only be tolerant, but understanding, compassionate. They well know it is our Christianity which sets us apart, our struggle to love our fellow man which allows them to live here in relative peace. If we lose our teaching, if our government goes mad and our people no longer care, there will be a firestorm on these plains such as none can imagine. Take this Gypsy girl as your own. And you will also learn from her."

"How did I let this happen?"

"You've thought only of yourself. You've satisfied a bodily need. Animals are free of moral decisions. But you are a man. Now you must think of her."

"I want to forget it all as one bad day."

"Do not make the mistake of thinking you will forget this. For it will fester. When we make a choice and act, we change ourselves as well as things. The world has changed for you today. You have changed. Indifference will destroy you if you trick your mind into making light of this deed. You are free to do what you will, now deal with the consequences. Evil enters the world through sin."

"I do not know which road to take."

"Our religion teaches we are an end unto ourselves and not a means. Faith springs from will and grace. You must pray. Pray to Mary. Balance your intellect and your emotions with the only sure map – your religion. As I said, Eve brought pain and suffering into the world through her disobedience to God. And since then women have suffered as temptresses of evil. This is why the Muslims veil their women. And this is how you see the Gypsy girl. You said your explosion of lust was not your fault, but hers. In the East there are many men who can afford to keep a great many wives to give them pleasure and to make new warrior sons. Their women are possessions."

"She just inflamed me, almost invited me into—"

"Mary brought the God of Love and redemption into the world. And Jesus explained to us how to live through his lone commandment to love one another as he had loved us. His Word is for all, coming through Christ and through His bride, the Church. This is the heart of Poland. This is why brave and honorable men will gallop to Vienna soon without a thought for their own safety or purse. You now stand upon your self-made precipice. Pray to Mary and the Holy Spirit will come to you."

Bolek rode off thinking long and hard before admitting Priest was right. He could not ride away from this, cut it with a sword or shoot it with an arrow. He could not embrace his mother or sister in honesty after what he had done. It must be made right. Dismounting, he fell to his knees in front of a *kapliczki*, one of the many Polish wayside shrines of worship, built and maintained by individuals for travelers to pray. As he looked at the stone image of Mary, he looked through it with inspiration and prayed. The girl had not come to him willingly. So what was the difference between him and the men who attempted to rape his mother and sister? Rozalia had been raped and worse. This Gypsy girl was a daughter to someone and perhaps a sister also. So he had followed in the steps of the evil ones. He had committed a grave injustice and was responsible for making amends or face being eaten up by guilt, for he was no better than the brigands, preying on the weak for his own needs.

Mary, hear my prayers.

That night he deserted his sleeping comrades and returned to the Gypsy camp. Tying his horse a hundred yards away, he walked to the ring of wagons, determined to speak to Alina alone. As fortune had it, he came across her huddled in the moonlight, sobbing against a tree, dressed in a simple woolen garb.

"You have returned so soon?"

Bolek was surprised, for she spoke in perfect Polish. He had expected a thick accent. He knew her body but not the woman.

"You are hungry for me again?" she hissed, pulling a dagger from beneath her robe. "I am ready for you. This time it will be you who feels the thrust."

"I've come to apologize for the incident," he replied, her blade at his heart.

"Incident? Like spilling milk or breaking a pitcher? I have been used and I am unmarried."

"I will marry you."

"My father is making arrangements to sell me. I am shameful to my entire family. None of the men in camp will ask for me."

"You told him?"

"You think I am a deceiver as well as a whore?"

"I was drunk."

"I have embarrassed my ancestors. I did not struggle hard enough. My body lives but I am dead inside."

"Marry me."

"I choose the Cossacks. My father will get money and the Cossacks will own an experienced wench."

"It wasn't your fault."

"Such a thing is always a woman's fault."

"Come with me. We can make a life."

"I once had dreams. Can you make them return? Is it you who controls the cards?"

"I can only do my best."

"The best is to leave. My one wish now is to become a proficient whore, to please the many men who will ride me, to trick them into believing I enjoy them. My father is not a cheat. I will give what my father promises of me."

"I . . ."

"You? You are worse than a beast. You cannot plow, give milk or meat. Leave."

"Marry me, Alina."

"What is your name?"

"Bolesław. Why?"

"So I can repeat it when I am in pain, as I am passed around from one drunken soldier to another. Each time I will whisper 'Bolesław,' and curse you to Hell."

"I . . ."

"Leave."

"Come with me."

"To dance for you? To use me as a dog? Leave."

"I am sorry. I was wrong. Together we can forget this. Make it right."

"Oh! What you don't know about women," she replied pushing the palms of her hands into her cheeks.

"I will make it right."

"Father! Brothers! Vardo! Help! He has returned! Help me!"

Bolek knew it was hopeless, he had done his best, the damage was done and the sin was on him. He needed time to think of the proper next step. Turning, he disappeared into the cover of the dark woods. Footsteps, torches and muttered curses followed him for some time but his training had made his body fit, outdistancing the Gypsy men easily. Vaulting onto Quo Vadis he galloped back to the cavalry camp with little satisfaction in his escape.

I would gladly turn and fight the brigands who killed my Rozalia yet I run from these Gypsies. But still, I cannot outrun my shame. I learn to fight like a warrior yet have no desire to die in Vienna. I am still the treed shepherd.

Chapter 42

"We are being hunted," Koyla told his brother Gustaw as they sat on a log munching on dried venison and crusty bread.

"Who this time?" the camp leader asked, his mouth full of food.

"A cavalry detachment. No more than four or five. I overheard villagers at the inn speak of them."

"So our missing comrades did not fall to a werewolf. Too bad. Killing a wolf man would be good sport."

"Should we be frightened of the soldiers?"

"Wary. This also explains the rumors of headless riders. Perhaps I have a history of one who is searching for us. We are more than enough for twenty or even fifty. There is only one way in here and we have our eyes on it day and night. We will just be more careful when we're hunting. We will go in force from now on and not send smaller raiding parties."

"Perhaps we should move on."

"Are you mad, you fool?" Gustaw shouted, slapping his brother's cheek with an open hand, hard enough to knock his brother's new green-feathered cap from his head. "The entire region trembles before us. We are like gods here. And you want to leave it all behind?"

Koyla gritted his teeth while massaging his cheek. "Soldiers, werewolves, headless riders. Too long in one place is not good."

"Go throw your live away to the army. You will be a shield for nobles. Go break my back on a farm. I am no serf. Trust in their invisible and powerless gods. Soldier, farmer, priest. Those are the choices we are offered. Here, I have drink for my head, food for my belly and women for my loins. What else is there?"

"Our booty."

"Look at your dirt-packed fingernails, brother, at your leathery blood-stained hands, your ever-growing belly. That's who we are. The booty speaks to our success."

"Something comes every closer to us."

"I visit the inns too, Koyla, but hear a different story," Gustaw told him between gulps from a pitcher of beer. "And do you know what I hear that pleases me? War comes again. The Muslims march into Austria. These cavalry geese who hunt us will soon ride south. And every man for miles around will ride with them. They make us presents of their wives, livestock, and crops and appoint us masters of the highlands. Unguarded wagons and carts loaded with supplies for the army will soon travel near us. And we will accept the opportunity, as well. These are exceptional times, Koyla. We are the kings. We wield absolute power. Grow fat with me."

"I have never had so much. It feels wrong."

"I am the lion. They are the lamb. Drink some of their vodka, eat some of their beef, and take one of their women. Here's to war, brother."

Koyla gulped his vodka to dull the pain in his cheek.

"We are kings by our own hand. And truly free."

Koyla, his head spinning, nodded at the wisdom of his brother.

"Now," Gustaw said, "in my travels I have spotted a wealthy merchant with a great wooden red spire topping his illustrious manor. It is well-guarded but I have a clever way to gain access. Listen."

Chapter 43

Miklos, a Hungarian Christian slave of the Ottoman Turkish sultan stood dizzily, his stomach empty and his mouth parched. A party of his masters rode up to the stable, tossing their horses' reins to their attendants. The beasts were allowed to drink gently before being fitted with feed bags. Miklos's eyes went in and out of focus; he was forced to squint as he contemplated his masters rolling out their prayer blankets, facing eastward, kneeling, and reverently bowing to their god. A paralyzing pain stiffened him. The lash of the whip reminded him he was remiss in his actions. Water and food for him would have to wait until sunset. Back to his labor.

The ancient Amber Way, *Szlak Bursztynowy*, winds its way through Western Poland, sometimes by water and sometimes by land. It runs south from the Baltic seacoast down the Vistula valley, through the Austrian Gap at Vienna and east along the Danube valley to the Black Sea, toward the Bosphorus, and Istanbul, once the seat of the Eastern Holy Roman Empire, called Constantinople. Abundant in amber for unknown reasons, the Baltic area produced stones so plentifully they could be picked up as one walked along the coast, especially after a storm where the tumble of waves over the sea floor freed the reddish gems from their hidden resting places.

These stones, the translucent petrified resin of ancient trees, were desired for adornment, to proclaim wealth, and to improve one's health. Marketed throughout Eurasia as necklaces, pendants, amulets, coins and healing agents, their fame spread for centuries. If crushed and mixed with honey, amber was said to cure headaches and toothaches. Burnt in fires and employed as incense, amber released an aromatic odor said to improve one's well-being and change a mood from dark to sunny. Cool to the touch, it was much lighter in weight than diamonds. Wealthy women often chose amber when adorning their bosom with jewels, preferring the warmth of the sun-colored amber to the colder, more burdensome diamonds. Wives demanded amber from their husbands, and the wise ones obliged, for throughout the world, an adorned fashionable wife was a symbol of wealth. The more beautiful your wife, the more decorated and embell-ished, the more successful you were.

There was a magically captive force in amber also, for if rubbed rigorously these stones would pull small objects to it, as if an invisible power was at work. Wealthy Roman women at the time of the Caesars rubbed amber on their clothes to pull lint from luxurious gowns. Solidified sunshine, golden pebbles, the gold of the north, amber was known by many names. Many thought amber once somehow freed itself from heaven and sunk into the sea.

For centuries caravans wore the earth into ruts along the widely dispersed trails to bring the sun gem from where it lay to whatever peoples possessed the wealth to pay for its rarity. For generations the monopoly on the amber trade was wholly controlled by Prussian tribes, but by the 13th century the Teutonic knights had all but wiped them out, forbidding the native survivors to marry. A history of blood continued as many vied to control the lucrative markets, for wherever a coin could be turned the business of harvesting the precious and hypnotic stone from its northern region in Poland sprang into existence. Kings, princes and mighty magnates paid tribute alike to local warlords, in gold or land or in a percentage of amber for permission to cross forbidden borders and private lands. Amber moved eastward, westward and to the south. Silk and spice moved westward, tin and vodka to the east. Europe became more Asian and Asia more European.

Miklos knew this history well, for he lived it every day. A Turkish raiding party had taken him and his wife, Bozena, from her father's farm in the north of their country, leaving the entire family behind, either dead or dying, deemed worthless by their conquerors as too old to work. Turkish wives and concubines of the seraglio demanded the highly prized adornment. By virtue of their youth and strength, Miklos and Bozena would now serve the Ottoman Empire on the Amber Road.

Barrel-chested Miklos was a capable 'amber diver,' able to jump off a boat and into the murky and cold Baltic to dig at the bottom with his small spade to harvest the precious stones. While many of his companions had succumbed to the dangerous currents or died writhing on the decks of the harvesting boats from horrible chest pains, Miklos was a survivor, somehow impervious to the inherent danger of the deep. He was also able to ride a horse well and worked in the northern marshes, identifying amber for his fellow captives as they collected the treasure. Root hog or die. With little rest, these prisoners filled unending streams of wagons driven to the south where Ottoman craftsmen fashioned silver and golden necklaces to surround and highlight the magical gems and display them to their fullest beauty.

Miklos's wife, Bozena, he saw rarely, for the slave men were camped separately from their women. He knew Turks used the slave women freely, but it was never spoken of on the few occasions husband and wife met. The penalty was death for attempting escape, death for attempting to keep any amber, death for resisting a command from a Turk, death for a slave husband to consort with his slave wife. When Miklos had been captured they had cut off his left ear with a scimitar, branding him as a Turkish captive, forcing him at sword's point to eat his own severed and bloody ear.

Too weak to hate, too worn down by pain to offer resistance, he trudged along in a self-imposed haze which blurred reality and fantasy, while the years slipped away unnoticed; chattel, less than human, enveloped by merciless scimitars and whips, a servant to these amber tears of the sun. Resistance was futile. Miklos knew well the power of these Muslims, for he had felt the cruelty of their sword, endured their constant goading to force their human property to submit, knew of their stifling taxes on the *dhimmi*, the Christians and Jews who were subject to humiliating laws so they would feel themselves subdued as the Koran demanded. He knew of the laws prohibiting churches and synagogues from being repaired, and once they crumbled they could not be replaced. Miklos agonized over the thought that his own Christian religion would be crushed in time, unless some miracle could stop this relentless and pitiless mistreatment of those who treated their horses better than their servants.

Miklos was tormented daily with concerns over his wife's well-being, yet well past the shame of having other men use her. The many swords of Allah and their belief that slavery was justified made Miklos and Bozena mere leaves captive in the current of a stream with only hopes and dreams of future release from their hell. Still, a rage sometimes burned deep within him when visions of his wife with a Turk, with one who thought of her as livestock.

The last time he had seen her, several months ago in the spring; she had been round with child and wore an expression of shame and helplessness. She had tried to shield her belly from him although she was too ripe with child for him not to know. He smiled at this attempt by Bozena, for through all her suffering and shame, she felt for his feelings. "I love you," he mouthed in his native tongue before she passed from sight as both were impatiently herded like sheep along a trail but in opposite directions. The child, he knew, was also destined for a life as human cattle.

"Holy Mary, Mother of God," he whispered as he curled in a dark corner, making a small sign of the cross. That night he dreamed of his Bozena, recalling when the most beautiful girl in their village had consented to be his wife, to go with him. Since her father had six girls, no sons, Miklos would join his father-in-law and work the farm as an adopted son, and plans were soon made to extend the cottage. But this all fell to nothing as the

Turkish raiders galloped over the hill. *Keep your faith*, he told himself as he lay with a goat hide under him and the flea-infested woolen blanket to cover his chest.

As part of a caravan he traveled many places and met many men, witnessed many strange customs, ate alien food seasoned with exotic spices to hide the rottenness, listened to many different philosophies, met pagans who worshiped dead images and animals, met those who believed their own bodies and all you could touch was evil. *Remember your story, Miklos.* And he repeated it this night.

A man stumbles into a deep pit and shivers there for many days. A holy man from east of the Indus passes by. The trapped man cries out for help. "You are ignorant. It is your karma, your fate," the holy man replies. "Your pit is merely illusion. Perhaps in your next life things will be better." A holy man from the great snowy mountains of the south and east peers down at him and again the suffering man in the pit cries out for help. "You crave. Learn how not to want to get out of the pit," the Oriental says, "for you are spoiled." Then a Muslim looks down into the pit, the captive meeting his eyes while begging for help. "It is Allah's will," the Muslim replies. "Submit. Honor Muhammad. Submit." The man collapses in hopelessness and prays for death.

A voice calls to him by name. "Miklos," Jesus says, "do not give up hope." And Jesus lowers himself down into the pit and lifts the helpless Miklos into his arms, then up onto his shoulder and Miklos pulls himself out of the black hole and into the light of day.

Crossing himself, Miklos fell asleep, praying the Prince of Peace would lift Bozena from her pit. And her infant child.

Camp rumors travel fast and Miklos knew before many that his horse and wagon should be made ready for a new endeavor. Slaves from all over the region were needed in the Christian city of Vienna to serve Grand Vizier Mustafa by digging trenches and setting mines to collapse the great walls and capture the infidels' city. This was an unusual day in camp, for word had come the entire Ottoman army now moved on Europe.

Later, as more news filtered through the ranks, Miklos learned the Ottomans had conquered and destroyed everything in their path on their march to Vienna. Soon all of Europe would be set ablaze. Yet Miklos could not see how such a thing could happen. No, much of it was just boasting, he told himself. What if the Europeans defeated the haughty Turks at Vienna? Would not he and the other Christian slaves be freed? New hope came as he reasoned out the possibilities. He knew no battle's outcome could be known in advance as certainty. He knew the stronger in size or number not always emerged victorious. He knew wars fought on too many fronts ended poorly for the aggressor. And he knew spirit and truth could overcome all. Something within a man made him unique in all of nature and an army of righteous spirits would eventually overcome all.

Amid the confusion of striking camp he found himself in a line moving in parallel with a group of slave women, the two columns separated by a small crumbling wall, with no guards in sight.

"Bozena!" he shouted, "Bozena!" And for one moment Miklos was able to run his calloused and filthy hand softly over the head of the infant she carried on her hip. He knew it was not his. But it was hers. Now theirs.

"His name is Miklos," Bozena said through a teary smile.

Without warning a mounted Turkish soldier kicked Miklos on the back of his head from horseback while shouting something Miklos could not understand as he collapsed. When he rose from the dust both his and Bozena's columns of slaves were gone. A veiled Muslim woman was kneeling next to him, dabbing at his bleeding head with a wet rag.

"Pray," the woman said.

"To whom should I pray?" Miklos asked, hoarse with emotion.

"To the god of Abraham, for we are all his sons and daughters. Those who put themselves above God for their own gains will suffer eternally. *'Which of you by taking thought can add one cubit unto his stature.'* Our slavery will end in Paradise."

Leaving a few coins in Miklos's hand, she was shooed away by a threatening guard.

The next morning as Miklos prepared his wagon, hope sprang anew when one of his fellow captives, a Pole well-familiar with deeds of his king, Jan III Sobieski, boasted nothing would stop the famed warrior from marching on Vienna; neither vast numbers of Turks, nor political intrigue, nor death itself. Sobieski, the Pole bragged, was a warrior of Christ, and therefore fearless. Miklos whispered a secretive prayer for this king, invoking the power of Mary to protect him and guide him to Vienna so Miklos could lay eyes on a flesh and blood warrior who was not feared but admired by so many.

He was unaware that at the same moment King Jan III Sobieski, far away to the east at Poland's holiest shrine, was praying for Miklos, Bozena, and for others like them.

Chapter 44

" . . . and also for the thousands of Christians enslaved by the infidel, unable to pray to you, to attend Mass, to praise You," the king whispered on the twenty-fifth day of July in the year of or Lord, 1683, as he knelt at the altar of the Black Madonna.

Ten days before this the Ottomans arrived at the walls of Vienna, an arrow shot over the walls bore a message in both Latin and Turkish. Demands were clear. Surrender the city; convert to Islam; safe conduct then guaranteed. Austrian Field Marshal Count Starhemberg gave no reply. The assault began that day.

At first word of the approaching Ottoman army, Charles V, Duke of Lorraine, Commander of the Imperial Forces retreated with the bulk of his force from Vienna, to wait for Sobieski. Reports ran as high as 500,000 Muslims besieged Vienna's fortress walls. Sobieski had stopped at a Roman Catholic monastery at Yasna Gora, near the Polish city of Czestochowa, at the head of a sizeable Polish army, all dedicated by a solemn oath to honor their pact with Austria and liberate the besieged Holy city. If the Holy League of the Emperor, the Republic of Venice and Pope Innocent XI could not overcome their petty power squabbles, Christian Europe would go up in flames. King Jan III Sobieski would not allow this to happen, political intrigue and economic opportunities be damned.

The king addressed his men as they stood on the ramparts of the fortress at Yasna Gora.

"God has given us the right to meet the invading hordes in Vienna. I ride proudly with you knights of Christ. Do not fear in your hearts. Are we Poles not already known throughout the world as the *Antemurale Christianitatis*, the bulwark of Christianity? Have we not sworn to defend our holy faith to the last drop of Polish blood?"

The three cannons standing guard over the icon of the Black

Madonna of Jasna Gora's Bright Mountain in the city of Czestochowa, Poland, stood nearly a thousand feet above the ground, protected by thick walls, bastions and a moat. The cannons had been named after three brave defenders of the fortress who, during the great Deluge, *Potop*, the Swedish invasion, defended their faith. Poland had at that time lost its collective spirit, its very soul, and the invading Swedish army marched easily through the country as Warsaw, Poznań and even Cracow fell with only token resistance. The Polish nobility, divided by personal and petty disputes, refused to fight. On November 18, 1655, General Muller's army of 3,000 Swedes reached Jasna Góra and demanded complete surrender. Jasna Góra's prior, Augustine Kordecki, with less than two hundred soldiers and half as many monks politely refused. The Swedes promptly attacked. It was then the three cannons, Augustyn Kordecki, Stefan Zamojski and Piotr Czarnecki roared with deafening voice, one which even the those lost in self-indulgence, in apathy, agnosticism, and those lacking the faith to believe in the worth of their country could hear and understand.

"Enough!" the Kordecki cannon roared.

"We give in no more!" the Zamojski cannon thundered.

"We retreat no more!" the Czarnecki cannon rumbled.

The Swedes besieged the fortress time and again, their battle of wills raged unsuccessfully, and after forty days, they gave up. The victory was due to the Mother of God's grace, for what other explanation to men of faith was possible? After such a brave stand and the miraculous victory at Jasna Góra, the whole country, noble and peasant alike, awoke from a long sleep of indifference, rising up against the Swedish invaders and driving them from their homeland. On April 1, 1656, King Jan Casimirus solemnly proclaimed Mary the protector of Poland, indeed, the Queen of Poland. Jasna Góra became the center of the religious and political liberty of Poland.

The Black Madonna, by tradition, was said to have been

painted by St. Luke the Evangelist as Mary told him of the life of her son, a story which Luke later incorporated into his gospel. The painting is known as the Black Madonna because of the smoke of candles held by devout worshippers over the centuries that had discolored it.

St. Helen, wife of Emperor Constantine, found the portrait in 326 A.D. in Jerusalem, She, in turn, gave the icon to her son, who built a shrine around it in Constantinople. During one battle with the infidels, the picture was exhibited on the walls of the city, and the enemy army fled. Clearly, the Black Madonna had saved the city from destruction. In 1382 when invading Tatars attacked Prince Ladislaus' fortress, the then protector of the sacred relic, an arrow lodged in the Madonna's throat, whereupon, the Prince immediately removed the painting to the safety of the citadel within Czestochowa Poland. In 1430, the church was invaded and a looter slashed the painting two times with his sword, but before the next blow, he fell dead.

King Jan III Sobieski pondered over these very scars, although his saddle awaited and every minute counted. He and his army were on its way through the Tatra Mountains by way of the Czchen Pass to engage the Ottoman Muslims at Vienna. The battle-hardened king was well-aware if Vienna fell to the Ottoman and the newly converted Hungarian Muslims, next spring would see them pour into Poland. He was certain this sacred Polish relic would then be destroyed, regardless of the reverence shown by the thousands who worshipped daily at its feet.

But this king tarried because he also knew the Black Madonna had been the source of miraculous healings, had repelled armies, and had been a motivating spirit for countless hundreds of thousands of pilgrims for centuries. Praying to Her for strength and courage he would lead his army toward Cracow to join up with Hetman Sieniawski and then take a southwest path across the Oder and Marava rivers and finally across the mighty

Danube itself. Saxon cavalry and infantry moved south, the Bavarians and Franconians moved eastward. All would meet to the north of Vienna sometime in early August, where they would confront their millennium-old foe.

Chapter 45

Grand Vizier Merzifonlu 'Kara' Mustafa Pasha, the chief political and religious administrator of the Ottoman Empire and advisor to Sultan Mohammad IV, the Caliph of Islam, fidgeted with the ornate blue cord dangling around his neck. It was presented to him as a warning when he promised his sultan this time Vienna would fall but only if Mustafa himself were at the army's head. If he could not fulfill this promise he was to be strangled with this very same cord. He took to wearing it in public as he commanded his huge army, a frown frozen on his face.

But today, as his army sprawled before him, camped and encircling Vienna, Mustafa was in rare spirits. There were twenty thousand Tatars in alliance with his Turkish force of 150,000, and though he reviled these Tatars, the compromise of politics told him they could be useful. The times were with Mustafa. Even Count Imre Thököly de Késmárk, proclaimed king of Hungary by the Sultan, in exchange for his acceptance of Islam, was revolting against the Hapsburg Holy Roman Emperor, Leopold, and soon all of Hungary would fall to Islam.

Christian Europe's last few grains of life were being drawn though the neck and to the bottom of the hourglass. The arrogance of kings, the wish to preserve dynasty, the apathy of the idle rich, the political beast seeking empty victories all weakened the West. It would crumble as Rome had, rotting and crumbling from within – until the right event would make it all collapse. That rotting selfishness, that self-interest, that is the thing that would keep the Poles in Poland, which pleased Mustafa since the Polish king was the one enemy he feared. Yes, indeed, there would be little if any threat to his master plan, and little resistance once Vienna fell. Mustafa would himself place that straw – the one that would break both the camel's and Europe's Christian back, here and now.

Mustafa's soldiers surrounded the city and controlled the

hinterlands as well. The Christian slaves, driven before the whip daily into the siege camp labored furiously to dig trenches to extend under Vienna's very walls. They dug deep tunnels for the miners who would set black power charges to explode under those walls, collapsing the mighty barriers, allowing his forces to stream into the wealthy Christian city. And it would be soon, for hadn't he accomplished the impossible before? Hadn't he taken Podolia and the Western Ukraine?

Once Vienna's walls crumbled it would be a simple matter to send his army through the breaches, put the garrison to the sword, take slaves, capture the booty, and enjoy the prestige of conquering Christendom's greatest city in the name of Allah. It would be Mustafa's honor to rename the city something more appropriate to the Ottoman ear and tongue, just as Constantinople had been renamed to Istanbul, its churches converted to mosques.

Because of these circumstances, the Turkish leader was a bit euphoric as he reclined in his tent sipping coffee, an exotic elixir unknown outside the Eastern world, from a delicate cup with a gold-lined rim which had been made especially for him by Chinese experts. Having just finished a meal of parrot tongue, peacock brains and a freshly killed lamb from his own herd, brought from south of the Black Sea in wagons, for the exertion of walking made the meat tough, he stretched and yawned.

He reclined on a red rug woven in India amidst his many pillows from the finest Turkish silk. The two voluptuous dancers, identical twins, who entertained him, were slaves from Georgia, personally picked from hundreds of women for their lithe and curvaceous beauty. They danced for their master adorned only in a golden silk patch to cover their pubic areas, with thin bands of golden chain holding the material in place, highlighting the feminine form. They clicked their brass finger cymbals as they moved, gyrating and twirling to the beat set by the three musicians who accompanied them, and all for the sole pleasure of the Grand Vizier. Gold powder as fine as dust covered their cheeks and buttocks. The master smiled as they twirled their breasts in time with the music, all four swinging in a synchronized pattern. He loved their aroma, for each had been anointed with the rare and costly frankincense, which was known to be the oil with which the crucified Christian god had been anointed. His women were worth at least ten horses but he would not part with them until they showed signs of age, whereby with a snap of a finger he would replace them as easily as bodyguards, cooks and horses.

Puffing lightly on his water pipe he began to dose. *One must enjoy these occasions,* he thought. *Life is good, attainment of Paradise uncertain.* His plan had almost reached fruition. His enemy, the Polish king, was too old and fat to mount a horse much less a campaign. This was the sole infidel who had ever halted a Turkish onslaught consistently. There was no strong enemy leader to emerge after Sobieski, for the Christian infidels to flock around. First, he would be victorious in Vienna, something the great Suleiman the Magnificent had failed to accomplish in 1529, and then on to Cracow and finally Rome, where the bastion of Christianity would soon be under the sword of the Crescent. Yes, this Vienna, it has always been our 'Red Apple.' And we will soon bite into it. For 30,000 troops now fought and dug their way into Vienna and 90,000 protected these troops.

He it is Who had sent His messenger with the Guidance and the religion of truth, that he may make it dominant over all religion however much the idolaters may be averse to it.

At that exact moment, over two hundred miles northwest of Vienna, thunder echoed through a mountain pass south of Opava, Silesia, sending all wildlife within the narrow pass on a stampede. Even the larger predators – wolves, lynx, wildcat, red fox and brown bear bolted from the ominous clamor. A myriad of birds circled overhead, shaken from the trees by the vibrations, seeking safety in the sky, hovering and gliding above the din.

Ten archers appeared first, each held bows in their left hands and several arrows in their right. They scanned the land before them for any sign of enemy forces. Then, a lone horseman appeared, maintaining a near-driven pace, shared the trail with deer, rabbit, and nocturnal fox as they scampered in terror, fleeing before the rumbling mass of man and equine that followed. He wore a 3/4ths length traveling joupan with an eagle, symbol of Poland's love of freedom, embroidered on his right chest, a cross, symbol of Poland's faith, embroidered on his left. He rode a bay Arab mare and carried a szabla, secured to his saddle, engraved with the words: *Bogu Jedynemu Chwala*, "Praise the one God". There was little to distinguish him from the numerous Polish horsemen in tow, except perhaps for his expression, a look of calmness mixed with a certain resolve. It was the look of a man who knew what he had to do and was ready to give all in its service.

Moving to a two-point position, as his horse leapt over a fallen sapling lying in his path, man and mount landed softly, riding out of the woods and into a seemingly endless prairie. A retinue of thousands followed closely behind: winged hussars in front, then pancerni, dragoons and foot soldiers. The horse soldiers riding shoulder to shoulder, crying out *Vivat Sobieski! Vitat Joannes Rex!* scaring up deer and wolf before them. Predator and prey found themselves running side by side, each fleeing in desperation from the barrage of Polish horsemen. For a time, it appeared man and nature had joined and rode together in relief of Vienna.

Kara Mustafa's contented reveries would have turned to violent hysterics if he had known the only opponent he feared, the one he deemed too old to fight, the one man who could construct a powerful alliance and lead it, was at that moment riding directly at Mustafa's position, his intent to end not only the siege but the threat of further invasion for all time.

Chapter 46

On their way to explore the mountain pass at Ciezsyn, to determine its feasibility as both a path to relieve Vienna or an invasion route suitable for Turk or Tatar, the Royal Guardsmen and Bolek rode at a faster than usual pace to cover the sixty kilometers from the Radok farm to the well-traveled mountain pass to the southwest. Riding near a large, ornate, well-kept manor house with an imposing tower topped by a wooden red onion spire with hammered shining copper, the group decided to rest their horses and themselves. Obviously a wealthy estate, judging by the large number of pigs, goats and horses, several outbuildings and well-tended fields.

Czesław had shot a few rabbits, and the five companions wanted to purchase some bread and vegetables to add to his planned *bigos*, a hunter's stew. The mood was anticipatory, mouths watering, and laughter abounding, until Czesław stopped his horse in his tracks, his comrades promptly following suit.

Other than a few scurrying chickens and geese, there was no activity around, no sign of people. The riders spread apart, ready to respond to anything, dismounting and walking their horses slowly toward the impressive manor house. Priest approached the entrance. A lanky, clean-shaven man appeared, holding a musket, taking two cautious steps forward before shouldering the weapon and leaning forward.

"That's far enough," he said, the musket aimed squarely at Priest's chest. "You are not welcome here."

"We are the king's Royal Guardsmen." Priest replied. "Point your musket elsewhere before you get yourself into trouble."

"I said you are not welcome here."

Czesław's hand sought his bow as three more muskets poked their barrels through the open manor-house windows.

"The muskets behind you tremble with fear," Priest said, as

calmly as if he had been in idle conversation. "And there is one chance in two your musket will misfire. If you do not lower it immediately, I will slice your arms from your shoulders!"

The man frowned, weighed his options and reluctantly lowered his weapon, signaling those behind him to do the same. "We want nothing to do with any of you, whether brigands, Cossacks or cavalry."

"I am here to protect you, ordered by the king himself."

"We do not require your protection."

"We are travelers in need of food," Priest said. "We seek Christian charity."

"Bring food," the man called out. Within a few tense moments, a servant came running from the house, her apron full of cabbage, garlic and beets.

"We will not bother you again, ever," Priest said, accepting what she offered him. "Enjoy your frail cocoon."

When the five horsemen were out of musket-shot range, a scowling Priest turned in the saddle and dumped the vegetables on the dirt road.

"Bah! I have seen this in the cities," Priest said to his comrades. "Poland was once based on God's law, on family. Now life is lived for comfort, for shiny objects. Each man is for himself only. The spirit is choked. Now, I see this in the rural areas. A mighty plague is upon us."

With that, Priest winced and prodded Mieszko riding away at a trot, as was his habit when disturbed.

"Why is he so upset by one ignoramus?" Bolek asked Piotr.

"The lord of the manor thinks more of his comfort and security than he does for his fellow man. In a sense, he slays his brother."

A blank stare from Bolek prompted more from Piotr.

"A government only serves those in power, not the people, and this is generally acceptable to most. They want protection, certainty. Freedom is a burden to many. Choice can be difficult, and mistakes have consequences. Let us put these things on the shoulders of our leaders. Our leaders are politicians. These men deal with matters of self-interests. States fail, our illustrious Saint Augustine shows us, because people fail. People fail because they love the wrong things. If a people are evil, the expression of their will in their democratic government will be evil."

"This cannot be so." Bolek said.

"Say it plainly," Czesław complained.

"As comforts grow our souls decay. As government grows our dependence breeds moral compromise. Those under that shiny spire back there crow with wealth and comfort; a culture of overindulgence. Priest sees us not only locked in religious wars, political and economic wars but a war within our own Polish society. Without a belief in the dignity of each soul, we will soon be defenseless in our campaigns. We have spent the last century acting as savages in Europe."

"That is your idea of speaking plainly," Czesław said.

Bolek spoke a statement that was part question. "If we lose virtue and think only of ourselves and our individual needs and deny Christian charity to others, our souls will wither and then so too Poland."

"Now that's plain speech, Piotr."

"Very good, Highlander," Piotr beamed. "Once you are back at Mass at home, Father Czarnota will give his sermon, and you will know him to be a wise man."

"True freedom binds one to following just rules," Bolek said, as if working it out in his head.

"So now you see our constitution is not founded on the illusion of emancipation for all, but on the limitations of those in power."

"And this is what you mean when you say the greatest of all paradoxes is that true freedom limits man."

"An apple for the student today, Góralu. The Age of Faith kept us from Reason; the Age of Reason keeps us from Faith. We shall again find the balance, I pray, but Priest is impatient."

"Why?"

"Perhaps for his own salvation."

"This lord here is in a prison of his own making. I spit on him," Tadek said.

"Can we at least pick up the vegetables," Czesław asked.

It took ten minutes for the riding companions to catch up with Priest. The steel-colored clouds laden with water, promised rain before sunset. The dry prairie grasses would drink; snow would blanket more of the distant peaks, eventually feeding the streams then the mighty rivers of Poland.

The five horsemen, rode as if without purpose, allowing the gentle motion of their mounts to sway their bodies, raising little dust on the wide expanse of grassland.

Neither could remember exactly how it began, but the consensus reached after a lively bout of the vodkie razor dance put the blame firmly on the shoulders of Tadek and Piotr. With no conversation and only an occasionally cry of a hawk, Tadek began goading Piotr, who lagged far behind the others, yelling insults at him for slowing down the patrol. He questioned Piotr's lineage.

This, of course, prompted the master horseman to proceed to the front of the pack while compelling Hector to perform some prancey-dancey footwork right next to Tadek's horse, Parabellum, declaring Hector was able to move faster in reverse than Parabellum was capable of achieving forward. Tadek laughed this off, but when Piotr asked how Tadek trained Parabellum to share his gassy constitution, Tadek deftly maneuvered his well-rested horse around Hector and sped off at a hefty canter. Priest, obviously thankful for a distraction to raise him out of his moody contemplations, gave a battle cry and followed Tadek's lead, as did Czesław, then Bolek and finally Piotr.

The quintet whooped as madmen suddenly possessed with a fever, raising sound and dust on a mute prairie. Galloping through the sea of knee-high grasses the world-weary company now raced with the wind as young spirits, effortlessly scaling small knolls only to hurtle down them with increased speed. Once they reached level ground, the men were no longer in command for the horses now knew the game and were in competition with each other, giant heads rocking back and forth, eyes bulging, enlarged nostrils snorting, the wind streaming through their manes, legs extended to their limits, man and animal moving full-out at an exhilarating pace.

"Where is the finish line?" Czesław shouted, his voice barely audible through wind racing past ears.

"First to water his horse in the Rhine," Priest called out in jest, as twenty galloping hooves pounded the earth and raised a trail of dust. Bolek, who held his own atop Quo Vadis, was not the only rider wearing a boyish smile. While he knew well some difficult decisions were before him, those were distant as if the mighty wind has pushed them to the back of his mind.

Chapter 47

That evening, as the group sat around a coaling campfire after a dinner of rabbit stew with some vegetables and spices purchased from a small nearby farm, the patrol unit agreed they had crossed the imaginary finish line together. The horses had been treated to some purchased high-protein forage, a rare treat, and groomed, hooves picked and tails combed and they now stood contented, near a grove of willows. Priest took out his violin and picked out a mournful song he had first heard in the Slovak south, with Piotr doing a decent job of matching Priest note for note on his flute, with Bolek nodding when pleased with his protégé's efforts or frowning on an errant note.

After the concert, they could see firelight to the north, which Bolek confirmed was the city of Szczyrk. Below lay one of the few breaks in the mountain walls, a possible invasion route which Priest and his company were charged with scouting.

"This is as far from my farm as I have ever been," Bolek said.

"You fear for your mother and sister, Góralu, as do I," Czesław said.

"I would like to head home," Bolek said.

"The boy is right, Priest," Piotr said. "To attack the Radok farm again, if even for revenge, is possible."

"This is good counsel," Priest said. "Perhaps you should head home, Góralu."

"Tadek," Piotr whispered, rising quickly. "Something is not right. Hector grows edgy."

"Up a tree, Czesław," Priest commanded, his head cocked, ears alert for something still unheard to Bolek. The giant bowman nimbly scrambled up a thick-branched pine and disappeared into darkness, the only sign of his presence a few swaying branches.

As Bolek's shoe scraped dirt to extinguish the fire, Priest raised his hand to halt the action.

"No need. Our presence is known," Priest said through a

broad smile. "Use your ears, gentlemen. Thunder approaches from the east and it is not coming from the sky."

A faint rumbling was indeed on the wind. But before speculation on its origin could be voiced, a lone rider appeared from between the shadows of two large pine trees, confidently sauntering directly into the camp.

"You are getting careless, Priest," the intruder declared, "allowing me to get this close."

An arrow hissed past Bolek's ear, lodging in the ground inches from the front hooves of the stranger's horse, forcing the rider to steady his mount.

"I should have known," the stranger chuckled as he dismounted with an open hand extended toward Priest. "I assume the fabled blue bow is aimed squarely at my back?"

"Not any more, Brother Lukasz," Czesław replied as he leapt from the tree. "I had you in my sight at twenty paces and recognized you at ten, merely waiting for Priest's orders."

"Come, my friends," Priest challenged his comrades. "Don't you remember Lukasz from Wadowice?"

"Of course!" Piotr replied, offering his hand also. "It was he who saved us during the fight at the inn with those Cossack braggarts two years passed. Well met."

"So Poland rides to Vienna," Priest said, offering this old acquaintance a log seat at the fire.

"Yes," Lukasz said.

"Góralu, meet Lukasz Kazimierz, scout, winged hussar retainer and patron of beer and women." "Bolesław Radok. Pleased to meet you."

"I forget you have another name than Góralu," Priest said, chuckling.

"A Góral highlander?" Lukasz replied, "An auspicious sign. Your people saved our King Casimir during the Deluge. I also hear your can drink as well as you fight."

"And we'll soon have some of both," Priest responded.

"Drink," passing a demijohn to their guest. "What news, Lukasz? What task are you set to?"

"I scout for the left flank all night," Lukasz replied, refusing the drink with a raised open palm.

"This explains the approaching thunder. A reconnaissance division, no doubt." Piotr said.

"God's blood man, where have you been?" Lukasz exclaimed, suddenly sitting up straight. "All of Poland rides. Three separate forces move south and west. Seven thousand of us now ride through Ciezsyn Pass and beyond. We moved on the fifteenth of last month."

"Tell us all," Piotr said, leaning forward to miss nothing.

"Nearly a fortnight ago the king ordered Grand Hetman Sieniawski to assemble his armies in Cracow. On August second, the king arrived at our capitol at the head of Grand Hetman Jablonowski's force. It was a sight to behold, my friends. Twenty-seven thousand men and twice this number in support personnel swelled the city. Sieniawski set out toward Silesia with twenty thousand. Later, the king rode at the head of the main force, with 8000 carts and carriages loaded with supplies in tow. The Germans marched toward Vienna on the same day. At Tarnowskie Gory, Sobieski split the army to join in Olomuniec. A three-fold advance will limit the impact of provisioning on the towns. Sieniawski rides by way of Biala, to here at Cieszyn then on toward Opawa. His Majesty rides at the head of 3000 cavalry in a forced march to join the army you see below. By the end of this month, we will all join at Nikolsburg. Then drive on to Vienna.

"Then it is time," Piotr said.

"It has been time for 150 years, as you well know," Lukasz replied. "These Muslims desire to extinguish the flame of our Christian faith. For a year, the Ottoman Sultan has been amassing a force to besiege Europe. His troops began moving in April, once the spring rains were done and the ground solid. They reached

Belgrade in May, crushing everything in their path, razing whole towns, taking slaves, raping, plundering the fields, taking all livestock, burning what they could not carry."

"What force do the Turks field?" Tadek asked.

"One hundred and forty thousand," the scout replied, forcing a moment of silence. "Some say two hundred thousand. On May 13, in Belgrade, the Ottoman Sultan Mehmed IV, proclaimed a jihad. He formally passed Islam's most holy standard, that of Muhammad, to his Grand Vizier, Kara Mustafa and marched across Hungary to Vienna along the western side of the Danube."

"I have fought against this Mustafa before," Priest said. "Kara means black in Turkish. A nickname he embraces. He has been called the beast of the Apocalypse. It speaks to his nature and not his complexion."

"So his will is the will of his people, then," Tadek stated as he prodded the fire with a thick stick. "Whether the Turkish people care or not."

"Vienna was prepared," Lukasz said, his audience leaning ever forward in rapt attention. "Her garrison has removed every obstacle in front of the great walls, clearing the land of every-thing for nearly two miles; all the houses, barns, any structure to give the enemy cover, gone. The invaders face a barren and scorched earth to the south and west of the city."

"The fortifications?" Priest asked.

"The holy city is well-protected to the north by the Danube, and the swampy land there and to the east. Those bastions of the city walls and the ravelins are in excellent repair. Moats, scarps and counterscarps are in place, leaving no cover for any who approach. An attack from the north would be suicidal. The Scottish Gate is secure. The Weiner Wald and the Hofburg gates stand strong, as always. The main Turkish force drives at the Lobl Fort, right at the Castle. But we have palisades and ramparts in place and any attack on these walls expose their army to slaughter from multiple angles."

"It must be a sight to behold," Priest sighed. "The ancient city besieged by countless thousands of men and their surrounding pitched tents."

"Yes. Mustafa pitched his tent prominently, for all to see. Scouts and couriers have told us those tents cover almost all of the ten miles of open space. His most elite soldiers, the janissary infantry, the deadliest of musketeer sharp shooters, face the walls for siege and the Spahis light cavalry raid the smaller towns and villages in all directions, killing everything before them. There is more smoke than air, more blood than water now, we hear."

"But the city still stands strong?" Czesław asked. "Hearts pound with resolve?"

"For now. But Mustafa's slaves labor day and night digging trenches, inching ever closer to the walls and gates. Their sappers, the mine experts, aided by French engineers, ignite their bombs under the walls. Others attempt to poison the city's water; some catapult stink bombs over the walls to spread disease. They drive our own Christian brothers and sisters, slaves of the Sultan, before their army, forcing us to kill our own people in our defense. It is heartbreaking. Vienna is desperate for relief."

"And it comes," Priest said, nodding his head toward the valley at the ever growing sound of rolling thunder.

"Aye, but time is critical," Lukasz cautioned.

"How many cannon do they sport?" Tadek asked.

"Their cannons are modest in size and few in number, no more than three hundred and not a serious threat at this time. It is not understood why Mustafa does not move. A full assault would surely gain access to the city."

"Mustafa lets his greed usurp his caution," Piotr said. "If the city falls in violence, the rules of plunder will be in effect. Many invaders will become rich, for the loot is shared. But if Vienna agrees to terms, the riches go to Mustafa and his sultan."

"But if those walls are breached, Vienna will share the same fate as did Constantinople," Lukasz said. "The sword. Perchtoldsdorf in southern Austria opened its city gates to Mustafa's force for the same promise Vienna was given. All were slaughtered. Vienna must not fall."

"Not while I draw breath," Tadek said.

"Well said, Tadek," Lukasz continued. "So we ride en masse. Never in my experience has an army moved so fast. We cover over thirty miles a day, stopping only to rest the horses and to fill our canteens. We tie ourselves to the saddle and catnap when we can. We force the wagons to keep the same pace."

"What of our troops in Vienna?" Piotr asked. "Who leads the resistance?"

"Charles IV Leopold, the duke of Lorraine and brother-in-law to the Emperor, has infantry in the city to protect the walls, as well as a sizable force garrisoned north of the city in Leopoldstadt. He is an honorable soldier."

"And the Emperor?" Czesław asked.

"He has left the city with many needed troops as his guard," Lukasz muttered. "He lounges safely in Prussia, at Linz, at last word. Over one hundred miles from Vienna."

All smiled at Tadek's imitation of a chicken, the sound of a coward.

"Who commands the garrison?" Priest asked.

"The German, Count Ernst Rüdiger von Starhemberg."

"Leopold made a wise choice there," Tadek said.

"He has no more than 11,000 troops, but veterans all. His artillery is concentrated at the heart of the attackers. Firefighters put out the incendiary bombs. We have three thousand Poles inside under Lubomirski. Starhemberg runs sorties outside the walls at the few opportune times. Fifty thousand Viennese residents have fled and only five thousand volunteer citizens are left, and fight as they can."

"It must be a hell within the city for the people." Bolek said.

"The Turks arrived in early July, high campaign season. The

shelling commenced on the fourteenth. When our king posed this same question you have, Bolek, about the status of people, through official courier correspondence, the emperor replied 'all trade has ceased. Salt no longer moves west and wine does not go east. Vienna starves.'"

Priest shook his head in disgust. Tadek spat into the fire.

"As of this morning, our latest report stated the city's resolve weakens. The cavalry is already eating their horses, some residents even trap mice. Lorraine continues to engage in small skirmishes against the Tatars to keep them off guard, but the shelling continues. The Imperial Palace lies in ruins."

"Sobieski marches to Austria and leaves Poland unguarded," Priest noted.

And I am here leaving my family unguarded.

"The king has sent a stern warning to *Imre Thököly*, Magyar leader of the Hungarians, not to move north. He warns if one straw of Polish wheat is burnt, the king will come with his hussars and burn *Thököly* and his family alive in their own house."

"May God bless Sobieski," Czesław said proudly.

"So Emperor Leopold's so-called Catholic war against the Protestants finally pushed the Hungarians into revolt and into the arms of the Muslim Porte," Piotr said, shaking his head.

"Worse news. The French king, Louis XIV, takes advantage of the siege and attacks Alsace in Germany."

"Why would the French king wish to see Europe invaded?" Bolek asked.

"To weaken the Austrian Hapsburg Emperor," Lukasz replied, turning his head away in shame. "Our diplomats tell us this Sun King, as he is called, is of the mind both Hapsburg and Turkish forces will be weakened, regardless of the outcome. The better then for him."

"Those damned self-serving idiots!" Priest shouted. "The Ottomans strike at the heart of Europe. To control Vienna is to control access to both Eastern and Western Europe."

"Madness," Piotr said, "like the man sinking deeper into quicksand but unable to let loose of his gold."

"And the news is still worse," Lukasz added. "In exchange for the Sultan granting *Thököly* the power to rule the Hungarians and the 'Kingdom of Vienna', he and his people have submitted to Islam."

"Submission to a foreign god in exchange for power and wealth. He sells his soul. And his people's," Piotr said.

Now Bolek could feel the very ground trembling beneath his feet and a steadily growing roar in his ears.

"Twenty thousand Polish crusaders ride to liberate," Lukasz said, acknowledging the rumble of the approaching army with a pointed finger. "And more coming."

"What of the Austrians?" Priest demanded.

"The Germans and Austrians number close to fifty thousand. Good men, all."

"Germans." Tadek repeated. "With Austrians."

"Another pact of mutual benefit," Lukasz replied. "Prince Georg Friedrich of Waldeck, leads 19,000 Franconian, Swabian and Bavarian troops. John George III, Elector of Saxony leads 9,000 brave souls also."

"Piotr," Bolek whispered. "All these foreign names, these alliances, these quarrels make my head spin. Do you understand all of this?"

"Saint Augustine said all of world history is simply a battle between two forms of love. Love of self to the point of destroying the world, and love of others to the point of renouncing oneself."

"So the invaders are the Muslims, and they seek to destroy the world?"

"In its current form, yes. Those in power in the East want the entire world to submit to their ways. They long to control, to set iron rules. First violent force, then control. Then, madness. One man in power. One man usurping God. It is evil incarnate. It is the old story."

"How did this all begin?" Bolek begged. "What kept my father in the saddle so long?"

"The one universal Catholic Church was cleaved in half many decades ago. You became either a German Protestant or a Roman Catholic, and this was decided for you primarily by where you lived within Europe. Catholic France fiddles in German politics and sides with Protestants to weaken Germany. Catholic Austria persecutes Hungary under the guise of persecuting Protestants. What he really seeks is to unite all of Hungary under his rule. Islam now stokes the fire again, desiring to tear down Catholic Austria and Spain. The politicians of each nation hatch cunning schemes to gain a stronger foothold in the old game of king of the hill. All this goes on under the false flags of religion. King Sobieski believes we have a right to preserve our faith, and he will soon ride into the gates of hell with no thought for himself."

"Look down there, Góralu," Czesław said, "the old army rides below toward the Ciezsyn Pass."

"Such a thing has never happened, Góralu," Piotr explained. "Our king has always fought with his own men, his own funds, and his own flesh and blood, always outnumbered by Poland's enemies. Now he rides at the combined head of the greatest cavalry in the world. This Polish roar is made by the most experienced of soldiers, veterans all, courageous and experienced men."

"We will meet Lorraine's cavalry at Stockerau," Lukasz continued. "The plan is to ride north of Vienna, cross the Danube at Tulln, and deal with the 25,000 Crimean Tatars our scouts tell us are massed there. They cover Mustafa's south and east."

"How the world conspires against us," Piotr proclaimed. "We must face these Tatars as we cross the Danube before scaling the mountains."

"The Crimeans have no love for Mustafa. They will bolt at the first clash," Priest said. "Note, Góralu, many of these thousands we speak of do not have the belly for this war. These men who ride past us now, most certainly do."

"And we have two pontoon bridges already built and will assemble them once we arrive in Tulln," Lukasz added. "From there, we will follow the Danube southeast in three detachments, advancing into the *Wienerwald*, the famous giant oak- and beech-treed Vienna Woods. With God's blessing, we estimate our arrival on September 9th, and we will engage on the 13th, moving down from the Kahlenburg Mountain, north of the city."

"That approach terrain is not horse friendly," Piotr noted.

"Which is why Mustafa rules it out as a point of threat and does not defend it properly," Lukasz replied. "The news that Sobieski rides to Vienna's defense at the head of a united crusader army has apparently not reached Mustafa's ears yet."

"Some vodka?" Piotr offered their guest.

"Thank you, no. If I do not report back within a certain time an alarm will go up, and our men will assume the worst. You do not want a large group of our own riding down on us, do you?"

"Understood," Priest said.

"When do you ride?" Lukasz asked Priest in return. "The Royal Guardsmen are needed now more than ever."

"Now," Priest answered, with a furled brow.

"Look down to the valley gentlemen," Lukasz said as he mounted his horse, "Soon the Polish cavalry, both light and hussar, flocks of pancerni, dragoons, generals and magnates all led by our esteemed Hetman Sieniawski will appear. We ride through the night with burning torches to light the way. *Dowvizenia*, comrades. Glory for God and Poland awaits you in Vienna." Lukasz saluted respectfully before disappearing into the forest.

"They ride to face one hundred and forty thousand Muslims," Bolek said, anticipating the sight of the Polish army. "If the Muslims were each a grain of wheat it would fill many bags."

"Rumors always bloat an army's size," Piotr cautioned.

"We have perhaps fifteen thousand battle-trained veterans riding below," Priest said.

"Pray it is more like twenty-five thousand," Piotr replied.

"We will be facing janissaries, the elite Turkish infantry." Tadek said.

"Turkish in name only," Priest replied. "It is an army made up of conscripts and slaves, since they've enslaved every fifth Christian boy from the Balkans, forcing them to submit to Allah, while training them to be servants, with no will of their own. They are not allowed to have wives or children. The practice is called *Devshirme*."

"The true Muslim cavalry, the spahis, are more like our pancerni – light armored," Tadek said. "They will be there attempting to show up their rivals, the Christian slave Janissaries."

"They are only guaranteed paradise if they kill enemies of Islam or die in battle," Piotr said.

"Are the spahis as good as we pancerni?"

"Yes," Tadek replied. "They know the secret Czeslaw has taught you. The best time to release an arrow on horseback is when all four hooves are off the ground."

"But they are meaner than our pancerni for all vodka and spirits are forbidden to them," Tadek replied. "And celibate, too. I get angry too when I have not been with a woman and . . ."

"Enough!" Priest shouted. "The truth is always an obstacle to power. Lies spread about our foes give us false superiority. Do you know what the Muslims say of our beliefs? Our god was an executed peasant. We celebrate his death by drinking his blood and eating his flesh. Those are not lies. But does this capture the true essence of Our Lord? If you close your mouths and open your eyes, you will see a sight reserved for few. Holy War."

With twilight already fading the landscape to gray and black, and the manmade thunder of approaching horses coupled with the fire-lit glow from hundreds of torches, all eyes were locked on the valley before them. Bolek's memory went to an image of molten steel being poured into a mold to make a sword blade. First a cloud of hazy dust, rising nearly to the tips of the trees, illuminated in ghostly, fire-lit shadows. A gust of wind moved the clouds and the moon revealed colorful pennants as legions of mounted soldiers rode out stretching the length of the valley below. They rode in columns of ten men across, all at a healthy canter.

So fast. How is it possible to keep such a pace for an extended period? And over such terrain?

Piotr read his mind. "See how they rise and fall in the saddle and match the rhythm of the horses? It saves both rider and horse from bouncing and jarring. Though our horses are bred for stamina, posting is the secret which allows us to travel thirty miles a day and more. No Turk, Cossack or the European army can move that far that fast."

Chapter 48

Bolek gazed in awe at the spectacle below. Here came the defenders of Poland, the mighty spirit of his country, those who were first to fight, the spear's tip against subjugation and terror. Goose bumps rose on his legs and arms as he spied the crosses visible on the pennons. And then there were eagles. Eagles of gold and silver and copper raised high and proudly on standards. Freedom. God and Freedom. Such Power! Such Glory! My country!

"There!" Piotr shouted, pointing toward the front of the center column. "See the standard there? There comes Hetman Sieniawski, God's hammer. Góralu, your father served with distinction under him. And was known to him."

Bolek was able to pick out the leader despite the great mass of riders who flowed like a raging river below. Hetman Nicholas Sieniawski, riding a well-muscled jet black Arab, sat his horse proudly, every inch a leader, with back straight, chest out, sitting his horse as if the two were one.

"There rides the most famous army in Poland," Czesław said, scratching his red beard. "Victors over countless Cossacks, Tatars and Turks encounters. They allow Poland to breathe freely."

"And he rides under the first true Polish king in our lifetime," Tadek added. "He rides for Jan III Sobieski, who in turn, rides for us and our god."

Bolek's heart swelled in his chest, for there, among thousands of warriors who forged through the valley without end, rode the man under whom his father and father before him had served, a man whose name he had heard praised throughout his life. And this extraordinary military leader and the forces he led, would soon unite with two more armies, one under Hetman Stanislas Jablonowski and one under the King Sobieski, the hero of Slobodyszcze, Podhaic, Kalish, Chocim, Lemberg, and countless skirmishes.

"To King Jan and Queen Marysieńka," Bolek had heard his father and grandfather say many times as they stood together and offered a toast at dinner. He remembered his parents, standing with cups raised, smiling proudly. And suddenly, here he was, young Bolesław Radok himself, of the same stock, the same family, the oldest male of the line, watching the very heart and soul of all that was Poland ride past him.

My father never abandoned me or our family. Father fought to protect our family. Father sacrificed all for me and Kasia and was away from Mother for so long. Still, their love endured. They kept my sister and me safe. Father forgive my ignorance. I have never been abandoned nor unprotected. This army of my fathers and brothers sacrifice all for the ignorant, the foolish, for those who care for nothing but themselves. All these men fear but do not run. They dream of family, of comfort but do not run. They ride for Poland. This is courage. God's love. God's truth.

"We leave you here, Góralu," Priest pronounced, hand to Bolek's shoulder. "Duty calls. Once Vienna is freed, and it will be, if God lets any of us here survive we will return to rout the brigands with you. I will pray for your safety."

"You think me a soulless coward, Priest? You see me fleeing back to the safety of my bed?"

"Think, Góralu," Tadek said. "I see your thoughts. But you will leave your mother and sister unprotected, the brigands unpunished and free to do their will."

"What does all this mean?" Priest asked.

"You are blind to your own redemption, Priest," Piotr said with a laugh. "Poland has just gained one more sword."

"And a deadly one it is," Czesław said, embracing Tadek.

"I serve God, my country, my family," Bolesław Radok said, pulling his szabla from its sheath and raising it to heaven. "Gentlemen, I offer you one more blade."

With glistening eyes, Priest drew his own szabla crossing it with his protégé's, the other's quickly joining suit with their szablas raised to heaven.

"Wait!" Tadek barked. "War is a wedding, boy. The wolves are your bridesmaids. Your szabla is your Best Man. Your bride is Death."

"Then on with the ceremony, gentlemen," Bolek hissed, "for I long to embrace my bride."

"Well said," Tadek, Piotr and Czesław shouted in unison.

"Hold!" Priest shouted. "Some questions remain. Can this Tatra Eagle ride? Can he shoot? Has he skill with a szabla? Does he love God and Poland above all?"

"Aye, Priest," the trio replied, again in unison.

"Bolesław Radok," Priest said in a deep, formal voice after clearing his throat, "as a captain in the King's Royal Guard, I offer you a commission in our brigade. I ask you to ride with us as equal, a Royal Guardsman of Jan III Sobieski. Do you accept this challenge?"

Bolek squinted, holding back tears.

"It is no challenge, but an honor, gentlemen."

Five more riders rode into liberating force, in like single mindedness, riding as one, determined to put a final end to one hundred and fifty years of invasion and confrontation within Poland. The fate of Christian Europe hung in the balance. Cross would soon meet Crescent at sword's point.

Chapter 49

An Ottoman Turkish Prayer

Eternal God and creator of all things, and thou O Mahomet, his sacred and divine prophet. We beseech thee let us not dread the Christians, who are so mean and silly to rely on a crucified god. By the power of thy right hand, so strengthen ours that we may surround this foolish people, on every side, and utterly destroy them. At length fulfill our prayers and put these miscreants into our hands, that we may establish thy throne for ever in Mecca, and sacrifice all those enemies of our most holy religion at thy tomb. Blow us with thy mighty breath like swarms of flies into their quarters, and let the eyes of these infidels bedazzled with the luster of our moon. Consume them with thy fiery darts, and blind them with the dust, which they themselves have raised. Destroy them all in thine anger. Break all their bones in pieces, and consume the flesh and blood of those who defile thy sacrifice, and hang the sacred light of circumcision on their cross. Wash them with showers of many waters, who are so stupid to worship gods they know not: and make their Christ a son to that God who ne're begot him. Hasten therefore their destruction we humbly entreat thee, and blot out their name and religion, which they glory so much in, from off the face of the earth, that they may be no more, who condemn and mock at thy law. Amen.

Chapter 50

On a clear and warm day in early September, 1683, a triad avalanche of thundering brownish clouds became one as three Polish cavalries merged, flowing westward as one. The dust choked and blinded, covering rich and poor, foot soldier and knight, horse and mule, uniforms, badges of rank, and equipment. Everything took on the same ghostly hue. This immense thunderhead would soon rendezvous with an equally powerful and opposing thunderhead as two mighty empires, one Muslim, one Christian, would soon collide within the fog of war.

Five of King Jan Sobieski Royal Guardsmen rode as one within the belly of the cloud. Bolek, his eyes burning, his throat parched, cursed as he squirmed in his saddle.

"What's this, Tadek?" Priest asked. "Is not war full of riches, glory and honor? Shiny medals? Góralu grumbles and frowns."

"Our highlander whines like a stuck piglet." Tadek replied.

"Why does my bottom hurt so?" Czesław teased in a falsetto voice.

"Why are there so many piles of manure in the path and poor Quo Vadis slips and slides?" Piotr added in a forced nasal tone.

"I only complain about the wisdom of our position," Bolek *snapped* back. "If we are the king's guards why do we not guard the king?"

"We soon will," Priest replied.

"What if the news our king riding toward Vienna precedes him?" Bolek shouted over the surrounding din. "What if Mustafa sends a wolf pack of his fabled archers and they sit even now high in the trees ahead, awaiting our king?"

Priest tugged on his mustache and frowned for a few seconds then shouted. "Move to the side for the King's Royal Guardsmen!"

Bolek smiled as the five comrades galloped outward from the thick living column of flesh and machine.

Even at the swift trot, they rode for nearly two hours to reach the army's front. They passed foot soldiers, camp followers, wagons and carts pulled by powerful draft horses, those in turn pulling everything from precious food, to critical fodder, to saddles, long lances, horseshoes and every instrument of war and maintenance. Bolek's eyes took in all, marveling first hand at what it took to move an immense military troop into a campaign.

An army moved not only on its stomach but on the collective experiences of veterans of past campaigns. This had been a trade for millennia. This ever-southwest-bound force moved as one gigantic fighting machine unto itself. Both strategy and tactic were essential for a successful campaign. Bolek could see someone experienced was responsible for each of the inner workings of this living force. Each man had expertise; each man counted. Retainers, servants and peasants, often with wives included, drove wagons, carts and mule trains at a furious pace. Wheelwrights by the score repaired wagons with broken wheel or axles, while others goose and pig greased the moving parts. Teams of men on their own initiatives assembled to push wagons through mud or to cut and haul trees blocking a road.

If a horse fell ill, became injured or lame, it was abandoned. Bolek lost count at thirty as he rode past a herd of these hapless animals grazing casually at the side of the road, thinking themselves at rest and lucky. He learned later from camp talk most of the poor mounts, knowing nothing but life with the army, trotted meekly at the hind of the campaign, desperately attempting to keep up with the only life they knew. They often ended up as meat for the troops or prey for wolf and bear.

In many ways, it was the same for the soldiers, for even the injured and ill were left behind to mend, compassion taking a back seat to the army's goals – relief of Vienna.

Later he learned disease was often a greater killer than combat. Many a battle had been lost, not by poor strategies or tactics or a lack of willingness to prevail, but from the dreaded dysentery, which could claim men by the armful. All this swirled past the naïve highlander as he trotted toward what he now felt was his destiny.

He fully understood the need for haste, but he did not want to be tired when he went into battle for the first time, for he was not simply weary now, he was exhausted. Lashed to and nodding in the saddle, head bobbing like waving wheat; he fought the line between being awake and asleep, having not stopped for over ten hours. The sweaty lather on his horse was an inch thick and spreading over her chest, her dry tongue dangling loosely from her parched mouth. He knew her thirst. But he would not shame himself and stop, nor would he embarrass the Royal Guardsmen, to which he now belonged.

The dust abated somewhat as the main Polish force slowed to welcome various contingent armies at predetermined locations within the Austrian Empire. His riding companions schooled Bolek in the rich and proud history of these often exotic groups which did not ride at the back of the main force, but next to it— each committed to the impending mission, but separate and distinct from the other as the blended force snaked ever-westward. *E pluribus unum*, Piotr said.

So many different flags and pennants, pennons, emblems, coats of arms, armor styles, clothing and equipment appeared as the army swelled steadily in rank, that Bolek's felt himself in another world or an unusual dream. Tadek pointed Bolek to his first Cossack banners in the distance, defining a warrior unit by district, clan, number and division of troops and on and on. The Cossack delegation joined as wild-eyed horsemen, shouting curses to any and all as they chugged vodka. For them, this seemed as natural as sport. The Vlach, warriors from west of the Black Sea, came quietly; sitting straight in the saddle, for them, this was serious. The Tatars appeared as rabbits, to Bolek, riding here and there quickly, suspicious of any and all, their eyes darting left and right as if an attack seemed imminent. The heavily armored Polish pancerni units announced their arrivals with drummers and trumpeters, each with unique melody and drumbeat rhythm. Soon Bolek was amid a multitude of strangers from strange lands, with strange customs and languages, but all riding with single-minded purpose.

Bolek's eyes caught those of a Cossack who rode next to him but part of his own contingent. He smiled and nodded in acknowledgement. With that, the Cossack's eyes went wild, kicking his horse with both legs, driving it right at Bolek. Madness was on his face, a scream of a beast on his tongue. Bolek readied himself for anything. At a few paces before impact, the Cossack deftly maneuvered his horse next to Quo Vadis, riding shoulder to shoulder with Bolek. Taking a healthy swig from a demijohn, the Cossack said "There are only three plagues. Typhus, Tatars and Poles." Then taking another swig he spit the mouthful into Bolek's face, momentarily blinding Bolek and burning his eyes.

Before regaining his eyesight, Bolek moved Quo Vadis into action with an unnoticeable pressure from his left toe. The white mare bolted in front of the Cossack horse, stopping it in its tracks and then, with a touch from Bolek's heel, his mount spun to its left, forcing the Cossack horse to stumble, knocking the crazy Cossack from his saddle and into the mud and horse droppings. Bolek looked down at the furious Cossack and spat. The red-faced madman screamed and jumped to his feet, a long dagger pulled from his sash. Three of his comrades spurred their horses, charging straight at Bolek, whose plan was already in his head.

Tadek rolled backwards off his horse's back, recovering with his szabla to the Cossack's throat; his three comrades reined in suddenly, their eyes to Bolek's left where a quick glance revealed Czesław's, Priest's and Piotr's drawn bows, pointing arrows at the three chests. The shamed and cursing Cossack who had challenged Bolek had no choice but to beg for mercy and guide his horse back to the safety of his banner, his boots stomping into the mud puddles in a childish display of temper.

"You bested your first Cossack," Tadek said.

"You saved my life just now."

"No. I saved his."

The pride Bolek felt from Tadek's compliment made his thirst and fatigue disappear for a time, but not enough to keep the exhausted Bolek from nodding off on the trail, dreaming about home, which now seemed a distant place from long ago. Someone was shaking his shoulder and he woke sluggishly. The column had slowed dramatically. He learned they were stopping to gather intelligence from the forward scouts, to wait for stragglers, perform maintenance on wagon and horse and to devise new reconnaissance missions. They could rest until morning. The Royal Guardsmen pulled away from the column to survey their surroundings.

"You expect these men from the flat lands to climb up there?" Bolek asked as he caught his first sight of the faint bluish Austrian Alps in the distance.

"The Turks will be of the same sentiment," Priest replied.

Each man dismounted, leading his horse off for some grazing, before drinking greedily from their water bags.

"To pull cannon over those mountains will take weeks," Bolek said in disbelief as imagined the sloping land ahead.

"We do not have weeks," Priest replied.

"These men are exhausted from forced march and we ask them now to heft iron into the sky," Bolek remarked, thinking aloud of the huge cannons he had passed in the last few days.

"Once the first saber is swung at your neck, Góralu, you will recover your strength with necessity," Tadek said. "We must conquer the mountains to win the right to conquer the Turks."

"We are near the great Danube," Piotr said, "the horses smell it. This means Tulln lies there to our west."

"And Vienna and a swarm of Turks just to our south, there" Tadek said.

"Our engineers are building the pontoon bridges as we speak," Priest said.

"Have you ever crossed a wide river on a horse, Góralu?" Piotr asked.

"It is only water," Bolek replied.

"Well said," Czesław offered. "If we don't fall into the Danube to be swept away by the swift currents, or crushed as we take our cannon up those peaks, then the hard part will be taking them down the other side."

"That is the point where men are killed and bodies crushed," Piotr added. "This is where horses give out and they must be abandoned and later eaten. At some point, you will be too tired to raise your arms and your thighs will burn, yet you must strain against the weight of cannon as you lower yours to the valley floor. If you succeed, you will learn something about your resolve."

"You are knights, why should you labor so?"

"We are knights of Christ," Piotr replied, "and we are no man's better."

"At that moment your will gives out, fellow Guardsmen," Bolek replied, "call to me if you need assistance and I will come, for the mountains are my home. I do not tire in them."

"Pity the Turks," Tadek said," when they meet this demon."

The ride to the banks of the Danube led through a mosquito-infested bog. Bolek overhead a few men discuss the threat of adverse weather, for this was an unusually wet September. Traction was so vital to move an army and the weather could be a fickle friend or foe. It was a common sight along the way to see cursing blacksmiths as they reshod horses, again and again, after the mud sucked off shoes.

"Why are our horses not shod?" Bolek asked Piotr. "All the rest are. And when you captured Quo Vadis you took her shoes off."

"Pooh!" Piotr said in disgust as he watched one smith

massage his aching back, a string of horses lined up in need of his service. "The Turks take their horses off the plains and pamper them in stalls built under tents. The poor beasts stand for hours at a time, motionless, caged against their nature. And as they stand for hours in their own excrement and urine, their hooves become rank with disease, crumbling and causing them to founder in considerable numbers. Thus, the horseshoe. Our horsemen begin to follow this practice also, but it is unnatural. The horses go lame easily. But wild horses are able to run for days without the benefit of iron shoes, are they not?"

Bolek could only nod.

"Which is why our horses go unshod. This is why we let them roam free at night. Do not control your horse, but guide him to acceptance and cooperation. He must learn of us as we must learn of him. Thus, our horses do not submit," Piotr, added with a wink.

Chapter 51

Bolek was unable to hide his awe at his first glimpse of the mighty Danube River. It was more than six widths greater than his own Vistula River. From the shore, he tensed as he noted how fast the water rushed by and did not look forward to having to traverse it on Quo Vadis. But the crossing was surprisingly uneventful due to the superb planning of engineers and the solid pontoon bridges they designed and assembled.

All were on heightened alert and cautious now, for this was the optimal time for the Tatars to attack since once a part of the army was across the river, a third would be engaged in the crossing and a third left waiting to cross, the force would be fragmented and vulnerable, their advantage in numbers markedly diminished. But the expected Tatar attack never came. By late afternoon, nearly 74,000 troops, 27,000 of them Poles, had crossed the Danube without incident. The only thing now standing between the besieging Turks and liberating coalition was a mere fifteen miles through the mountainous Vienna Woods.

Bolek sat upright in his saddle as he rode over his first cobblestone street through the city of Tulln, to the music of clackety-clack hoofs on a stone avenue mixed with the welcoming church bells coupled with those from around the necks of the sheep and goats as the herds were driven off the road by the shepherds to make way for the advancing army. He made a point to smile as he caught the eyes of the awe-struck shepherds, knowing more about the intimate details of their lives than any of them could have ever imagined.

Having never seen anything larger than his own village, entering Tulln was beyond his imagination – exotic, and many things unknown no matter where his eyes fell. It struck him as odd that he was now a soldier in an Austrian city where the construction, the language and the clothes were so strange. It made him proud as he entered the canyon of stone houses on the narrow streets of the city proper. Voices and hoof beats echoed like in his mountains. The liberating force was greeted by the grateful townsfolk lining the road, hanging out from windows, waving handkerchiefs, cheering and clapping, men bowing and women curtseying to those who came to fight the invaders. Mothers with babies on their hips smiled as their precious little ones cried because of all the noise. One beautiful girl, a dark-haired maiden with laughing eyes, held out a single flower to Bolek and his blush matched hers as he leaned down to grasp it. Holding it reverently to his nose, he recalled his beautiful Rozalia. He felt melancholia for his past and yet a burst of resolve to help stop the approaching evil. If the Muslims planned on reaching the girl with the flower, they would have to deal with Bolek first.

Riding deeper into the city, soldiers and laborers, horses and wagons, merchants and onlookers were everywhere, all completely involved in specific tasks. Bolek had never seen so many people in one place. He could hardly believe this disorder could somehow be turned into an orderly army, an army of one purpose, to strike at the heart of evil. So confused. So much urgency. This was all so removed from a safe farm bed or a secluded mountain meadow. He felt trapped within a crowd of humanity. Dutifully following his companions in single file in the blackish water ruts of a muddy road, he could no longer recognize the treed shepherd in him. The two Boleks, the one he was in the mountains and the one he had dreamed to be, were daily becoming strangers to the other.

That night he dreamt of the Rysy Mountain, and the high pristine alpine Morskie Oko Lake he had visited with his father, wishing with all his might to be there now, to be able to wash the dirt and sweat away, and to swim and rest on its peaceful shores. He dreamed, as well, of his own village, its only defense the old church on the hill, famous for its towering wooden steeple, a village where he knew every face and name. The mountain lake would have to wait; it might even never be, for Vienna called to him, by name, for help. Yet another Radok was called to Poland's aid and to wield yet another Polish szabla.

Chapter 52

Before the sun rose over the peaks, Bolek and his comrades followed Priest as he entered the Wienerwald, the fabled Vienna Woods, looking up the mountain known at the Kahlenburg, its mist-covered summit hidden somewhere above them, the last obstacle blocking their way to the relief of Vienna.

"Up and over," Priest said, dismounting.

The Guardsmen handed over their horses to a young camp follower who promised their mounts would reach the top uninjured.

"Why are those men cutting the saplings down?" Bolek asked and they began their upward journey.

"To wedge between the wheels of the cannon so they won't roll back down the steep grades. The saplings will brake the iron monsters."

Bolek became more familiar with this strategy as he became part of a twenty-five-man team to 'adopt' one of the cannons to haul up the mountainside. Heavy ropes were strung around trees, and the cannons were both reeled up by a team of men pulling on the rope and also by a team pushing the cannon by its wooden wheel spokes. The saplings were shoved through the heavy oaken spokes to secure the cannon wheels in place to prevent gravity from pulling the cannon back down the ravine. The brakes allowed the men to rest. Some lucky teams with the gift of foresight employed mules to pull the ropes. A whole day and night was spent assaulting the mountain with their burden of cannon, hand-carried weapons, supplies and food, all needed to face the Muslims. All carried on the backs of men, all straining actively knowing full well their labors could soon bring them to their deaths.

As Bolek finally gained the summit he and his team smiled and patted each other's back as they looked down triumphantly past the deep ravine below, taking in the vista of the Danube

Valley as it lay long and wide far below them. Yet, after a few quick breaths and a bit of libation, the realization of their next mission exploded in their minds. They now had to repeat their task in reverse; they had to move the cannon down the mountainside.

This mountain, Bolek thought as his eyes surveyed it, was like a giant extended hand. It was their job to move up and over several finger-like ravines within the Vienna Woods, which was the gateway to the famed city they had come to liberate. Their reward, if they succeeded in the bone-breaking work, was to meet several hundred thousand resolute Muslims in mortal combat.

This new effort, true to prediction, tested Bolek's resolve as much as anything he had ever experienced. Death may be quick, he thought, but this struggle seemed never-ending. But he did not quit, nor did the man next to him because the man next to *him* did not. And so it went down the line. Each man knew the Turks could not believe an army laden with cannon would attempt to drive over the mountains. The liberating army did believe it. And it would be so.

As others made camp, his duty finally completed, Bolek tramped into the privacy of the woods as nature urgently called. Encircled by bone-white birch with vivid green leaves, a twinge of pain from the scar on his right shoulder brought old memories. Peering deeper into the woods, he tensed as two cold eyes peered back at him, from no more than thirty paces. Man and beast appraised each other. Neither looked away nor blinked. It was the large grey wolf that eventually showed its teeth before loping off into the darkness.

After 4 days of effort, sapped of most of his strength, Bolek collapsed on his blanket in the dark makeshift campsite, moaning as he pulled his bearskin blanket around himself. The last thing he heard before sleep took him was the voice of a messenger, summoning Priest to a meeting with Hetman something-or-other.

He awoke to a misting rain, an uncommon event for mid-September. But there were few puddles and little mud. Fortunately the ground was dry enough to absorb much of the water and it did not pool. This was the morning of September 11th, a Saturday.

"A bad sign," Piotr complained to Priest as he attended to morning duties. "Only cavalry has a chance to win this battle and cavalry does not do well in mud, or in grape arbors."

"Enjoy our baptism of rain, Piotr," Priest said grinning, his face dripping. "It is our renewal, a gift from God."

"*Jezus Maria!*" Bolek heard a strange high-pitched voice shout. "Will no one rid me of this troublesome priest?"

Rising from his camp bed, Bolek saw a priest in a dusty and worn black habit walking with a younger man toward Priest.

"Well, bless me!" Priest exclaimed, "It is Father Woynowski, the warrior turned priest."

"And here is Krzysztof, priest turned warrior," the other arms.

"We meet only at weddings and funerals, my brother," Priest said.

"And which is this to be?" Father Woynowski asked.

"A Turkish funeral."

"Spoken like a priest who *should* be a warrior, Krzysztof. Who is the greatest sinner? You or I?"

"We have both been raised from the darkness and called to serve. And between the two of us we find the balance, the middle ground somewhere. Swords and crosses."

"*Let him who has no sword sell his mantle and buy one,*" Piotr stated, quoting Saint Luke.

"We are resolved to promote peace and have been slow to resort to war," Priest replied. "I feel no sin, Father."

"You are absolved then, warrior, for unchecked evil threatens us all," the silver-haired Father Woynowski replied. "Here we are fighting Muslims arm and arm with our Protestant brothers.

Would that Leo had taken an early grave and Luther had become Pope. Then, perhaps, no schism. Look at the cost the squabbles of Christian against Christian has weakened our collective European strength. Will there ever be an end to it?"

"We are still surrounded by Christ's warriors, are we not?" Priest asked. "One mighty trunk with multiple limbs still bears fruit."

"I'll accept that," Father Woynowski replied, his hands clasped behind his back. "As for the Muslims, if we all eat the same hearty stew but someone has added poisonous mushrooms, do we not all die? Is it not better to remove the offending mushrooms than to throw out the stew?"

"Islam's bloody borders," Priest said. "A better justification for war has never been spoken."

"Men who use their religion for personal gains be damned!" Father Woynowski shouted, fist to the sky. Then in a perfectly calm voice: "May I introduce Jacek Taczewski," changing the subject and losing some of the beet color in his face. "A virtuous man from an ancient and noble family. Jacek, meet Priest."

The two men shook hands as Piotr whispered to Bolek that the Christian borders were sometimes bloody also.

"Priest?" Jacek asked politely, the young man of medium height and build, a strong face and pleasant demeanor. "Name or title, sir."

"Nickname," Father Woynowski replied. "There may well be only one path up life's mountain, Jacek, but Priest and I use different footholds. I found God after the sword, and he found the sword after God. There is only one thing we agree on."

Priest took his cue, knelt with Father Woynowski and recited in unison:

Saint Michael the Archangel,
defend us in battle.
Be our protection against the wickedness and snares of the devil.

May God rebuke him, we humbly pray;
and do Thou, O Prince of the Heavenly Host -
by the Divine Power of God -
cast into hell, Satan and all the evil spirits,
who roam throughout the world seeking the ruin of souls.
Amen.

"Well met, young hussar," Priest said as both men rose and Priest took Jacek's hand.

"Father Woynowski you remember Piotr, Czesław and Tadek."

"Of course. Greetings all, you worthless drunkards and wayward fools," said with good-natured humor, blessing all in attendance. "Come Jacek, now here's a swordsman," pointing out Tadek. "Jacek is trained, better than excellent, Tadek, but one can ever be too good. Perhaps you two could practice together?"

"Let's save their fire for the Turks," Priest cautioned.

"Not even for a wager? The winner paid in vodka?" Woynowski challenged.

"The Turks can wait," Priest replied with a smirk. "Father, may I present Bolek Radok, our ward in sword and Cross and soon to be the newest member of the Royal Guard when I can get an audience with our king."

"Well met, sir," the priest replied. "From where do you spring?"

"He's a highlander, Father, one who carves bears and flutes," Piotr said. "And rides as if he were born in a saddle."

"Wields the szabla like a demon, deadly on both sides," Tadek said.

"Shoots the Tatar way, accurate and quickly, ta, ta, ta, ta, ta," Czesław said, pulling an imaginary bow.

"Goodness," Father Woynowski replied. "Such bragging, and from those who are parsimonious in their praise. Do you have any words of your own, son?"

So taken by the unexpected praise from his comrades Bolek's mind raced to find words to speak.

"*Non nobis, Domine, non nobis, sed nomini tuo da gloriam!(Not unto us, o Lord, not unto us, but unto your name grant glory!*"

He recited, remembering the great Knight Templar battle cry he learned from his father's own lips, which once seemed meaningless but touched him to the bone.

Father Woynowski eyes grew wide, as did his smile. "We'll said, Highlander. Jacek and you should be friends."

"I am no hussar, Father," Bolek replied. "That is a great achievement." Bolek was quick to return Jacek's polite bow.

God curse me for fighting with Green Hat, who was such a man as this.

"Well spoken, Góralu," Priest replied. "While we fight six days a week, the *Husarstow* is for Sunday. Wait until you see them charge."

"What is your business today, Priest" Father Woynowski asked.

"Today we ride quickly through the woods to evaluate the battlefield and the enemy troops for weakness on orders of the king."

"Would you mind if Jacek and I road with you?"

"Mount up. Gentlemen, we fly up the Kahlenburg."

Chapter 53

Bolek first heard the faint echo of thunder, knowing it to be cannon fire; then, an awareness of activity and a low murmur of voices. Finally, he smelled it. On reaching the Kahlenburg at the right flank position of the Christian relief force, the men dismounted and strode out onto a relatively treeless overlook. The ground fell at a gentle slope, to reveal a sprawling valley, ringed within both gentle hills and framed by the mighty Danube. Each man was silent as he witnessed what he had only imagined, yet was all the more unreal.

At first, Bolek's eyes could only take in a mass of smoking and scorched, brown and blackened land adjacent to a huge area of reds and blues. They soon became flags, tents, pennons.

As the wind came his way he could smell campfires smoke, and pick out the acrid odor of black powder from cannon, mixed with animal offal, and the smell of sweat. The ground, which lay before and below him was filled with precipice and ravine. It was, in all certainty, no place for a horse. A spider web of trenches marked the ground for perhaps three bow shot in length from the Ottoman's to the Lobl Gate. Thousands of men labored, either digging, heaving dirt out of the myriad of trenches or moving wagonloads of dirt. These trenches allowed men to move freely, immune from gunfire, to dig tunnels underground, under the very walls of Vienna. The sappers would place mines, set fuses and the explosions would collapse sections of the mighty walls. The trenches were at the very walls now, from what Bolek could see.

But before the walls could be breached, the Turks had to negotiate protective palisade fencing, then deal with massive arrowhead-like structures which protected the walls, looking like giant saw teeth to Bolek. These were large siege-defensive ravelins, triangular-shaped fortifications each manned by archers and dragoons who left any attacker exposed to arrow or musket ball on every side. Then, a moat.

Beyond all of this, stood Vienna, wrapped in a protective cocoon of walls. The city reminded Bolek of a castle he had once carved from wood, as his eyes rested on the seat of the Holy Roman Empire. The famous vaulting spire of St. Stephan's was clearly visible. This elegant beauty, now teetering on the brink of destruction, reminded Bolek of the Pitry Manor, only a thousand times more grand. Hundreds of cannons belched and puffed white smoke, hurling iron and whatnot against the walls, and over the walls and into the city. Manmade thunder.

"There are your 140,000 Turks," Priest told Bolek. And there, 100,000 tents, spread around Vienna like a crescent."

"Perhaps half are conscripts," Father Woynowski added. "I'd say no more than one in four is battle-tested. Look there, sweet Jesus!" He exclaimed his clutched fists to his heart. "There are Christian slaves, poor souls forced to dig trenches and tunnels. Look at them, beaten, bruised, the women prostituted, taken and used in public as if they were animals. The men broken, health gone, faltering. More than a thousand times a thousand are in such bondage. Most would face the sword rather than submit to Allah. So they live as slaves. And there! The Muslims taunt the defenders of the city by parading a line of naked slave women. Gaze upon the aim of the worldwide Caliphate. Would that I could wield a szabla again. Christ forgive me. It is a madhouse. Death to all fanatics."

"It is not too late to get you a horse and a sword, Father," Priest said with a smirk.

Bolek and the others followed the lead of the ordained priest as he made the sign of the cross and fell to his knees.

"Lord, as brother is about to fight brother, forgive us for our corruption of your commandments. We pray for our Christian brothers, who squabble over material wealth, for our Christian brothers who seek earthly power. We pray for our invading brothers who seek revenge for no sins which we know to have committed against them, other than the land we inhabit and our devotion to You. And we ask your forgiveness for our lack of timely courage and action, our lack of striving to gain the knowledge to prevent this conflict and how it soon squanders Your precious gift of life."

"So, Master Bolek," Father Woynowski said as he rose after the *Amen*, pointing west. "There are the Tatars."

Bolek's eyes followed with utter curiosity as the priest spryly walked to the edge of their vantage point that opened to the valley below, for though he had fought hundreds of Tatars in his dreams, he had never actually seen one.

"They do not mix well with the Turks and are kept sequestered off to the side," Priest said. "By the counts our king gave us last night these Turks and Tatars field one hundred twenty thousand men and horses and almost as many carts for supplies and support, surrounding the city in a near death grip."

"And look there, Master Bolek,' Father Woynowski said. "Have you ever seen a camel? Well there are a thousand more for good measure. Camels are the ships of the desert, able to run for miles in the ever-shifting sands, without water, in the winter for up to a month."

"*Czlowiek nie wielblad napic sie musi!*" (Humans are not camels, they must drink), the priest toasted as he pulled a small flask from his breast pocket and shared it with all.

"But they boast the foulest temperament of any beast created by God. And there! There is the pasha's tent. The most ornate among the 25,000 on display."

"His Majesty's intelligence reports tell us the Sultan of the Ottomans is off hunting game and women in the south," Priest said. "Mustafa is here to do the dirty work. He sees himself as a great man, but the Sultan sees him as only one who serves. Fool. And as for his military skills, well, they have too few cannon and they place them badly. Their army is split. Some stay with the siege to the south and the majority await our troops. A huge mistake. They smell of overconfidence and arrogance. Hubris."

"It smells of something else to me," Bolek noted, his eyes constantly scanning the besieged city. "It is a wonder they endure it?"

"And we are still miles away," Priest noted. "And soon the odor of blood and fear will be added to the mix."

"So many will die. For what purpose?" Bolek asked. "Mustafa must know he will lose many."

"God made the heavens and earth and proclaimed them good," Father Woynowski said. "But us, young Radok, we believe the only way to maintain order is through violence. We make our own bed."

"Mustafa's men are nothing to him. He is captive in man's futile will to power." Priest added. "Their government is run by those who use their religion for personal gains. We know that story only too well. All that matters to them is what they can see or touch. Finally, we have the self-serving Mustafa who seeks to usurp God. At first the Dark One whispers in his ear, softly preaching that if there was but one nation on the earth that peace would surly ensue. This sits well with Mustafa. His mind soon leaps to his religion for justification. He reads the wisdom of his prophet with Satan as corrupted interpreter. This mighty army is assembled here to ensure Mustafa's authority is felt. Now these mavens of death choke the air with dust and life from the living. He misuses the command of his prophet to enslave the world."

"A willful blindness," Bolek said, "I know the strategy well."

"We are at war with each other because we are at war with ourselves." Father Woynowski said. "We are at war with God. We are such of little faith."

"Satan is the only victor in war," Priest replied. "Soon he will call the tune and command the Turks, our European armies and you and I to dance. That smell from the offal below is his essence. Thousands of souls will be extinguished within hours of the first blows. One army will conquer and one will flee. There will be too many bodies to bury. Below you lay the wolves' harvest."

Tadek always says, "Without the shedding of blood, there is no forgiveness of sins," Bolek said.

"Often misunderstood, son" Father Woynowski said.

"Love always costs," Priest added. "And voluntary suffering has a great power over evil."

"Our sacrifice here transforms a necessity into a choice," Bolek said, and was pleased with Father Woynowski's reaction and Priest's prideful smile for his protégé.

"Krzysztof, you duplicate yourself with your protégé here, and make a warrior-philosopher, I see," Woynowski said.

"It would seem we are outnumbered," Bolek said, unconsciously moving his lips as he tried to count the enemy.

"We are of limited power, but immense ability," Father Woynowski said.

"We will soon thresh the wheat, each man a stalk," Priest added. "These Muslims come to dominate, with a thirst for blood. But they come with large numbers of conscripts and slaves. Those who have no will to fight. Each man among us fights for personal freedom. See the Christian slaves down there?" Priest shouted as he pointed. "Most have not submitted to Islam. They only wear the world's chains. The truth must come from deep inside and then radiate outward."

"Again, Christ's teachings." Bolek said. "Why are the words suddenly so clear?"

Priest and the priest smiled at each other as two satisfied schoolboys might.

"War is an ancient extension of politics," Priest said. "On our side it stems from apathy, petty dynastic squabbles, and yes, also the will to power. You see below you the eternal destruction of nations. All these European and Asian armies are ruled by a few men of self-interest. The leaders of our nations care nothing for their fellow men, believing they themselves are above all. All their temples will burn and crumble to dust. They are blind to the obvious outcome of the love of oneself – chaos."

"Even our king?"

"His Majesty does not fight for private Poland but for public Poland. *Tranquillitas ordinis.* Sobieski is here to repel Ottoman invasion, free the slaves and then march home."

"While the wolf licks his chops and bides his time for the inevitable outcome," Woynowski added.

Never taking his eyes off the spectacle which lay below him, Priest chuckled. "Do you remember that selfish and trembling mountain boy, Góralu, we found those many months ago."

"Yes."

"Well, I have not seen or heard from that boy in many weeks."

"Good riddance," Bolek shouted spitting on the ground.

"Sobieski will put the fear of hell into Mustafa," Piotr said as he joined his two comrades.

"Our king's grandfather, Hetman Zolkiewski was killed by Muslims at Cecora in 1620, as my grandfather told me many times." Bolek said. "His brother, Marek, died on the plains of Batoh in 1652. And the king himself was a hostage in the Tatars' Crimea. He knows the cruelty of Turk and Tatar alike. He fights for Catholic Poland."

"It is neither glory nor booty he seeks," Priest said, nodding in agreement. "It is the will that follows reason and not the other way around, as many think." This was said with a clenched and trembling fist at the center of his chest.

What a fool I've been. Perhaps it is a blessing my father did not return to see what an idiot of a son.

Priest smiled while tussling Bolek's hair.

"As long as there are men like our king," Bolek continued, "Poland will never fall."

"We will delude ourselves to justify this war."

"We are God's madmen." Bolek said.

"By heaven, son!" Priest exclaimed, "I do not know what you have taken to better, the sword, politics, or your catechism."

"Still, some sanity tells me death is something to fear." Bolek admitted.

Piotr raised his eyebrows to Priest and walked away.

"There has only been one who has triumphed over death. And it is his sacrifice that gives us a path to immortality."

Bolek spoke softly. "If you die here who fights for us, who will show us the way?"

Priest put his long arm around his protégé. "By God's breath you have been listening, sir. My fear exactly. Who indeed will carry out that fight when I give all for it? What are your thoughts?"

"Poland will not fall as long as truth lives. I pray for courage."

"If you believe this truly, then your fears will not cripple you. At this moment, the Lord of Lies cowers. This cadre of fools spread below us is Satan's doing. But ours also, for our greed and our indifference. Yet a few among us, a few who believe and can stand without fear, will prevail."

"Then we fight together, our heads held high," Bolek said with chin to the sky.

"Our wisdom shall be trust. His gift to us will be Providence."

The two men grasped hands, a pact sealed in an iron grip.

"Down there it will be like a great village dance, son," Priest cautioned, switching to tactical advice garnered from years of experience. "You will only have knowledge of that around you, no more than ten paces in each direction. You will experience your own dance with your own partners and not know what the rest of the great party is about."

"It will be like the werewolf," Bolek said. "Before the encounter I imagined him an invincible giant, indestructible and all-powerful. But after I slew him, I saw him for what he truly was."

"So it will be in this struggle. You see many armed and terrible foes below. But you will fight individuals, and most will be weak and afraid."

"I will kill infidels, free slaves; relive Vienna, shoulder to shoulder with my brothers."

"Remember the tale of Lech and the Polish eagle?" a squinting Priest asked.

"Freedom and responsibility." Bolek repeated.

"Yes. Remember your gypsy girl."

"In sin and shame, yes." Bolek admitted.

"Now imagine just a few short months ago how life would have been if there were no raiders. Then imagine if Rozalia had chosen you."

"That cannot be. I buried her with my own hands."

"But imagine another young boy and another beautiful and innocent young girl with your same story. But know they are real, live on this earth and draw breath. They are behind us, and whether they know it or not, they rely on us. Do not hate those in front of you, Góralu, rather love those behind. Fight not with the madness of anger but with a righteous determination. We are noble eagles, white eagles that fight to preserve our souls. If today is the day of engagement, remember Saturday, September 11th, in the year of our Lord 1683 always, Góralu. Something still troubles you?"

"One thing. Perhaps a nit. When I look at the Turks, well, they look so organized, like colorful dolls, each an image of the other in their bright blue uniforms and red hats. It troubles me. Our hussars look plain."

"Plain?" Priest said with a roar. "Our men wear travel clothes now. Their battle suits follow behind on the backs of retainers and camp aides who scaled the mountain with you. It is a lesson well-learned from when we defeated the Teutonic Knights at Grunwald in 1410. Our wise king, Wladyslaw Jagiello, who brought Christianity to our people, refused to engage in combat during most of the day, leaving his proud and arrogant chain-armor foe, Krzyzacy, to stew in hot armor and be burned by the sun. When we finally engaged them, they were already fatigued.

The lesson is that we do not dress for combat until the proper time. Wait until tomorrow, Góralu," Priest said with a wink as he turned.

"Plain," Bolek heard Priest say whimsically as he walked away, shaking his head in disbelief.

Chapter 54

Priest walked up with both arms full of armor and weapons, unceremoniously dropping the bundle in a heap before Bolek's feet.

"You don't intend to engage the Turks like that," he said as he sized up his protégé from his Magyar cap to his grandfather's yellow boots.

Bolek stooped and began sorting through the cache. Chain armor for chest and arms, a silver misiurka helmet with a protective veil of chain, just like the one his father had let him wear as a boy; a spiked iron hammer; a bearskin cape; a bright red *kalkan* shield. Bolek Radok would go into a holy war as a *pancerny*, an armored cavalry Royal Guardsman.

"You let me borrow this?" Bolek asked as he sifted through the treasures. "No. They are yours to keep," Priest said sternly. "Just keep in mind they are here because their former owners are not. Keep your head at all times. Honor your fellow Guardsmen."

"Nice hammer," Tadek said as he also began to rummage through the heap. "You already have your mountain ax. I'll trade you even for my dagger." A handshake sealed the deal. Warriors of the East and West had been trading armor, horses, stories, drink, and spices for centuries.

"Your bearskin cape is really two sewn together," Czesław said. "It is too cumbersome for you, Góralu. It may impair your sword arm. I offer you a trade for my smaller one but of better quality."

"What, a cape to fit our archer?" Piotr laughed. "But take the deal, Góralu. Czesław's cape has always looked like nothing more than a handkerchief on his oversized and deformed back. We Poles are famous for our attention to fashion."

Yet another trade was completed.

"We engage today. There is no going back," Priest told his

companions, in those early hours of the morning of September 12th. "Our king must not fall this day," he whispered as he turned Mieszko and rode away.

"It means we will protect out king at the expense of our own defense," Piotr said to Bolek. "If he dies, so does Christian Europe."

"No doubt he will take the lead," Tadek added.

"If the Turks see Jan Sobieski, the man who has beat them time and again, lead the charge, they will be disheartened," Piotr said.

"And if he breaks through the enemy line behind the Husaria," Czesław added, "the Turks will quickly show us their backsides."

"The waiting is maddening," a pacing Bolek admitted. "This is an old enemy of ours. *'From the fury of the Mohammedan, spare us, O Lord,'* he repeated, invoking an old prayer. "My fathers, for a thousand years, feared these men."

"In the morning, we will face an enemy who has absorbed half of what once were Christian cultures," Piotr said. "They invaded Spain, Italy and Sicily and sacked Naples and Ravenna and even Rome itself, with vast numbers put to the Saracen sword. They enslaved all in their path and cheapened life for all who were not like them."

"Grandfather said even the Roman churches of St. Peter and St. Paul were sacked," Bolek said.

"Rome has an enormous wall, which, though now in ruins, once encircled the city. Called the Leonine, it was built to protect The Eternal City from Islam," Tadek said.

"See how European Christians have watered down our unifying faith with schism, heresy, and reformation," Piotr said his hand on his szabla. "Islam moves because we are complacent. Those we face today do not only want our lives, but all we value and love." Suddenly, Piotr ran to his horse, retrieving an old dusty book from his saddlebag.

"And future ages groan for this foul act; Peace shall go sleep with Turks and infidels. And in this seat of peace tumultuous wars shall kin with kin and kind with kind confound; Disorder, horror, fear and mutiny shall here inhabit, and this land be called the field of Golgotha and dead men's skulls. O! if you rear this house against this house, it will the woefullest division prove that ever fell upon this cursed earth. Prevent it, resist it, let it not be so, Lest child, child's children, cry against you 'woe!'"

"Great words from a wise man," Piotr said as he snapped the book shut. "One Master Shakespeare from England wrote this a century ago. It is a certainty he must have lived the experience we feel now. Our mission is to protect the king when he takes the field. You and I will deal with any Turk who nears him. If our weapons fail, our bodies will shield him.

Chapter 55

Later the five comrades sat under a leather tarp, drawn tight between three pine trees and tilted to direct the rain away. It had been decided early in the day it was too wet to attack and the forced march had left the men too tired. One more night of rest was mandated, something Bolek thanked heaven for as he reclined on his deerskin, daydreaming of home and hearth as Priest softly played his violin.

"What is this tune, Priest?" Bolek asked. "I've never heard it."

"It comes from Italy. A man named Monteverdi wrote it. He's passed on now, but we still can hear and feel his essence. Isn't this extraordinary?"

"I know a hundred folk tunes and yet never met a man who wrote one. Are they like us, the ones who write books and music, the creative sort?"

"Only God creates. We imitate Him. Music can be turned into ugliness, singing to your loins, as the Turkish drums do for them. These musicians, poets and painters, if true to their art, seem to have the capacity to remind us what is most precious in life. That old crust of bread we take for granted comes alive with some butter and some salt."

Priest sighed as he pulled his blanket around him. Each soldier gazed into the fire, watching it coal and smolder, hearing the sizzle as raindrops hit the heated wood, all mixed with the sounds of snorting horses and the occasional scream from some tortured wretch far below, his tortured plea unanswered. But there was always tomorrow.

Soon the sound of cannon fire echoed around the hills, set off every night by the Turks at a variable time after midnight.

"They do this to keep the besieged citizens of Vienna off guard, edgy and weary from lack of sleep," Tadek said, poking at their campfire with a smoldering stick.

"Perhaps in the morning we will awake to find the Turks have abandoned the field and gone home," Bolek said.

"They only do what their commanders tell them to do."

"But I am free to leave right now," Bolek stated.

"Yes. But the crazy boys, the janissaries, know they cannot go home. They are taught to fight as the Golden Horde did and the Tatars still do," Tadek replied. "The core unit is ten men. Next, one hundred. Next, one thousand. Next ten thousand. If any unit abandons the field without orders to do so, each man in the unit is put to death. I have seen one thousand men beheaded in one such instance. These Janissaries must fight or die. Their enemy is before them, among them and behind them."

"I remember celebrating *Wielkanoc*," Czeslaw suddenly declared, his red hair enhanced by the redness of the fire. "The great night of our Lord's birth. But I used to hate *Adventum Domini* as a boy. *Czterdziestnica*. No meat. Fasting was not to my liking."

"Forty days," Priest said. "But still we had the Feast of St. Martin to prepare us for what lay ahead. A reprieve. For creed, commandment and sacrament."

"Roast pork at my home," Czesław said, throwing another branch on the hungry fire. "I can taste the first sample, sliced from the spit when none were looking, the salty crust dripping with fat and the promise of thick white meat. But milk was forbidden."

"Time slowed to a crawl then," Tadek reminisced. "The Lord was coming, and we were made to remember, to suffer, but still a pittance compared to His."

"There was always *Wigilia*," Bolek said. "And the *Pasterka* mass."

"From the Latin, *vigilare*. To watch. Christ is coming.," Priest said, puffing on his pipe. "Be ever *en garde*."

"We woke at midnight," Bolek added, fully stretched out, the fingers of both hands locked behind his neck to cradle his head, his dreamy eyes on the heavens. "We sprinkled cold water on our faces. Kasia loved to sprinkle me, to baptize me."

"We would spend much of the day visiting friends and neighbors and making prayers and good wishes for all," Piotr said. "All was peace for a time."

"We did the same," Czesław said, "and from the other side of Poland. I did not know you Lublin heathens had any customs."

"We even had fire, Czesław, a discovery still unknown in Poznan, I think," Piotr growled.

"We would hang grain upside down over our Christmas Eve table," Priest said. "So long ago."

"Still done," Bolek assured him.

"And is there still straw thrown on the floors to remind us of where He was born?" Tadek asked.

"That and hay under the tablecloth, Tadek." Bolek answered.

"Burning amber on St. John's night to chase evil spirits away?" Czesław asked.

"Frowned on by our priest, but still done," Bolek assured again.

"Do they still make Easter egg soup, *barzscz*?" Piotr asked, with a smack of his lips. "My recipe was famous. Thick-cut bacon, thumb-long slices of kielbasa, sliced ham and creamy horseradish, sharp as my szabla."

"Zupa *chrzanowa – horseradish soup in Silesia.*"

"*Kiszka*," Priest said, his memory jogged, "with good Polish beer, from Zwiec."

"*Pisanki*," Tadek said. "I bet my painted wooden Easter eggs could even compare with Góralu's."

"You painted eggs?" an incredulous Bolek asked.

"I was like you once," Tadek replied, "and I, I . . ."

"Our family *kapliczki* shrine was famous in our region," Czesław said. "Ours was a roadside shrine to Mary that none could rival for beauty or reverence." There was a long pause before Czesław continued. "A soldier's life is so bleak. Christmas Eve spent in a barracks. All my family is . . ." He struggled with the words, trailing off with a sigh.

"You shall all dine with me at my home this Christmas," Bolek declared.

"Jacek will be invited too, and Father Woynowski will give us the Shepherd's Mass, for shepherds like me were the first to greet the Lord formally."

"You are no longer a shepherd," Tadek reminded him. "The wolves will run when they smell you, and you will eat all the lambs yourself to keep your sword arm strong."

All laughed.

"*Przednówek*, the last weeks before the new harvest," Czesław said, "when our supplies from the previous season are exhausted, and we dream of fresh food."

It was clear from their expressions the bowman's words sparked a flood of memories.

"Then the twelve days of Christmas," Piotr said, "with each day predicting the weather for the next month in turn, starting with St. Stephan's Day."

"Can we reminisce about a summer month," Czesław pleaded. "I'm feeling chilled."

"Before the harvest," Priest said, "in August," nodding to Czesław, "when the weathered old men knew the time was right, our wives and mothers and sisters would begin baking mountains of bread to keep us strong for the labor we faced. We cleared whole fields."

"And the butter flowed," Tadek said, "Tell me, what is better after a hard morning of work than a crust of buttered bread and cool stream water?"

"Choose another month, Tadek," Czesław ordered, "now I am hungry."

"If we cannot reminisce about food, the weather or religion, well there is nothing else, Czesław," Priest said.

"On Christmas Eve, you are all welcome at my home," Bolek said. "And whether you come or not there will be a place set to honor each of you."

"We will be there, Góralu," Piotr said, his eyes shining with tears. "In one form or another, we will be there."

A Guardsman appeared, calling for Priest, telling him His Royal Highness wished to speak with him. Priest quickly rose and followed the Guardsman.

"An audience with the king?" Bolek asked Czesław.

"Priest's advice is highly respected," Piotr replied.

"Ensure the horses are healthy and are fed well tonight, Góralu," Tadek said. "Tomorrow will be hard on them."

"The horses? And what about us?" Czesław asked. "In only a few short hours most of the soldiers of Europe and Asia are going to clash and attempt to kill each other in this place. It will not only be hard on the horses, brother Tadek."

"May this truly be the last Crusade," Piotr prayed.

Chapter 56

The night was unending for Bolek and dawn couldn't come too soon. He felt guilty trying to get some rest while the king and the hussars were riding through the night to reach his position. At about 4 a.m. Bolek saw Priest move to the assembly point, and he followed.

"The Austrians are stirring," Priest said. "They will assemble soon. Let us pray that for glory sake, they do not engage too early."

"If they do?"

"If our left flank marches down that hill, the right flank of the Ottomans will attack. Then the Germans at the center would have to engage also, so Lorraine's men are not flanked."

"What of our right flank."

"Exactly. Our flank is still navigating the forest and hills to get here. All we can do here is wait."

As the eastern sky lightened, more than one quarter of a million men readied themselves to maim and kill and be maimed or killed. Some would fight for personal gain, some for glory, some for politics, some for religion, some as forced conscripts and slaves, while others were as leaves caught in life's current, brought to Vienna by mere happenstance. "So many men," Bolek said to Piotr, as both men looked in all directions from their high vantage point.

"Don't bother yourself with counting. Nobody can know exact numbers in clashes such as this. For you and I, there are only two. Us and them. And we shall soon see which of us has the greatest spirit."

"I hear so many rumors."

"The men are anxious. They imagine, they hope, they talk. Right now many of us wish we had three times the men we currently have. But with victory, some will tell the story that the enemy outnumbered us seven to one. And not one of us was ever frightened. Some of the great Hetman, leaders of these throngs, if God graces us with success, some will believe it was their strategies that won the war. Such as our overly anxious Lorraine on our far left."

With dawn, the Austrian relief force under the Duke of Lorraine assembled at the left flank atop the Kahlenburg. The Germans, under Starhemberg, took the center, soon after. This was where the Ottoman generals put their strongest force. Sobieski and his Winged Hussars were still navigating their way through the most difficult part of the Vienna Woods and had not arrived yet.

The Christian left flank under Charles V, the Duke of Lorraine, true to Priest's words, gave orders to move his men down the mountain and toward the awaiting Turkish right flank. And so, on a glorious sunny day, began *Bitwa pod Wiedniem,* the Battle of Vienna. Over almost impassable terrain, a struggle through Vienna's famous tangled vineyards, down slopes and up ravines, fighting for a few feet at a time, Lorraine engaged. He was forced to utilize his infantry in a musket strategy of stand-shoot-attack method for hour upon hour, face to face with the enemy, shoring holes here and taking fast and full advantage in breaches in the lines, fighting up ridges and down into valleys, constantly blinded with smoke, sweat and blood. Field commanders lost sight of whole dragoon units only to see them pop up on a ridge where they least expected them. Pancerni cavalry eager to join the fray stood impatiently in reserve, choking with their horses and sweating in their heavy mail armor.

Men shouted their brothers onward, and ever upward, encouraging, exposing themselves to enemy fire, exhibiting bravery, courage and resolve. 'I offer my life for this cause' their body language proclaimed as they killed, bled, died, as a mass of flesh staunchly moving forward over heaps of dead flesh to shoot from a higher position; anything to gain ground.

The morning was well spent before Lorraine's cannon was

able to push the Turks back enough to capture some high ground, holding back his forward momentum for a time, both to give his men a brief respite and to allow the Polish right flank to join them. But there was no sign of Sobieski. Starhemberg and his German musketeers at the center now engaged, using the same tactics as Lorraine.

"If that is indeed 120,000 men, Góralu," Priest said, waving his arm across the valley below, "then Mustafa employs only one in three in the trenches. He must be indeed close to setting off a mine to collapse that wall. These troops he sends at ours are, therefore, equally grouped in three groups of 30,000 each. This matches up well with Lorraine's left flank and Starhemberg center. The Ottoman left flank awaits our cavalry. There are the sipahis cavalry and only one line of janissaries with cannon. If our hussars could break that line and get behind it, it would be a godsend."

"But the ground is so uneven, and our army isn't even here yet."

Chapter 57

At four in the morning on September 12th, Sobieski assisted in the Mass among the ruins of St. Joseph's convent and church. Padre Marco of Avoano, a papal legate of Pope Innocent XI, joined him. The king then rode out before the assembled armies to take leadership at its front. Orders were shouted back and forth, and groups of soldiers raced to take their place behind the Polish king.

Padre Marco, mounted behind and to the left of the cavalry, held a crucifix to the lines of Muslims before him, shouting, "Behold the cross of the Lord! Begone, enemy troops," then falling to his knees, he began to sing the ancient *Bogurodzica* song, and was soon joined by more and more voices until the entire mountainside rang with the full rich voices of king and peasant, noble and serf alike, faithfully chanting the prayer that had been sung for over four hundred years.

> *Mother of God, Virgin, by God glorified Mary,*
> *From your son, our Lord, chosen mother, Mary!*
> *Win over for us, send to us.*
> *Kyrie Eleison. Lord have mercy.*

"Non nobis, no nobis Domine exercituum sed nomini tuo da gloriam (not unto us, not unto, but to Thy name, o Lord of Hosts, be ascribed the glory)" the king of the Poles prayed, in communion with his hussars, all heads bowed.

It was slow going for the Poles, who navigated the most uneven ground and thickest of woods. The forced night march had been slow, difficult and frustrating. Sobieski was unaware that the battle had already begun

At about 3 P.M., a soft murmur from behind turned Bolek's head as he sat mounted, watching the action below. The very spirit of that which was Poland rode out from the darkness of the trees from above and behind. The sunlight on shimmering armor wrapped the lone knight in a golden aura which warmed Bolek from within. A fabled Polish hussar appeared; a giant of a man on a behemoth of a bay horse strutted down from the apex of the hill as light as a feather, his horse prancing sure-footedly at an angle so all could see. Bolek was not alone in the ranks as pride and confidence swelled in his chest.

The brilliant flags and pennons of Poland burst from the dark woods in red backgrounds with white crosses as retainers followed. The wind, as if on command, rose up to billow and flap them, as if awakening and filling them with a new spirit and strength.

"*Boże, coś Polskę* ! God for Poland!" Bolek shouted, repeating the oath he so often heard at home.

The famed and feared Polish Winged Horsemen – the Husaria – marched out of the forest to assemble on the right side of the mountain. As if by practiced signal, roars and cheers exploded in a single instance and echoed through the mountains and to the very walls of Vienna. Poland was on the field of glory. The chorągiew, or companies, were each lead to their field positions either by a *rotomistrz* (captain) or a *porucznik* (lieutenant). He controlled one hundred and fifty hussars, the *towarzysze* companions, each a noble, able to afford the expensive arms and armor, remounts and campaign retainers. Pułks (regiments) were organizational units, later divided into tactical units (szwadrony).

Each szwadron, a unit with a chorągiew of hussars in the center and a chorągiew of pancerni on each side, were tasked with protecting the flanks. Eight thousand heavily armored pancerni, Bolek Radok among them, stood ready to deliver the second deadly punch, that of quickly filling the breach with deadly speed, deadly darts and sharpened steel. Bolek counted twenty-three Hussar banners. Nearly three thousand hussars stood visible to the bruised and burning but defiant Holy Roman

City of Vienna, at the ready, on command from its king, to drive through the Turkish defensive front line.

Next in procession came the venerable nobles, the landowners, the wealthy merchants took the field. Each man was resplendent in dress, carriage and mount. Diamonds, emeralds, sapphires and rubies sewn into fabric and cemented into sword hilt and helmet sparkled as each caught the sunlight. Every color on God's earth was on display, every horse decked in gold, some even painted various shades of red. Many of the warrior's shoulders were covered with skins of leopard, bear, lion and wolf. Feather of hawk and goose, dyed gray or brown, flapped in the wind on helmet and horse. Kopia lances, nearly twenty feet in length stood facing the sky, the pennons flapping and hissing in the wind, the bright reds and bright white colors of Poland unfolding in full display. Bolek knew for certain this sparkle would quickly heat up, then glow then burst into a flaming and unquenchable spirit.

As twenty-eight additional cannons appearing just outside the Vienna Woods set up to fire, yet another cheer rose from the liberating army. What Grand Vizier Mustafa had believed was impossible was now before him. A Christian army had crossed impassible mountains with cannon and cavalry and stood, united, before his astounded eyes. And it was led by King Jan III Sobieski, the Lion of Lechistan. Two standards appeared, one with the Jania coat of arms, the other, a lance with a falcon wing attached – the sign of the commander-in-chief. The Polish king, rumored to be too old and fat to even mount a horse, had just come over the Kahlenburg Mountain. Dressed in a white joupane coat of Chinese silk, covered by a dark blue kontush, a large red cap spouting egret tail feathers and a diamond pin, he rode out to the field atop a large white Arab charger, its mane streaming in the wind.

"Many here were once wealthy men," Priest explained in a whisper. "All their wealth has been traded for their armor, weapons, mounts, jewels and retainers. This is what to be noble means. They give all for Poland. Are you able to follow such men, Góralu?"

This drove Bolek into deep thought. What would indeed inspire a noble to risk all in combat and leave a rag-bare family behind?

"A line has been drawn," Bolek whispered back to Priest. "Animal instincts, greed and selfishness stand on one side. Faith and reason on the other."

"And your will, young warrior?"

"Steeled," came a trembling reply.

As Sobieski moved forward, his twenty-six thousand additional warriors became visible to the Turks on their own left flank. On the Polish right flank, Grand General Stanisław Jabłonowski commanded the place of honor. Hetman Kontzki manned the center and on the left stood Sieniawski. Kontzki commanded 7500 infantry, Sieniawski 6000 cavalry, Jablonowski 8000.

"Relax, Góralu," Priest said, leaning over to Bolek. "We are still three miles from the walls and about one from level ground. Our services are not required as yet. Not until they trample out the vintage," he added, pointing to the vineyards that were being crushed under the feet and bodies of the infantry as the mass of men moved closer to the walls of Vienna.

Bolek Radok, shepherd boy from the Tatry Mountains, watched the struggle of death and knew his turn would come soon. Hour after hour of screams, of spilt blood, tore at his resolve. He began to imagine himself slaughtered in the manner painfully acted out below. Perhaps his mountain retreat was the place to be, he reasoned. In the confusion all around, I could escape and be home in mere days. I could find the brigands and slaughter them. Then life would return to the way it was. Oh, I was such a fool to wish for more than a farmer's life. But then images of his mother and sister entered his head. He knew if the

Muslims triumphed today on this field, the mayhem would reach the Radok farm. Bolek searched for his father and grandfather as spirits, somewhere quite near. They smiled at him. They were proud he was at the walls of Vienna. They had sacrificed, not taken. They had given and had not run.

Mary, please make me worthy to sit at their table.

Chapter 58

Bolek, having time on his hands, watched in amazement at how the troops readied for battle, for once they left the forests they would immediately need to fall into ranks, and line up appropriately. The retainers worked efficiently to prepare the hussars, and the general chaos of shouting, rearing horses, gallows humor, and a general air of anticipation set the mood. He spied Jacek, preparing for the engagement, aided by three retainers.

"Good morning, Bolek," Jacek said as his polished mailed armor was tied to his chest from behind. "As you see, it takes two men to ready a hussar, but once prepared our horns will scatter the enemy like a bull against sheep and our teeth will grind on their front lines while their back lines stand and watch, awaiting their turn at death."

"I itch to silence those drums," Bolek replied, sensing the time for battle nearing and anxious to get into action.

"They hammer to unnerve us. Soon our trumpets and bagpipes will drown them out. Then we will silence the drums one infidel at a time. And once a few lose their nerve and turn tail, the infection spreads."

"They ready themselves now, as we do."

"They will have their long spears in front, no more than four rows, and their infantry behind with their muskets, then mounted Tatar archers and ultimately their regiments of horse guard, the Spahis, behind that. These are the deadly musketeers who will shoot at us in volley salvos. They will be the ones in bright blue with the linings of embroidered gold. And turbans. They all dress the same in issued clothing, while each of us, responsible to pay for our own battle garments, dress in our own style. A treasured custom."

"We will have these pennants on display," Jacek continued, pointing to the silk, two-pointed flags hanging from the lances which jutted well out from the bags carried by retainers, longer than a man was tall, one point in red with a coat of arms sewn into it and the other in red with a green dragon breathing red fire. A Christian cross spanned the width of the banner where it attached to the lance. The attendants scurried from one bag to the next, assembling each knight's armor and weapons in a mound. The wagons were left at Tulln, and all equipment had been carried up and over on the backs of each knight's entourage.

"This banner identifies my troop," Jacek explained. "The length helps unnerve enemy horses, for unless your horse is trained for such a banner flapping around its eyes and obscuring its vision it will cause him to rear or bolt. Nothing is left to chance, not when I ride at a full gallop toward impalement," he added with a dry laugh. "There, look at my kopia, my lance. While mine are only fifteen feet long, they can be made even longer. The Turks do not fight with pike today, so this length is ideal. It is the color of my group and the pennon I will apply will further identify me and strike terror into the enemy horses. The Turks will not recognize these things until it is too late."

"Remarkably light," Bolek said as he hefted the long wooden lance, wrapped in red felt decorated in white felt stripes, ending in a deadly steel-pointed tip.

"Steel and silk," Jacek said as his men brought his horse to him. "My point will reach them first. Its length belies its weight, no? It is made of spruce and hollow to the wooden handle guard. Only fit for one thrust but sometimes a broken one can skewer a Turk. I support it in this *tok*, a leather cup attached to the right base of my saddle. And I charge either holding it to my side or with the *kopia* resting in the *tok*, giving me added weight on impact. If the Turks who are unlucky enough to stand ready to repel my charge are not wearing body armor, this kopia is capable of impaling two of them, one behind the other as I contact them at a full gallop."

"Whereupon you move to sword, pistol, steel *czekan* hammer," Bolek said.

"I do not use a pistol. The powder too often flashes rather than propels the missile. But once we break the line then you will be there, Bolek, firing arrows, slicing infantry, carving a red path to the very walls of Vienna."

The two men took stock of each other, Bolek in his simple quilted zupon coat, and Jacek, the first-time hussar, in *karcena* scale armor, riveted to a leather-padded jacket under shining armor of overlapping steel scales, replete with matching arm guards and a skirt of steel that protected the thighs from saber thrusts. His pants were bright red; his knee-length boots a pale yellow.

Next, the retainers armored up, for they rode with their hussar lords. Each differed from the hussars in only one way. A double, lyre-shaped wooden arch, much like a shepherd's crook, lined in red silk and covered with a single row of light gray dyed goose feathers ran vertically along Jacek's retainers' backs, looping forward, above their heads. When caught by the wind at a full gallop, these wings began to mourn, then chant as the pace picked up, and finally, they shrieked; a united shriek, like that of a large raptor. Horses unaccustomed to this sound often bolted. Hussars armed with lances three to four times the length of a man, coupled with winged retainers at a full gallop became Lech's eagle; the sharp talons and the hiss of the wind on its feathers reaching for its prey, the enemy's cavalry.

Jacek's horse's head was even adorned with a light gray plume. The animal had been groomed so its coat shined like polished chestnuts and its mane and tail glistened in the sun. Red felt covered reins, and a red-tasseled martingale attaching to the gold inlayed bridle, at the horse's chest, together with a brightly colored saddle blanket, rimmed in fringe, and ornate deep-seated saddle, in matching colors made horseman and his mount as one.

"I will be there, Jacek. I will follow you through those gates of Hell," Bolek promised. "My arrows will protect your back and your sides."

The sun sat low in the west as Bolek watched the mayhem below when Priest cried, "There! There it is! The Turks pull men from our right to shore up their center. A great victory for the heroic Germans and brave Austrians; a crucial mistake for the Turks. They now have their backs to the River Wien. His Majesty will soon give direction to push harder on our side."

A lull in the fighting came within the hour as both armies regrouped. Bolek heard one old and grizzled general tell the king he expected to dine and sleep in Vienna tonight, and there was much laughter in response. But the king held himself stoic and straight on his white charger, constantly gazing below through his telescope.

"Turkish troops are moving there," Priest called. "See the red tent? Behind it is a standard with horsetails. Those are Mustafa's personal troops moving to fight."

Once the Christian generals realized Mustafa had committed his personal troops to the fray smiles of delight came to them. This was a welcome respite from the deafening roar of these Janissaries mixed with the constant Boom! Boom! Boom! of their huge drums, which sorely tested Bolek's nerves.

"Priest!" The king shouted without taking his eyes from the raging battle below.

"Here, Your Majesty."

"The Tatar Khan, Girey, did not strike at Tulln, nor does he attack our right wing now. What say you to this?"

"Sire, you have always defeated him, even when he had ten times your numbers. He has seen you now with a larger army and will soon abandon the field and ride home to the Crimea, his oath to Mustafa conveniently forgotten."

The king twisted himself in his saddle and looked directly at Priest. "Is this courtly flattery?" he asked.

All in earshot were silent. Only the reverberation of the Turkish drums could be heard.

"Sire," Priest replied, "it worries me that an old man, servant to his calculating French queen, too fat to even mount a horse, will soon gallop down this hill to engage the entire Ottoman Empire."

Even the horses quieted after this remark until the king shook with laughter. All who could hear the remark laughed the laugh of gratefully released tension.

"Try and keep up, cousin, just try," the monarch replied before summoning a messenger. A short command and the retainer galloped off toward Hetman Jablonowski's hillock.

Bolek noticed Jacek, his winged retainers and other hussars moving to position themselves in front of their king while checking armor, weapons, adjusting tack and saddle.

"Volunteers," Priest said in a hushed voice. "These are the souls of our country. Now come magnates, senators, the high born, the wealthy and powerful nobles. Each has said his confession at St. Josephs, each has an image of the Virgin painted onto his armored chest, and each carries a red and white cross on his pennant."

Bolek recognized Lukasz Kazimierz, the hussar scout who had strolled into their campfire as the grand army came. "God's blessing, Bolek," the winged horseman retainer said, winking as he rode by to take his rightful place in the front lines.

The massive Turkish drums continued to pound out their sinister Boom! Boom! Boom! But the Turkish din was soon drowned out with the sound of fifes, drums, horns and Polish bagpipes. There were even a few mounted hussar retainers carrying bright blue and white striped kettledrums riding among their brothers, beating out their own rhythms as they rode. The retainers of this first volley of winged horsemen lined up in two rows behind their lords, each carrying extra lances and various other weapons, ready to offer their weapons, horses and lives after the first contact.

At 4 P.M., 150 hussars volunteered to test the ground before them, to determine its suitability for cavalry, having to traverse grape fields, stone fences and the Turkish spahis cavalry. A squadron of hussars were sent to cover their retreat. The king received a report that the ground before him was hard and flat enough for cavalry.

At five in the afternoon, a single cannon shot rang out from Jablonowski's Hillock. Unknown to the Turks, this was a prearranged signal for the besieged garrison to throw open the gates of the city and attack the Turks. Thousands of Christian Ukrainian Cossacks had been joining the liberating army and with many capable of speaking the Turkish language well, were able to move one brave spy in and out of the city to deliver the vital message.

Within moments of the cannon shot the first of Vienna's cavalry streamed out from the fort at a gallop, followed by the starving and battered citizens, women and children included, who attacked the Turks with pitch forks and anything heavy, mad with a vengeance after sixty days of siege, of sixty days of bombardment by cannon, of sixty days of facing war, death, disease and starvation.

"There! There is the enemy," King Jan Sobieski shouted, pointing to Turkish pasha's finely embroidered red tent where Mustafa sat calmly, for all to see. "*Jezus Maria ratuj*! Lord deliver us. We ride for that point."

"Now, Góralu," Priest whispered. "Ready yourself. The Turks are giving up ground, we are herding them, and packing them closely so only the few on the edge can actually fight. A flanking maneuver will tip the scale in our favor. Our lines must hold now as the steel hammer of the Husaria will break the front line and the enemy spirit with it."

Bolek moved and twitched in his saddle, searching for the proper position, the right steeling thoughts. He sat with a nervous energy as the front row of the hussars moved as one, their horses in a slow walk, when the king spurred his Arab onward to engage. The Royal Guardsmen shadowed each move the monarch made; thousands of hussars did the same. Rank and file, spirits boiling but disciplined, maintained field positions. Several thousand pennoned lances heralding their presence, their culture, and their god were proudly displayed. Hetmans Sieniawski and Jablonowski moved up to Sobieski's flanks, matching the king's pace and direction, step for step.

"Now it comes," Priest said to Bolek with a great smile, his eyes as wild as the prairie. "Your king sets the pace."

Three groups of Polish Hussars and one group of like Austria cavalry, twenty thousand mounted men in all, initiated perhaps the longest cavalry charge in history, trotting boldly at first toward one point – the green Standard of the Prophet which flew above the red tent in the distance. This was to be the last crusade.

Four ranks of hussars and five hundred light cavalry ringed the king, all brilliant in color and terrible in gleaming steel. Each kept one horse length between rank and column. Once locked in an embrace with the invaders a fallen comrade in the front row would be replaced by another from the second row, the replacement often having to leap over a wounded or dead horse, for in battle the gallant equines bore the greatest brunt of bullets, arrows and spears. The retainers followed with spare kopia lances, *pocztow,* also ready to smash into armor and flesh. Priest tossed two additional quivers of arrows to Bolek while mouthing, *"Trust me."*

The charge of the three thousand Polish Hussar right flank began from one thousand feet away from the awaiting line of bodies, the Turkish spears and muskets readying for embrace, their commanders futilely attempting to shout final orders over the din. The hussar horses were held to a slow deliberate pace to save the horses from tiring too early. Let the Turks tremble with anticipation. Lances still pointed to heaven, horse, rider and a fifteen-foot lance appeared to the Turkish front line as a swarm of approaching giants. On a raised sword signal and holler from the king, who rode in the center of this wall of death, the hussars commanded their steeds into a slow canter, all lances driven as one downward, parallel to the ground, aimed at the hearts of the Turkish front line of defense. The field commanders shouted another command and the hussars pulled together, knee to knee, into a fast canter.

Chapter 59

There was no going back now. The die was cast, for neither horse nor man could turn away. With momentum in body and soul, the committed mass of human and equine, sword and spear charged as one.

One hundred paces before contact with the seamless and deadly barbed Turkish line, the hussars flew into a frightening gallop, nostrils flaring on horse and rider, eyes wide. The ground rumbled, the field alive with an eerie sound as the air moved rapidly through the tall, feathered wooden arcs attached to the retainers' backs, hissing like a giant snake as they gained momentum. Hundreds of hooves pounded the ground yet the hearts beat as one.

Neither Mustafa nor his generals had expected the Polish cavalry to commit to a gallop charge so quickly and from so far away. The Husaria was always used as a last attempt to break through an enemy line. But here they came early, and from so far away. The Muslims felt confused, pressured. What was the Christian plan?

"Holy Mary, Mother of God, pray for us sinners now and at the hour of our death," many charging Polish and Austrian warriors chanted.

Taking up the rear with the king's Royal Guards, riding on the back rim of the elliptical phalanx of attack, Bolek also prayed. Confusion reigned as some of the galloping men were shot off their mounts, thrown under the hooves of their comrades' mounts. Horses fell, impaled with spears and arrows. Quo Vadis leapt and twisted this way and that, sturdy and true, no obstacle too difficult. The rumbling of hooves continued as Bolek could see now see the sweat pouring down individual faces before him, eyes wide with terror as the steel wall approached them.

"God for Poland!" was the last thing Bolek heard before the wave of men and horses collided with the enemy line, the deafening roar of two thousand shattering lances signaling contact. Splintered wood rained down as snowflakes, filling his dry mouth.

The janissary Turkish defense line was hurled backward as a cloud of red mist rose into the air and enveloped them. Quo Vadis reared behind two dead Polish steeds, giving Bolek a quick view of what lay ahead. He saw the backs of many Turks as they ran for the safety of the Danube, their spirits broken by the vicious embrace. Many of them lay flat with lance points in their backs, their courage broken seconds before impact. Many hussars had broken through the single line of infantry and cannons to engage the sipahis cavalry.

Quo Vadis leapt over a screaming mass of flesh and Bolek spun her around, clearing a space for him to fire his bow as the hussar war steeds muscled their way through the second line of defense. Sabers, war hammers, pistols, maces and points of broken lances slashed, smashed, pummeled and gored, sung to a chorus of screaming men and horses in horrifying pain. Live Turkish bodies immediately replaced the dead to fill the gaps as the hussars hacked forward with brutal efficiency and commitment.

Some Turks fought at eye-level with mounted hussars, standing on the dead and dying bodies of their comrades and horse carcasses. Hussar field commanders vied with their janissary counterparts to shout orders and words of encouragement to their troops, each echoing the other, but in tongues foreign to the other. "Forward, men!" and "kill the infidel!" War, a revolt against civilization itself, forced each man to awaken the beast within.

The forward momentum quickened as pancerni joined the hussars, peppering the maw of Hell before them with deadly arrows and spears, hundreds launched at point-blank range in an unending stream.

The front lines of the hussars, now hedged on three sides by the Turkish infantry, turned attention to the attacks coming from the left and right, goading their horses forward, some fighting on foot, each maintaining a forward moving pace, creating a living, flying phalanx of death. Bolek stayed with the fight, often forcing Quo Vadis forward, often commanding the magnificent beast to spin round and round in a tight circle, knocking attackers who came too close off their feet. All was a blur, a roar of screams, an indescribable odor as he was forced to stand in his stirrups, firing downward into the blue coats.

"I am here, Father! I am for Poland, Mother!"

In his peripheral vision he caught sight of a familiar figure and turned to it, freezing briefly in disbelief as his king, atop his white charger, hurdled over a pile of bodies which littered this area of the melee, jumping forward, over and through the Turkish front line. Though horrified, Bolek instinctively followed the living breath of Poland, driving his heels into Quo Vadis, forcing the horse to leap over the waist-height obstacles as he fired arrow after arrow, hitting target after target of those who threatened to unhorse, shoot or impale his king, while leaving his own body defenseless, vulnerable to enemy spears and battleaxes. He realized he was next to a comrade, a hussar with the same goal. A quick glance. Jacek!

The king reared his horse for friend and foe alike to see, cutting the air with his szabla, shouting inaudible words, spurring his troops forward. Follow me! A thundering cheer rose from behind Bolek, but his excitement was brief as four mounted Saphis appeared, riding directly at the king. Jacek prodded his horse to his king's left, Bolek to the right.

"You take Pestilence," the king shouted to Jacek, and to Bolek: "and you Famine. Leave War and Death to me!"

Inspired by the fearless challenge, Bolek shot an arrow straight into the face of the closest armored rider. Jacek threw his broken lance at the other three as a distraction, giving himself time to draw his szabla and war hammer. While the king charged with saber in his left hand and mace in his right, Bolek raised his mountain ax. All three Turkish riders fell, as if they had ridden into a low-hanging branch.

More enemy cavalry chased the advancing trio, as the king refused to slow his charge, driving straight at the red tent. Bolek raised his legs as high as he was able, twisting in the saddle, until he rode backwards on Quo Vadis, firing the last few arrows from the last quiver into the pursuing infidel bodies.

A mass of blurry horsemen charged the trio from the smoky flank. Dropping his now useless bow Bolek drew his saber, only to find Polish Royal Guardsmen emerge from the smoke and dust, quickly dispersing the attacking Turks, encircling the king and his two bodyguards.

Righting his body in the saddle while taking a second to look about, Bolek took in the chaotic results of his king's rash bravery. Once the much-feared Jan III Sobieski had hurdled over the Turkish front line for all to see, he had broken the spirit and resolve of the enemy. Nearly the entire Turkish army, looking like a stampede of herd animals, ran for the supposed safety of the mighty Danube, with the aggressive Polish horsemen at their tails.

Hundreds of hussars and pancerni galloped and slashed their way toward the red tent which stood under the green standard of the Grand Vizier Kara Mustafa. The Crescent had been bent and now was to be broken by the Cross. With the Husaria and pancerni cavalry now behind the Turkish center, the will of the Ottoman army broke.

Danger was still near as many Turks turned and fought in desperation, knowing a soldier's death was their only option. Small groups of resistance formed, arrows whizzed on all sides of Bolek, but more and more Poles reached the fray at the front-most point, most on blood-spattered horses. Bolek continued to protect his king with his body as a living shield as the famed fighter and symbol of his people fearlessly rode ever forward.

Jacek was there too, but Bolek saw no sign of his other comrades. Suddenly the king reined his horse to a halt and Bolek realized he stood before the Turkish leader's opulent red tent. Pride-filled shouts came from all directions.

A roar of praise mixed with relief erupted from the walls of the city also as hundred of arms waved in tribute to the new owner of that garish tent. After sixty days of siege, the constant bombardment of cannon balls and near starvation, the lightning charge and quick victory was like the sun bursting through ominous black clouds. Thoughts of death were replaced with those of hope and thanksgiving. People clanged pots together, smashed helmets into the stone walls of Vienna, fired off cannon, and pounded on armor in a childlike elation. Others fell to their knees and cried out in disbelief, thanking God for this miracle. All eyes were on the king of Poland as he graciously nodded toward the defiant walled city, while sweeping his szabla in a great circle, to honor his hussars, cavalry, infantry and retainers.

Anxious to share in triumph with his friends, Bolek looked around through smoke and dust for familiar faces to no avail.

"Go," Jacek told Bolek, "I will shadow his majesty. See to your friends."

Chapter 60

Tracing his way back to where he separated from his comrades, to the spot where his king had hurdled over the Turkish line, Bolek found himself surrounded by hellish scenes as Quo Vadis picked her way over dead and dying bodies, her hooves sloshing through a sickening mixture of hacked flesh, spurting blood, mud, sweat and urine. Both victor and vanquished, all too human now, somehow fell into themselves. The war became personal. Bolek locked eyes with a dying Turk who no longer radiated hatred, but acceptance, readying himself silently for the inevitable. A Pole, eyes wild and face bloody, continued to hack at the long-dead body of a Turk. Another walked along in a whimpering daze, cradling his severed left arm in his right.

Bolek fell heavily in what was once a man's entrails, his curse lost in the confusion of men dying in pain. Tadek's body lay a few feet away, three arrows sunk deeply into his chest, his mouth contorted, frozen in death as he lay among seven dead Turks, szabla in hand, killed of necessity from a distance, for no man could have bested him at arm's length. His magnificent horse Parabellum stood patiently next to its master, waiting for him to rise.

Czesław lay at the edge of a heap of human and horse flesh; a pale-faced fallen giant lying in a pool of his own blood, his stomach ripped open from an ax which lay at his feet, its handle still clutched by the hand of its slain owner. A bulging-eyed Ajax panted shallow and fast, lying next to its master, blood spurting from belly and mouth with each labored breath.

"Am I still invited for Christmas Eve?" Czesław gasped, as Bolek covered his body with a nearby horse blanket.

"Yes, Father. First guest on the list."

"Are horses allowed in heaven?" he whispered, his once plump and ruddy face now pale and drawn. He died with a child's innocent expression frozen on his face. It somehow pleased Bolek that Ajax's panting stopped with Czesław's.

A few feet on he found the red beard's blue bow, No Arc, taking it for his own. No battle ghoul, those who rummaged after battles, would touch it. Sobbing, he found Piotr a few yards away, lying on his back, a single arrow lodged in his chest. The faithful Hector perhaps five yards away, snorting, awaiting more Turks.

"The others . . .?" Piotr asked through a gasp.

"With the king in the pasha's tent," Bolek whispered, "their szablas each dripping with Turkish blood."

"Hector crushed a skull with one mighty kick. Góralu, I've lost my flute."

Bolek reached into his coat, extracting his own flute and putting it into Piotr's hand. "May God bless you."

Before Piotr could finish crossing himself, he passed. Bolek took his hand and softly finished Piotr's final task for him.

Looking up as if to find some deep meaning above, Bolek screamed to heaven. The sky was obscured by smoke and ash. The smell that enveloped him was a corrupt mixture of the odors of flowing blood and acrid sulphur.

A moan to his left. A man with one eye hanging down to his cheek, leaning against a pile of bodies, an arrow in his neck, looked with horror with his remaining eye at the dangling one.

A curse from a familiar voice brought him back from Hell to the battlefield as he recognized Priest struggling to emerge from amid a pile of bodies; his head and armor bloody, an arrow in his right breast.

"How did we fare?" he asked hoarsely.

"The Turks are on the run, the king commands from the pasha's tent. The thunder in the distance is the shouts of celebration from the walls of Vienna."

"Innocence no longer graces you eyes, Góralu."

"Some things should not be seen," Bolek mumbled."Or spoken of."

"The wolves bide their time; patiently awaiting their feast; the eternal harvest. What of our friends?" Priest asked, wincing and shuddering as Bolek helped him to his feet.

"All gone."

Two wild eyed Janissaries, running blindly in panic, charged Bolek, swords drawn, mad screams from their throats. Bolek dodged left then right, confusing the two sufficiently to get under their guard. Knocking the first to the ground with No Arc, the other he dispatched with a left fist to the jaw.

"Look at this!" Bolek shouted. "These are boys, not men."

Summoning his beloved Quo Vadis and Tadek's Parabellum to him, he slapped the young Janissaries conscious then hefted one atop Parabellum, the other atop Quo Vadis.

"Ride! He commanded. "Go home! Remember this!"

The two boys needed no more prodding and galloped from the carnage.

Priest's warm smile was unexpected. "Góralu, the four of us had the honor of watching our king break the Turkish line. And we saw you at his side. It was our destiny to find you."

"Don't die, Priest," Bolek begged as he caught his slumping master.

"After this, there is only one choice; faith or despair? Which will it be for you, my son?"

"Father in heaven, please let him live. Please," Bolek prayed as he helped Priest recline atop the body of a dead horse.

"Góralu, they say heaven is a feast. And I am hungry for it. I move not to death but through it."

"I am losing my father and grandfather all over again."

"Vodka."

Bolek found the flask Priest pointed to and helped him drink.

"Bah!" Priest cursed. "I'll not die in the mud. Mieszko!" he shouted, before whistling feebly.

"You can't be moved. The surgeons must save you."

"By God's grace, I will die as I've lived, in the saddle."

Mieszko appeared on command, Piotr's Hector at his side, head low, realization that his master was no more had come.

Bolek cut off the arrow shaft and then dug out the barb as Priest emptied his flask. Mieszko bowed his front legs, his chest almost touching the ground, allowing Bolek to raise Priest to the saddle with as little pain to the wounded soldier as possible.

"Give me Czesław's bow," Priest ordered. "I will pick up my violin back at camp. Take my szabla, Bolek," he said, weakly pulling his saber from its sheath. "Come down from your mountain, son. Z gory jedz. You will be closer to God among his people than in the clouds."

"You leave me here amid the greatest evil ever to plague the earth?"

"I just saw you give your precious Quo Vadis to a sworn enemy. Your soul is primed to stand and confront evil."

A cheer from behind the walls of Vienna made Priest shake his head and grimace. Bolek watched as the old soldier surveyed the carnage all around them.

"Evil is a mystery, Bolek. We face it with faith, reason and grace. Always follow the One who has defeated evil, sin and death."

"I will, Father."

"One day a great Pole will rise and show the world how to resist evil – but peacefully, without all of this death and sin. Be not afraid."

Bolek put his head to Priest's thigh and embraced him at the waist, as the wounded warrior rested against the mighty Mieszko.

"Hector is yours, young Bolesław Radok. You two shall fly like the wind over the unbridled plains. May your love of Poland be wider than the sky."

The Royal Guardsman leader gently nodded before turning Mieszko eastward. Bolek could only watch as the image of the slumped body atop the grand and faithful horse, bathed in the soft rosy glow of sunset, trotted away, eventually to merge with the mountain shadows of earth and sky, on his way home.

Chapter 61

A letter from Jan Sobieski to his queen, written from the Vizier's tent on the 13th of September, 1683.

Only solace of my heart and soul, my most beautiful, most charming and most beloved Marysienka!

Our Lord and God, blessed for all ages, has brought unheard of factory and glory to our nation. All the guns, the whole camp, uncountable spoils have fallen into our hands. Having covered the trenches, the fields and the camp with corpses, the enemy now flees in confusion. The camels, mules, cattle and sheep, which he kept nearby, are only today being rounded up by our troops, who also drive herds of Turks before them.

Others, particularly des renegats, flee to our camp from the Turks of their own accord mounted on fine horses and in beautiful dress. Such is the unbelievable nature of events that there was an alarm today both among the town's people and here in our camp, no one being able to think or believe other than the enemy will return. There is enough powder and ammunition alone for a million men. This past night I saw also what I had always longed to see. Our marauding bands put light to the powder in several places; it seemed as if Judgment Day was upon us, but no harm was caused; we watched the smoke forming clouds in the sky. Yet it is most unfortunate that there should have been such wasteful destruction.

The Vizier took such hurried flight that he only had time to escape with one horse and in the clothes he wore. I have succeeded him, for the greater part of the riches has fallen to me; chance would have it that being first in the camp and close on the Vizier's heels one of his servants betrayed his allegiance and pointed out to us his tents, as extensive as the cities of Warsaw and Lwow within their walls. I have all his personal insignia which are usually borne before him, and the Mahometan banner which his Emperor gave him for the war, and which even today I sent in the care of Talenti to the Holy Father in

Rome. *I have all the tents, carts et mille d'autres galanteries fort jolies et fort riches, mais fort riches and a vast array of other things still unseen. Il n'y a point de comparaison avec ceux de Chocim. Several quivers, studded with rubies and sapphires, are alone worth several thousand red zlotys You will not be able to say to me as the Tatar women do to their husbands when they return empty-handed: 'You are no warrior to return without booty' because he who captures booty must be at the front. I have the Vizier's horse with all its caparison; he himself was hotly pursued but managed nonetheless to escape. His kihaj, i.e. second in importance only to him, was killed, and no small number of his pashas. Gold swords and other military equipment lie in abundance. The night prevented a conclusion; furthermore, in retreating they put up fierce opposition et font la plus belle retirade du mond. They abandoned their janissaries in the trenches, who were put to the sword during the night because such was their arrogance and pride that when some of them were fighting us in the fields, the others were storming the town, as indeed they had the equipment to do.*

I estimate their numbers, excluding the Tatars, at some three hundred thousand; others put the numbers of their tents alone at three hundred thousand and take an average of three to one tent, which would make an unheard of number. I, however, reckon there to be at least a hundred thousand tents, as there were several camps. For a day and two nights anyone who cares to has been dismantling them, but I warrant they will not pull them all down this week. They left behind them a mass if innocent local Austrian people, particularly women, but they butchered as many as they could. Bodies of dead women lie in great numbers, but there are also many wounded and those who might yet live. Yesterday I saw a three-year-old child, a most pretty little boy, whose face and head had been savagely slashed by an infidel.

The Vizier had captured a marvelously beautiful ostrich from one of the Emperor's palaces here; but this too was killed so that it would not fall into our hands. What luxuries he had surrounding his tents, it is impossible to imaging. He had baths, he had a garden and fountains, rabbits, cats; there was even a parrot, but as this flew about we could not catch it.

Today I was in the city, which could have held out five more days, no more. Eyes have never seen such damage as the mines have caused there; the fortified towers, which were once enormous and high, stand like rocky crags and are in such ruins that they could have withstood no longer. The Emperor's palace is completely ruined by shot.

A;; the armies, which gave such good account of themselves, give praise to God and ourselves for this victory. When the enemy began to retreat and allowed himself to be broken – the Vizier, with whom it fell on me to do battle, turned his entire forces against my right wing, leaving our middle or main guard, like the left wing, with nothing to do, with the result that they sent me all their German reinforcements – the Princes, such as the Elector of Bavaria and Prince Waldeck, rushed up to me clasping me around the neck and kissing me on the mouth. The generals did likewise on my hands and feet; imagine what then the soldiers! The officers and all the cavalry and infantry regiments cried out: Ach, unzer brave Kenik! They listened to me as our soldiers never do. I dare not speak of the delight of the Princes of Lorraine and Saxony this morning (I did not have occasion to see them yesterday, since they were on the extreme of my left wing where U had sent the Marshal of the Court several squadrons of hussars) nor of Starhemberg who is commandant here. They all embraced me, congratulated me, and called me their savior. Afterwards I went to two churches. All the common people kissed my hands, my feet, my clothes; others only touched me saying: 'Ach, let us kiss such a valiant a hand!' They would all have liked to cry 'Vivat' but it was plain that they feared their officers and superiors. One group could not resist and timorously cried out 'Vivat' which I saw was frowned on. Therefore, having dined with the commandant, I left the city to return to camp and the people waved and accompanied me to the very gates. Relations, I notice, are not very good between Starhemberg and the city council, for when they greeted me, he did not even bother to introduce them. All the Princes have now gathered and the Emperor has sent a message ahead that he is only one mile away. This letter draws on into the early morning, but they will not allow me to finish it and share my happiness longer with you, my love

There are many dead on our side; notably the two, God have mercy on them, about whom you will have already heard from Dopont. As regards the foreign armies, de Croy is dead, his brother wounded and several eminent fiures also killed. Padre d-Aviano who could not cover me with enough kisses, tells me that he saw a white dove flying above our armies.

Today we shall move off after the enemy into Hungary. The electors do not want to leave my side. For all these blessings of the Lord, may praise, honor and glory be His for ever. When the Vizier saw that he could not withstand our attack, he summoned his sons and cried like a baby. Then he said to the Khan, 'Save me, if you can!' To this the Khan replied 'We know the king, nothing can be done and we must think how to save ourselves.'

This letter will make an excellent news-sheet to send out to all the world, adding que c'est lat letter du Roi a la Reine. The Prince of Saxony and Bavaria have promised to accompany me to the ends of the world. We must move some two miles from here because of the great stench coming from the corpses, horses, cattle and camels. I wrote a few words to the French king, addressing them us Roi tres Chretien and informing him de la bataille gagnee et du salut de la chreitiente. The Emperor who is sailing down the Danube is now just a mile and a half away; I can see, however, that he is not too keen to see me, given his pomps and vanities; on the other hand, he would like to arrive in the town as soon as possible pour chanter le 'Te Deum'. I withdraw in his favor, most happy to avoid these ceremonies, which is all the reward we have so fare experienced.

So I must end, kissing and embracing my most beautiful Marysienka with all my heart and soul. A. M. le Marquis et a ma souer mes baisemains. May all

rejoice and give thanks to God that He did not let the pagan as us, 'So where is your God?'.

The morning of September 13th found some of the victorious warriors in celebration while others tended to the wounded and buried the dead, still others lost in deep mourning. Rank determined one's place and, therefore, one's duties. Losses had to be tallied. The dark battlefield humor demanded the enemy's losses be doubled while your own were halved. But the reality on the field was dealing with slain comrades, now frozen in death, soon to be bloated and stinking bags of gaseous flesh to be burned in a community pit or, if in rough terrain, merely covered with rocks, hoping the creatures of the night would not feast on the dead.

Wounded in the thousands were brought to a central location, well away from the camp, where they were tended to by a small army of surgeons; the screams from the makeshift hospital often loud enough to cause a horse to bolt.

"Are you Bolesław Radok?" A pancerni captain asked as he and a detachment of cavalry soldiers rode up to Bolek who was burying the bodies of his fallen friends.

"I am," Bolek replied, resting on his shovel, using the sleeve of his coat to wick the sweat away.

"You are burying a horse," one asked with a chuckle.

"And its rider," Bolek replied without looking up.

"His Majesty asks for you."

"I have an important task to complete."

"A command from the king demands immediate response," the leader fired back.

"Tell his majesty I will finish burying three of the men who gave all for our victory," Bolek replied. "And then I will come."

The captain scowled and moved to dismount but was stopped by his lieutenant.

"Wojiech," he whispered, "This is the guardsman who was first through the line with the king."

The pancerni captain's expression softened. "May we help?" he asked.

"I would be grateful," Bolek said. "And later I shall help you with your dead."

"Thank you, sir," the officer nodded. "I will tell my youngsters of the sight of the king of Poland charging directly at the entire Ottoman army, hurdling over the line first, a Royal Guardsman and a hussar at each flank."

"And if I am blessed with a wife and children," Bolek replied, "I will tell them of the twelve hours you and your comrades stood against the grinding teeth of the Janissary units' front line, wearing it down an inch at a time." And there, thinking of how Priest would say it, "By God, gentlemen, watching the enemy wither was like watching a young man aging before one's eyes, his sharp teeth changed to a set of toothless gums. You were the relentless surgeons."

"Ha!" the pancerni captain exclaimed, "we have here a warrior poet."

The exhausted men shared a laugh and became fast friends. Many hands soon made short work, dirt was packed, the graves blended with the ground, so no battle ghouls would defile them. Bolek accompanied his new friends to the richly colored and embroidered red tent, now the encampment headquarters of the Hero of the Relief of Vienna.

The mood of the army was much-changed from the days before victory for the booty was unbelievable. The Turks had abandoned their precious cannons, weapons, and hordes of horses, camels, oxen and sheep, pig and goat. Mountains of exquisite clothing stitched with gold, made of materials the Poles had never seen or felt before, large and ornate rugs worth fortunes, cavernous tents, and sacks of money requiring two men to lift littering the tent floors. Many soldiers were sampling the exotic foods of the East. The mood-elevating effects of a drink that the newly freed slaves and servants called coffee was a particular favorite.

More heart-warming still was the gratitude of the Christian

slaves, freed and being tended to as well as humanely possible. They were treated as human beings now, each deserving of his own measure of dignity, and their expressions were more than enough thanks. Shouts of joy, thanksgiving and oaths to God rang like thunder as former slaves were encouraged to dine on the pasha's own food stocks.

Bolek's heart pounded as much as it had before the battle had begun as he rode past the famed hetman generals and captains, the leaders of Poland's formidable army who had just crushed the best the Ottoman Empire could muster. The king's generals, their aides, strategists and their captains were working around an outdoor table with maps strewn everywhere. Bolek spied Jacek next to the king himself, and his friend motioned him to his side.

"Sire, this is Bolesław Radok," Jacek said.

The king stunned Bolek with a bear hug embrace from the Hero of Vienna and a kiss on each cheek. As the king spoke to Jacek, Bolek had an opportunity to study the revered leader. Taller than he appeared from a distance on horseback, he wore his hair closely cropped, in a campaign cut, his thick brown mustache finely trimmed. The king was not fat, but stoutly built, with a protruding belly. A bull. It was no wonder, Bolek thought, that the hearty campaigner could still lead a charge at the age of fifty-six. As he smiled at Jacek, he seemed quite noble. When he touched on a dark subject, his face darkened and Bolek could see the fear this great king could inspire.

Mustafa's heart must have fallen to his embroidered slippers when his saw this Polish veteran lead his troops into battle.

"Gentlemen," the king said, addressing his generals. "I wanted to introduce each of you to my temporary left and right flank at the very end of the charge."

The others laughed without offence as their king and then each of them extended his hand first to Jacek and then to Bolek.

It was with pride that Bolek took the hand of Grand General

Jablonowski and his lieutenants Kontzki, Wielopolski, Lazinski, Sieniawski, Potocki, Galecki, Lydzinski, Wisniowski, Mionczynski, Zbrozek, Zamojski, Szczuka, Dobczyc, Malachowski, Polanowski, and Charczewski. His one regret was his comrades could not share in this moment, for it was they who had forged the man who now stood next to their king.

"You do all the planning, the strategies, the execution and you allow me and my two young friends here the esteemed honor of the cutting of the ribbon. I salute you." As his captains returned the compliment, the king graciously bowed.

"Now back to work, my noble staff. I want to put an end to these invasions once and for all. This time we must break the swordsman, not the sword. Let us chase these Muslims back to the Black Sea then deep into Hungary."

When the formal meeting broke up, Bolek Radok, former Górale shepherd found himself and his friend Jacek alone with their king.

"And so here is our triumvirate again, our Christian troika," the king exclaimed. "I humbly thank the Queen of Heaven for a mailed hussar on one arm and a deadly pancerni archer on the other. Who taught you to shoot and ride like that?" the king asked Bolek.

"Czesław, the bow; Piotr the horse. . . . . I do not even know from what clan the spring from," Bolek admitted.

"Adamczyk. Then you've been taught by the best. They both trained my son, Prince Jakub, in said skills."

"And Priest. He taught me . . ."

"I am sorely distressed at the news of him. He and his comrades, my honored Royal Guardsmen, devoted to God and Poland, all. *Dulce et decorum est pro patria mori!* (*It is sweet and fitting to die for one's homeland.*)"

Bolek bowed his head and relayed the story of lashing Priest to his horse and how he disappeared over the horizon, toward the Poland he so loved.

"A service to Poland, young Highlander," the king replied. "We have no concrete evidence of his death. Perhaps God will favor us and allow his spirit to haunt these hills for five hundred years or more. As for you, you have done your part to create a new myth. Beware evildoers, beware of the warrior priest who rides the hills and mountains of Poland, protecting the innocent and defending the truth. Beware his terrible swift sword, his deadly arrows. The faint sound of a violin will alert you of his coming. I will repeat this story in Cracow, myself."

Bolek and Jacek smiled.

"Grieve not, gentlemen. It is fitting for God to sacrifice the best for the good of the whole. Sons, there is booty here and responsibility. I have need of you both."

Both men swore allegiance to any task.

"First, Jacek of the ancient line and feeble purse," the king said, snapping his fingers, to which an aide promptly appeared at his side. "I want you to take this captured Turkish standard to his Holiness in Rome. The standard is not Mustafa's but there is no need to share that with him. Tell him *Veni Vidi Deus Vicit*, (I came, I saw, God conquered). Let the Pope grasp his crucifix, say his prayers. Then you must add that Emperor Leopold should be sailing on the Danube, back to his city from Passau in a few days, once things have settled down, and throw in a wink once the realization the Emperor was not part of the melee comes to His Holiness."

Jacek repeated the message and promised quick fulfillment.

"Then say to His Holiness that if he wishes to graciously honor Poland for her service in Vienna, to please excommunicate the French king for attempting to bribe our politicians."

"Bolek the Góral highlander, fearless friend of patriots who gave all, you are every inch a noble gentleman. Poland and especially her king are indebted to you. Time and circumstances prevents formalities at this moment, but in front of all here, I say your heart is as noble as any in Poland. I embrace you and call you my peer."

Bolek froze.

Once I would have given my soul for these words. Now . . . Rozalia, dead. My crime of rape. My comrades gone. Those I've killed.

He tried to form words but the king went on as if he had just announced a dance.

"I will guide the knighthood through the Sejm personally. Our victory today saved many noble necks and purses and all will cheer my decision on this," he said with a wink. "Lands suitable to your liking will be granted. I adopt you, young Radok, into my own clan, that of Janina, and my coat of arms is also yours."

"Your Majesty, I . . ."

"The Grand Vizier Mustafa had to leave Vienna suddenly and was negligent in forgetting his horse. Take this silver stirrup to my queen who awaits me in Cracow and tell her who it belonged to and how I came by it. Give her this letter."

A German cavalryman rode up, dismounting before his horse had fully stopped, handing his reins to a nearby servant.

"Sire," the soldier said with a deep bow, "the Duke of Lorraine respectfully requests your presence outside the city's main gate."

"Tell him I come," the king replied.

The German remounted with a leap and drove his horse toward Vienna's main gate.

"You see, gentlemen, duty call for me also," Sobieski said with a smile. "So, quickly to some additional business concerning you two. By the hand of God, we three broke through the Turkish line first and thereby crushed their spirit. Your deeds have spread through these ranks like the wind on the Steppes. And so you now pass from mere men and into the world of myth and symbol. Symbols of Poland. Symbols of sacrifice. I know you are both of high moral character for you never wavered from your duty in this great test. But from now until your last breath you must both remain Polish heroes. Act as such. Give me two stouthearted men like you in our front lines and we'll soon have a thousand more under saddle. You represent our ideal."

"Your majesty, you are too kind," Bolek said.

"These are not kind words, young sir, but a command. You both must strive to be exemplary Poles from this day forward. For your parts in the battle, I grant a sizable share of the booty to each of you. These fortunes will be recorded in Cracow within the month, accounts created and filled. Draw on the accounts at your pleasure."

"There is no need, Sire for—"

"Not your choice, Jacek," the king replied sternly. "I understand your Anulka, our beautiful Sieninska ward, whom my wife favors so well, has agreed to a marriage."

"Yes, Your Majesty." Jacek replied.

"Raise good Christian sons and daughters. Our enemies will never dry up and fly away. God tests us always, for how do we learn without these tests? What we have is worth the sacrifice, no?"

"Yes, Your Majesty," Jacek replied.

"Young Radok, has God put a feminine prospect in your path?" the king asked.

"No, Your Majesty."

"Not to worry. Once word of your heroics and of the booty I am awarding to you spreads it will draw maidens to you from each cardinal direction. You'll see nothing but painted faces and carefully combed hair, hear nothing but the rustle of skirts and smell nothing but perfumes. Choose wisely."

"Yes, Your Majesty," Bolek said, bowing deeply.

Neither an illustrious king nor the wealth of the Turkish army can restore my loved ones to me. Who was I and who am I now?

"Now to another obligation. When the Turks ran like scared chickens, it seems there was no time to take their women with them. The Muslim treats his women as possessions. And rather than leave their slave wives and concubines to their Christian conquerors the Muslims slit their throats. We awoke this morning to witness the sight of female bodies littering the riverbank. Those with newborn babes were not spared, and many poor infants were seen still sucking at lifeless breasts. This is inhuman. I charge both of you to take one child each and raise it as one of your own, in good Polish Christian tradition. Give them a God of peace and love, of salvation."

Both men agreed, glancing quickly at the other, speechless, as only two bachelors could be with such an obligation in front of them.

"I thank you both, deeply. When it is time for marriage, sons, come to Cracow and I will act the godfather. I want to honor you both for you were first through the breach at your king's side, first for Poland. God's blessing." The king crossed himself. "Wodek over there is assigned to help you with all the details. *Dowvitzenia*. Go with God."

Jacek and Bolek could hardly maintain their demeanors as the king abruptly ended the audience and disappeared into another part of his newly acquired palatial tent. This warrior king who had just saved Christendom had spoken to both men in familiar tones. They would be known and honored for their deeds in battle and their weddings would be affairs of state. Even more astounding was the size of their share of the booty captured from the luxury-loving Eastern Ottomans. Now both were rich beyond reason, and together they vowed to remain fast friends, to found illustrious families, to be active in the political affairs of their country, to meet in the Sejm and stand for truth and Poland.

"Bolek, the test for you and I will be to see if these riches and honors color us in the wrong ways."

Jacek and Bolek met with Wodek, the man assigned, by the king, to work out the details of their new responsibilities. Jacek had to leave immediately for Rome and an audience with the Pope. His new daughter, chosen at random by Wodek, would be taken back to Cracow along with a freed slave woman to serve as a nurse until further arrangements could be made.

Bolek accepted responsibility for his new son also. A freed Christian slave, named Joanna, would care for the child on the long journey home to the mountains of Poland. She had known the poor orphaned child's mother, and mournfully related the story of how the woman told Joanna she and her husband were willing to die for their faith, knowing fully the worship of Jesus and his teachings grew through martyrdom and not through slaughter.

"I have turned my other cheek," Joanna told Bolek the slain woman said as she handed Joanna her precious baby. "I know in my heart my husband, and I must defend the life of our child now, our fellow slaves, our brothers and sisters." Joanna told Bolek also how she had watched as the couple fell to their knees and swore an oath between them to assist the crusading force. At that point, Joanna turned and walked away from the child's parents, their most precious possession in a stranger's hands and keeping.

"They sacrificed all for this innocent child," Joanna said, holding the child out to Bolek. "His name is Miklos."

Taking an infant in his arms for the first time ever, Bolek lovingly kissed the dark-haired child then promptly gave it back to Joanna, pleading he was not experienced in such.

So much frailty and innocence after so much brutality and carnage. Lord God allow this child to grow up in peace.

Chapter 62

Before leaving for Cracow, he spent some time with his new friends from the pancerni, sharing stories and promising correspondence and future meetings. Although he enjoyed the awed respect of his fellow soldiers, he was adamant that he simply found himself at the front of the battle and did what any one of them would have done in his place. His fellows, representing every region of Poland, good-naturedly made up impossible stories of the Goral's deeds, with Bolek laughing the hardest, swearing each was true.

The regular army left early in order to join those who shadowed and cut down the fleeing Turks, now on the full run, an army in turmoil, and like a boulder careening down a mountainside, a danger to all in its path. But the Turks still had teeth. Numerous minor battles and skirmishes were fought to the south, and the east as the retreating army struggled for its life as the Austrian, Polish and German alliance tried to put a final end to a one hundred and fifty year threat of Turkish invasion, murderous raids, and Christian enslavement.

Bolek, along with his newly adopted son and the nurse Joanna, left the camp on the morning on September 14th. Although he would have preferred to remain in camp for a few days to partake in more festivities and enjoy the spectacle of watching Emperor Leopold ride in triumph into Vienna, he was under orders to bring news of victory to his queen. While nurse and child were off by wagon to the Radok Manor, Bolek rode ahead on the mighty Hector. He flew toward Cracow at a remarkable pace, resting only for man and mount to eat and drink.

Seeking the fastest route to Poland's famed capitol, he navigated a winding path through his Tatry Mountains. His was a route few would have chosen. One known to only a very few locals, a treacherous endeavor because of the numerous narrow and stony paths and the tricky rock-laden hills and deeply slanted ravines that needed to be traversed. But Bolek knew these paths well, for it was near both his confrontation with the werewolf and his shameful encounter with Alina, the Gypsy girl he had so abused.

Even in the full sun of the September afternoon Bolek felt alone as he raced along on his well-lathered mount, his letter of victory for his queen and souvenir of the splendid victory tucked safely away.

His thoughts turned to his companions. In many ways, they had been fathers to him, and yet in many ways, he had not known them at all. They had bent their personal lives into service to their faith and their country, offering all. They had chosen their path of humble service, foregoing all the pleasures of wife and family, of home and hearth. Yet now they lay in unknown graves. The world would never shout their names or praise their contributions and sacrifices. Nor would Bolek's father's or grand-father's name be shouted in praise. Nor the fathers before them. Nor the truth they stood for.

Invasion, slavery, politics, lust for land, ignorance and apathy toward the rights of the free. There is so much to do, and I am but one man.

But Priest's words echoed in his mind.

See the difference one man can make? One to lead the way. Then there will always be a Poland. You cannot control every situation you face, but you can control your reaction to it.

Bolek reached up to run his hand against the eagle feathers in the Magyar cap Priest had brought for him. The Lech tale, the balance of reason and faith, the wisdom of Solomon – to act with your heart. Now he lies in an unmarked grave.

As he passed Vardo's abandoned Gypsy camp, he slowed his energetic pace at the sight of his brief triumph and greatest failure. His feelings that night which seemed so long ago had led him from elation, to pride, to lust, to shame in a few short hours. The memory of the Gypsy girl, Alina came to him, and his jaw tightened. He attempted to force the image from his mind, but failed. What if the camp were there now? What if he rode into the midst of her father and his men? He asked himself if he had not been on his mission, would he seek out the Gypsy's new camp and confront her father on her whereabouts, find out to whom she had been sold; where she had been taken. He had listened closely to the stories the freed Joanna had whispered of the horrors of slavery, the depraved acts she had been forced to commit, the humiliation of being treated as an animal, devoid of any dignity.

But this was idle dreaming, for nothing could keep him from his mission, an assignment from his king. He put Alina out of his thoughts. Reaching into his pocket, to ensure the precious war trophy, the silver stirrup, was still in his possession, he touched the sealed letter given to him by the king for his queen. Once the word spread through the great city the newspapers would proclaim the thrilling news, and soon all of Poland would know of the great victory. Poland was saved! The church bells would ring in every corner of the land, perhaps even the mighty Zigmunt Bell atop the Wawel Hill in mighty Cracow might awaken.

As he turned onto a little-known trail he knew, that offered a steep but timesaving passage through the mountains, a faint sound reached his ears. There it was again. A scream, Bolek thought. A third time it rang out. His stomach turned as he recognized the scream as the one that haunted his nights and tortured his soul. As he nudged Hector forward at a wary walk the horse paused and snorted. Bolek nudged him to move, but he sniffed the air and snorted again. Despite another nudge, he stood motionless. He sensed something.

Bolek, on full alert, noted motion in two tall pines directly ahead. His mind raced to what lay ahead. Of course! The great cave. Once the lair of a hulking bear and now that of the brigands. The pines hide archers. Bolek's next move was instinctive.

Simon, a former Cossack archer, banished from his village for abusing young boys, squinted and smirked as he focused his attention on the Gypsy girl's writhing and the music of her screams. From his well-disguised platform set high in a pine, he guarded the exposed entrance to the cave his fellows used as a base of operations for all their raids. This was where the captive dark-haired beauty was being prepared for the enjoyment of all. The hot knives applied to her back would weaken her resolve. She would submit soon, and gladly. Broken women were the best. Like horses.

By the angle of the sun, Simon knew his shift as sentry was nearly done. His eyes stayed on the girl, and he bided his time in anticipated lust, for there was little chance of danger. Every able-bodied Pole was occupied in Vienna, and it would take at least thirty soldiers to threaten his camp. And a band that size could be heard for a mile. A sentry could rest, could daydream.

Besides, Simon's fellow sentry, Bela, an escaped Ukrainian prisoner convicted of cheating rich merchants with fraudulent shares in amber caravan profits, sat a hundred paces away, across the path and high up in another pine. Together these men could spot and kill a trespasser through a deadly crossfire of arrows from above. Any hapless traveler who wandered too close to their encampment was a dead man. These sentries could also provide early warning of an attack, if an army patrol was spotted.

Simon tore his eyes from the girl as Koyla, easily recognized by his finely plumed green cap, rode between the mountain and the cave, on patrol. Here was a bold and cruel master, one known both for sword and horse skills, and one eager to engage in battle. A protégé rode behind him, learning the tactics of the experienced warrior.

"When you ride at your mounted opponent, each with drawn sword, at the last instant ram your horse into his body," Simon remembered Koyla once say while training his protégé in tactics. "You will knock him from his mount. Then, the easier to slaughter."

"But what of your horse, Master Koyla?" The raw recruit asked seconds before Koyla's strong arm knocked the boy to the ground.

"What of your horse? Take your opponent's. That is war."

A memorable lesson, Simon thought as he grinned and swayed in his perch, seeking a more comfortable seat. Simon often watched the mentor and student pass the time during his boring watch shift. The boy was learning well, coming along day by day, profiting from Koyla's training. These two constantly practiced and patrolled, praying for an opponent to challenge them. As Koyla locked eyes with Simon, the sentry raised his hand quickly, signaling the all clear. A nod in recognition from Koyla pleased him, and he looked to the sound of the lingering scream. The gypsy girl, partially obscured from the smoke of the fire beside her, her back arched like a bow as she attempted to avoid the glowing knife, was coming along nicely. Simon gauged the height of the sun and frowned. His shift could not end soon enough.

A whistle past his ears was followed by a thump. Familiar, but out of place. Simon turned in his perch just in time to witness his co-sentry's body plummeting limply toward the pine needle-carpeted forest floor twenty feet below. Instantly placing shaft to bow string, Simon sought the source of the arrow, only to hear another, much closer whistle. A burning pain deep in his chest deflated his lungs. He lost control of his body, and it followed his falling bow to the forest floor. His death throe was the blurred glimpse of a giant eagle flying over the head of a Polish pancerni soldier, flying as one down the path to the camp and the cave. The last thing he heard was the wailing of an eagle.

Chapter 63

The Tatra Eagle

'And he hath made my mouth like a sharp sword: in the shadow of his hand he hath protected me, and hath made me as a chosen arrow: in his quiver he hath hidden me.' (Isa 49:2).

Alina, struggling to stay conscious through her pain, looked to a snapping sound high into the tree line.

An eagle. Flying at me.

As the giant raptor grew larger in her sight, the one they called Koyla, he with the beautiful green cap with hawk feathers, charged at it, his student at his heels.

As the eagle reached level ground, Alina felt she had gone mad as the fleet raptor flew into a fog at the mountain's foot and reappeared as a man on horseback. Koyla readied a long *koncerz* for impaling his opponent and rode at a measured pace at the eagle-man, who rode at a full gallop, sword in hand. An instant before contact the eagle-man veered his horse to the brigand's unguarded left side, nimbly tossing his saber from his right hand to his left, the stiff-armed blade instantly slicing Koyla's unsuspecting head from his shoulders, to spin about in a splash of red, as it bounced lightly along the ground. One shout from the eagle-man and the second rider veered off the attack at a gallop toward the safety of the forest.

The camp sprang to life with shouts of alarm. Everyone, including Alina, looked up the mountainside and to its steep path, but there were no other attackers. A volley of arrows spat through the air at the lone man. Standing in his stirrups, he returned fire. While the defender arrows touched only air then earth, the eagle-man's shafts pierced flesh and bone with an uncanny accuracy and at a horrifying rate. To fire at the intruder brought instant death.

As the lunatic rode straight for her, Alina imagined there may be life for her beyond this day. But five men sprang from the brush, rushing man and horse with battleaxes and spears. In an instant, the horse gave a heroic bellow, spinning in circles, the attackers swept to the ground by the half-ton steed then trampled. As the last survivor rose, rear hooves crushed his skull. The eagle-man continued riding at Alina, sliding his horse to a full stop, its hot breath on her face, bulging eyes inches from her own. Her bounds were slashed. She collapsed in a heap.

A voice. A question. Back to reality. *Can you stand?* shouted into her ear. The face of yet another nemesis floated in front of her eyes. The dog, Bolesław. A sudden fury gave her the strength to stand.

"I will stand," she told him, through bloody spittle, brushing his supportive hand away.

"Then fly!" he roared, putting his horse's reins in her hand, then dropping his bow and his quiver of arrows.

He rolled backwards, off the back of his horse, a saber in each hand, turned and ran straight at the approaching wasp's nest of brigands. Her legs numb, her back on fire, she defiantly grabbed the horse's stirrup and pulled herself up. As clarity came, she knew this dream to be real. She was not mad. The beast, Bolesław, the madman, Bolesław was here, attempting to rescue her. Her brief hope of respite quickly melted into an eddy of shame, anger and contempt. She would wait and watch him die.

But why does this madman risk all for such as me?

Unable to blink, she saw him rush into a score of men wielding sabers, pistols, battleaxes and spears.

A pistol shot missed him at point-blank range, as pistol and hand fell to the ground. A scream of pain. Another pistol fizzled. Another shriek.

The madman disappeared within a crowd of enraged brigands. The sound of steel on steel reminded Alina of the metal wind chimes her father gave her as a gift on a day long ago. How it rattled and clanged against itself in a windstorm as it hung on the gypsy wagon that night.

A red mist engulfed the cluster of swirling bodies as one after another screamed and fell. The lone warrior now visible through the thinning mob, moved at lightning speed, sometimes as a dancing shadow leaping from a block to a thrust, sometimes as a hammer, slashing aggressively downward with commanding might, taking an ax and arm at the forearm, sometimes simply stepping a half-step backward or to the side, then aggressively moving forward.

One dropped his ax and ran. Then a second bolted from the fray. Then two ran for the safety of deep forest, another jumped on an unsaddled horse and galloped away. Bolek slipped in blooded grass, severing a brigand's foot at the ankle as he steadied himself on one knee, a deep slash to another's face as he rose. A handful of remaining brigands tightened the ring and renewed their attack.

I taste the vodka. I am tempered fury, Father Tadek.

A glancing blow to the head sent him to the ground. He lost his grip on both blades. Rolling on his back, he looked up at a Tatar ax raised high above and into the luminous eyes of the giant, Gustaw.

A Thump! The fierce eyes dimmed. A second thump! The eyes faded, then closed, the ax fell from his hands. Gustaw collapsed heavily face first, two arrows sunk deeply in his mid back.

Bolek stole one glance as he rose with his ciupaga. There, next to Hector, stood Alina, naked, eyes afire, Bolek's bow in her steady arms. As he turned to fight on, he looked only at the backs of men as they scrambled in any direction away from Bolek. Motion to his right caught his eye and he readied himself.

A single bowman. Enough time to see but none to react.

A scream of pain. An arrow appeared in the brigand's shoulder, and he collapsed.

No man challenged Bolek now. The camp was in complete

disarray with only the sounds of the wailing wounded and whines of those scattering in full retreat. A few begged God for mercy, some begged the eagle-man, others cried out Uciekaj! Run! There is a werewolf in camp. Vilkodlak! Uciekaj!

A triumphant Bolek turned to Alina. She stood with his bow, its string drawn to her ear, cocked with an arrow aimed at his chest. Falling to his knees, and offering his chest, he said, "You have every right," before closing his eyes.

The zip of an arrow past his ear made him flinch. But the thump and shutter as it lodged in a nearby tree relaxed him. He opened his eyes as Alina collapsed in tears. Running to her, he pulled his bearskin cloak from his saddle to cover her.

"I prayed to the Christian god to save me, and he sends you."

"Perhaps for us to share our lives."

"You have defiled me, tormented me, ruined my life with my family and now save me. Yet I cannot kill you. I cannot even hate you now. But you do not know me."

"I've seen your struggle. I've felt your anger. I know of your deeply wounded honor, your shame, your love of family. I also see your nobility and courage. I know you well enough by far."

"We are not to be together," she told him. "It is not our fate."

"There is no fate, no destiny, no magic or meant to be. There is only our wills. And this is what makes love possible. I choose. You choose. I came here willingly, Alina. For you. To trade my life for yours. And somehow, together, we have won the right to live. Take my love for your own. I will honor you until my last breath."

Looking to the sky, perhaps for some sort of sign or imparted wisdom from heaven, she moaned deeply before burying her face in Bolek's breast. They huddled there for some time, holding to each other, oblivious to all that went on around them. Finally, looking up at him, her tangled black hair and watery eyes only enhancing her beauty, she shook her head slightly.

"I am so tired of being scared," she said. "This is such a

wretched world. We are only flesh."

"*Only* flesh? Today our flesh united to defeat iron. And our united flesh is invincible, immortal, because of the spirit within us."

"What will become of me? Where will you take me?"

"Home. My family will welcome you with open arms as our own. As for the rest, well, you will learn all of it shortly."

"Then bring me behind your armor and your iron will."

Mounting a bowing Hector, Bolek lifted Alina up into his arms.

"You know you are a very strong and deadly bowman," he said, urging Hector into a trot. "Those were great shots you made, especially the last."

"You left me three arrows. I fired the last past your head."

"What? Then who—"

"I do not know. But it came from there, far up in the mountains."

"No man could make such a shot."

"A few moments ago I thought not even your god could save me from torture and death. But yet, I am here, eagle of the Tatras, but I may have something to teach also."

"And I will listen. For yes, I do have friends up there, higher than the mountain peaks, watching over us. And they are in my heart, as well. Forever."

"You are a strange man. As much spirit as flesh. How can such a thing be?"

As Bolek nudged Hector toward home and the couple held onto each other, he whispered into her ear: "My love for you, Alina, is wider than the sky."

Jeszcze Polska nie zginęła,Kiedy my żyjemy.

Roundfire Books put simply, publish great stories. Whether it's literary or popular, a gentle tale or a pulsating thriller, the connecting theme in all Roundfire fiction titles is that once you pick them up you won't want to put them down.